PRAISE FOR GAYLE

Winter Winds

"In *Winter Winds,* Gayle Roper creates memorable, lovable characters and places them into an exciting, fast-moving plot that kept me turning pages to the end. It's laugh-out-loud funny all the way through, and yet the message of hope and faith flows from the pages like a healing balm. This is Gayle's best yet, and I've been an avid fan for years."

HANNAH ALEXANDER, AUTHOR OF THE HIDEAWAY SERIES

"Romance, suspense, and feisty characters, coupled with important lessons in perseverance and forgiveness, make Gayle Roper's *Winter Winds* an interesting read."

SYLVIA BAMBOLA, AUTHOR OF *REFINER'S FIRE,*
TEARS IN A BOTTLE, AND *WATERS OF MARAH*

"Skillfully blending humor and suspense, Gayle Roper explores the turmoil of relationships gone awry in a rapid-fire series of twists and turns that keep you turning pages. *Winter Winds* is a wonderful read!"

CAROL COX, COAUTHOR OF *TO CATCH A THIEF*

"Gayle Roper's *Winter Winds* was a wonderful blend of heart-warming characters, hometown setting, humor, and intrigue. I loved this book and wanted to marry the characters off to my own kids!"

COLLEEN COBLE, AUTHOR OF *WITHOUT A TRACE*

Autumn Dreams

"*Autumn Dreams* takes readers on a delightful off-season vacation to the Jersey shore of my childhood—complete with an ocean view and a delicious menu of characters. Cassandra and company face more than one stormy night before this romantic mystery concludes with a sunny splash. Enjoy the trip!"

LIZ CURTIS HIGGS, BESTSELLING AUTHOR OF
BOOKENDS AND BAD GIRLS OF THE BIBLE

"When Gayle presses her peopled pen, a cast of heart-lively folks emerge. Colorfully arrayed in real-life pressures, you'll recognize their struggles and feel their emotions. My greatest challenge was not to peek ahead, but I didn't want to 'awaken' from this *Autumn Dream*."

PATSY CLAIRMONT, WOMEN OF FAITH SPEAKER AND
AUTHOR OF STARDUST ON MY PILLOW

"Gayle Roper has written another wonderfully entertaining book with characters that endeared themselves to me in the first few pages and a neatly woven theme that shows the wisdom of waiting on God's perfect timing. *Autumn Dreams* was my third 'season' in Seaside and I can't wait to return for the winter."

DEBORAH RANEY, RITA AWARD-WINNING AUTHOR OF
AFTER THE RAINS AND A SCARLET CORD

"Gayle Roper spins a memorable tale of romance and intrigue, embellished with a cast of heartwarming characters armed by faith and united by love against a threat to one of their own."

LINDA WINDSOR, AWARD-WINNING AUTHOR OF
ALONG CAME JONES AND DEIRDRE

"Master of romantic suspense Gayle Roper has delivered another winner in *Autumn Dreams*. Real characters with all their flaws and all their baggage fill the pages of this well-written book. Once you pick it up, you will not be able to put it down until you have come to the dramatic end!"

LINDA HALL, AUTHOR OF STEAL AWAY,
SADIE'S SONG, AND KATHERYN'S SECRET

"I loved the first two books in Gayle Roper's series. Now she's done it again—wielding her powerful pen, creating captivating and compelling characters, a page-turning plot, and stirring action that inspires me to say, 'More! More!' I'm so glad this isn't the end. Write number four quickly, Gayle!"

KATHY COLLARD MILLER, SPEAKER AND
AUTHOR OF *PRINCESS TO PRINCESS*

Summer Shadows

"Once again, Gayle Roper shows herself to be a master at creating compelling characters."

NANCY MOSER, COAUTHOR OF THE SISTER CIRCLE SERIES

"Suspenseful drama, sweet romance, and breezy seaside setting...Gayle Roper's *Summer Shadows* is ideal for summer reading."

DEANNA JULIE DODSON, AUTHOR OF
IN HONOR BOUND AND *TO GRACE SURRENDERED*

Spring Rain

"*Spring Rain* is a heartwarming love story that doesn't shy away from tackling tough subjects like homosexuality and promiscuity. Ms. Roper handles them with grace and compassion, never compromising the hope-filled truth of God's Word while giving us a bang-up tale of romantic suspense!"

LIZ CURTIS HIGGS, BESTSELLING AUTHOR OF
BAD GIRLS OF THE BIBLE

"*Spring Rain* contains all the mystery, suspense, and romance a reader could want. I also appreciated the story's 'something extra': realism and candor. Thank you, Gayle, for speaking the truth in love!"

ANGELA HUNT, BESTSELLING AUTHOR OF *THE NOTE*

"This is a realistically portrayed story of love and forgiveness, filled with emotion and grace… A compelling read."

ROMANTIC TIMES MAGAZINE

"*Spring Rain* weaves powerful lessons on contemporary moral issues into a wonderful story—a very powerful combination!"

BOB DAVIES, NORTH AMERICAN DIRECTOR, EXODUS INTERNATIONAL

"Gayle Roper is in top form with *Spring Rain*. Her storytelling skills make this one a page-turning experience readers will love."

JAMES SCOTT BELL, AUTHOR OF *BLIND JUSTICE* AND *FINAL WITNESS*

NOVELS BY GAYLE ROPER

SEASIDE SEASONS:

Spring Rain
Summer Shadows
Autumn Dreams
Winter Winds

THE AMHEARST MYSTERIES:

Caught in the Middle
Caught in the Act
Caught in a Bind

Winter Winds

SEASIDE SEASONS BOOK FOUR

GAYLE ROPER

Multnomah® Publishers *Sisters, Oregon*

WINTER WINDS
published by Multnomah Publishers, Inc.

© 2004 by Gayle G. Roper
International Standard Book Number: 1-59052-279-6

Cover image by Garry Black /Masterfile

Unless otherwise indicated, Scripture quotations are from:
Holy Bible, New Living Translation © 1996. Used by permission of
Tyndale House Publishers, Inc. All rights reserved.
The Holy Bible, New International Version (NIV) © 1973, 1984 by International Bible
Society, used by permission of Zondervan Publishing House

Multnomah is a trademark of Multnomah Publishers, Inc., and is registered in the U.S. Patent and Trademark Office. The colophon is a trademark of Multnomah Publishers, Inc.

Printed in the United States of America

For information:
MULTNOMAH PUBLISHERS, INC. • P.O. BOX 1720 • SISTERS, OR 97759

Library of Congress Cataloging-in-Publication Data

Roper, Gayle G.
  Winter winds / by Gayle Roper.
        p. cm. — (Seaside seasons ; bk. 4)
  ISBN 1-59052-279-6 (pbk.)
  1. Clergy—Fiction. 2. Spouses of clergy—Fiction. 3. Separated
people—Fiction. 4. Seaside resorts—Fiction. I. Title.

PS3568.O68W56 2004
813'.54—dc22

                                    2004000276

04 05 06 07 08 09 10—10 9 8 7 6 5 4 3 2 1

For Frank and Margaret Wilder
who exemplify the gift of hospitality
and model the love of Jesus

Acknowledgments

My deepest thanks to:

Nancy Ferguson Notaro, owner of Harbor Light Christian Bookstore, Ocean City, New Jersey, who was so gracious in sharing the workings of a resort town bookstore and hosting a book signing for me.

Josie Haines, manager of the Mustard Seed Christian Bookstore, Exton, Pennsylvania, who let me wander around her store and eavesdrop and who introduced me to the pink sheet.

Chris and Peggie, pharmacists at the Ocean Pharmacy, Ocean City, New Jersey, who shared their pleasure with life in a nonchain pharmacy.

Reverend Don Phillips, Ocean City Baptist Church, Ocean City, New Jersey, who told us all about life as a pastor in a resort town church with its fluctuating summer attendance and stable winter congregation.

Julee Schwarzburg, my editor par excellence, who makes everything better.

My prayer board, who encourage me, keep after me, and most important, pray for me.

Chuck, my husband, who wandered around Ocean City with me one winter weekend, asking all the good questions that I hadn't thought of.

Be kind and compassionate to one another,
forgiving each other, just as in Christ God forgave you.

EPHESIANS 4:32, NIV

One

Come on, Trudy, sweetheart. Stand tall. You can do it."

As she raised her hand with the treat in it, Dori MacAllister smiled encouragingly at her little Dandie Dinmont. The dog in turn cocked her ears, watched the hand with the treat, but didn't move.

"Come on, Trudy, baby. Do it for Mommy."

Do it for Mommy? Gag! Dori had promised herself when she spent way too much money to buy Trudy that she'd never become one of those weird ladies who talked to their animals like they were mentally impaired babies.

And here she was, talking to the little beige terrier as if she were a canine Rain Man.

Dori cleared her throat. "Stand tall, Trudy," she ordered in the sternest voice she could muster.

Trudy immediately went up on her hind legs.

Dori blinked. That was all there was to it? She thought of all the time and money she'd spent on dog obedience classes and the mixed results. Trudy always performed wonderfully before everyone there, but at home she only obeyed when she felt like it.

Dori pictured herself in class. She had always spoken firmly there, and Trudy did as asked. It was only at home she made a fool of herself with baby talk. With a sigh of disgust, she got to her feet. Just another proof that she needed a life.

The phone rang, and she stared at it for a moment. What if it was Bill Fralinger asking again for a date? Couldn't the man take a hint? Five refusals ought to make him realize her disinterest, or so one would think.

The answering machine kicked in after the fourth ring. "Dori, I've got to talk to you! It's an emergency! Call—"

She launched herself at the phone, heart in her throat. "Phil! It's me. What's wrong?" *Not Trev. Please let it not be Trev.*

"You've got to come at once," Phil said without preamble. "It's Pop."

Dori's stomach dropped. Before hearing *"It's Pop,"* she'd thought that a stomach dropping was just a phrase writers used to convey distress. Now she knew it was a real sensation. "What's wrong?" she managed to whisper.

"Heart attack, we think."

Fear shafted through her, and she leaned against the wall to keep herself upright. Pop! Sturdy, invincible Pop, the man who with his wife Honey had raised her, the man who stood as grand-father to her, as close as or closer than any blood grandparent could ever be.

"How bad?" She held her breath, afraid of the answer.

"It's too soon to tell." Phil's voice shook. "He's got tubes and wires and oxygen and…" He had to stop and clear his throat before he could continue. "You've got to come, Dori."

"N-no, I can't." Not even for Pop. Her conscience and her emotions clashed, and she began to shake.

"He asked for you."

Was that anger she was beginning to hear in his voice? "Oh, Phil."

He must have heard her hesitation, her distress. "Look, Dori, you know I've never pried." Yes, he had. Scads of times. "I figured whatever happened was your personal business, but it's time to come home. He needs to see you."

"Phil, you just don't understand." She heard the slide toward whining in her voice and flinched.

Trudy whimpered. Dori turned and saw her standing on the

sofa, front feet planted on the arm, watching intently. Somehow she had caught Dori's distress and was worried. Dori swooped her up and cuddled her close, drawing comfort from the animal even as she dodged her relentless pink tongue. There was no question; the little sweetheart was worth every penny.

"I can't leave Trudy," Dori said, then flushed at how inane and unfeeling that comment sounded, given the circumstances. But she knew how to worry over Trudy. She had no idea how to respond to the devastating news about Pop.

"Who's Trudy, and why in the world not?"

"Who would take care of her?"

"Dori, is Trudy your dog?"

"I told you about her last time we talked, didn't I?"

"Yeah, I just forgot her name. Now listen closely because this is what you do. You put her in a kennel. You give her to a friend. You take her to the pound."

"What?"

"Dori, she's a dog. We're talking about Pop here."

"You think I'm a terrible person." Dori found she had tears in her eyes. She hated to cry because it meant losing control, but if she was going to shed tears whether she wanted to or not, she might as well make use of them. She sniffed loudly into the phone.

"Are you crying?" Phil demanded, outrage clear in his voice.

She gave Trudy a teary grin. Worked every time. Someday he was going to be putty in the hands of the right woman.

She looked around her small living room with the soft peach walls; the moss green carpet; the peach, russet, and green floral love seat; and the two white wicker chairs with pillows that matched the sofa. She didn't want to leave its security and safety, but with an inward sigh, she admitted she had to go east.

"Come on, Dori. Enough is enough."

She closed her eyes and nodded, even though he couldn't see her.

She'd been seven when she met Pop, nineteen when she left him. She had taken her heart and run to save herself, and though she hadn't intended it, she knew that Pop had paid a stiff price for her emotional retreat. Honey, too. For six long years, she'd stayed away, and, coward that she was, she'd planned to extend her absence indefinitely.

But how could she do that in light of, "He asked for you"?

She sighed. Much as she hated to admit it, Phil was right. Enough was enough. "I'll catch the red-eye."

"Good girl. Let me know your arrival time, and I'll meet you."

"You needn't bother. I'll rent a car."

"I'm picking you up. No arguments."

Dori stood unmoving in the living room of her San Diego apartment long after Phil hung up. It wasn't until Trudy complained about being hugged too tightly that Dori moved. First she called for her airline ticket and got a compassionate fare leaving at eleven-thirty that evening, arriving in Philadelphia at nine-thirty tomorrow morning. Next she called Meg Reynolds, owner of Small Treasures and her boss.

"Oh, Dori, I'm so sorry," Meg said as soon as Dori told her about Pop. "Take as much time as you need. I'll be fine."

"Thanks, Meg. I—" Dori stalled. Meg knew more of her story than anyone, and she alone could understand Dori's mixed feelings. She tried again. "I want to be there for Pop, but—"

"But you're afraid you'll see Trev."

Dori closed her eyes. There it was, spoken brazenly and boldly. "I'm scared to death," she confessed, her voice a mere whisper. "What would I say? What would I do?"

"Ah, Dori, don't underestimate yourself. You'll manage fine. I have every confidence in you."

The affirming words were a balm on Dori's unsettled spirit.

When she'd first moved to San Diego six years ago, she was in dire need of a job. She went to a mall, thinking that surely someone there would need a sales clerk. What she found was Small Treasures, a gift shop with the most creative inventory she'd ever seen. She spent two hours looking at all the lovely items, yearning for the money to buy some of them, knowing it would be a long time before she had discretionary money of the type she was used to.

Then she'd taken a deep breath and forced herself to ask for a job. "Your inventory is so wonderful, even I could sell it," she said. "Please."

Meg Reynolds, a short, dark-haired woman of indeterminate age, not only hired her; she trained her, taught her, and gave her ever greater responsibility until Dori was now Meg's right hand with a small percentage of the store in her name.

But most important, Meg had given her love. She became the mother Dori no longer had, the anchor that held her stable in the hurricane-tossed sea her life had become. Meg invited Dori to dinner frequently, sometimes with just her and Ron, Meg's big bear of a husband, sometimes with her three sons and two daughters-in-law, too. They weren't Pop and Honey or Trev and Phil, but they were wonderfully accepting of the quiet, wounded young woman she'd become. Slowly Dori learned to relax, to smile again, then laugh freely.

It was Meg who found the small apartment that Dori lived in, and Meg who gave her a used bedroom suite that had belonged to one of her boys. Dori was so grateful she wouldn't have to bunk on the floor that the Batman sheets, which came with Meg's gift, seemed like the finest of bed linens.

"I'd give you more," Meg said, "but the boys cleaned us out when they married or moved." She grinned. "I still had the bed because it's a single and these sheets because for some reason the wives don't want to sleep on Batman."

Perhaps Meg's greatest kindness was that she never pressed, never probed. She waited patiently for the time Dori was willing to trust, willing to open her heart. When Dori finally talked and talked and talked about home, about Trev, Meg just listened, her eyes full of tears when Dori told of Trev's betrayal.

"Ah, lamb, I'm so sorry." She wrapped her arms around Dori. "Unfortunately, not every man's as wonderful as my Ron. I'd make it better for you if I could. Since I can't, I'll just love you."

And Dori cried. The unequivocal acceptance helped heal her as nothing else could have.

When the tears abated, Dori smiled at Meg. "I bet you regret the day I walked into your shop."

"Never. Not for an instant."

"Why did you hire me if you weren't looking for help?"

"It was the *please* that did it," Meg said. "That and the desperation in your eyes." Her warm smile took any sting from the words.

Dori never wanted to be that needy again. That was why she feared the trip east.

"What are you going to do with Trudy?" Meg asked.

"I don't know."

"Let us keep her for you. We think she's the cutest thing there is."

"Oh, Meg, would you?" One problem solved.

"You just get your stuff together and go to the airport. Ron and I will collect Trudy. We've got your key, remember?"

With a strange mix of anxiety and excitement turning her stomach upside down, Dori made it through security checks twenty minutes before her flight left. She walked right down the Jetway and sank gratefully into her seat, prepared to sleep until Chicago's O'Hare and her plane change. She grabbed a pillow and a blanket and tucked herself in. All over the plane passengers were doing the same. The only difference between the others and her was that they slept.

Instead, she remembered.

Her mother and Phil's had gone to college together and become fast friends. Even geography, marriage, and parenthood hadn't diminished their friendship, and joint vacations were an annual event. Dori vaguely remembered Disney World, Yosemite National Park, and the Rocky Mountains, all shared with Phil and his younger brother, Trev. Every other year, they all trooped to Ocean City, Maryland—the MacAllisters from Chicago and the Trevelyans from Amhearst, Pennsylvania.

Then came the year she was seven. They were vacationing in Ocean City when the police came to their rented condo to tell the three children that their parents, out together for an evening, had been killed by a drunk driver. With no grandparents still living and with her parents both only children, Dori had had no family to come to her aid. In fact, in her little girl's mind, she had nobody but Phil and Trev.

The authorities sent a woman officer to get her and take her to social services. Even today she could feel her child's heart hammering against her rib cage, desperate and terrified. She remembered her valiant attempts to stop crying and be brave like the police lady said. Her nose had become so stopped up that she couldn't breathe through it, and she felt sick to her stomach from all the phlegm she swallowed.

It was Trev who changed everything. She could picture him, a skinny nine-year-old with ribs you could play like a xylophone, staring at the officer.

"You aren't taking her anywhere! She's ours!" He'd pushed Dori behind him to protect her.

When he came for the boys, Pop asked, "What will happen to her?"

"Foster care, I imagine," the officer said. "She'll be just fine."

"Not adoption?"

The officer shrugged. "She's probably too old to be adopted."

"We'll adopt her," Trev yelled, his voice shaking with emotion. "You can't have her."

"Don't let them take me," she whispered as she hid behind him again. "Don't let them, Trev." She wrapped her skinny arms around his waist and buried her face in his back. They'd never pull her free. She would be like one of those barnacles that encrusted the big pilings that went down, down into the bay where they'd rented Jet Skis yesterday. Daddy scraped his leg against one, and the barnacle hadn't been hurt at all. Daddy had bled.

Phil sidled up beside Dori and put an arm around her heaving shoulders.

Pop, Honey, and the policewoman stood facing the three orphans. The officer held out her hand. "Come on, sweetie. The Trevelyans have to go home."

"No!" she screamed over and over. "No!"

Pop moved then. He reached over Trev's head and pulled Dori up and into his arms. Try as she would to hold on to Trev, she couldn't fight Pop's strength. Her heart was already broken because Mommy and Daddy were never coming back. She was surprised when it broke a little more. She turned her weeping gaze to Trev.

Help me! Help me!

But he wasn't even watching her. He was looking at Pop. So was Phil. They were both smiling.

She realized suddenly that Pop hadn't handed her to the

police lady. He was holding her close, patting her back, and Honey was stroking her arm. They crooned to her. "Shh, sweetheart. Everything will be fine. The boys are right. You're ours. You can come with us."

The police lady protested. "You are not a relative."

Pop pulled her closer, an arm under her bottom, a hand splayed over her back. She wound her dangling legs around his waist. A barnacle, glomming on to Pop.

"Her mother was my daughter's best friend," Pop said.

"That does not count."

Pop scowled at the woman. "This little girl belongs to Honey and me as much as our two grandsons."

"Mr. Trevelyan, there are laws."

"We're taking her." He began moving toward the door. "You cannot stop us."

The policewoman hurried after them. "There may be a legal guardian named in the will."

"She's ours." Pop said again and carried Dori out the door. Honey and the boys followed. Dori buried her face in the bend of Pop's neck and shoulder and held on as tightly as she could. He put her in the middle of the backseat of his shiny black car and buckled her in.

"You've got to let go now, sweetheart."

She tightened her grip on his neck.

"I've got to go drive the car, Dori. You've got to let go. It's okay. You're safe now."

Reluctantly she released her death grip, and Pop backed out of the car. Trev climbed in on one side of her, Phil on the other. Honey and Pop climbed in the front seat, and off they drove, the policewoman watching helplessly from the curb. Trev put his arm around Dori and patted her shoulder.

She didn't stop shaking until they pulled up in front of the brick Colonial in Amhearst.

As always with this memory, the burning sensation of both gratitude and loss lodged over her breastbone. Absently she rubbed at the ache as she watched the landing strip lights flash by as the plane touched down at O'Hare. That had all happened eighteen years ago. Unbelievable.

Dori blinked her gritty eyes as she deplaned. They didn't call these flights red-eyes for nothing. She located the gate for the final leg of her flight and found herself in the middle seat of the next-to-the-last row with a big man on either side, each reading a full-sized daily. She pulled out a paperback, small, compact, and easy to handle. She studied the girl on the cover. Dressed in a blue robe, she looked back over her shoulder as she ran toward the safety of an old house. Her long blonde hair streamed behind her, every curl in place. Dori's hand went to her own dark mane, and she sighed as she opened her book. Models never seemed to have bad hair days or crammed-in-an-airplane nights.

But she couldn't concentrate enough to read. She dropped the book to her lap and put her head back. She closed her eyes as worries about what she'd find in Pennsylvania clawed at her.

What if Pop needed a heart transplant? Could a donor be found in time? What if he was permanently incapacitated, confined to bed or a wheelchair for the rest of his life? What if he died? She wrapped her arms around herself as she went cold all over.

Then there was Trev.

In California, she felt safe from thoughts of him. He had no part in her life there. She could forget him, go days at a time feeling, if not happy exactly, at least satisfied with the life she'd carved out for herself. It was only when she was overly tired or upset that he appeared in her dreams and daydreams, a ghost who haunted her with memories of his charming smile, his promises, his touch. Some days she feared he'd never be completely exorcised. He was like a virus swimming through her blood, just waiting for the right circumstances to reinfect her.

If her susceptibility to Trev-itis frightened her when she was bustling around Small Treasures or training Trudy or trying to get a good night's sleep in her cozy blue and gold bedroom, it terrified her as she approached Philadelphia. For how could she see Pop without seeing Trev?

Even agonizing flights eventually end, and Dori eyed the luggage circling the baggage carousel in Terminal A at Philadelphia

International Airport. Hers would undoubtedly be the last piece off. It was the traveler's equivalent to the shopper being in the line that moved most slowly at checkout.

"Come on, come on," she muttered at the unseen baggage handlers, then brightened. Here came her black bag. In the sea of black bags she knew it was hers even before it got to her because it had the red yarn tied around the handle. She settled her laptop against her small roll-on and shouldered her way to the slowly moving belt. As her suitcase slid past, she reached for it. She bumped into a young woman also reaching for the bag.

"Sorry." Dori gave her a wan smile. "This one's mine."

She dragged her suitcase off the belt, pulled up the handle on the case, and wheeled it to her other luggage. The ads said that she could take this baby onto the plane too, but she'd stuffed it with not only her clothes, but gifts from Small Treasures for everyone in her Pennsylvania family.

She collected things whenever she saw something she thought one of them might like, mailing them for any and all occasions— birthdays, Christmas, Arbor Day, the Fourth of July. She'd recently been collecting Valentine's Day presents, and there were several gifts inside, even one for Trev. As a result, every expansion zipper on the suitcase was open, making it too fat to fit either under or over a seat. Not that she would ever have been able to lift it into the overhead bin given its weight. It had been all she could do to pull it off the carousel.

She found the attachment thingamabob stored in the front zipper pouch and clicked it to the bag. She clipped the other end to her small roll-on. Gripping the laptop in one hand and tugging her luggage behind her with the other, she walked out the automatic doors and to the curb.

She shivered inside her chenille jacket as the frigid January air wrapped around her. She hunched her shoulders and thought with longing of the green down-filled parka she used to have back when cold Pennsylvania winters were an annual event in her life. And the warm gloves. And the knit ski cap. Six years in San Diego had thinned her blood.

She shuddered again, wishing she didn't have to deal with what weather.com had told her would be a week of single-digit temperatures all through the Mid-Atlantic states. Maybe, she thought hopefully, Pop still had her red Lands' End Squall, the one with the navy lining. Grandparents kept things like that, didn't they? After all, it had meaning for him where the green parka didn't. He'd bought the whole family the red jackets one year for Christmas, Trev's senior year in high school if she remembered correctly. They'd all told Pop he was nuts, they weren't some athletic team to be dressed alike, but they'd all worn the jackets with pride, even Honey.

Like he'd kept a coat for her for six long years.

Just when she was certain she was going to be struck down with pneumonia as she waited for Phil, she heard her name called.

"Yo, Dori!"

She looked in the direction of the voice and saw a man waving to her from the end of the line of cars pulled to the curb awaiting passengers.

Her heart sputtered. Trev!

Two

H*E WON'T COME FOR YOU*, she'd told herself again and again all through the long flight. *He won't meet you. And you don't want him to. You don't even want to see him.*

But he had come! Delight washed warm through her.

When in the next heartbeat she realized it wasn't Trev after all, but Phil, she had to turn away, blinking at tears. To buy time, she made a production of being certain her suitcases were secure. When she finally felt dry-eyed, she turned toward Phil and made her way slowly through the press of people all anxious to leave the airport.

She was appalled at herself. The height of her elation when she thought Trev had come both shamed and frightened her, as did the depth of her subsequent disappointment.

Don't think about Trev. Don't look for Trev. Don't expect to see Trev. He means nothing to you. You've cut him out of your life—and with very good reason. Let it go. Let him go.

It was that black hair and the size of the man that made her think Trev, but the closer she got to Phil, the less he looked like his brother. Though both men were handsome by any measure, there was about Phil the softness and charm of a puppy gamboling at your feet, anxious to please, while about Trev was a toughness, a strength that made him a combination of Sir Lancelot, Prince Valiant, and Buzz Lightyear.

"Dori!" Phil cried, running to meet her, leaving his car in spite of the Do-Not-Leave-Your-Car signs and the watchful police presence. He grabbed her in a bear hug and swung her around, then planted a great smacking kiss on her cheek. "It is so good to see you!"

She had to smile as she kissed him back. Sweet Phil. He'd come to San Diego several times to visit her, making her laugh, taking her places, reminding her of his brother. Such bittersweet visits.

"Welcome home," he said as he picked up her suitcases from where they had fallen when he grabbed her. He began walking toward the car, and Dori followed, thankful she had managed to keep hold of her laptop when he grabbed her.

Home. Visions of the brick Colonial flashed across her mind, Honey's carefully pruned and tended azaleas mixing with rhododendrons across the front of the place, the giant oaks shading the deep backyard. She could practically feel Trev and Phil pelting her eight-year-old self with acorns from those trees, grinning with delight when she shrieked that they hurt, then kneeling beside her in distress when they reduced her to tears. At least Trev had knelt beside her, wiping her cheeks, soothing her. Trev, her white knight.

Swallowing the lump at the base of her throat, she turned from Phil, who was putting her bags in the trunk. No remembering! No reminiscing. It was the only way she could keep the regrets from overwhelming her.

"I'm freezing!" She shivered again and pulled the passenger door open. "You don't happen to have another coat in the car, do you?"

"Wimp." Phil grinned at her over the roof as he walked to the driver's door. "Don't worry. I'll crank the heat up. You'll be warm in no time." He pulled off his leather aviator's jacket and passed it across the car's roof.

Dori shoved her arms in the sleeves and wrapped it close. Immediately the retained body heat eased her chill, and her shoulders dropped back toward their normal alignment. Not that all the tension left her. Not at all. But at least she wouldn't freeze to death before she even saw Pop.

She climbed wearily into the car and rested her head against the back of her seat.

"Long night?" he asked.

"Very. I'm absolutely beat."

"Couldn't sleep on the flight?"

She shook her head. "Two big men reading newspapers on either side of me." She held out her hands in demonstration.

"Poor baby," Phil mocked gently.

"You know it."

Once Phil had pulled clear of the airport congestion and they were driving south on I-95, Dori turned to him. "So how bad is it?" she asked as they sped through Chester and past the Commodore Barry Bridge ramp.

"I don't really know." Phil swung onto 322. "You know how hard it can be to get answers out of doctors. But Honey won't leave his side."

Dori flinched. That didn't sound good. *Oh, God, please!*

The prayer was out before she could catch it, and it wasn't the first one since Phil's call. She smiled in self-mockery. Old habits, no matter how long unused, surfaced in times of duress. Well, maybe God remembered her. Maybe He'd deign to answer. After all, she was asking for Pop, not herself.

She leaned her head back once again and closed her eyes. The next thing she knew, Phil was shaking her.

"Dori. Dori, wake up. We're here."

Dori blinked and sat up, expecting to see their home on its acre lot in Amhearst. Instead, she realized they were in the hospital parking lot. Of course. She climbed out and followed Phil who seemed to know where he was going.

As the sleep cobwebs fled, she found she didn't want to go in the austere-looking building. She had so many emotions whirling around—fear, regret, distress, love, longing, reticence, uncertainty—that she could barely think straight. She glanced at her watch. Eleven AM.

Reprieve! She could call Meg. She'd be at the store by now.

"I've got to call my business partner," she said, stopping outside the hospital's doors.

Phil blinked. "It can't wait?"

Of course it could wait. "I've got to let her know I arrived safely," Dori said as she pulled her cell phone from her purse. It sat dark and dead in her palm, turned off for the flight. She flicked it on and hit the office number.

Phil wandered to a bench and sat.

"Hello. Small Treasures. Meg Reynolds here."

Dori could picture Meg sitting in the cramped space in the back of their store, coffee cup steaming beside her, Krispy Kreme donut sitting beside the cup. Just hearing her voice eased some of Dori's anxiety. "Meg, it's me."

"Ah, you made it. Good trip?"

"You don't want to know."

Meg laughed, a wonderful sound that always cheered Dori, even on her black days. But she was serious when she asked, "So how's Pop?"

"I haven't seen him yet," Dori admitted.

"Ah."

Dori narrowed her eyes. "What do you mean, *ah*?"

"You're procrastinating."

"I am not. I needed to call you."

"Right. The store couldn't run for even one day without you checking in. Where are you?"

"At the hospital."

"And you haven't been to his room yet?" Dori could imagine Meg shaking her head in disbelief. "Procrastinating."

She hated it when Meg was right. "No, I'm not." *Liar, liar, pants on fire.*

Meg's sigh echoed through the air. "If you say so, girl. But listen to me. You go in that room and kiss that man and hug Honey and tell them you love them. Masochism should never last six years."

"I am not masochistic."

"Dori, sweetie, do you honestly think ostracizing yourself from the people you love most in the world is normal?"

Dori glanced at Phil who was studying the parking lot with great seriousness. Still, she turned her back completely on him and said in a voice just above a whisper, "But Trev..."

"Forget Trev," Meg said. "This trip is about Pop. Get in that room. Now!" And she was gone.

Dori was torn between anger and laughter. Meg loved to play parent, and it irked Dori to no end when she did, especially since

Meg was usually right. Like now.

Dori sighed, clicked off her phone, and dropped it back in her purse. She turned to Phil. "Let's go see him."

Phil didn't say, "About time," but it was written all over his face. Well, it wasn't that she wanted to be an emotional coward. To her severe embarrassment, she just was. Even though she recognized that her cowardice was the result of the losses and hurts of the past, her parents and Trev especially, it was still humiliating to be so spineless.

An elevator disgorged them on the third floor where Phil turned left. He stopped in front of a door that had a tag naming Seth Trevelyan as the room's occupant. He turned to Dori. "Pop looks old."

She blinked, trying to absorb that information. While Pop was old, seventy-six if she remembered correctly, he had never looked old. He had broad shoulders and a barrel chest. His hair, though gray, was thick, and the wrinkles on his face only made him more ruggedly handsome. There was a time when Dori imagined Trev looking like Pop when he was old. Now she no longer cared what Trev would look like, but she was glad Phil had given her this warning about Pop.

"He always seemed invincible," she said, her voice soft, sad.

"Yeah." Phil took a deep breath. "That's why seeing him like this hurts so."

Dori made no move to enter the room. She didn't want even a glimpse of him in one of those hospital gowns with no back, infirm and vulnerable. She wanted him to always be strong and wise and *there*.

"I remember the first time I saw him." A small smile tugged at her lips.

Phil nodded, remembering along with her. "He walked into the condo that day and took over."

"I was so scared." She gave a puff of humorless laughter. "Make that terrified."

"Me, too. I had no idea what was supposed to happen to you when your parents died, but I was sure it had to be very, very bad."

As if anything could be worse for a child than being told you'd lost your parents. *Boom!* Just like that, her mother and father with their wonderful laughs and enfolding hugs were gone. Even now, eighteen years later, it was still painful. "Remember the lady cop they sent to tell us about the crash and to take me away?"

Phil shuddered. "She was probably a very nice lady, but just thinking about her gave me nightmares for months."

"We must have been three pathetic mites," Dori said, "all huddled together on the couch that was so deep that when we sat back, our legs stuck out straight like six skinny, knobby branches."

"You were the skinny one," Phil said. "Not me."

"That's right." Dori grinned. "You were in your chubby stage then, weren't you?"

He threw her a fake scowl. "That's not how I remember it."

"What I remember is Honey coming right over to us and kneeling."

Phil nodded. "Then she gathered all three of us in her arms."

"That's when I started to cry. Again."

"I thought you'd never stop."

"Me, too. I knew this was a nice lady, but she wasn't my grandmother. She was yours. And I didn't have one. In fact, I didn't have anybody but you and Trev." Her mouth filled with the metallic taste of that long ago fear. "I was Little Orphan Annie without Daddy Warbucks. And I knew Miss Hannigan was waiting for me just around the corner."

Phil grinned. "That's when Pop said, 'She's ours,' and told Honey to grab our clothes. She strode to the bedroom like Joan of Arc onto the fields of Orleans, opened drawers and scooped out clothes. Trev and I helped, grabbing up toys and those baseball caps reading Ocean City, MD. Remember them?"

She nodded. "Our fathers bought them for us on the boardwalk." Her lips quirked in a soft smile. "I still have mine."

Phil stared at her. "You're kidding."

"It was the last thing Daddy ever bought me, so it's sort of sacred. It's hanging from the post of my bed."

"You've always been a sentimental fool, haven't you?" His expression was gently mocking and full of affection. "I bet you have the corsage from your senior prom, and you actually know where your high school yearbook is."

"Of course. Anyone of character has a big box of keepsakes."

"Dori, baby, keepsakes are things like heirlooms, not squashed corsages."

She shook her head. "Keepsakes are anything that causes you to remember special times or people. The baseball cap makes me remember my parents, especially on the days when they seem more a figment of my imagination than real people who loved me."

They were both quiet for a minute as they studied the name written by the door. Seth Trevelyan. Somehow both she and Phil had survived a devastating loss to become healthy adults, and it was largely due to the man lying ill in that room. Dori shuddered to think what her life might have been without Pop and Honey stepping in.

"I remember that the policewoman threatened all kinds of legal repercussions when Pop carried me out to the car," Dori said. "But nothing happened, did it? At least nothing we know about."

"There must have been some legal actions. After all, they became your legal guardians." Phil gave her a quick hug. "That's when you became a Trevelyan. Best sister a man could want."

Dori hugged him back. "I may have lost my parents, but I found a substitute family that couldn't have been better."

That was the simple truth. From that day in Ocean City until today, she had never doubted that they wanted her and loved her, though she was the only one in the Trevelyan house named MacAllister.

And she'd repaid that love by staying away for six years. Guilt slammed into her afresh as she pushed open the door to Pop's hospital room.

Three

WHEN MAUREEN GALLOWAY went to the Philadelphia airport prepared to follow Joanne Pilotti and the black bag, the last thing she expected was to find herself deep in Chester County, Pennsylvania, sitting in a hospital parking lot, waiting for some unknown person who had blithely left a treasure worth millions locked in the trunk of a white Saturn.

What was going on here?

She punched the memory button on her cell phone and listened to Greg Barnes's phone ring. She couldn't wait to tell him the latest news.

Two hours ago she'd been sitting casually reading a book at the gate where the American flight from Chicago debarked, her Seaside PD credentials allowing her through security without a boarding pass. When Joanne appeared without a suitcase, Maureen had turned cold all over. Had their information been wrong? Had the bag been passed to someone else?

Two weeks ago when Greg Barnes, a lieutenant with the Seaside police department, had gotten the anonymous phone call about the stolen goods being transported to Seaside, he'd been skeptical, as well he should be. He recorded the conversation and replayed it for the rest of the department.

"I never heard of any such robbery," Greg said to the caller.

"You haven't been listening at the right places. Do some checking, and you'll find the goods went missing from a prominent West Coast gallery in October. They've just been bought by Neal Jankowski."

Jankowski! "And you know this because?"

"Let's just say I know everything."

"Right," Greg said. "But why are you telling me this? What do you get out of it?"

"Neal Jankowski," was the answer.

"Ah," replied Greg who wanted to bring Jankowski down too. He was a loose cannon, at once vicious and stupid, driven and without conscience. "Let's hear some details."

"You do some checking first. Verify what I've said. I'll call back in a few days."

Greg checked and found there had indeed been a major robbery in October. The stolen goods had been neither seen nor heard of in the ensuing three months.

"Talk to me," Greg said when the anonymous source called back.

"On one condition. No feds. If you contact them, this deal is off, and Jankowski will move more and more of his operation to Seaside. He likes the quiet of your delightful little town as opposed to the noise and chaos of Atlantic City."

So here Maureen was, waiting at the airport for Joanne Pilotti, the woman the tipster said would have the goods in the suitcase she wheeled off the plane. But there was no suitcase.

Her heart pounding at the possibility of some gigantic mix-up, Maureen stuck her book in her purse and walked purposefully with the crowd. She kept Joanne in sight, staying a careful two or three people in back of her, and followed her to baggage claim.

In the crowd at the baggage carousel, Maureen stood behind and slightly to the left of Joanne so she could see the suitcase when it came down the chute. She couldn't believe that Joanne had blithely checked it through instead of taking it on board with her. But then Joanne probably didn't know what was in it.

Please, Lord, let it come. *Please, Lord. Help us get these guys!* The idea of someone like Neal Jankowski setting up shop in Seaside was too terrible to contemplate.

When the black bag slid onto the belt, Maureen felt limp with relief. With its red yarn tie around the handle and the clearly visible white chalk streak down its side, it was easy to identify. The operation would continue as planned. The net would finally close around Jankowski, and one of the scariest of the bosses would go down.

As Joanne Pilotti reached for the bag, Maureen hit the memory button to call Greg Barnes back in Seaside. She stepped back farther so there was no possibility of Joanne overhearing her.

Greg picked up immediately. "Yeah, Galloway?"

"The bag just hit the carousel, and Joanne's going for it." Maureen blinked and went cold all over. "Wait a minute. Another woman's taken it. Practically pulled it out of Pilotti's hands." Was this some elaborate plan for passing the baton? One that Pilotti wasn't in on?

"What?" Greg's agitation was clear. "Who?"

"Never saw her before in my life."

Greg hissed. "And Pilotti just let her take it?"

"She did. She looks startled, sort of like you do when some unexpected and terrible thing happens, and you don't know how to respond."

"When Jankowski gets hold of her, *terrible* will be the right word."

"Wait! Here comes another black bag with a red yarn tie. Pilotti's going for it."

"Then that's the bag." Relief washed through Greg's voice.

"I don't know, but I don't think so. The one the unknown's got has the chalk mark on the side. She's wheeling it out to the curb. She's also got a small carry-on and what looks like a laptop."

"So she's got the bag we want."

Maureen only hesitated a second. "I think so."

"Then follow her."

"What about Pilotti?"

"I'll give her to Fleishman."

Maureen bit back a smile. *And won't he just love that!*

She struggled through the crowd and out to the curb. She easily found the unknown woman with the bag, a brunette about her age who stood with her arms wrapped about herself, shivering. As if the lightweight jacket weren't clue enough that

Philadelphia in January wasn't her home, the still-vibrant tan indicated some warm climate. All who lived here were wearing their pasty white winter complexions.

"Greg, some guy just called her name. Dori."

"Dori what?"

"Come on. People don't yell full names." She shook her head in exasperation. "He's hugging her, swinging her around. The suitcase just went flying."

When the guy finally put Dori on her feet and bent for the case, Maureen reached into her large purse and grabbed the small camera she always carried. It had been a gift from her parents when she graduated from the police academy.

"To use to document situations," Dad said. "You can take photos either day or night if you buy high-speed film with an ASA of 800 or higher."

Trying to be both quick and casual, hoping desperately that no one would notice, she raised the little camera and took a couple of quick shots of Dori and the man.

"He just picked the case up," she reported as she dropped the camera back in her bag. "They're going to a car, and he's loading her luggage, all of it, in the trunk."

"What kind of car?"

"White Saturn. This year's model, I think."

"License?"

"Can't see it. Others are parked too close, blocking the view." Maureen began walking toward the car. A sliver of the plate came into view. "It looks like one of those with the lighthouse on it. You know, the New Jersey save-the-seashore ones?"

"That narrows it to only a few thousand."

"Yeah, but it makes you think Seaside, doesn't it? Coincidence only goes so far."

Greg grunted.

"What do you want me to do?" She kept walking toward the car. "They're about to get in."

"Keep following the girl. Don't let her out of your sight."

Maureen nodded, turned, and raced toward the black Camry waiting on the far side of the island across the street. In it sat Cary Fleishman reading a magazine.

"Out, Fleishman," she said. "Greg wants you to follow Pilotti, and I've got to follow the unknown who grabbed the suitcase."

"What unknown?"

"I don't know. That's why she's an unknown."

Fleishman looked at her without moving. "How can I follow Pilotti if you've got the car?"

Maureen socked him in the arm. "Come on. Out. And hurry!" She watched as the white Saturn pulled into the flow of traffic. "You know Pilotti's going to Seaside. Go rent a car and catch up with her. But get out before I lose my girl."

"Where's she going?"

"I don't know," Maureen growled through gritted teeth. "That's why I'm following her."

"Alone?"

"Yes, alone," she said, counting to five. Counting to ten would take too long. "I do know how to do surveillance, you know."

Fleishman raised an eyebrow in doubt, tossed his magazine onto the floor, and slid out of the driver's seat. "Call me when you need me."

Like it was a given she'd need him. Thanks goodness Greg Barnes didn't think like Fleishman. Neither did Chief Gordon.

With a puff of irritation and a vague wave, she pulled out, looking wildly about for the white Saturn. She had to find it before it exited the airport or she'd lose it. There were just too many ways it could go, though she imagined it would head to Seaside. She sped past Terminal B into the chaos that was Terminal C, the major US Airways hub. There she spotted the Saturn caught behind one of the buses for economy parking, forced by the crush of traffic to wait there, exhaust fumes condensing around it in the frigid air.

She slowed, maneuvered behind the Saturn, and followed, surprised when the car turned onto I-95 south instead of turning north toward the Walt Whitman Bridge and the Atlantic City Expressway and Seaside.

As she cruised down 95 two cars behind the Saturn, Maureen called Greg again and gave him the license number.

"Stay with them," he ordered. "There's a lot more than recovering stolen goods at stake here."

Maureen shuddered, knowing that was true. She'd only been

in Seaside for a couple of weeks, but already she loved the town. The thought of someone like Neal Jankowski corrupting it was unbearable. She set her jaw. She would not fail. She hadn't come this far, survived this much, to go down in flames.

She had wanted to be a cop for as long as she could remember. Her father was one as were her two brothers and a sister-in-law. It ran in the blood.

"You sure you want to do this?" Dad had asked when she filled in her application for the police academy.

She looked at him in surprise. "I've always wanted to be a cop, Dad. You know that."

He ran his hand over her shining fall of black curls. "Sure, I know that, lovey. But it wasn't real to me until today. It's potentially dangerous work, and I'm suddenly thinking I don't want my girl anywhere where she might be hurt."

She smiled and kissed his cheek. "Now, Dad, don't turn chauvinistic at this late stage. And you know as well as I do that most cops never even fire their guns in the line of duty."

"That's no great comfort," he said. "Because there are many who do. And many who get hurt."

And killed, but he didn't say it, and she was grateful for that.

In the long run, it hadn't been any of the Galloways who got killed in the line of duty but bright, shining, lovely Adam, her love, her life, her fiancé. And it hadn't been in keeping the peace in New Jersey but in Bosnia.

He'd gently chided her for crying when they parted. "I'll be back before your tears dry, sweetheart."

And he almost was, in his box draped with a flag, the random victim of a land mine.

How her father had worried about her then. She was in her final months at the academy, and she'd thrown herself into her training to keep the grief at bay. Thanks to the rigors of training, it worked during the day, but at night she wrapped her arms around her middle and curled up in pain.

"God, I don't understand. He loved You. And he loved me. Can You at least tell me why?"

He hadn't. All He'd ever whispered to her was, "Trust me, Maureen."

And she tried. Some days God seemed real, the One who cared for her above all. Other days He was as far from her as the east is from the west. She stood at graduation choking on tears of grief, anger, and loss.

Lord, I believe. Help my unbelief. And help me be a good cop in Adam's memory.

Because she knew she was fragile, Maureen chose to seek a position on a force in a small town where the pressures would be less. She worked in the little town of Audubon, just the Jersey side of Philadelphia, for two years, then, feeling stronger emotionally and spiritually, moved to Camden, a small city looking for someone to work in the juvenile division. She spent three years in that particular emotional wringer, working with the small victims of heartbreaking crimes and their families. Then the job in Seaside opened up, and she grabbed it. For some reason, it just felt right.

"I don't remember you worrying like this about Bobby and Joe," she teased her father the day she moved to Seaside. "And if you say they're boys, I'll have to hit you." She smiled to show she wasn't serious.

"Well, they are," Dad said, his black Irish eyes suddenly tearing as he ran a hand through hair as dark as hers but fringed at the temples with gray. "Your brothers are big strapping men, like me. You're this tiny thing and skinny as a rail. I don't think you've eaten since Adam died."

"Dad." Maureen shook her head at his exaggeration. It was almost six years that Adam had been gone, and the pain at the mention of his name had passed. Her heart was still full of what-ifs and whys, but time had worked its healing magic, something she had originally thought impossible.

"And you're so cute," Dad continued as if she hadn't interrupted him. "Like your mother. What big bad perp's going to listen to a sweet little thing like you?" He sniffed.

"Now don't go all gooey on me." She hugged him, and he hugged her back, his bulk, as always, making her feel secure, safe. "You taught me to pray about decisions, and I've done that about this choice. In fact, I've done it for years. And I can't think of anything else I'd rather do." *Except be Adam's wife.* The thought came automatically, and she pushed it aside, amazed and guilty at how easy it had become.

Dad sighed. "It's your mother's fault."

Maureen had to laugh. "What?"

He nodded. "If she weren't so independent—"

"If she weren't so independent," Maureen cut in, "she'd bore you to tears."

Her father grinned. "Haven't had a boring day since I met her."

"Since you met who?" Mom asked as she walked into the room. "You have another woman hidden away somewhere that I don't know about?" She walked to her husband and wrapped an arm about his waist.

"Wouldn't dare." He wrapped his arms around her, rocking her from side to side.

He wouldn't want to, Maureen knew as she felt again the warmth of knowing her parents loved each other. Their marriage was just what she had wanted for herself and Adam. Sparks after more than thirty-five years.

"He's blaming you for my wanting to be a cop," Maureen said. "You infected me with your independent spirit."

"I did?" Mom drew back. "Why, Sean Galloway, that's the nicest thing you've said in a long while, even if it isn't true. It was you and how handsome you looked in your uniform."

Now Maureen grinned as she sat in the hospital parking lot. What a wonderful heritage. She'd hoped to pass it on to her own children, but in the absence of that possibility, she'd just make her parents proud.

With that thought in mind, she studied the white Saturn. She'd watched the occupants, Dori and a very handsome man, go into the hospital. Their faces had looked so serious that she almost believed they had someone in there they were worried about. Well, maybe they did; even bad guys had family members who got sick. She climbed out of her car and walked to the white Saturn. She called Greg. "Any word?"

"The owner is one Phillip Trevelyan, 3142 Oystercatcher Way, Apt. 4B, Seaside."

"Ah." So the handsome guy lived in Seaside. Interesting. She bent and peered in the windows of the car to see what she could see. "What else have you got?"

"He's a pharmacist."

She straightened. "He's what?"

"You heard me. He owns the pharmacy at Ninth and Asbury."

"Across from the Christian bookstore?"

"That's the one."

"What do you think? He borrowed the money to buy the store from Jankowski and is working it off by running his errands? Or he's low on funds now and likes to eat, so he's earning food money by running the errands? Or maybe he's just a corrupt pharmacist who makes more money with illegals than in his store?"

Greg grunted noncommittally. "His brother's the pastor at Seaside Chapel."

Maureen frowned, not sure what to do with that piece of information. "That's nice."

"Well, sit tight and don't let them out of your sight."

"You know, Greg, I could break into the trunk and get the goods in a flash."

"If getting the stuff back were all there was to it, I'd say go ahead. But—"

"But it's Jankowski."

"Right. So be a good little shadow, and I'll see you when I see you. Just keep in touch."

Maureen climbed back into the Camry and slouched in her seat. Was there anything as boring as surveillance? *Look, Dad, no guns.* She made a little face. *No clue either, but we won't talk about that.*

Four

$\mathcal{P}$ASTOR PAUL TREVELYAN walked in the front door of his house in Seaside, New Jersey, and froze. "Ryan! What are you doing home?"

The thirteen-year-old who had been lounging on the sofa watching TV stared wide-eyed at Trev but said nothing. His face was a study in conflicting emotions: shock, distress, antagonism, fear.

It was the fear that hit Trev the hardest.

Belatedly, the black lab who had been sprawled across Ryan's lap jumped to the floor and raced to Trev. The dog wiggled and made little welcoming sounds in his throat. When Trev gave him the merest pat on the head, the dog butted him in the hip.

Trev looked from Ryan to the dog and grinned. He loved this dog who'd seen him through a lot of lonely times. "Hey, Jack. How's my boy?"

Jack went wild with delight as he reveled in Trev's energetic ear scratch.

As he rubbed the animal's head, Trev tried to decide what to do about Ryan. The boy was supposed to be in school, not draped across the sofa watching daytime TV.

"What's up, kiddo?" Trev finally asked. "Aren't you feeling well?"

"How come you're home?" Ryan Harper countered,

fake bravado coloring his voice. At least Trev thought it was fake. "You're supposed to be at work."

Trev glanced at the clock. 10:30 AM. "Yeah, I am, but I just got an emergency call from my brother. Pop's in the hospital. I've got to go to Pennsylvania for a couple of days."

Ryan sat up at that, his teen defiance giving way to uncertainty. "What about me?"

Trev knew exactly how the boy felt. He had felt that same way when his parents had been killed. *What about me?* "Do you want to come with me?"

"How sick is he? Hospital?"

"Yeah, hospital."

"And you'll be visiting there?"

"As long as they let me stay."

Ryan made a face.

"That's what I thought." Trev dropped his jacket on the stuffed chair. "That's why I spoke to Todd's mom. She said you could stay there through the weekend."

Ryan brightened and seemed to relax. A weekend with his best friend wouldn't be too bad, though he was careful not to admit it. "So, when are you coming back?"

"Today's Friday. Probably sometime late tomorrow night. I have to preach on Sunday."

Ryan looked satisfied as he collapsed once again on the sofa, slumped so far that he was almost sitting on his neck. Trev marveled at the kid's suppleness. Ryan was a little guy, skinny, undeveloped, and he hated himself for not growing. At his age he didn't appreciate the fine mind he possessed, wishing only for a bigger body and some athletic prowess. Poor Ryan suffered from the curse of the nerd.

Trev had seen pictures of the boy's mother, Lucy, and she was a real looker. He expected the boy would one day be quite good-looking too. All he had to do was survive the years of growing up, an experience fraught with untold pitfalls even without the instability of Ryan's present circumstances.

Trev fought back the wave of sympathy he felt for the lonely boy. Even when your life was in the toilet, you had to go to school. The fact that you were smarter than many of your teachers didn't alter the law. Neither did the fact that for you every day was an exercise in anxiety and social failure.

Hooky was unacceptable.

Ryan kept his attention firmly on the TV, apparently mesmerized by commercials for hemorrhoid ointment and denture fixative. Trev bit back a smile. Any topic was preferable to the lecture the kid knew was coming.

"We'll talk in a minute," Trev said. "I want to get packed first."

Ryan grunted as denture cream gave way to Scrubbing Bubbles. "Whatever."

Trev made his way to the second floor. He pulled his duffel from the shelf in his closet and threw in enough for an overnight stay.

Pop was in the hospital. Unbelievable. The man was never sick. The young Trev had secretly thought him invincible, the one man in history who would live forever. With his barrel chest and deep, hearty voice, he exuded strength and character.

When Trev's parents died, Pop was his lifeline. He and Honey wrapped him and Phil and Dori in a giant security blanket and stabilized a world gone madly atilt. Pop taught them love and responsibility. He taught them life.

And now he was sick. A heart attack. An old person's ailment.

Oh, Lord, please don't let Pop become an invalid. He couldn't take it. I couldn't take it.

It was almost impossible to think of Pop as an old man, though Trev knew he was. People his age were subject to all kinds of ailments—strokes, heart attacks, cancers. But that was people in general, not Pop the Indestructible.

Trev blinked against the sudden wash of tears that stung the back of his eyes. He grabbed his toothbrush and shaving tackle. Maybe this heart attack wasn't all that serious. Maybe Phil had exaggerated.

"When did this happen?" Trev had asked as he talked to his brother on the phone in his church office.

"Last night about nine." Phil sounded tired. "Honey and I've been at the hospital with him all night."

"And you're just now calling me?"

"Honey tried to get you last night, but there was no answer.

When she got me, I drove right up. At midnight she decided to stop calling you, to wait until morning so you could have a good night's sleep."

"But I was home all night," Trev said. "Ryan and I watched some TV and ate ice cream."

"I don't know, Trev. Maybe Honey called the church number by mistake. I never thought to ask."

"Yeah. There were a number of hang ups when I checked the messages this morning."

"He-he looks so vulnerable, Trev. Weary." Disbelief filled Phil's voice.

Trev's hand went to his heart, and he rubbed there as if he could make the pain of those words go away. "Maybe all they'll have to do is Roto-Rooter his arteries or bring down his blood pressure or something equally doable." *Please, Lord, may it be so!*

"If the doctors know, they haven't told us yet. When can you come?"

"I'll be there in a couple of hours. I've got to take care of Ryan first."

The brothers hung up, and Trev quickly cleared his calendar for the next two days. Then he rushed home to pack and caught Ryan.

Now he zipped his bag shut and went downstairs. Ryan hadn't moved, and Jack had climbed back onto the sofa and draped himself over the boy's lap.

"Will you and Todd stop by a couple of times tonight and tomorrow to take care of Jack?"

Ryan reached a hand to Jack's silky black head and fondled an ear. "You want me to take care of you, boy?"

Jack grinned his doggie grin.

Trev smiled at the dog. The one thing that had gone right since Ryan came to stay three weeks ago was the mutual affection between the boy and Jack. In fact, Jack had deserted Trev's bed to sleep with Ryan, a fact that pleased the boy immensely.

It was a simple case of someone caring, and Trev couldn't begrudge the need for an extra blanket at night to replace Jack's body heat. He knew all too well Ryan's uncertainty because he'd felt it himself when his parents died, and he'd had Phil and Dori to help him get through it. Poor Ryan had no one. Well, he had Mae Harper, his grandmother, but she wasn't available at the moment.

The boy's father had gone AWOL two weeks after Ryan was born and hadn't been seen nor heard from since. His mother left her then two-year-old toddler with her mother so she might go to New York and become a famous Broadway star, an ambition she had still not achieved after eleven years. She deigned to visit Seaside once or twice a year as the mood struck her, but then she only stayed a couple of hours.

For years Ryan's only security had been his grandmother. Now Mae was in the rehab center on the mainland, trying to recover functions damaged in a terrible fall at her bookstore. Breaks in both hip and leg had required surgery and guaranteed it would be some time before she could return to work. All attempts to find Ryan's mother to tell her of her mother's injuries and her son's need had failed.

Trev went to the kitchen to get himself something to eat on the trip to see Pop. He opened the refrigerator and stared. There were no two ways about it: The worst part of living alone was having to feed yourself. And having a hungry Ryan around did not simplify the matter. For a little guy, Ryan ate an amazing amount of food. In fact, Ryan reminded Trev of a younger Jack, all big feet and unbelievable appetite.

Finally Trev shut the fridge and pulled the trusty jar of chunky peanut butter from the cupboard. He slathered bread with it and a cholesterol-defying amount of butter and slid the sandwich into a plastic bag. He grabbed an apple, a pack of chocolate Tastykakes, and a bag of Herr's chips. He went back to the refrigerator. There were two twenty-ounce bottles of Coke chilling there, and he grabbed one. He made a mental note to buy more.

He stood quietly in the kitchen for a moment. What was he supposed to say to Ryan? His natural tendency was to make light of the crime, to be flip, to make it a joke. One day out of school was not going to ruin Ryan's life nor cost him admission to a good college.

So where was Lucy Harper when you needed her? Of course, she'd probably do a worse job than Trev if her past record was anything to go by. Missed birthdays. Unkept promises of visits.

And Christmas might as well not exist for all the attention she paid her son at that time of year.

No, the kid was probably better off stuck with an ignorant guy like himself, an ignorant guy who had no idea what to do but at least was present. Somehow Pop had always known how to handle him and Phil. So, what would Pop do?

Who knew? Neither he nor Phil had ever bagged school. But if they had, there would have been plenty of sound and fury. He was sure of that.

Sound and fury. Okay, Lord, give me the right words, please!

His mental loins girded to deliver a telling lecture on school and responsibility of the thirteen-year-old kind, Trev walked from the kitchen. He stopped short at the sight of Ryan with his head buried in Jack's neck and his arms wrapped around the dog. The boy's nape looked so vulnerable, his skinny shoulders so fragile, that the lecture died before one word was spoken.

Ryan straightened when he heard Trev's footsteps. He tried to recapture the bravado he'd had when Trev first came home but failed miserably. All he managed was to look woebegone with a capital W. "I can just stay here with Jack. I can take care of myself, you know."

"I'm sure you can," Trev said.

"In fact, I can take care of myself all the time. Then I wouldn't be a bother to you."

Trev blinked. "You aren't a bother to me."

Ryan looked skeptical. "Whatever. But if I took care of myself, I wouldn't have to go to school if I didn't want to. Or church." Ryan's resentment at what life had dealt him bled out in every word. "I wouldn't have to do anything I didn't want to."

Trev nodded. "But how would you get to the store to buy your food? And where would you get the money to pay for it?"

Ryan frowned.

"And what about paying the rent on your apartment? Or getting new clothes as you grow? Where would that money come from? Even if someone was willing to hire you at your age, how would you get to the job?"

"But I just want to call my own shots! I just want to do what I want!"

Trev looked Ryan square in the eye as he bit his lip to keep from smiling. "When you have the money and the transportation to care for yourself, then you can do as you want. But in the meantime, I'll drop you at school on my way out of town."

The unhappy face somehow managed to become unhappier. "You're going to make me go back?"

Trev didn't answer.

"Yeah, you are." Ryan gently pushed Jack aside and got to his feet. With a sigh he grabbed his Eagles jacket from the chair where he'd tossed it. When he pulled it on, it swallowed him whole. Mae had undoubtedly bought it for him to grow into. It would probably only take five years.

Trev zipped his red Lands' End Squall and grabbed his duffel. The two walked in silence to the car.

They were almost to the school when Ryan spoke, his voice barely above a whisper. "I'm sorry, Pastor Paul."

Trev reached over and patted Ryan's knee. "Sometimes life stinks, big guy. There's no other word for it. But we have to keep going."

Ryan nodded, a picture of dejection.

"Did you know that I'm an orphan?"

Ryan looked at him, surprised. "Then who's Pop?"

"My grandfather. After our parents died, he raised my brother and me." And Dori.

Interested in spite of himself, Ryan asked, "How old were you when they died?"

"Nine. Phil was twelve." And Dori was seven.

"How'd they die?"

"Drunk driver."

"Yuk."

"You can say that again."

Ryan was quiet for a minute. "At least they didn't leave you on purpose."

Trev's heart stumbled. "No, they didn't. But, you know, Ryan, God's our Father who never leaves."

Ryan sat up straight and stared out the windshield as Trev pulled to the curb in front of the school. "No offense, Pastor Paul, but I'm not sure I believe all that God stuff anymore."

Trev nodded. "I understand." And he did. He remembered all the years when he blamed God for everything that had happened to him. How he had teased Dori when she "got religion" at a Young Life meeting back in high school. He wondered, as he frequently did, whether she still followed the Lord. Whenever he called her, she kept the call so short that he didn't have time to probe. The few times he'd visited her, she always made certain someone else was with them, so again no time to talk about anything of substance.

He rubbed absently at his chest. Would the pain that speared through him whenever he thought of her ever go away? But how could it? When you lost your heart, you were bound to feel the ache of its absence.

Ryan climbed reluctantly from the car. Trev felt like an ogre even though he knew the boy had to go back to school.

"I'll see you Sunday," Trev called after Ryan as the boy dragged himself up the walk. A weak little wave over his shoulder indicated that he had heard. When the school door swung shut behind the kid, Trev drove away.

He worried and prayed about Ryan as he crossed the Ninth Street Causeway and made his way to the Garden State Parkway. Taking the boy in had seemed such a logical thing to do when Mae got hurt.

"Just until your grandmother comes home," he'd said to Ryan at the hospital that first night. "We don't want her worrying about you unnecessarily."

"I can take care of myself," Ryan had answered.

Trev looked at the determined set of the boy's jaw and nodded. Pride was about all the kid had left. "I'm sure you can, but do you want to? It's always nicer to be around another person. And you'll love Jack."

At least he'd been right about that. It was hard to tell who trailed who, Ryan Jack or Jack Ryan. He just knew that where one was, there was the other.

As he turned north on the Atlantic City Expressway, Trev's mind turned to what awaited him. Pop. A heart attack. Unbelievable.

When he and Honey had come to rescue Phil, Dori, and him

the day after their parents died, Trev had responded immediately to Pop's strength.

I want to be just like him, his boy's mind had thought. Little had happened to change his mind. Even when he found Christ in college, Pop was still a model of common sense and reliability to him. *If I can be just like him with the added depth of knowing Christ, I just might be a man worth knowing. And, Lord, please help Pop come to know Jesus as Savior. Honey, too.*

Pop had run a tight ship. He and Honey expected the three of them to obey regardless of their feelings on a matter.

"This home is not a democracy," he frequently told them. "It is a benevolent dictatorship. I am the dictator, and Honey is the dictatrix or whatever the female counterpart is. What we say is law."

There was always so much fun and love mixed with the law that none of them minded. Still, he never had any doubt that to cross Pop was to ask for it.

Trev smiled to himself. Whenever he thought of the summer he was fifteen and Dori thirteen, he knew he had the quintessential Pop.

It was the first Trev noticed her *that* way. Up until that day in June, he'd loved her like a sister. He considered himself her protector, her guardian, her big brother, the one whose job it was to tell her what to do and how to do it. He could pick on her as much as he wanted, but let anyone else, even Phil, bother her at his peril.

Then that day as he was mowing the lawn, she'd walked into the backyard in her new bathing suit.

Trev looked up from following the faint marks in the grass that showed where he'd last mowed and almost swallowed his tongue. He stood, paralyzed by the vision before him. When had she grown that figure? When had she turned from a skinny, scrappy little girl into a femme fatale? He couldn't stop staring.

Pop was working in the garden, and when the lawn mower seemed stuck in one spot, he looked over to see why. He got to his feet, walked to Trev, and tapped him on the shoulder.

"Turn it off," he mouthed, pointing to the mower.

Trev blinked himself back to reality and let the machine die.

"Come with me," Pop said. "You need a break."

Still feeling as if he'd been hit over the head, Trev followed Pop into the kitchen. Pop went to the refrigerator and pulled out two cans of Sprite. He handed one to Trev. They popped the tabs and took long drinks.

As if his head were attached to a lead that pulled him, Trev turned to look through the sliding glass doors at Dori, spreading a towel in the freshly mown grass.

"Trev."

"Um?" She was going to lie there and sun herself. Suddenly he felt a need to get a tan too.

"Trev." Pop's voice was more insistent.

"Yep?" She lay on her stomach, her head pillowed on her arms. Her dark hair was pulled high on her head in a ponytail. Her face was turned in his direction, her brown eyes closed against the sun.

"Paul Michael Trevelyan!"

Trev jumped and turned to Pop, Dori momentarily forgotten. All three names? What in the world had he done?

"Look at me, boy, and listen closely."

Trev blinked and nodded. "Yes, sir."

"Dori's becoming a very beautiful young lady."

Trev grinned.

"And if I ever catch you looking at her like that again, I'll send one of you away."

The grin disappeared. "What?"

"You heard me. I will not have any romantic folderol in this house."

Folderol? "Send her away?"

"Or you."

Trev knew implacable when he saw it. "Pop!"

"I want your word that you will leave her alone."

"You'd actually send one of us away?"

"Swear to me, Trev, that you will stay away from her in any way romantic whatsoever. Swear."

And so for years he said nothing about how he felt.

Did she know about Pop's illness? Had Phil or Honey called her? Surely she would come, wouldn't she? As he pulled up to the hospital, his heart was thudding wildly, and he wasn't sure which scared him most—seeing Pop or perhaps seeing Dori.

When he reached the third floor, he saw Phil leaning against the wall outside a room whose door was closed.

"Phil." The brothers shook hands, then hugged awkwardly. "How is he?"

"I don't know. We haven't seen the doctors yet today. I'm hopeful though. His pain level has gone way down. He knows what's going on around him. He's cranky and giving orders."

Trev laughed. "I'd say that last is a very good sign."

Phil grinned back. "That's why I'm out here in the hall. 'Go away, Phil. I want to talk to her by herself.'"

Trev nodded. He'd always enjoyed watching the love between Pop and Honey. She was his second wife, his first having died from uterine cancer. Pop was fifty-two and Honey forty-eight when they married. They had five years together before Trev, Phil, and Dori arrived, putting Pop through a second stint at parenting and Honey a first. Their affection for each other filled their home and had given the young orphaned Trev the family every kid needed. "How's Honey taking it?"

"She's doing fine. She's a strong lady. She's down in the cafeteria getting coffee and something to eat. We had to practically throw her out of the room."

Trev's gut clenched. "If Honey's in the cafeteria, who's in with Pop?"

"Brace yourself, little brother."

"Dori?" Trev tried to be casual, but he feared he was failing miserably.

Phil nodded. "Dori. I called her last night. She flew in on the red-eye. I picked her up at the airport." He slanted a glance at Trev. "She looks great, by the way. Prettier than ever."

Trev wondered how that could possibly be true. She'd always been beautiful to him.

"Look," Phil said. "Do you know what happened that made her bolt? I've never pushed for somebody to tell me what happened, but I've always wondered."

Trev had to grin. Phil had pushed and pushed for information, not that he'd gotten any from Trev.

Phil looked at the door to Pop's room. "I always figured it must be something Pop did, and I'd probably be happier not knowing."

"Pop?" Trev couldn't hide his surprise.

Phil nodded. "He can be awfully heavy-handed sometimes, and she could be easily hurt."

"Pop didn't do anything." Of that Trev was certain, even if he wasn't certain about much else.

"You sure?" Phil looked amazed.

"Absolutely."

"Well, I certainly didn't do anything, and Honey couldn't hurt anyone if she tried." Phil narrowed his eyes at Trev. "That leaves you." His voice grew hard. "Just what did you do to her?"

Trev gave a sad half smile. "I married her."

Five

JOANNE PILOTTI STARED at the contents of the black suitcase in confusion. Paperbacks. Millions of them, or so it seemed. What was this, a bookstore on wheels?

She pulled the books out and stacked them neatly on the table beside her. Eight of them with titles like *Don't Look Behind You* and *You Can't Run Too Fast* and *Shadows at Stillburn Keep*. All the covers had women running, and they all ran looking over their shoulders. Some ran from a mysterious shadow or dark woods. Some ran toward an old mansion and some an old castle, all with one light lit in the attic window or in the top of a castle tower.

Joanne snorted. Give her a good horror film any day. Besides, if she was going to read, which she wasn't if she could help it, she'd try Stephen King. Fortunately, she hadn't had to read anything since the last book cover she read for a book report back just before she quit school in tenth grade. That was three whole years ago.

Still, it was very clever of whoever sent the suitcase. If some security guy checked like they did sometimes these days, he'd think she was some smart lady who liked to read. A lot. They'd never think courier. Never in a million years.

"Want to earn some big money?" Vinnie'd asked when he came to her house a week ago.

"Big money? Sure. Who doesn't?" she said, but she wasn't completely dumb. It was a rough world, and a girl couldn't be too careful. "What do I have to do?"

"Pick up a suitcase."

She stared at him as he reached in her refrigerator and got out the first of many beers. She kept it stocked for him. "Just get a suitcase? That's all?"

Vinnie nodded as he tore the tab from the can and sucked out the contents.

Joanne eyed him, trying to see the catch. There had to be one somewhere. She had never been one of those pampered princesses like some of the girls she had gone to school with, the ones who got everything they wanted, the ones who somehow attracted all the breaks. Not her. She attracted all the hard knocks.

Of course with Vinnie's new job, they were hoping things would be different. Maybe sometime soon they could even get married, not that Vinnie had actually asked her. Still, she was hopeful.

And suspicious about the suitcase gig. "Why aren't they sending you to get the suitcase?"

He let out a loud, "Ahh!" of satisfaction as he crumbled the beer can in his hand. A loud belch followed.

"You aren't setting me up to carry on a bomb to blow up the plane, are you?" She looked at him with sudden fear. "'Cause I don't want to get blown up."

Vinnie looked at her like she had just crawled out from under a rock. "Geez, Joanne, where do you get your crazy ideas? The idea of a courier is for the courier to deliver something safely."

"Yeah, well," she said defensively, "I just gotta be sure. So, why aren't you taking the job?"

"Well, you see," he began, and Joanne went on high alert. *Well, you see* was a warning. He always gave himself away when he was trying to weasel out of something.

"It's like this." He grabbed his second beer. "Mr. J is looking for a woman to be the courier, and he asked me if I knew anyone I could trust."

Mr. J. Neal Jankowski. Now there was a name that made all

Atlantic City quake, Vinnie told her, and Vinnie knew what he was talking about. After all, Mr. J was Vinnie's new boss.

"He's already asking your advice?" She felt so proud. Maybe she had been wrong about the *well, you see.*

Vinnie nodded, trying to make believe he didn't feel proud too. "So, you interested?"

She nodded. "Yeah. How much money, where do I get the suitcase, and where do I got to deliver it?"

"One thousand dollars, Chicago, and to me right here in Seaside," Vinnie told her.

At first all she heard was the one thousand, and she could hardly breathe at the thought. How many tables did she have to wait on in that little bitty restaurant before she had a thou free and clear? She giggled. She could already imagine all the new clothes she'd buy with her payment, and not from Wal-Mart, oh, no. This time she was going to Sears or Penney's to get really good stuff, maybe even stuff made in the USA.

Then she heard the rest of the deal. "What? I gotta go to Chicago?"

Vinnie was halfway through can number two. "Sure."

"And just how do I get there?"

"You fly."

She stared at him in disbelief as she started to hyperventilate. "No way. I can't! You know I can't. Planes crash and all the people die! In little pieces!"

Vinnie shook his head in exasperation. "Jo, what do you care about little pieces? I mean, dead is dead."

Gasping for air, she began pacing, wiping her sweaty palms over and over against her jeans. "I care, especially if it's me!"

Vinnie stepped in front of her and stuck his face in hers. "You're going to Chicago. I told Mr. J you would."

His voice was soft and lethal, and she closed her eyes against it. "I can't," she whimpered. Not even for gorgeous new clothes. Not even for Vinnie.

"You don't have no choice, Jo." Vinnie grabbed her hair and forced her to look at him. "Mr. J is counting on me." He gave an extra tug and she winced at the pain. "And you."

So she'd flown to Chicago yesterday, so zoned out on tranqs that she barely noticed the takeoff, the flight, or the landing. It was all she could do to get out of her seat and walk off the plane, dragging her big purse with her clean underwear in it behind her. Her thighs were all black and blue from where she kept bumping into the seats, and she literally bounced off the walls of the Jetway, but she didn't care. She was on the ground again!

She finally found her way to the transportation stand and climbed in a cab.

"Where to, lady?" the cabbie asked.

"Chicago," she said.

He turned around and stared at her. "Can we be a bit more specific?"

For a minute Joanne didn't know what to say. Then she remembered the piece of paper in her pocket. Vinnie had stuck it there. "Give this to the cab driver. He'll take you here."

And he did, right up to the door of the Holiday Inn O'Hare. She dragged herself out of the cab and slapped one of the five twenties Vinnie had given her into his hand. "Thank you, and keep the change."

He blinked, then looked at her with a wide grin. With a wave, he was gone.

She felt like a high roller with two queen-size beds and a gleaming bathroom with enough towels for a small army. There was a big TV with a remote, and by playing with the buttons, she found she could get all kinds of movies right here in the room. She decided to watch every single one to keep the fear of tomorrow's return flight at bay.

When the third movie ended, she thought about going out to eat all by herself. Nasty. Everybody would think she was some ugly person that no one liked. Then her eye fell on an ad for pizza delivered right to your room. She watched the next three movies as she chomped her way through a large pizza with everything including anchovies, which she could never get at home because Vinnie hated them. She fell asleep happy.

Now she was happy again, back home in Seaside in her little third-floor apartment, checking out the suitcase before Vinnie came for it. She wanted to see what was in it. Nosy her mother always called her. Personally, Jo liked the word *curious* better.

Under the books were women's clothes—sweaters and sweat-shirts, jeans, slacks, a denim skirt, tops in lots of different colors, pajamas, and at the bottom some very pretty underwear, very pretty indeed. Too bad it wasn't her size. Last came two pairs of shoes with deodorant tucked in one of the shoes, a bottle of perfume in another. Clever.

Slipped in among the clothes were several pretty things. She liked the glass ball with lots of different colors swirled through it. She didn't know what you did with it, but it would look pretty sitting on a table or something. She put it on her end table under the light. It sort of glowed, and she loved it.

The silver and gold picture frame was just the right size for the picture of her and Vinnie taken at the beach last summer. He looked so handsome with his curly black hair and great tan. She didn't look too bad either in her red and white bikini. Since she never went into the ocean, her hair was just right, and her nose wasn't even red from the sun.

There were a couple of neckties in the suitcase too. One had pill bottles all over it, spilling colorful pills onto a bright red background. Who would ever wear an ugly thing like that? The other had books and more books in lots of colors on a bright blue background. Well, maybe a teacher might wear that. She tossed them in the general direction of the wastebasket.

The door opened and Vinnie came in with a six-pack in his hand.

"Hey, what are you doing?" he yelled, dropping the beer and rushing to her.

She blinked, scared. "J-just looking. I didn't hurt nothing! Honest!"

Vinnie fell to his knees and flipped up the lining at the bottom of the empty suitcase. He stared, not moving for a minute, then turned to her, his face white with horror. "What did you do with them?"

"I didn't do nothing with nothing." She backed behind the stuffed chair. "Unless you mean that glass thing." She pointed a shaking finger at the table.

"You dumb—I should never have trusted you!" Vinnie grabbed the glass ball and threw it as hard as he could against the wall. It didn't break, but the wall did.

And she knew she was in very big trouble.

*Y*OU WHAT?"

Trev would have laughed at Phil's horrified expression if the subject weren't so painful. "I married her," he repeated.

Phil was outraged. "But she's our sister!"

Trev shook his head. "She's not."

Some of Phil's anger dropped away. "Or as good as."

"Yours maybe." Trev thought of Dori's vibrant, laughing face. He thought of the wrenching pain of her long absence. "Not mine."

Phil ran his hand through his hair. "I can't believe you fell in love with her *that* way."

"Big-time, big brother. Big-time."

Phil still looked poleaxed. "Why did I never know this?"

Trev shrugged. "You're not very observant?"

"Don't give me that. I'm as observant as the next man."

Trev didn't say anything. What was there to say when you had kept your feelings under tight rein for years, then let them loose in one glorious weekend, only to have the sweet, fizzing wine of love turn sour before its time?

"When?" Phil demanded.

"When what? When did I fall in love with her, or when did I marry her?"

"Both."

Trev looked at his disgruntled brother. "I realized I loved her when I was about fifteen."

Phil shuddered. "This creeps me out."

Trev leaned against the wall and crossed one foot over the other. "Yeah, I guess it does sound weird."

Suddenly Phil's fists balled, and he leaned in Trev's face. "Did you ever take advantage of her? Is that why she left?"

Trev held up a hand in the sign of peace. "Easy, Phil. Relax. I never took advantage of her in any way. I might not have been a Christian back then, but I'd like to think that I still had some integrity. After all, Pop raised me."

"So when did you marry her?"

"The weekend before she disappeared."

"That was six years ago!"

"Close your mouth, Phil. Flies will get in."

Phil frowned. "You're nuts."

"I know. Was, am, and always will be nuts about her."

"Then why in the world do you live in New Jersey and she lives in California?"

"That's the big question, Phil. And I don't know the answer."

"You mean she's never told you why she walked? Come on, Trev. You're not dumb. You must know what you did."

Trev pushed himself off the wall and began to pace. "She told me I broke my vows to her."

"You were unfaithful? You? Mr. Squeaky-Clean Christian?"

"I wasn't a Christian then."

"Oh, yeah, you weren't. You were the quintessential ladies' man."

Trev eyed his brother. "Look who's talking."

Phil shrugged, not denying he had a similar reputation. "But back to this Dori thing. If you were only married for one weekend, how'd you have time to be with another woman?"

"I was never with another woman."

"Never?"

"From that moment to this."

"Did you tell her that?"

"Of course I told her, but she kept saying she knew what she knew, and what she knew was that I'd broken my vows. If I cared so little for her, I didn't deserve her."

"And this makes sense to you?" Phil asked.

"No!" Trev rubbed between his brows to ease the tension. "No," he said more gently.

"So when did you get your divorce?"

Trev turned to him, startled. "We're not divorced."

"What?"

"We're not divorced."

"You haven't lived together for six years, but you're still married?"

Trev shrugged. He had no idea how to explain. All he knew was that he would never, ever institute divorce proceedings against Dori, and for some reason known only to her, she had never moved against him either.

He'd talked about this strange situation with Dr. Quentin, his seminary professor and the man he considered his mentor.

"I love her," he'd told Dr. Quentin several times. "I want to be married to her. I want her with me."

Dr. Quentin nodded. "What if she doesn't ever want to be with you?"

"If she divorces me, there's not much I can do about it, is there?" He heard the self-pity in his voice and flinched inside.

"Probably not. But you do know that being divorced will affect your ministry, don't you?"

"Oh yes, I understand that." And he did, all too well. There were many churches that wouldn't even consider a divorced man for their pulpit. "I just keep praying that she comes back, and not just because of its effect on my ministry. I love her."

"Just be careful of that anger if she comes back." Dr. Quentin smiled. "It could sink your love boat before you're even out of port."

So he continued to hope that one day she'd come home, that one day she'd be willing to talk to him about whatever it was that was stuck in her craw, that one day they could straighten things out and have a marriage like Pop and Honey.

An amused smile began to curve Phil's lips. "Does Pop know? Because if he doesn't, I want to be there when you tell him. That way I can bind up your wounds when he realizes you're the reason his baby girl left home."

"He knows I love her, but I never told him we were married." Trev didn't know if Dori had said anything, but he doubted it. Surely Pop would have indicated he knew, wouldn't he? "In fact, I've never told anyone but Dr. Quentin until right now, not even the elders at the chapel."

Phil looked at him strangely. "You never told anyone at all?"

"It's sort of awkward to say, 'I'm married, but my wife left me three days after our wedding.'"

"Yeah." Phil nodded. "I see your point. But what's going to happen if men like Jonathan Warrington find out? He's not the sort to take news like this lying down."

Trev shuddered mentally. To say Jonathan Warrington was an elder of strong opinions was much like saying a cheetah was an animal that liked to run. Jonathan didn't hesitate to use his position to unleash lethal attacks any more than the cheetah debated using his speed to overpower a weaker animal.

"And then there's Angie." Phil was laughing now. "Whoa, baby, are you in trouble, Trev."

"Shut up, Phil." Trev spoke without heat. Poor Angie. She'd had a bad crush on him ever since he came to the chapel two and a half years ago, straight from seminary. She was a nice person, cute, amazingly pleasant considering that Jonathan Warrington was her father. She was a college senior this year, and she clearly saw herself as a wonderful candidate for pastor's wife.

When Phil cocked his head and looked at him with narrowed eyes, Trev braced himself.

"Is this marriage why you haven't been willing to take the pastor's position permanently? Does it make you feel unqualified?"

Trev leaned back against the wall again and stared at his crossed ankles for a long minute. Phil was touching on a very thorny issue, one about which he knew there would be much debate if his situation were known. And it should be that way. A pastor's marriage was a key issue in his suitability for the job.

"Yes, I'm married, but I haven't lived with my wife for six

years," was hardly the answer any church board would want to hear from a candidate for their pulpit.

"When they asked me to come to the chapel over two years ago," Trev said, "it was basically for the summer. Their former pastor had left rather abruptly, and they were caught with the summer season coming and no minister. I came with the idea of being there three, four months. What I would do at the end of that time, I wasn't sure. Probably make use of my undergraduate degree in business somehow."

"That's right," Phil said. "Back before you got religion, you were going to be a very rich businessman."

Trev shrugged. "What can I say? I was young and immature. I thought money was the way to happiness."

"Then you found true love and lasting happiness." Phil's smile was sad.

"Then I found Christ and true happiness," Trev corrected.

"And Seaside Chapel."

Trev nodded. "Every couple of months in the two and a half years I've been there, the elders ask me to take the job permanently, but I can't. How can I be a pastor with a marriage like mine, and how can I ever explain the situation? Maybe I'm splitting hairs. I don't know. All I know is that my conscience allows me to be the interim but not the permanent pastor."

"You're as good as permanent, bro. I don't see them looking for anyone else to fill the pulpit."

"I don't either." Trev couldn't decide whether he was pleased about this or not. It was a compliment that the people of Seaside felt blessed by his ministry, but Phil was right. It might as well be a permanent thing. He'd have to prod the elders to look for someone else.

"And I don't think they will look, Trev. You've done too good a job. The church is growing, the people like you, and you're dynamite in the pulpit."

Trev blinked. "You mean you actually listen?"

"I always listen to my younger brother," Phil said, face straight, eyes twinkling. "He always knows what's best."

Trev grinned. "Yeah, right."

Phil grinned back. "It drove me nuts growing up. Which brings me back to this present strange situation, which is anything but your standard modus operandi."

Trev agreed, pushed himself away from the wall, and went to stare glumly out the window. The parking lot had mounds of snow pushed to the rear to open as many parking slots as possible. None had melted. Cold out there and cold in his heart.

How had his life gotten so messed up? He hadn't expected things to be any different than usual that fateful spring weekend when he was a junior and Dori a freshman at college. The evening had started quietly enough. She'd come to the apartment he and Phil shared to cook them dinner, not an unusual occurrence.

As she poured spaghetti sauce into a pan, Trev had pulled a beer from the refrigerator. He leaned against the counter and watched her. She had on jeans and a long-sleeved T-shirt and clogs. She wore no makeup and her hair was pulled up into a slightly off-center ponytail.

"What?" she asked as she put the pot on the stove.

He tossed the empty bottle in the trash. He pulled another out and twisted the cap. "I didn't say anything."

"You're staring."

He shrugged. How could he tell her what he felt when she was around? "You're nice to look at."

She turned to him, her cheeks red. "Trev."

"Are you blushing?" He grinned and took a long swallow. Maybe the cold liquid would cool the heat in his blood. *Yeah, right.*

She watched him drink and frowned. "How many bottles have you had today?"

He blinked. A lecture about drinking would kill any amorous thoughts more quickly than a dozen cold showers. "How should I know?"

"That's what concerns me," she said. "These days I never see you without a bottle in your hand."

"So what? It's only beer."

"Beer can make alcoholics too, you know."

"Come on, Dori. You're overreacting."

She walked to him and took the bottle from his hand. "I'm not overreacting. You drink too much, Trev. It worries me. You know what drinking did to our parents."

He glared at her. "I am not irresponsible enough to drink and drive."

"So you say." She looked at him with those amazing dark eyes. "Please promise me you'll stop."

Much as he hated to admit it, he knew she was right. He was drinking very heavily. It was what college guys did. They hung out together and drank. They played football, basketball, or baseball and drank. They scoped out the babes in the park and drank. They went out for late night pizza and drank. They turned the air blue with their jokes and drank.

She laid her hand on his arm. "Please, Trev."

He tried to save face. "I'll cut down. How's that?"

She shook her head. "Stop."

"Stop? As in totally?"

"As in completely. Please? For me?" She moved her hand to his chest. "Please?"

Something inside him shifted, and suddenly his thoughts had nothing to do with beer. Maybe it was the look in her eyes. Maybe it was the way she stood so close, her hand on his chest. Probably it was him reaching his limit to the rigid discipline he'd practiced for so many years where she was concerned.

Until that moment he had scrupulously honored Pop's order about leaving Dori alone. *No more,* he thought as he covered her hand with his own where it rested against him. *Never again.*

He reached an arm out and wrapped it around her waist. As far as he knew, she had no idea how he felt about her. He also had no idea how she'd respond to any physical advances from him. Well, he'd never know unless he made a move. Slowly he pulled her against him, giving her time to resist. To his intense pleasure she didn't.

When there was barely a breath of air between them, he released her hand and drew a knuckle down her soft cheek. "I love you, Dori McAllister." And he kissed her before she had a chance to protest.

After a startled moment during which he feared she'd pull away, she threw her arms around his neck and kissed him back with an enthusiasm that surprised and delighted him. When they came up for air, Dori leaned her head on his chest. "I love you too, Trev. I've loved you for years."

It was the most wonderful weekend of his life, but by Monday evening she was gone. Once again Pop had been his bulwark as the waves of despair and depression threatened to drown him.

"Why?" Trev had asked over and over again. "Why did she go away? And where?"

Pop didn't have the answers, at least to the first question. No one did except Dori, and she wouldn't talk about it.

"I can't discuss it yet, Trev," she'd say in a thick voice when he phoned her. "So just don't ask."

"But, Dori—"

"I mean it. If you keep asking, I won't talk to you at all."

"Give her room, Trev," Pop said. "Let her work it out for herself."

"I love her, Pop," he blurted out. It was the first time he'd told anyone but Dori.

Pop nodded, and Trev realized that his secret had been no secret after all.

"And she loves me."

Once again Pop nodded. "I know."

That was six long years ago, years during which she lived in San Diego while he lived in Seaside. They spoke on the phone on average once a month. She made certain his calls were short and the conversation innocuous. It was as if their words of love had never been spoken, their marriage never taken place. He knew far more than he wanted about Small Treasures, about Meg Reynolds and her family, and almost nothing about Dori herself, certainly nothing about why she was there and he here.

Phil walked to the hospital window and stopped beside Trev. He studied his younger brother through narrowed eyes, and Trev braced himself.

"If you didn't want to get divorced," Phil asked, "why didn't you make her come home?"

"Believe me, I wanted to. I went out to get her when I finally found out where she was, but you can't *make* someone come home."

There was a small silence as Phil thought about that. "I still say you should have made her come home."

"Make your wife be your wife?" Trev shook his head. "Being a wife has to be voluntary, a love offering, as it were. I was young and dumb when she left, but I knew even then that I couldn't force her to live with me, to love me, and I haven't changed my mind." He shrugged. "So I wait and I pray."

Phil shook his head. "Who would ever have believed that my little brother would become a living soap opera?"

"You're enjoying this, aren't you?" Trev asked without rancor.

Phil nodded. "I wouldn't say I'm exactly enjoying it, because it's obvious you're a man in pain, but it isn't often you fall off your white horse."

Seven

ORI LOOKED UP as the door opened, expecting to see Phil or Honey. When Trev walked in, she felt all the breath leave her body.

He looked wonderful. He'd always been a good-looking boy and a handsome if unfinished teenager, but now as a man, the skinniness that had followed him through his growing years had been replaced by a lean maturity. His black hair was thick and shiny, his shoulders broad, his blue eyes brilliant, and his jaw firm. He exuded strength.

His eyes went directly to her, and their gazes locked. She swallowed involuntarily. Slowly his mouth curved in a self-mocking smile.

"Hello, Dori. Nice to see you." His voice was cool, neutral.

She nodded, swallowed again to be certain she could speak. "Hello, Trev. It's good to see you too." She gave what she hoped was a polite smile. She would match him lack of emotion for lack of emotion or die trying. No way would she allow him to know the raw power his mere appearance had to unnerve her.

Trev blinked and turned his attention to Pop. Like Dori he had to be distressed to see their rock lying listlessly with a nose cannula supplying oxygen and an IV line feeding nutrients, but he didn't let it show. He walked to the bed, leaned over, and planted a kiss on Pop's forehead. Then he took the man's hand, the one with the IV inserted in the vein. Trev held it carefully, just as Dori held his other hand.

"How are you feeling?" Trev asked.

Pop raised an eyebrow. "How do you think?"

Trev grinned. "Yeah, I know. Dumb question."

"I'm lying here on my deathbed—"

"This is not your deathbed!" Dori rose to her feet in protest. Her chest felt as if it were being crushed in a vise. She could hardly draw a breath. "You are not dying. You're not! You aren't allowed!"

Pop smiled sadly. "I wish it were that simple, dear heart. We know that's not the case. God does with us as He wills." He closed his eyes, worn out. Even with the oxygen his breathing was labored. The gray cast to his skin scared Dori almost as much as his abject weariness.

Oh, God, we can't lose him! How will we manage without him? This time she didn't even apologize for bothering God. *Make him better!* she demanded, then apologized and added, *Please!*

She closed her eyes, determined to hold back her tears. The last thing he needed was a weepy granddaughter. But it hurt so much seeing him like this. She brought her free hand to her heart, her fist clenched so tightly that her nails cut into her palm. She started when she felt a hand on her back, rubbing gently, making small soothing circles.

Trev. He'd come to stand behind her, to care for her. Her already jangled nerves kicked up a notch, but the panic over Pop slowly receded.

"I'm going to be sick," Pop said suddenly.

Dori grabbed the call button and pressed.

"That pan," Pop muttered, swallowing. "Get me that pan. Fast." He pointed to the plastic washbasin resting on the windowsill.

Trev grabbed it and held it under Pop's chin. Pop tried to raise himself on his elbows. Dori moved to support his shoulders and hold him steady.

Pop made a distressed noise and out gushed a fountain of bright red blood.

Terrified at what this evidence of a hemorrhage might mean, Dori turned horror-filled eyes to Trev who was staring in distress at the pan.

With a sigh, Pop went limp under Dori's hands, and she helped him lie back down. She grabbed some tissues, dampened them in the water jug by the bed, and wiped his mouth.

"Feel better," he said.

"Where is that nurse?" Trev demanded, still holding the pan full of scarlet fluid.

Dori bolted from the room and raced to the nurses' station. "We need help! Mr. Trevelyan is vomiting blood!"

A nurse nodded. "Be right there." She turned and spoke to the man making notations on a chart. "Dr. Rosen, Trevelyan in 326."

Dr. Rosen nodded his white head without looking up. "Be right there."

Hurrying to Pop's room beside the nurse, Dori asked, "Has this happened before?"

The nurse waved her away. "Wait out here." And the door slid shut in her face. In a minute Trev was beside her, ejected too, and Dr. Rosen rushed in.

Dori stared at the closed door, her hand pressed to her lips to hold back a sob. Her Pop!

Trev slid an arm about her shoulders and pulled her close. Without a second thought, she burrowed against him, needing his comfort, his warmth to ease the chill around her heart. She slid her arms around his waist and held on, feeling almost as lost as the little girl who had clung to him all those years ago. Fatigue and jumbled emotions brought tears to her eyes, more than could be contained, and they poured down her cheeks.

Trev lowered his head and rested his jaw against her hair. "Shh, Dori. Don't cry. I can't stand to see you cry. I never could."

Dori sniffed and smiled sadly. He should have seen her when she first moved to San Diego. And with that thought came the memories and the resentments, the hurts and dashed expectations. She straightened her shoulders and pulled away from him.

"Thanks, but I'll be all right." She heard the coolness in her voice, and so did he. He stepped back, and she saw a flash of hurt in his eyes before he shuttered his expression. Deliberately he stepped back again, putting an even greater distance between them. If he stood much farther away, she'd have to yell to him.

Sighing, Dori turned and walked down the hall toward Phil who, blissfully unaware of the latest crisis, stared intently at the parking lot. Trev followed. Phil didn't become conscious of them until they were beside him. Then one look at their faces erased all interest in whatever had occupied him out the window.

"What?" he asked, his body tense, his voice brittle.

"He's vomiting blood, lots of it," Trev said.

Phil grimaced and started toward Pop's room.

Trev caught his arm. "We're not allowed in at the moment. The doctor's looking at him."

Behind them the elevators opened, and Honey stepped out. Again their faces gave rise to fear. "What?" she whispered.

Dori hesitated, hating to tell such bad news, but Trev told the situation straight out. "He's vomiting blood."

Honey shut her eyes and swayed. Phil threw his arm about her waist to steady her. "Easy, Honey. Easy."

"I'm all right." Honey centered her fist just below her ribs. "Right here is where it hurts him. He had a lot of pain for a whole day before he told me. Last night it finally got so bad he couldn't deny it anymore. It had spread upward, and he was finally willing to admit he might be having a heart attack. He still didn't want me to call an ambulance. Then he threw up. I thought it was the first time, only to learn later that it wasn't. Aggravating old man." The affection in her voice made the pejorative statement sound like a compliment. "Anyway, while he was occupied, I called 911. They were there before he was back in bed, and he threw a fit. But I don't care. I can be as stubborn as he is if I have to be."

Trev leaned down and kissed her cheek. "He'll forgive you."

Honey made a snort of disagreement. "I don't know. Maybe. Eventually." Then she turned to Dori. "Come here, sweetie. I haven't had a chance to welcome you home." She held out her arms.

Dori fell into them. Their comfort was uncomplicated and real. "Oh, Honey, I'm so sorry."

Even Dori wasn't certain what she was sorry for, but everyone acted as if it was Pop's illness she spoke of.

"Aren't we all," Honey answered, she, too, addressing many issues.

"Excuse me."

They all turned to find Dr. Rosen standing by them, his wire-rimmed glasses and white hair making him look like a scholar. Dori would settle for a very smart, very competent physician.

"We're going to take Mr. Trevelyan up to surgery immediately." Dr. Rosen gestured toward Pop's room.

They all nodded and began walking toward his room with the doctor.

"What do you think it is?" Honey asked.

Dr. Rosen shook his head. "I'm not certain, but it's not an aortic blowout. That would obviously be the most dangerous, but if that were the case, he'd have been gone before now." He shrugged. "We'll know soon, and you'll know as soon as I do." He waved briefly and was gone.

Honey nodded. "Thank you," she called after him.

The four of them filed into Pop's room and found him already on a gurney, sides raised, ready to be wheeled away.

"One minute." Pop held up his hand to stay the orderly ready to roll him off to somewhere in the depths of the hospital. "There's something I have to say."

"Please, Seth," Honey said, taking his raised hand in hers. "Just go along with the plan for once in your life. We'll deal with that other issue later."

Dori swallowed her grin. It was rare that Honey challenged Pop, but when she did, the role reversal always tickled her.

Pop smiled at Honey, love for her bright in his eyes. "Now. I have to say this now. You know that. What if I don't get another chance?"

She flinched at his last words but nodded her head. "Okay, go ahead. I know you won't have any peace unless you do."

"I love you, sweetheart," Pop whispered to her, his eyes bright with tears.

Honey laid a tender hand on his head. "And I love you, Seth. Now go ahead. Say your piece, and get to wherever it is they're taking you. I want you fixed up and out of here. It's too lonely at home without you."

He gave her one more weak smile, then turned his eyes on Dori. She blinked at the intensity of his gaze. He might be weak and pale, but his will was as strong as ever. Then he switched his concentration to Trev who looked as startled by the force of his will as she had.

"It's time for you two to stop playing whatever game it is you're playing."

Dori stiffened. "What-what are you talking about?"

"As if you didn't know." Pop looked at her with disappointment, something she'd rarely ever seen, and it shook her deeply. She dropped her eyes.

"I know you two are married," Pop said.

How strange it sounded so bluntly stated. And how did he find out? She'd never told anyone, and she doubted Trev bragged about the fiasco.

Pop's weary voice continued relentlessly, all the more compelling because of its weakness. "I know you love each other."

Dori pressed her lips together. That was a debatable thought if ever she'd heard one.

"I want you to reconcile."

Yeah, right. Just like that.

"I want you to live together as husband and wife for the next six months."

Dori's mouth fell open. Live together for six months? They'd barely been able to manage a weekend. How would they ever manage six months? She snapped her mouth shut. The answer was simple. They wouldn't.

"It's what I wish more than anything in the world. In fact, it may be my dying wish. I'm going to be sick again." The last was fast and panicky. He turned his head and more blood flowed from his mouth all over the gurney and onto the floor.

Honey grabbed an unsoiled corner of the sheet and began wiping his face. "Easy, Seth." She leaned over and kissed his sweating forehead. "You go on, dear heart. I'll deal with the children from here."

He gave her a tired but grateful smile and closed his eyes. "Please," he whispered. "For me."

As the orderly pushed Pop down the hall and into the elevator, Dori knew she and Trev had the proverbial snowball's chance in that eternal hot place to escape Pop's machinations. Whether they liked it or not, they were doomed to six months of excruciating cohabiting.

God, what have You done?

"Honey," Trev said into the silence that followed Pop's leaving, but Honey cut him off.

"Whatever you planned to say, Trev, I don't want to hear it. I want you to be quiet and listen to me for a change."

Dori stared at Honey. She'd never heard the woman speak with such an edge before.

"Pop has waited patiently for you two to come to your senses." Honey looked from Dori to Trev and back. The warmth of her welcome was now gone, replaced by a determination that made Dori shiver. "He's agonized over your foolishness, as have I."

Foolishness! Dori felt her temperature rise. Honey went on relentlessly. "In all this time, neither of you has moved for a divorce. That says something to Seth and me, and it should to you two, too."

Phil spread his arms wide like an evangelist sharing the truth of the gospel. "They still love each other."

Both Dori and Trev turned on him. "Shut up, Phil," they barked, almost in unison. Phil merely grinned.

Honey nodded. "I agree. They still love each other."

So what's love got to do with anything? Dori shut her eyes. She felt so weary. Besides, the issue was trust.

"How did Pop find out?" she asked. Any topic to get away from the subject of love.

Honey looked at her. "We've known of your marriage almost since the day you two said *I do.*"

"And you never said anything?" Dori was floored.

Honey shrugged. "We were waiting for you to come to us."

Dori shook her head. "Not after you and Pop told me—" Her voice drifted away as Trev spun to her.

"You too?" he asked. "One of us would have to leave?"

Dori nodded.

He turned back to Honey. "Not a good basis for sharing our secret, you'll have to agree."

Honey didn't look the least embarrassed or repentant. "We did what we had to do. You were kids. But even though you had your share of boys chasing you, Dori, and you had an eye for a beautiful woman, Trev, it was obvious that for each of you there was no other."

Dori felt the blood drain from her face at hearing her feelings stated so baldly—and correctly. But Honey was wrong about Trev. Once a ladies' man, always a ladies' man. She knew that all too well.

"Marriage is such a private thing," Honey said, "and marriage troubles are even more so. Every couple has to work out their problems themselves."

"Then let us," Dori cried.

Honey looked her in the eye. "Maybe if we saw either of you trying, we would. But you're too stubborn and Trev's too accommodating. We've gotten tired of waiting. In fact, I'm now convinced we waited much too long. We kept hoping you'd come to your senses on your own." Honey snorted, a strange sound coming from a classy woman like her.

Trev shook his head, his mouth turning up in a sardonic smile. "I wonder why we ever thought you wouldn't find out."

"What we don't know," Honey continued, "is why Dori took off almost immediately."

Dori smiled with tight lips, hugging herself against the ever-expanding pain of this conversation. All she knew was that she was not about to tell Honey or the eagerly eavesdropping Phil what had driven her as far from Seaside as she could get. She'd gone to the airport, backpack in hand, and looked for the most distant destination available. The choices were southern California or the Seattle, Washington area. Warm and sunny versus cool and rainy. With her spirits so drear, the decision was easy. San Diego. And she hadn't regretted the choice even once. The reason for the need to choose, yes, many, many times, but the choice itself, no.

"When you left, Trev went to pieces," Phil said suddenly.

"What?" Dori blinked at him.

"That's enough, Phil," Trev said in a tight voice.

Phil smirked at Trev. "That was the semester he almost flunked out of school."

He almost flunked out of school? Dori looked at Trev in amazement. He'd always been Mr. Honor Roll and Dean's List in spite of his love of a good time.

He shrugged. "I was too busy sending you e-mails, worrying about you, and trying to figure out how to get you to come home to pay attention to something as unimportant as school."

Dori flinched. She had thought he was probably glad to see her go. It had never crossed her mind that his life had gone as topsy-turvy as hers. And those e-mails. She had erased every one without reading it for six months, wishing she could erase him from her mind as easily.

Keeping pace with the depth of her anger at Trev was her bitterness at God for letting her be so hurt. He'd snatched happiness from her twice, first with the death of her parents and then with Trev's treachery. How could she ever trust Him again?

When she finally allowed herself to read Trev's e-mails, e-mails that broke her heart with their poignancy, she responded with such trivia that his pleas eventually stopped. From then until now, all communication was as bland as Dori could make it. Some days she felt that if she ignored the wedding, the marriage wouldn't exist.

They stood silent for a moment. All Dori wanted was to be home in her apartment with its filled-to-overflowing bookcases and plants covering all free surfaces, curled up on her bed with the gold-on-gold quilted spread, hugging Trudy and keeping herself safe.

Phil broke the silence. "That's also the semester you became a Christian, Trev, if I remember right."

Trev nodded. "I was trying to figure out what I'd done that was so terrible that my wife of two days would leave me." He gave Dori a hard stare. "As I started down the list of possible offenses, I realized just how rotten I was and how much I needed a Savior."

The stare softened. "Just like you used to tell me, Dori."

What irony. He had come to Christ just as she had turned from God in anger and disappointment.

"Such a bittersweet time," he said. "I knew the joy that comes with finding Christ and the agony of losing my wife."

Dori's heart exploded. She felt it let go, felt all the blood drain to her feet. She swayed with the wave of guilt that inundated her.

But he was the one who was wrong! He was. Let him feel the guilt.

"Well, you've got enough time now," Phil said, grinning. "You've got six months." He rubbed his hands together. "And I for one can't wait to see what happens."

Dori wanted to slap him. This situation was anything but funny. It didn't matter that her deepest dream was to reconcile with Trev, to make the terrible separation go away, to know his love again. But it needed to happen because Trev came to her, fell to his knees, and begged her forgiveness, not because they were manipulated into it.

She sighed inwardly. She had thought she had these ugly feelings of unforgiveness under control, that the spitefulness had faded, indeed had all but disappeared. Blame their resurgence on proximity, she thought. The yearning too.

She stared at Honey, stony faced. "I have a business in California to run. Trev has his work here."

Honey was unmoved. "You and I both know that Meg is more than able to manage for a little while without you."

"Six months is hardly a little while."

"Honey." Trev's voice was too calm, too reasonable, a fact that fed Dori's anger. "You can't force people to live together, to love each other."

"Six years and neither of you filed for divorce," Honey reminded. "Six years!"

Dori shut her eyes. That didn't mean anything. They'd just never gotten around to it. That was all.

But *six months* together. More than enough time to love him all over again. More than enough time to open herself to the same kind of pain, only somehow she knew that when it fell apart this time, it would be much, much worse. "Honey, please," she managed. "Don't."

"We want your promises, Seth and I." Honey's eyes flashed with purpose. "Your promise, Dori? To a sick old man who's loved you since the day he met you."

Dori sagged. How could she fight that burden of gratitude? She sighed. "Oh, all right. I promise."

Honey turned to Trev. "Well?"

Trev nodded. "I promise."

"Six months. Not a day less."

Both Dori and Trev nodded, careful to avoid each other's eyes.

Honey smiled, looking far too pleased with herself in Dori's opinion. She reached into her purse and pulled out a sheet of paper. As she held it out, Dori noticed for the first time that several of her knuckles were swollen with arthritis. When had that happened?

Pop might be dying. Honey showed signs of getting infirm. Trev was going to live with her. And Phil was smiling like a monkey, enjoying the whole mess, at least the part about her and Trev.

God, what are You doing? I was doing fine on my own. Just butt out!

Honey handed the paper to Trev who scowled at it, then handed it to Dori. It was the directions to a motel on Route 100 in Exton.

"I made the reservations for you as soon as Phil said you were coming," Honey said. "You and Trev can go on over and get yourselves settled."

"I can't leave—" Trev began.

Honey raised an eyebrow. "You can come back here to the hospital or not as you please." She looked from one to the other, suddenly smiling. "You've made us very happy."

You maybe. But what about us? Dori thought as Honey continued to watch them with a sweet smile on her lips.

Sweet like a crocodile's grin.

Eight

JOANNE COWERED BEHIND THE CHAIR as Vinnie fell to his knees and searched the suitcase again. He muttered, "It's got to be here," over and over.

"What's missing?" she managed to whisper. She tried so hard not to do anything that would upset or disappoint Vinnie because she was afraid of his anger, but she'd really done it this time. But what had she done?

"The pictures!" he yelled. "Where are the pictures?"

Jo pointed to the silver and gold frame she'd found in the suitcase. "Is that what you mean?"

Vinnie glanced up, hope in his eyes. When he saw the frame, he turned to her with a terrifying sneer. "Not pictures like that, you idiot! Pictures like in a museum."

"A museum? But I didn't go to a museum, Vinnie." Her underarms ran with nervous perspiration. "Was I supposed to?"

He gave her a disgusted look. "No, you wasn't supposed to."

Relief flowed through her. She hadn't messed up after all, at least with the museum. A new thought made her shiver. What if Vinnie found out she had let the suitcase out of her sight?

When he saw her off for the airport yesterday, he'd said, "Whatever you do, don't let that suitcase out of your sight."

She nodded as she looked at the big black car that was going to drive her to Philadelphia. Wow. Mr. J sure knew how to treat a girl. "Don't let it out of my sight," she repeated absently. Was that a TV in the car?

Vinnie grabbed her chin and forced her to look at him. "Our future depends on that suitcase, Jo. Do not let it out of your sight for even a minute."

She'd let it out of her sight for hours.

What if Mr. J found out? She went dizzy at the thought.

She'd been the last person to walk down the Jetway for the trip back to Philadelphia, her stomach in turmoil at the thought of the flight. Usually a Just Say No person because she didn't want a fried egg brain, she stopped halfway to the plane and grabbed the tranqs Vinnie'd given her, much like a person too far out in the waves grabs the lifeguard who has come to save her. She swallowed them with the bottled water in her purse and hoped they kicked in before the plane took off.

She continued to the plane and bumped into a group of people at the door. She tried to go around them.

"Excuse me, miss," a lady in uniform called to her. "We'll need to take your bag."

"What?" She couldn't let the lady take the bag. Vinnie'd kill her. *Don't let it out of your sight!*

The lady smiled. "The plane is very full and all the overhead space is taken. Don't worry. Your suitcase will be waiting for you in Philadelphia."

Now as she stared at an infuriated Vinnie, she knew she'd lie until she died.

"Did you let this out of your sight?" Vinnie demanded, his shaking finger pointing to the bag. "You did, didn't you?"

"What?" she squeaked. "Of course not! You told me how important it was. I did just what you told me. I swear."

God, if You're there, I'm sorry for the lie. But I got to.

"Then where's the paintings?" he roared.

"I don't know!"

Vinnie pulled out a penknife, flicked it open, and began

slicing the suitcase lining to pieces. Jo swallowed a yelp of distress at the fury of his slashes. She couldn't tell whether he thought he might find the paintings in some other hiding place or whether he was just good and mad.

"What were the pictures of?" she asked.

"I don't know." Grunt. Slash. "Just real old stuff by some French guy." Grunt. Slash. "Masterpieces worth millions."

Millions? She'd been carrying around stuff worth millions? Vinnie reduced the suitcase to strips of black fabric, but he didn't find anything. When he straightened and looked at her, she saw his anger was spent, and fear had taken its place. That scared her even more than the missing paintings. Nothing made Vinnie afraid.

He fingered the red yarn, his face pale. "We're dead men walking."

Joanne started to cry.

"Shut up," he muttered.

She sniffed and tried to be quiet. She wrapped her hand over her mouth to stifle the sound. It didn't work. Little gasps and sobs escaped.

"I said shut up!"

Joanne grabbed a pillow from the chair and shoved it against her face.

The phone rang. Joanne didn't move. She was afraid to.

On the third ring, Vinnie turned on her. "Answer it!"

She grabbed it up on the fourth ring. "H-hello?"

"May I speak to Vinnie, please? He is there, isn't he?"

"Y-yes, he's here." She held out the receiver to Vinnie.

"Who?" he mouthed.

"I don't know," she mouthed back.

He took a deep breath and said, "Hello, this is Vinnie."

He turned pale. "Hello, Mr. Jankowski. What a pleasant surprise. I thought you were in Aruba."

Vinnie listened. He glanced at the ribbons of black nylon. He wiped beads of sweat from his forehead. "Don't you worry one bit, Mr. Jankowski. Everything is going like clockwork. The paintings will be waiting for you when you get home next Sunday. Oh yes, I'm sure. You just relax and have a good time. Yes, sir. Just trust me, sir. I'll see to everything. Good-bye."

He held the phone out to Joanne with shaking hands. He collapsed into the stuffed chair.

"What, Vinnie? Are you in trouble?"

"We," he snarled. "Not me. We. You're the one who lost the paintings, not me."

Jo licked her lips. "What does he do to people who lose millions?"

Vinnie snorted as if the question were dumb. "What do you think?"

She could think of lots of things, and her heart went *kathump!* "K-kill?"

"Let's just say that people who disappoint him are never seen again."

Jo groaned. Without thinking, she bent and began picking up the pieces of suitcase. She tossed them into the plastic trash can as she wondered how Mr. J did away with people.

Please let it be painless, God. And don't let him throw me overboard way out in the ocean. Please!

She gathered another handful of black nylon, putting the hard plastic name tag lying in the mess on the end table beside Vinnie's chair.

"What's this?" He picked up the luggage tag. "Dori McAllister. Who's that?"

"I don't know." Jo's voice shook as she thought of all kinds of fish nibbling on her, maybe even a shark taking a big bite. She shuddered. Then she remembered a pretty lady with big brown eyes who reached for a suitcase with her, a suitcase with red yarn tied to the handle.

"Sorry. This is mine," the woman had said. And Jo'd automatically stepped back.

If she'd been sweating before, it was nothing to the cold film of terror that coated her whole body now. She'd let someone else take Mr. J's million-dollar paintings.

Nine

MAUREEN SLOUCHED IN HER CAR, parked nose out in the hospital parking lot for a quick getaway. She was thoroughly bored. She hated surveillance because she hated inactivity. Unfortunately, much of police work was step-by-step and methodical, hours spent on the phone and at her desk. But sitting in a car on a frigid winter day was the worst. She had the motor running and the heater cranked, but still she felt stiff with cold. She could see pneumonia in her future as clearly as clairvoyants saw dark, handsome men in the lives of their rich women customers.

There had to be a better way to catch a thief. There had to be. She just wasn't sure what it was.

Then they walked out of the front door, Phillip Trevelyan and the girl. And another man. He was big and dark haired and looked like a rougher version of Phillip. His brother, the preacher? He must look very impressive in the pulpit.

Maureen quickly turned off the motor so plumes of exhaust wouldn't attract their eyes to her. The last thing she needed was for them to know they were under surveillance. The cold immediately bit more deeply, and she shivered in her down anorak. The girl in her lightweight jacket must be freezing.

The three walked to Phillip's car and opened the

trunk. Maureen sat up straight. Another transfer of the Matisse paintings? They were small, one a rectangle of five inches by eight, the other larger, nine inches by ten. Their size made them much too easy to transport or to pass off to another.

The brother—what was his name?—reached into the trunk and pulled out the black suitcase. Even from here, five cars down and one aisle over, Maureen could see the red yarn tied around the handle. He set it down and pulled up the handle. The girl reached into the trunk and pulled out her laptop. Phillip reached in and grabbed the carry-on. Together they walked to a dark green Caravan parked almost directly across from Maureen's car.

She muttered under her breath and slouched to hide behind the steering wheel. If she slid any lower, she'd slide right off the seat. She lowered her window, hoping she could hear some of their conversation. The biting air swept in and froze her breath in her lungs.

For extra cover she grabbed the magazine Fleishman had been reading back at the airport and held it in front of her face. She blinked as she caught sight of the photo of a naked woman just inches from her nose. Not that she'd never seen such a magazine before. After all, she'd been a cop for several years now, and she knew more than she wanted to about real life. Rather, she never read such magazines herself, just like she never opened the porn sites that appeared regularly in her e-mail. She threw the magazine on the floor in disgust and went back to depending on the steering wheel for cover.

The preacher opened the side door of his van, and all the luggage went inside. The chalk streak on the side of the black bag was clear as it disappeared into the vehicle.

Then he opened the passenger door, holding out a hand to the woman.

As he did this, Phillip turned and looked directly at Maureen. *Directly* at her. He smiled slightly and raised an eyebrow as their gazes met through the steering wheel.

Maureen's eyes widened. It was like he knew she was there, like he knew she was watching them. She forced herself to nod, just a slight incline of the head, then made herself look away. She was just a bored woman slouched in her seat, waiting for someone she was supposed to pick up at the hospital, nothing more. She had just been watching them for something to do. That was all.

The girl said something, her voice drifting across the space between the cars but not her words. Phillip turned from Maureen to her, and Maureen sagged. Greg would have a fit if she was made. Surely Phillip's glance—well, it was more than a glance; it was like a long stare—was just an accident. It meant nothing, impacted the case in no way.

She watched as Phillip took the girl in his arms and gave her a great hug and a kiss on the cheek. He turned to his brother and said something. The preacher gave a rueful smile. The woman climbed into the van; the preacher closed the door and walked around to the driver's side, Phillip walking with him.

The preacher turned. "You've got my cell phone number. Call if anything happens. We can be back here in just a few minutes."

Phillip extended his hand and the brothers shook. "Just go, Trev. If I didn't know better, I'd say you were stalling."

The woman inside must have said something because both men looked into the van. Phillip laughed and Trev—for Trevelyan? Certainly no one would have named him Trevor Trevelyan—climbed into the van. Phillip stepped out of the way, and the van pulled from its parking place, then from the lot.

Maureen raised her window and turned the key in the ignition, preparing to follow. She slid into first gear and put her foot on the gas, only to slam on the brake.

Phillip Trevelyan stood directly in front of her, legs spread, arms akimbo.

She frowned at him. He stared impassively back.

Maybe she could back out and still have time to follow the preacher and the girl. She glanced behind her. Aside from a concrete parking buffer, a silver SUV sat with its nose to her back bumper. She wasn't going anywhere that way.

Muttering to herself, she turned back to Phillip Trevelyan. Opening her window and leaning out, she called, "Excuse me. I was just leaving." She began to inch forward.

He didn't move.

Father God, please make him move!

She threw a desperate glance toward the green van, disappearing down the highway. If she was ruthless and nuts like Riggs, the Mel Gibson character in the *Lethal Weapon* movies, she'd just gun the motor and force Phillip out of her way. In the movies everyone always jumped out of Riggs's way. But what if Phillip Trevelyan didn't know the rules? What if he didn't move, and she ran over him?

She turned pleading eyes to him, but all he did was put one foot on her front bumper and drape his arm over his raised knee. He looked like he was posing for *GQ*, except for his nose turning red in the cold.

She closed her eyes and leaned back on the headrest, failure washing through her. It was too late to catch the green van now. There were too many roads, too many possibilities.

And it was all his fault!

She straightened. She should arrest him for impeding the progress of an investigation. Maybe that would teach him a lesson. Or for transporting stolen goods.

"What is your problem?" she shouted at him.

"I could ask you the same question," he called back calmly.

"What?"

He lowered his foot. "If I come close so we don't have to yell at each other, will you promise not to drive away when I step to the side?"

She looked again at the empty stretch of road that ran from the hospital and sighed. Like it mattered what he did now. She reached out and turned the car off. She had to hand it to him. He was good. He had effectively caused her to lose their best lead, their only lead, in the Matisse investigation.

Apparently taking her turning off the Camry's engine as an affirmative, he walked to her open window. She pushed the lock button, though what good it would do with her window wide open was debatable. He heard the snick of the depressed locks and, grinning, nodded. He stopped beside the car and looked at her. Just looked. She in turn stared impassively back. Suddenly he blinked, shivered, and turned his collar up. "It's cold out here."

Maureen wiggled her frozen toes and silently agreed.

He leaned down, resting his arms on her window ledge, his hands dangling inches from her face. Eying him warily, she leaned back. Hadn't he ever heard of personal space?

"Want to let me in so I don't freeze?" he asked, his voice halfway between a question and an order.

Right. Like she'd ask a strange man with ties to Jankowski into the car with her.

He nodded. "Didn't think so. Smart girl."

There was a power about him, an air of command that filled the car and made it hard for her to breathe. If she'd let him in, he'd probably asphyxiate her whether he meant to or not. Yet he didn't seem overbearing or scary. In fact, if she didn't know better, she'd never, ever imagine him to be the sort involved with the theft of such valuable property, not that criminals followed physical or personality stereotypes.

Of course, maybe he wasn't a thief. Maybe it was just the girl. Maybe he was only the driver of a car she rode in.

And maybe the moon was made of green cheese.

"What's so interesting about us Trevelyans?"

She feigned surprise. "Who are the Trevelyans?"

His look said he was disappointed in her. "As if you didn't know."

She merely stared at him. The silence didn't bother her one bit. She'd outwaited many a petty troublemaker. She'd outwait him.

"Why did you follow us from the airport?"

She started. How did he know? She hoped that her surprise looked like disbelief at the accusation rather than distress at being found out. "Now why would I do something like that?"

"I might have been meeting Dori, but I always notice a pretty woman, especially one who seems more than a bit interested in Dori and me, even takes our picture, then runs like crazy to her own car when we start to drive away."

"It sounds to me like you're just a teensy bit paranoid." She put everything she could into her sneer, though she was thrown that he'd noticed the pictures.

He gave a smile that was both beautiful and more than slightly condescending. "I might agree with you if I hadn't watched you search my car."

She stiffened. "I did not search your car."

"Maybe you didn't force any locks, but you walked around it long enough, peeking in the windows, studying the license plate, talking to your contact on the phone as you did all this."

She glanced involuntarily at all the hospital windows and inwardly grimaced. She should have been more careful.

"Yeah," he said. "I watched from that big window on the third floor." He pointed.

"Maybe I just like the looks of your car. Maybe I just like the lighthouse license plate."

He shook his head, not deigning to respond to such obvious cavils. "Maybe you're planning to rob me."

She sat up, stung by the charge. "What? Are you nuts?" She was a cop, for Pete's sake, not that she could tell him.

He leaned closer, invading her personal space again, forcing her to back farther into the car. "Then why were you spying on me?"

She crossed her arms over her chest and met him steely look for steely look. She reminded herself to take slow, deep breaths. He wasn't really taking up all the oxygen in the car; it just felt that way. "How well do you know the woman you drove here?"

She could tell he didn't expect her question. He frowned, then pulled back a bit, and she could breathe again.

"She's my sister."

"Really?"

He gave a half smile. "You needn't sound so skeptical. She's my sister."

"And the man who just left with her?" And the black suitcase.

"My brother."

"And their names?"

"Paul Trevelyan and Dori MacAllister. And I'm Phil Trevelyan, as if you didn't already know that." He grew thoughtful. "Though I guess Dori's name is really Dori Trevelyan now. And has been."

"MacAllister was her married name, and she's reverted after a divorce?" Clarification would help with tracing her.

"No, Trevelyan's her married name."

Maureen looked at him. "I think you'd better explain."

For some reason he did. "Well, she's not my blood sister, but the three of us were raised together. Then Trev married her."

"Your brother married your sister."

"But not my blood sister," he repeated hastily. "Or Trev's."

"So your sister is now also your sister-in-law."

Phillip stared at the place where the van had been, smiling vaguely. "I still can't believe it."

"Recent marriage, huh?"

He shook his head. "No, six years ago. I just didn't know it until today."

That surprised her. "I would have thought from the way you pounced on me that you didn't miss much. How'd a marriage of six years get by you?"

"Simple. They don't live together. Dori's been in California ever since they married, and Trev's been here."

Maureen snorted. "Strange marriage."

He gave her a decidedly unfriendly look. "You don't know anything about it."

She felt herself flush. He was right. "Sorry."

He held up a hand. "Me, too. You're right. It is a strange situation. Now they have to live together for six months."

"Have to?"

Phil grinned. "Yeah. Have to. Because of Pop and Honey."

And that was supposed to make sense? "I take it the three of you were visiting someone here?" She pointed at the hospital.

He nodded. "Pop. And I've got to get back. I need to be with Honey when the doctor tells her what he found." He straightened, then hesitated. Bending to her again, he turned on that charming smile, this time without the condescension. "What's your name, sweetheart?"

Maureen's heart kicked. *Sweetheart?* The man was dangerous, thief or no. "Why should I tell you?"

He shrugged. "Because I want to know?"

A good reason if she ever heard one. "Maureen Galloway. What do you know about Matisse?"

He looked surprised at the question. "The artist?"

Maureen nodded.

"That's what I know, all of it. He was an artist. I assume he painted in a particular school and lived somewhere—France?—

and had a first name and a family." He spread his hands. "No clue. Why?"

She shook her head again. What else would she expect him to say? That he was somehow involved in the theft of two of the artist's paintings?

"You're an interesting one, Maureen. I still don't know what your game is or why my car fascinated you so much or if you did indeed follow me from the airport. Or maybe it was Dori you followed. But you can find me in Seaside, New Jersey, at the Seaside Pharmacy."

"And why would I want to find you?" Maureen retorted.

Phil studied her for a minute. "I have no idea. But I think that I'd like you to find me."

She stared at him, dumbfounded. "Why?"

He shrugged. "Because?"

On that note, he walked off. She watched him until he disappeared into the hospital. What game was he playing? What did he want from her? And why did the first man who had interested her even the slightest bit since Adam's death have to be involved in one of her cases?

Ten

THE AIR IN THE CARAVAN was thick with tension. Dori felt it twining around her like the tendrils of the heavy fog in an English mystery movie.

Six months with Trev! Even the thought stole her breath. How could she survive? She'd barely escaped intact last time, and that had only been three days. She knew she'd never survive a hurt like he'd inflicted before if it happened a second time, at least not the parts of her that were truly her. Her spirit, her soul, her personality, all those intangibles that made her who she was.

A pillow over her face would be kinder, smothering the life from her body. Then she wouldn't have to learn to live with the unbearable ache of rejection and betrayal again.

A tear slipped down her cheek, and she turned to look out her side window so Trev wouldn't see. He must not know the power he had over her. To protect herself she would be polite but distant, pleasant but withdrawn. In other words, there but not there. Maybe then she could cope.

Trev finally spoke. "So how will Small Treasures survive without you for six months?" He gave her a wry smile.

She couldn't help but return the smile in kind.

"Meg managed before I showed up. I'm sure she can manage again." Polite but emotionally uninvolved.

"How did she get started in the business?"

"She'd always wanted a store of her own, so when her three sons were in high school, she opened Small Treasures with Ron's financial help and blessing."

"Ron's the husband?"

Dori pictured Ron and smiled. "He's a great guy, a big bear of a man like Pop. He and Meg have been married for thirty-one years."

"Do their kids work at Small Treasures too?"

"I think they did when they were in high school or college— stock boy type of stuff—but they're all established in their own careers now. Ronny is a teacher, Chaz is a CPA, and Randy, the baby, is a musician, a starving one to hear his father talk."

"And they're all married?"

"Randy's not. Someday if he ever matures, he'll make some woman a fine husband, but not now. He's definitely not ready."

Like another person I know, she could have said but didn't. It wouldn't help anything.

Trev turned into the motel parking lot, and Dori felt the tension revive, at least as far as she was concerned. Trev looked the picture of cool unconcern, which somehow irked her. He should be feeling as awkward as she. It was only right.

Honey had reserved them a lovely deluxe room with a king-size bed that dominated the room and rasped on Dori's already strained nerves. It might as well have had a note leaning against the pillows that read, "Reconciliation starts here."

She walked to the window and stared at the parking lot and Dumpster. A stray buff-colored cat jumped to the edge of the Dumpster and sat, studying its contents. She shivered at the thought of the animal out in the cold fending for himself. Where did he sleep so he didn't freeze to death? If he jumped into the Dumpster, how did he get out?

"Are you all right?" Trev asked from behind her.

She turned, surprised. "What made you think I wasn't?"

"You were shivering."

She pointed out the window. "A stray cat. I was shivering for him living outside in this weather."

"Ah." He looked out the window, then down at her. "Speaking of cold, we need to get you a warm coat."

She raised a hand. "No, it's all right. I won't be here lon—"

Trev smiled sympathetically. "Six months, Dori. And since it's only January, three of those months are guaranteed to be pretty cold."

She spoke without thinking. "You know, if Pop were here right now, I'd happily sock him in the nose, even if he is sick." Appalled at what she heard herself say, she clamped a hand to her mouth. "That sounded so awful!"

"I know exactly what you mean, so don't feel bad."

He hated this as much as she did? Somehow that made her feel both comforted and affronted.

Trev indicated the room's door. "Come on. Let's go get your coat."

She followed him out, only too happy to leave the confines of the room. They drove to the Exton Mall and bought her a coat, a black parka lined in red and filled with so much down that she felt like the eight ball in a game of pool. She didn't care. It would keep her warm.

On their way to the cash register they passed a sale table holding gloves and hats. Immediately Dori was taken with a red felt beret. She grabbed it and tried it on, pulling it so it draped more on the right side of her head. She looked around for a mirror but saw none.

"It looks wonderful," Trev said, watching her with a smile.

She looked at him skeptically.

"It does," he insisted. "It looks good with that hairdo of yours, and the red perks up the coat. Get it."

Deciding that for nine dollars she could afford to believe him, she rooted on the table until she found a pair of red leather, fleece-lined gloves, another nine dollars. When she went back outside, she might have felt like a checkerboard, but she was wonderfully toasty for the first time since she'd gotten off the plane.

They drove back to the hospital and spent the afternoon and early evening with Honey and Phil. Pop returned from surgery around dinnertime.

"He's going to be fine," Dr. Rosen said, nodding his white head in satisfaction.

Looking at the sleeping Pop, still much too pale, Dori hoped and prayed Dr. Rosen was right. Even she knew heart attacks were tricky things.

Honey pulled up a chair beside the bed and took Pop's hand. She rubbed her thumb back and forth over the age spots and ridged veins. Once she leaned over and pressed her forehead to his hand. Her lips moved in soundless prayer. Another time she lifted Pop's hand and held his palm against her cheek.

As she watched, Dori's eyes blurred with tears. That was the kind of love she wanted, dreamed of, yearned for. Trying to hide her tears, she turned to the window and stared blindly out.

She felt an arm drop over her shoulders and looked up in surprise, ready to step away. But it was Phil, and she let him draw her close, resting her head on his chest.

The sound of a chair scraping back brought Dori's attention to Honey who stood and looked at her.

"Go back to your motel, Dori, and get some sleep. You've got to be absolutely worn out."

"No, I'm all right," Dori insisted even though her brain felt mushy with fatigue. "I don't want to leave you and Pop." *And I don't want to go back to the motel.*

"Take her, Trev." Honey's tone brooked no argument. "Get her dinner and a good night's sleep."

Trev nodded and picked her new coat off the wide windowsill and held it out to her. When Phil gave her a gentle push in Trev's direction, she knew she hadn't the ghost of a chance to escape. She went with as much dignity as she could muster, given her circumstances, the red rims around her eyes, and the dark circles under them.

They went to Cracker Barrel for dinner and managed to make innocuous conversation. "Movie?" Trev suggested when they finished.

Dori jumped at the idea. Anything to keep from returning to that room with that huge bed. But inevitably, unavoidably, they had to go back. Once in the room, the first thing Trev did was call Phil for the latest on Pop while Dori flicked on the TV. Noise, news, other people in the charged atmosphere.

When he hung up, Trev stood quietly for a moment, and Dori

almost thought he was praying. "What?" Fear made her voice tight. "Is Pop worse?"

He smiled slightly and shook his head. "If anything, he's better. Much better. He'll be going home tomorrow."

"What? How can that be? Twelve hours ago he looked like he was dying! He acted like he was dying."

"They determined that the bleeding was from a tear in his stomach near the place it joins the esophagus. They cauterized it, and the bleeding has stopped. They decided he was also suffering from a massive attack of indigestion."

"Indigestion?" Her life had been turned upside down by an upset stomach?

"The indigestion mimicked a heart attack. Apparently it made him vomit rather violently, and that in turn made the stomach tear."

Dori didn't know whether to laugh or cry.

"Phil said Pop had a message for us."

"Well, I have a message for him!" Indigestion indeed!

Trev gave her a sympathetic look. "Pop says we're to remember that a promise is a promise."

All the air whooshed from her lungs at the old man's gall. She stared at Trev, words piling upon each other in her throat but no sound emerging—which was probably a good thing considering what was running through her mind.

"We did give our word." Trev looked calm, controlled, and much too handsome.

She scowled. "Under false circumstances."

They stared at each other for several silent moments. Dori had no idea what Trev was thinking, but if he was half as confused as she was, it didn't matter. It wouldn't make sense anyway.

So Pop wasn't dying. That was a good thing. When he had asked for their promise, he'd thought he was. Hadn't he? Her jaw tightened and her eyes narrowed as she thought back to her visit. It hadn't struck her at the time, but now she realized he hadn't been in a coronary unit, nor had he worn a heart monitor. In retrospect she was willing to bet that the doctor she'd assumed was a cardiologist was in fact a gastroenterologist.

"He knew!" she shouted. "Trev, he knew. They both knew!"

"That he wasn't dying of a heart attack?" Trev nodded. "Probably."

"He tricked us. I can't believe it." She flopped down on the side of the bed, mind racing, emotions rioting. She no longer knew which end was up, which person was trustworthy, which choice was right.

Trev hunkered down in front of her and took her hands in his. He turned his brilliant eyes on her, eyes she'd always thought the most beautiful she'd ever seen, though of course she never told him. Guys didn't like hearing they had beautiful anythings.

"Dori, we can't make any decisions tonight. I know I'm worn to a frazzle, physically and emotionally, and you are too. We might too easily say things we'll regret. Let's get a good night's sleep and see how we feel about things tomorrow."

She looked into the face of this man she had once loved so deeply and nodded. "You're right. I am so exhausted I can barely stand, let alone think straight." She looked down at their joined hands. "Tomorrow."

He gave her hands a slight squeeze. "Good girl. And Father God, we ask you to direct our thinking. Help us see beyond our anger and resentment at being manipulated."

Dori started and stared at Trev's now bowed head. He was praying! Right here, just like that, he was praying. Out loud!

"Help us make wise choices, ones that in the long run will honor You. For that is our heart's desire, Lord. To honor You."

Oh, yeah?

He stood, dropping her hands. She clasped them in her lap, missing the warmth of his grip and mad at herself because she did. "Do you often do that?"

He looked at her. "What?"

"Pray at the drop of a hat?"

He looked thoughtful. "I hope so."

"Huh." She got to her feet and went to the window again. It was dark outside, though the lights in the parking lot shone brightly on the Dumpster. Dori wondered in passing where the buff-colored cat had gone. "I guess that proves you're a pastor."

"Um. I suppose it's as good a marker as any."

She watched his reflection in the window as he studied her,

unaware she could see him too. He looked sad, thoughtful. Yearning?

It's just your imagination, the distortion of the reflection.

She pulled her eyes from him back to the night beyond the window, but her thoughts stayed on him, his prayer, his comment. She slid a finger through a line of condensate along the bottom edge of the window sash.

"It's hard to get used to you praying." She turned to him. "All I remember is you teasing me about my naiveté when I trusted Christ back in high school. And now here you are, a seminary grad and all." She gave a wan smile. "Wonders never cease."

"You can thank yourself for my believing. When you left, I was so devastated that I turned to God." On those words he grabbed his duffel and went into the bathroom, closing the door behind him. She stared openmouthed after him.

Devastated? Trev? Sure Phil had said his brother had come close to failing out, and maybe she almost believed him. But for Trev himself to say he was devastated? That couldn't be. *She* was the one who had been devastated.

Again the thought flashed that the pain that had driven Trev to God had driven her from Him. What that said about each of them she didn't want to contemplate.

She grabbed her cell phone. She had to talk to Meg. Meg would sympathize. Meg would understand how trapped she felt. Meg would tell her to come home.

She did not find the sympathy she expected.

"But six months, Meg! And he tricked us."

"Good for him."

"What?" Dori felt betrayed. She had been so sure Meg would understand.

"Listen, my girl, and listen closely to Mama Meg. For six years you've held resentment and hurt in your arms like they were precious friends."

Dori made a protesting sound, but Meg continued as if she hadn't heard. "It's well worth six months to rid yourself of these pernicious cancers. They are robbing you of life. You've got to let go and forgive."

"But, Meg—"

"No buts, Dori Trevelyan. Stay. Please, stay."

When Trev came out of the bathroom, freshly showered and wearing a T-shirt and jeans, she was still sitting on the bed, staring into space, trying to come to terms with Meg's perfidy.

Without a word, she collected her things and went into the warm, steamy room fragrant from his shower. She looked at herself in the mirror over the sink and saw blue-black smudges under her eyes, a pallor that equaled Pop's, and a pinched, angry look around her mouth. She sighed. She'd be lucky if Trev wanted to keep her, looking the way she did. She turned away and rummaged for her toiletry items.

Though they'd brought all her luggage to the room, she'd only needed to open her small carry-on. Because she'd been afraid of losing the bigger case, it landing in Timbuktu while she landed in Philly, she'd packed enough for a couple of days in the smaller bag. The only thing she would normally have needed out of the large bag was her pajamas, but there was no way on earth she was wearing them tonight. Those little shorts and that skimpy top would send entirely the wrong message, even if they were just a washed out, tired pink cotton knit, not a slinky silk.

Tonight she was sleeping in her jeans. Maybe tomorrow night too, and every night into the foreseeable future.

When she came back into the bedroom, Trev was leaning against the headboard, pillows stuffed behind him, reading a Bible, its navy leather binding creased and worn. He looked up and smiled at her. "I was just getting ready to pray for Pop. Want to pray with me?"

No! I don't pray anymore, not even for Pop. "Sure," she forced out. "That's a good idea."

He shifted over a bit and patted the bed beside him. She glanced at him, then down at the bed, then back at him.

He held up a hand, palm out. "I'm only asking you to pray with me, nothing more. I won't ask anything more. I promise."

Her face burning because he had read her so easily, she sat gingerly on the edge of the bed. She folded her hands primly in her lap and bowed her head.

Nothing happened. She opened her eyes and looked cautiously over her shoulder at him.

Trev was studying her with an inscrutable look on his face. "I won't hurt you, Dori. I would never do anything to hurt you."

The sincerity with which he spoke was a knife in her heart. She turned her back to him again and bowed her head.

"We're going to have to talk about it sometime, you know." His voice was gentle, meant to be soothing. "Otherwise, it'll be a big pink elephant in the room with us, stepping on our toes, knocking into us, getting in our way, obvious but ignored."

The thought of talking about her pain made her breath hitch. "Just pray, will you?" *And let me alone!*

When morning finally came, Dori had a horrendous headache and felt as grouchy as she ever had in her entire life. She'd tossed all night, falling into periods of fitful sleep as she hung on the edge of her side of the huge bed. Dreams of Trev, of the joy of the last night they'd spent together in bed, swirled with the heat of summer only to be interrupted by visions of another glimpse of Trev in bed, this time with a blonde head beside him. Then she'd start awake, only to hear Trev's deep, easy breathing and his occasional woofle snore. She couldn't decide which was worse: Her too-vivid dreams or the thought that he was blasé enough about their situation to actually get a restful night's sleep.

She lurched out of bed, a gorgon in a wrinkled T-shirt and jeans. Trev took one look at her as she snarled her way to the bathroom and swallowed whatever jolly greeting had been on his tongue. When she saw herself in the mirror over the sink, she wondered why he hadn't just bolted from the room before she turned him to stone. Her hair rivaled Don King's with its finger-in-the-electric-socket look, and her left cheek was a mass of sleep lines, interesting since she'd not slept much. If she pursed her mouth any more tightly, by tomorrow she'd have those lovely little radiating lines into which lipstick bled so becomingly.

If she remained this ugly, he'd be happy to send her back to California and soon.

She climbed into the shower and let it beat her into at least a semblance of a decent person. She spent a lot of time on her hair and makeup, not because she wanted to impress Trev, oh no, never that. She needed to look good as part of her armor, as a means of giving herself strength. She had to remember that she could manage without him. She would manage without him.

By the time she was ready to leave the safety of the bathroom, she had come to a decision. So what that she'd promised Pop? She'd already disappointed him big-time. What was one more hurt? She was good at giving pain and receiving it in return. And Pop, well, he was good at being magnanimous. So was Honey. They'd both forgive her in time, and she'd avoid the humiliation she was certain awaited down the road.

She threw all her notions and cosmetics into her small bag and walked into the bedroom with her shoulders straight and her chin high.

Trev turned from stuffing things in his duffel. When he saw her, he smiled, a full, appreciative male smile. "You look lovely this morning."

She allowed herself only a small, tight smile though his words felt like a gentle rain on a parched soul, far too soothing, too necessary.

"Thank you," she said with as little emotion as she could manage and watched his smile turn wry as he answered his chiming cell phone.

She listened as she again stared out the window at the Dumpster. It was obvious that the call was from someone in his church about someone else in his church.

He punched off with a sigh. "We're going to have to leave immediately, I'm afraid."

"Trouble in River City?"

"Barry Sanders, our church flasher, went at it last night and is in jail. And Mary Jensen is in the hospital with kidney stones. I've got to go see both of them, especially Barry."

Dori barely heard the second emergency. "You have a flasher in your church?"

Trev nodded and gave a soft snort. "And he loves my preaching. He tells me so all the time."

"I can see that it must be doing him a lot of good," Dori said solemnly.

Trev grinned, then sighed again. "It's sad really. He's been in jail several times for the problem, been to all kinds of court-ordered counseling and therapy, both Christian and secular. He meets with me once a week for accountability."

"And while you were away, the mouse played."

"Apparently so. I'm worried that one of these times they're going to throw the book at him, and he won't get out for years, if ever. Of course, the upside of that scenario is that he does best spiritually in the regimented circumstances of jail. No chance to give in to these strange urges of his, so he stays clean and really grows as a Christian."

Dori was fascinated by the fact that Trev, popular, one-of-the-good-old-boys Trev, spent time with a flasher. Willingly, no less. "Does he have a family?"

"A mother who has washed her hands of him and a wife who left long ago."

"Can't say I blame her." Dori thought about what it must have been like married to someone who ran around town without his clothes. She shuddered. "Just how old is this guy?"

"Old enough to know better." Trev's tone was acerbic. "I'd say he's forty-five, forty-eight."

"Old enough to know better is right. And it was cold out there last night! The guy's nuts. He's got to be."

"Definitely different, but in most other ways a very nice guy."

Dori's stomach growled. "Do we have time to eat before we go?"

Trev grinned. "Never could stand to miss a meal, could you?" He zipped his duffel shut, then turned to grab his coat.

His red Lands' End Squall.

She'd been so absorbed in her misery yesterday that she hadn't even noticed the coat. Now it hit her hard. He still had his Squall, though it couldn't still be the same one that Pop had given him that long-ago Christmas, could it? He must have bought another of exactly the same model. She blinked. Trev was a sentimentalist.

Well, she wasn't. She was a realist. As she slipped on her parka, she said, "Trev, I've been thinking."

He opened the room door and said, "Hmm?" He reached to take the handle of her larger suitcase from her.

"This isn't going to work." She picked up her laptop and the handle on her small carry-on bag and started out the door after him. She was so intent on what she was saying that she was only vaguely aware of others passing their door and the sudden, surprised, "Pastor Paul! What are you doing here?"

She pulled the door shut behind her, rattling it to make certain it had caught. "We can't do this again. At least I can't."

She felt rather than heard a sudden thick silence. She looked up and saw three people staring at her: a man and a woman she supposed were husband and wife, and a buxom Betty Boop blonde who was a younger, souped-up model of the mother and who looked like she'd just been shot.

The vaguely heard words came back to her. *Pastor Paul!* These people were from Trev's church. Dori's face flamed as she thought about what she'd said and its possible and highly inaccurate reading. She looked at Trev in consternation. Talk about an imbroglio.

Trev was once again wearing his wry look. "Dori, I'd like you to meet Jonathan and Judy Warrington and their daughter, Angie. They're members of Seaside Chapel. In fact, Jonathan is an elder."

Trev slid an arm around Dori's shaking shoulders. "Folks, I'd like you to meet my wife, Dori."

Eleven

ALL TREV COULD THINK as he watched the incredulous faces of the Warringtons and the beached-whale expression on Dori's face was that he was extremely glad Phil wasn't standing in the corridor with them. Of course Phil's hysterical laughter would have gone a long way in relieving all the awkwardness, disbelief, and uncertainty that was swirling about their little gathering with more chilling vigor than the winter winds howling outside.

"We were just going to get some breakfast before we started home." Trev was pleased that his voice sounded ordinary in spite of the weight pressing his chest. Of all the people from church to run into, the Warringtons were by far the worst.

Jonathan Warrington thought Seaside Chapel belonged to him. Of course he'd never say such a blasphemous thing—"This is the Lord's church!"—but he acted it. All decisions had to be his or at least have his agreement. Every time he talked about the past three pastors and how he had purified the church by scripting their leaving, Trev flinched. Of course Jonathan didn't phrase his machinations so baldly. He said things like, "It became obvious that he was no longer spiritually qualified to lead us" or "The Lord just showed us that he had to go." For *us*, read Jonathan Warrington.

Trev had managed to avoid any heavy disagreements with Jonathan, though it had taken some fancy footwork a few times. Trev understood that Jonathan hadn't bothered or attacked him because he was only the interim. As Jonathan saw it, he still had more power than Trev, so he was happy. Goodness only knew what he'd think of Dori's sudden appearance, and when he learned of the six years—Trev paled at the possibilities.

Then there was Angie, smiling bravely at Trev in spite of her tear-sheened eyes. For two and a half years she'd been after him and not very subtly. In fact, her hand had been resting on his arm when Dori stated her decision to never do "this" again. He didn't even want to think about how those words sounded to suspicious ears. Angie's fingers had tightened, her nails becoming talons digging through his jacket and sweater to make what he feared were little red marks all over his arm. Just how much of her father's vindictiveness was in her Trev wasn't certain, but he was afraid they would soon find out.

He put his hand in the small of Dori's back and began pushing her toward the exit. "See you tomorrow." He smiled broadly.

Dori let him push her, but at the last minute she looked back over her shoulder and called gamely, "Nice to meet you."

"You too, Laurie," said Judy Warrington stiffly. Significantly missing were polite nothings from Jonathan and Angie.

As Trev sat in the motel restaurant and ate the breakfast that tasted like sand, he tried to keep up pleasant, meaningless conversation with the woman seated across from him. His wife. His unhappy, unwilling, twice-trapped wife, ensnared once by Pop, now ambushed by the Warringtons. She didn't need to be a genius to know that if she left now, his ministry was finished. He would be assumed to be having an affair, and no amount of talking would convince people otherwise. Only her presence would defuse the situation, though undoubtedly causing other difficulties.

Like how was he ever to explain her sudden appearance to the congregation?

The very best scenario was one in which no one asked any questions and happily accepted the marriage as a fait accompli. Then they could smoothly meld Dori into church life. However, he'd been a pastor long enough to know wishful thinking when he thought it. There would be questions, rumors, and gossip. He shuddered to think what was ahead for both of them, and not just from the Warringtons.

In his mind's eye he saw the three Graces, little old ladies he called his grace builders because they considered it their Christian duty to speak to him about every perceived fault, failure, or poor sermon. Without venom and with sweet smiles they corrected him and cosseted him. Without doubt they would ask endless questions about Dori, questions that could cause great harm, given the information they were bound to uncover.

"How long have you known each other?" they'd ask, eyes bright and sparkling with the romance of it all.

Well, he could deal with that. So could Dori. Answer: always.

"When did you decide to get married?"

How would the old ladies take six years ago as the answer? Of course he could dodge the question and say he'd fallen in love with her when he was fifteen and she thirteen, but that led to another logical question.

"Well, what took you so long? And why did you keep her existence secret? No one even knew you had girlfriend, let alone that you were engaged." They'd look at him with hurt in their eyes because he had not shared his great good news with them. "When did you get engaged?"

He could tell them that they decided to marry without going through the usual engagement thing. After all, it was the truth.

"Where did you get married?"

"In Las Vegas in one of the tacky Elvis chapels," he'd say.

They'd stare, stunned. It seemed so out of character—or what they thought should be the character—of their pastor. Of course it hadn't been out of character for the kids he and Dori had been six years ago. It had been a great lark, a wonderful laugh, a story to tell to their children and grandchildren.

Not that it presently looked as if they'd ever have any progeny to tell.

"But what about Angie?" one of the old ladies was bound to ask. "I thought you and she had something going." Wink, wink.

He had been absolutely faithful to Dori, but the fact that he had never, ever given Angie any encouragement whatsoever wouldn't mean anything if she chose to wear a broken heart on her sleeve. The damning truth was that he'd never told Angie he was married either, just like he'd never told any of his people including the church's elected elders. Some things were best kept private.

Like a pastor has the luxury of privacy.

He sighed. If anyone did any checking, it wouldn't take long to find out the whole sorry truth. Then would come the big questions.

"Why did your wife leave you?"

"How could you take our pulpit without telling us?"

"Why has she come back now?"

He set his coffee cup down and leaned back in his chair, closing his eyes against the headache he'd had since he'd first felt Dori's reluctance yesterday.

Ah, Pop, I know you meant to help, but what a mess!

"Are you okay?" she asked from across the table.

Do you actually care? "Headache. I didn't sleep well last night."

She pulled her purse to her lap and began rooting. "You slept fine. I know because I didn't." She pulled out a small vial of aspirin and handed it to him. "You still make that soft little woofle sound when you sleep on your back."

"I do, do I?" How pathetic that he was pleased she noticed he snored.

She turned rosy, presumably because of the intimacy inherent in hearing someone snore, and became very interested in the contents of her purse. Smiling to himself at how pretty the blush made her, he took three pills, downed them with a drink of water, and passed the vial back.

"The people from your church are sitting over there in the corner, and they keep staring at us," Dori said, self-consciously straightening the collar on her denim shirt.

Trev suddenly felt he should have taken four aspirin. He shrugged. What would have been the use? Even the whole bottle wouldn't cure what ailed him. "I'm afraid you'll have to get used to it, sweetheart, being a surprise bride and all."

Dori frowned, poured two aspirin into her hand, and downed

106 ~ Gayle Roper

them with a Coke. He'd forgotten that she drank Coke for breakfast. How she could daily perform such an abhorrent act was
beyond him. Coffee strong and hot was the only acceptable breakfast beverage, except for a glass of orange juice, of course. He was
certain he'd find the biblical proof to support his beverage position
any day now. In the meantime, he drank his hot caffeine on faith.

"They seem like nice people," Dori said hesitantly.

She'd always been inclined to look for the good in people, but
they were talking about the Warringtons here.

To lie and pray like crazy that none of the potential problems
he feared came to pass, or to tell the truth and burden her with
more worries? He sighed. The answer was obvious.

"Beware the man who meets you at the airport," he said, his
back prickling under Jonathan's relentless gaze. Given time, Trev
felt he would look down and see a hole in his middle where the
concentrated glare had bored right through him from back to
front.

"Beware what man at the airport?" Dori looked confused.
"Beware of Phil?"

Trev had to laugh. "That's not a bad thought, knowing Phil,
but it's not what I meant. It's an old seminary saying. It means look
out for the guy who thinks he runs the church, often the guy who
wants first crack at the new candidate or new pastor, so he meets
your plane. Such men have their own agendas, and they aren't
always the pastor's or the church's."

"It's about who has the power?" Dori suggested.

Trev was pleased at her insight. "That's it in a nutshell.
Sometimes these people are mature enough that you can work
through your problems and disagreements; sometimes it's a matter
of neither of you being wrong though there will never be agreement, so you separate; and sometimes it's a matter of a genuine
power struggle with all the nastiness that implies."

"And Mr. Warrington is the last kind of man?"

Trev neck hairs prickled anew, and he squirmed under
Jonathan's continued scrutiny. "I'm afraid so."

"And my coming has complicated matters for you immensely."
Dori looked troubled.

Trev nodded. "But your going would be even worse."

Dori swallowed, put her napkin beside her plate, and pushed her chair back. "I realize that." She stood. "I'm going to the ladies' room before we leave."

Trev watched her cross the dining room, his emotions in a giant tangle. He felt as knotted as his fishing line the time Jack decided to tie himself up in it. That he still loved Dori was a given. She had taken his heart years ago, and nothing had changed. He could be happy as a clam spending the rest of his life protecting her, loving her, possessing her. The problem was that she had to allow him to protect her and possess her. He guessed he could continue to love her unilaterally, but where was the joy, the pleasure in unrequited affection?

Oh, Lord, can there be reciprocity in this relationship? Can I win her back? Can I undo whatever it was I did?

Whatever it was he did. He snorted sardonically. He knew what he'd done. He just couldn't understand why she became angry enough over it to sunder their marriage.

Still, he remembered Dr. Quentin's advice given during their talks all through his three years at seminary. "Just be careful of that anger if she comes back. It could sink your love boat before you're even out of port."

At this point he had no idea whether they were sailing or not, but he vowed to do everything he could to get them out to sea.

Phil had been right about one thing though. She was so much more beautiful now. There was a maturity about her that was riveting. Gone was the bouncy enthusiasm of her youth when she had seemed a perpetual cheerleader. In its place was a grace of movement that drew his eye. Her figure was a woman's: slim, elegant, appealing. A short, sophisticated, and very becoming haircut replaced the waist-length hair of high school, hair he'd always loved to touch. For years he'd had to satisfy himself with pulling it as he teased her or wrapping it around his hand and yanking just to make her lose her balance. She'd always flown at him in mock fury when he'd done it, and he'd loved the game of holding her off as she made believe she was beating him up.

Then for three glorious days, he'd been able to stroke that beautiful hair, run his fingers through it, feel it fall across his chest as she curled next to him in their bed.

He stood abruptly. That way lay madness and pain.

Dori fell asleep almost as soon as they left the motel, her head resting half on the headrest and half on the car door. She didn't wake up until they made the turn off the Atlantic City Expressway onto the Garden State Parkway. She sat up with a groan, rubbing the back of her neck.

"Stiff?" Trev asked.

She didn't reply but bent her neck to both sides, front and back, then rotated it in circles. "Where are we?"

"Almost to Seaside. Our turnoff is just a couple of miles away."

She looked out the window at the salt marsh they were driving past. Even in the closed car, the distinctive, briny scent of the marsh was obvious. Dori wrinkled her nose. "I'd forgotten how the shore smells here in the East."

Trev inhaled. "I love the smell. I think one reason is that it always makes me think of my parents and that long-ago vacation. Now it makes me think of home."

"Home," Dori echoed, her voice hollow.

Trev's heart sank. His home, not hers. "I'm sorry, sweetheart." He stopped to toss his coins in the automatic toll station and left the Parkway. "I know this can't be any fun for you."

She merely gave him a sad smile.

In moments they were driving over the Ninth Street Causeway into Seaside. There were few cars and fewer people about, especially when compared to the chaos of this section of town in the summer. Trev drove down Ninth to Asbury where a red light stopped them. He pointed to the close left hand corner.

"That's Phil's pharmacy."

Dori bent and leaned toward Trev to see out his window. "I have a hard time imagining Phil as responsible enough to count out the right number of pills, let alone mature enough to run his own business."

Trev grunted. "He's still the jokester he always was, but he's very good at what he does."

Dori laughed. "He was so excited when he phoned to tell me he'd bought the store. I asked him where he got the money. 'Rob a bank?' I asked. He said he bought it with the bulk of his share of the life insurance he got from his parents."

"I think they would be pleased." The light changed and Trev turned down Asbury.

Dori looked at him. "I didn't know you two were beneficiaries of a policy of that size. No one ever told me anything about it."

"We didn't know for years either. Pop kept tabs on the money, investing it on our behalf while we were growing up. He always told us Dad had left us money for college, but not that there was more. He got around to telling us when we each reached twenty-three, though the law says he should have told us at twenty-one. By then I was almost finished working my way through seminary, and Phil was working for a chain pharmacy not far from Honey and Pop's. When I came to the church here, Phil followed, looking for some fun in the sun. It turns out he loves Seaside almost as much as I do, so he settled here."

As they drove slowly down Asbury, heading south, Trev looked at Dori. They were almost home, and she needed to know what awaited her. He took a deep breath. "I guess I'd better tell you about Jack and Ryan, hadn't I?"

She looked at him sharply. "Jack and Ryan?"

Trev nodded. "Jack's my dog—our dog. He's a black lab. I got him about five years ago." He didn't tell her that he'd bought the little black ball of curls with sharp puppy teeth and a loving tongue so that he'd have someone to care for, someone to talk to, someone to be his companion after he lost her. Obviously Jack didn't replace her, but he had been truer than she, never failing to delight in Trev's company or to forgive him for all faults.

Dori looked at him. "I remember that you always wanted a big dog, not the little yappy ones that Honey loved. So how big?"

Trev shrugged. "His head comes to my waist."

Dori's eyes widened. "Big."

"But a lover."

"That's what they all say as the animal bites your head off. I have a little beige Dandie Dinmont. Trudy. I paid way too much for her." For a minute she looked lost. "If I stay, I guess I'll have to have her sent."

Jack and Trudy. There was undoubtedly a pair for the ages. "Is she yappy?"

Dori shook her head. "Rarely barks."

"That's what they all say as the shrill sound drives you insane."

They looked at each other and grinned. Trev's heart filled with hope at her natural response, but only for a moment. She turned to the passenger window and watched Seaside slide past, withdrawing behind her cool façade.

"So tell me about Ryan." She almost sounded like she cared. "Is he your cat? Or your guinea pig?"

"Ryan's a thirteen-year-old boy who's living with me."

She turned and stared at him. "You have a teenaged kid living with you?"

Trev was slightly miffed at her total surprise. Had he never been kind before? "Someone had to care for him, and it fell to me. I was glad to do it." He heard his mock humility and flinched.

"Um," she said thoughtfully.

They pulled to the curb in front of 112 Heron Lane. He'd bought the place new with a huge chunk of his parents' insurance money because he knew it was a good investment, even if he was in Seaside only a short time. Already it had risen in value several thousands of dollars in the two years he'd lived here.

"This is where you live?" Dori studied the pale gray house. "Wow. Seaside Chapel must be doing very, very well to have this nice a parsonage or manse or whatever they call it."

"This isn't the church's house," Trev said. "It's mine. I own it."

She nodded and continued to stare. "It's absolutely beautiful, Trev. Beautiful."

Trev tried to see the gray house through her eyes. He knew he liked the white porch that ran from the off-center front steps across the left side of the house, and he liked the upper-class feel of the white French doors that opened onto it from the living room. French doors from the master bedroom opened onto a similar porch on the second level. The arch over the front door was repeated in the arched window of the second-floor room he'd made his office.

The lawn was small and winter ugly, but the builder had been only too happy to include excellent plantings across the front at an undoubtedly inflated price. Trev hadn't cared that he was paying extra at the time because he was anxious to get out of the no-pets-allowed apartment he was staying in and retrieve Jack from Honey and Pop and their latest little white yappy dog. Jack had been jittery for a good two months after he moved home. He was going to love having Trudy invade his space.

The front door with its oval of etched glass flew open, and Jack surged out with Ryan hanging on to his leash for dear life. Todd followed, slamming the door with a vigor that made Trev flinch for the glass panel.

"I think you're about to meet the troops." Trev opened his car door. "Hey, guys," he called as he stood.

"Pastor Paul! What are you doing back so early?" Ryan let go of Jack's leash. "Get him, boy!"

Like Jack needed any encouragement. He raced to Trev and lunged, his paws hitting Trev in the chest and knocking him back against the van.

"Get down, you great big horse," Trev said, laughing. He raised his knee and gently pushed at Jack's chest. Jack dropped to the ground and stood, panting happily, eyes on Trev. Trev bent and rubbed Jack's ears and neck. When he stood, the dog leaned happily against his leg.

"So how'd it go last night?" Trev asked Ryan. "You guys have a good time?"

"Great! Mr. Marlowe gave us each a gazillion quarters and took us to the arcade. Then he took us to Mack and Manco's for pizza."

Trev, who wasn't a great fan of arcades because of some of the older kids who hung out there, said with forced cheer, "Sounds great. Did Mr. Marlowe play some games too?"

"He tried," Todd said. "But we whopped him good!" He and Ryan high-fived.

Trev relaxed. Mr. Marlowe was definitely salt of the earth.

"Hey, Pastor Paul, did you hear that Barry got arrested again last night?" Ryan started to giggle. "He was walking around the parking lot at the Acme with nothing on!" The boy was obviously both impressed and appalled. "What's with him? I mean, it was below freezing!"

Apparently appalled won the day, a good sign, though the reason wasn't exactly what Trev would have hoped for. Still, he couldn't expect moral and spiritual issues to be at the head of a thirteen-year-old's reasons for behavior, and he had to admit that the temperature had given him pause too.

Suddenly the boys noticed Dori standing quietly at the front bumper of the van. They looked from her to Trev. Then Ryan leaned forward and whispered, "Who's she?"

Trev turned to Dori and held out his hand. She came toward him and took it. He felt immense relief. It was going to be hard enough explaining to Ryan why he was sleeping in his office while his "new" bride slept alone in the master bedroom. At least he assumed those would be the sleeping arrangements, given her ice princess demeanor. He threaded his fingers through hers. Holding hands in front of the boy was one normal thing a married couple could be expected to do.

"Ryan—and Todd—I'd like you to meet Dori Trevelyan."

Ryan looked at Trev in surprise. "I didn't know you had a sister. I thought you just had Mr. Phil."

Trev had to smile. "Dori's not my sister."

"Though I sort of am," Dori said, laughter in her eyes.

He gave her hand a tug, drawing her against his side. "Don't complicate things."

"You're holding hands," Ryan accused.

Trev lifted their joined hands and looked at them as if surprised. "So we are." He let their hands fall, though he still held tightly to hers. "That's because Dori's my wife."

"Your wife?" Ryan squinted at Trev. Then he folded his arms over his chest and studied Dori. He looked back at Trev, accusation in his gaze. "I thought you went to visit your sick Pop. That's what you told me."

"And that was true," Dori said. "I know because I was there too. Pop's my Pop too."

Ryan's eyes widened. "Jeepers, she *is* your sister!"

Trev shook his head and tried to clarify the situation for the first of what would undoubtedly be a million times before they were finished. "Pop raised both of us, but we aren't related."

"What?" Both Ryan and Todd looked confused.

"I'm adopted," Dori said. "That's the easiest way to explain it."

"Oh." Both boys nodded, satisfied.

Still Ryan eyed Trev uneasily, and Trev knew exactly what was on his mind. *What about me? Do I have to go now that you've got a wife? Go where?*

"Do you want to come home now?" Trev asked the boy. "Or do you want to spend the night with Todd as planned?"

A tension in Ryan eased at Trev's words. "I'll stay at Todd's."

"Yeah, my parents are taking us bowling," Todd added.

"Sounds like fun. Have you ever bowled?" Trev asked Ryan.

"Nah, but what's to it? You just roll the ball down the alley and knock over some pins."

Trev didn't laugh. Ryan would learn soon enough that it wasn't quite that easy.

Todd bumped Ryan with his elbow. "Let's go."

Ryan looked at Trev who nodded. "You guys go on. I'll–We'll walk Jack."

The boys took off at a run, but Todd's words drifted back clearly.

"Wow, wait until I tell Mom about Pastor Paul's wife! And poor Angie."

Twelve

ORI TOOK HER HAND BACK as soon as the boys turned the corner. "Poor Angie?" That buxom, blonde Betty Boop from the motel?

Trev looked her straight in the eye. "There is nothing between Angie and me. There never has been. There never will be. In case you've forgotten, I'm a married man."

The snap in his voice took her aback, but she refused to let it show. "Does anyone here know you're married?"

He shook his head. "No one. Even Phil only found out yesterday."

"So if we hadn't met the Warringtons this morning, I could have gone back to California." Fate could be so fickle. She wouldn't even consider the idea that the Lord had put the Warringtons there to keep her here.

"If you wanted to go back on your word again." His tone was sharp.

She held her chin high, making believe that the words didn't hurt. "Like you'd care."

"Oh, I'd care all right."

Her heart jumped. He'd care!

"Pop doesn't deserve to be treated so shabbily a second time." The chill in his voice matched the chill in the air.

Anger welled in her. "Don't you make me the fall guy here, Paul Michael Trevelyan. I'm not the one who broke his vows."

"No, you're the one who ran like a coward before I even had a chance to talk with you and work things out."

The word *coward* shot straight to her heart. She hadn't been a coward. She had been a young wife who didn't know what else to do. "You thought a few words would erase the betrayal?"

"*Betrayal?* Don't you think you're blowing things a bit out of proportion?"

Dori glared at him. The man had no shame, no sense of guilt, no life ethos. That she had pined for him for six years suddenly seemed the utmost in pathetic. "Just because you think Christ forgave you doesn't mean I have," she spat.

"No, you haven't." He spoke through clenched teeth, the muscle in his jaw jumping. "You've wound your self-righteous hurt around yourself like Lazarus's grave clothes, and just like Lazarus, you've begun to stink."

Dori stepped back as if she'd been struck. "How dare you!"

Suddenly Jack whined. Dori frowned down at him. He looked from her to Trev and back, his agitation plain to see.

"What's wrong with you?" she asked the dog, her voice abrupt. Jack stared at her, his soft brown eyes full of worry.

Then awareness hit and her head jerked up. She and Trev were fighting like fishwives right out on the sidewalk for anyone to see and hear. A great image for a pastor and his wife, but she refused to blush. She had right on her side.

"Open the trunk," she ordered. "I'll get my suitcase and go inside."

"I'll take it in for you," Trev said, voice brusque.

She threw a scorching look his way. "Don't bother. I can manage fine on my own. I've done so for six happy, trouble-free years."

However it was quickly obvious that apart from a tug-of-war right here in the street, Trev was carrying the suitcases. She grabbed her laptop and followed, muttering imprecations all the way up the walk.

He took her things upstairs to what was obviously the master bedroom, dropping them on the beige duvet that covered the queen-size bed. Jack hairs covered the duvet. Beyond the bed she saw the French doors and the white-railed porch. In other circumstances and seasons, it would be wonderful to lounge out there and enjoy the sea air, but not today. Now the chill outside was only slightly lower than that inside.

"I'll sleep on the couch in my office," Trev said, his voice still stiff with anger. "I'll clean my things out this evening,"

"Good. You do that." She was very glad he didn't plan to share the room with her. She couldn't deal with more nights like last night.

"That's Ryan's room." He pointed across the hall, then waved toward the room at the front of the house. "That's my office."

She glimpsed the couch he'd sleep on against one wall, and turning her back to him, she began fiddling with her small roll-on. They stood, mere feet apart, as estranged as they'd ever been. She thought she heard him sigh. It was all she could do not to cry.

"I've got to take Jack for a quick walk before I go see Barry and give Mary a quick visit."

She gave a curt nod. He hesitated a minute as though he had something to say, but on another sigh, he left. She listened to him and Jack thump their way down the stairs, and she heard the front door close quietly.

She sank to the bed and buried her face in her hands. What had just happened? She and Trev had never said ugly words to each other before. Never. As adults they were behaving worse than they ever had as kids. Less than twenty-four hours together, and they'd attacked each other mercilessly.

Feeling defeated and sad and unaccountably to blame—*Wait a minute here. I'm the injured party!*—she left the master bedroom and wandered slowly around the house. The only room she avoided was Trev's office. It felt too personal, too private to invade.

Ryan's room was awash in strewn clothes and boy toys. A small TV sat on a card table with PlayStation 2 hand controls leaning against it. A pile of game CDs made a small Leaning Tower. Another pile of CDs, music this time, and a portable CD player had been thrown on his pillow. A backpack lay just inside the door, its sides bulging with books. A small wire bookshelf was filled with paperbacks including *The Chronicles of Narnia*, *The Hobbit*, *The Lord of the Rings*, and several Stephen Lawhead,

Randall Ingermanson, Kathy Tyers, and Karen Hancock fantasies. All were obviously read and reread.

In the bathroom, ugly, mud-colored towels were tucked helter-skelter into racks, but at least they weren't on the floor. Dori automatically straightened them. She noted that the sink and the tub were clean as were the toilet and the floor around it. A cleaning lady was the only possible answer.

She slowly went downstairs. She'd been so upset and angry when she stormed into the house that she'd seen the living room through a red haze. Now she studied the dark green sofa and matching chair. They were angled to give a good view of the TV, a surprisingly old-fashioned unit.

Beside the chair on an end table sat a pile of books, the top one open and splayed facedown to hold Trev's place. For they were obviously his. Some were popular Christian titles she was vaguely familiar with, but several were theological books of a highly academic nature. She picked up the top one and read some of the parts he'd underlined in yellow.

She replaced the book with a thoughtful frown. Never in a million years would the old Trev, the Trev she remembered, have read a book about the implications of the Incarnation. Or—she glanced at the second book in the pile—a book on bioethics and the evangelical community. In a flash she comprehended a fact she had acknowledged but not understood before.

Paul Trevelyan was not the same man she had known and married.

Just as she wasn't the same woman.

She sank into his chair and stared at the blank TV screen. What did these changes mean to her? What did they mean to the next six months?

After a few minutes with no answers, she got up and wandered into what was supposedly a dining room but had been made into a weight room. A weight bench sat along one wall, the bar resting on its supports, large disks attached to the ends. Along another wall other weights of varying sizes lined a shelf shaped like a V.

Well, that explained the broad shoulders.

She walked to the bench, glanced over her shoulder even

though she knew no one was home but her, and yielding to curiosity, lay down on the bench. She placed her feet flat on the floor and her chest under the bar. She gripped it with both hands and pushed upward. Nothing happened. She rubbed her hands together, gripped the bar again, and pushed. Nothing budged, not even an inch. *Wimp!* She climbed to her feet and turned to the kitchen.

Again neat and clean but barren. She opened the refrigerator. A half-full half gallon of 2 percent milk. A container of Philadelphia Cream Cheese and a tub of cottage cheese. She pulled out the cottage cheese and checked the date. Only three weeks past. She slipped off the lid and found no interesting green growth inside. Somehow she felt tricked. There should be green slime, lots of it, so she could sniff at Trev and his life.

On the kitchen table sat a leather-bound copy of Oswald Chambers's *My Utmost for His Highest*. It was as obviously used as any of the books in Ryan's bookcase, as the navy leather Bible Trev had read last night. She could see Trev sitting here each morning, his coffee beside him, as he read one of Chambers's thoughtful devotions. Did he read them aloud to Ryan? Would he read them aloud to her? Did she want him to?

What a warm, cozy, domestic scene that was, even in the starkness of the unadorned kitchen. For a minute its appeal was overwhelming.

What are you thinking, woman? Taking herself firmly in hand, she opened all the cupboards and examined what was in them. The least she could do while Trev was off pastoring was go to the grocery store. She would show him that she was not a cowardly runaway but a competent woman who was more than up to the challenge before them.

List finally compiled, she looked around the stark kitchen and thought of her warm, inviting kitchen in San Diego with its yellow and white gingham curtains, yellow plaid wallpaper above the countertops, and the white cabinets with their glass doors that showed off her yellow dishes. She thought longingly of the plants that sat on the windowsill above the sink and the African violets that bloomed continuously before the sliding glass door that led to her minuscule deck, where she grew containers of cyclamen, salvia, gerber daisies, trailing ivy, and petunias.

She'd have to call Meg and make arrangements for the care of the plants while she was gone. Or should she have them shipped here along with Trudy?

No, that was too much of a commitment, one she wasn't yet willing to make. Not until Trev got down on his knees and begged her forgiveness.

She eyed the phone resting on the counter. Should she call Meg on that phone or her cell? Put the bill on Trev's tab or hers? She grinned. He might as well get used to paying for her. She didn't have a job anymore to pay for herself.

"Dori, sweetie!" Meg's voice warmed the air waves. "I'm so glad you caught me. I was about to leave the shop in April's capable hands for a couple of hours."

"You and Ron going out on the town?"

"I wish. No, we were going to your place to pack it up."

"What?" Pack it up?

"Randy has a gig in New York City starting Wednesday, and he's going to drive all your things east for you rather than take a plane. That way you'll have your car and Trudy in no time at all. And your clothes and plants."

Dori didn't know what to say, but she felt panic rising in her chest. Why was everybody making her choices for her? And choices that seemed so final.

"Randy and a musician friend will be coming together, so they can drive straight through." Meg laughed. "They have to be in New York by Wednesday, so you'll probably see them sometime late Tuesday, bleary eyed and weary. You can put them up for the night, can't you?"

"Sure," she answered weakly.

"They'll be so tired that the floor will be fine," Meg assured her. "Oops, got to go. Ron's beeping for me."

Slowly, carefully Dori set the phone back in its cradle. Her hand was shaking. When had she lost control of her own life? And how had it happened?

She felt like the prisoner in Poe's "The Pit and the Pendulum" when the walls started closing in on him. She shuddered. She had to get out of this house! But where would she go?

The list fluttered in her shaking hand.

The grocery store!

She grabbed her coat, hat, gloves, and purse and was out the door before she remembered that she didn't have a vehicle. With a snarl she went back inside and grabbed the phone book. She looked up car rentals and was surprised to find one in Seaside. She dialed the number.

"Sure, we got cars to rent," said the man who answered. "Come on down and look."

"If I could come down and look, I wouldn't need to rent a car, now would I?" Dori said, the very soul of reason.

"Oh. Yeah."

She waited for him to offer to bring her a car, but no such luck. "What kinds of cars do you have available?"

"You name it, we got it," he said with pride.

It had been a long day, she was feeling ill-used, and he wasn't helping any. "Do you have a Mercedes ragtop? In green?" She didn't even know if there was such a car.

There was a brief silence. "Uh, no. We only got American cars."

"How about a gold Cadillac convertible then?" Again she had no idea whether there was such a car. "Or a silver one. I'm not particular."

"Well, uh, uh." He sounded frantic.

Suddenly she regretted baiting him. "So what do you have?" she asked in a gentle voice.

"Fords," he blurted.

"Fine. A Taurus would be nice. Do you have one available?"

"Yeah. How long you want it?"

"Until Wednesday. Then it will get driven to New York City."

"Well, I got a red one, this year's model, great condition. And there are lots of drop-offs in New York. Cost you more though if you don't return it to the point of origin."

"No problem. How about you deliver my car to—" She stopped. "Wait a minute. I have to run outside and see what the address is." When she returned to the phone, panting, she was more than slightly surprised to find him still waiting. She gave the street and number. "Can you deliver the car right away please? I need it immediately."

"Can you pay me right away?" he countered. "I need the money immediately."

"Got my credit card right here."

In a half hour she had a red rental Taurus at rates that sounded like a giveaway after what she was used to in California. She drove the salesman back to his office, passing the grocery store on her way. She did the necessary paperwork, bid him good-bye, and returned to the store.

As she pushed her cart up and down the Acme aisles, Dori tried to imagine what quantities she should buy for Trev and Ryan. How much did Trev eat? She remembered a teenager who consumed quantities that would have felled an ox. But how did he eat now? And Ryan. He was a small, skinny kid, but did he eat like the kid he was or the kid he would become, if and when he grew?

She decided to get spaghetti because she could always cook more noodles and pour more sauce out of the jar. An extra bag of salad could also plug lots of hollow legs. And Amoroso rolls, good, crusty Italian rolls, the kind no one made on the west coast.

She looked at her basket, pleased. One meal taken care of. What about a rump roast with potatoes, carrots, and onions? Add a green vegetable and you had a feast. Leftovers, if there were any, would make good hot roast beef sandwiches. And a Perdue Oven Stuffer Roaster. Throw in stuffing mix and a different green vegetable and bingo.

Maybe this shopping bit wouldn't be so hard after all. She threw in a loaf of bread, a carton of orange juice, a half gallon of milk, a box of cereal, and a twelve pack of Coke. She swung into the aisle where the cookies were and promptly bumped into a cart coming the other way.

"I'm so sorry," she said, trying to get out of the other cart's way. With an apologetic smile she looked up and found herself staring at Angie Warrington and her mother.

Thirteen

O H, HI," DORI SAID, smiling brightly. "Imagine bumping into the only people I know in Seaside."

"Small world," said Judy Warrington, her mouth pinched and hard. "And twice in one day."

Dori smiled, trying to project warmth in spite of the chill that flowed about her like the fog from dry ice. These women were very angry, and she felt pretty sure she was the reason.

"Have you known Pastor Paul long?" Angie asked, her hands wrapped around the handle of the cart so tightly her knuckles showed white.

"Pas—Oh, you mean Trev." She grinned. "Forever, I think. Our families have been friends since our mothers met in college."

"Oh. I don't think I ever heard him mention you," Angie said, hurling the barb with obvious relish.

Dori suddenly felt the need to move on. A catfight was the last thing she wanted. "Could be. I wouldn't know." She tried to angle her cart around the Warringtons. "If you'll excuse me?"

Angie's move to block the aisle wasn't subtle. Dori looked at her in surprise and saw genuine dislike mingled with true hurt. It was obvious that Angie cared deeply for Trev.

"Pastor Paul has been in Seaside all week." Judy

suddenly entered the conversation. "When did he have time to get married?"

Dori prayed her face didn't reveal her panic. Or her anger at Trev. Instead of running out to care for his flock, he should have stayed home. He should have helped her figure out the questions people would ask and the answers they would give.

Her conscience suddenly jibed. In all fairness, he hadn't expected her to leave the house. But she had left, and she needed a fast but true answer, one that wouldn't come back and bite them later.

"Getting married was an impulsive decision." That was very true. "Spur-of-the-moment romantic."

"But how did you manage it so fast?"

"We eloped."

"Our pastor eloped?" Judy managed to make it seem the equivalent of murder.

"Pastors aren't allowed to elope?" Dori asked with a mix of defensiveness and curiosity.

"Pastors are to set an example." Judy folded her arms over her chest. "A good example."

Dori swallowed her own rising anger. "What's wrong with eloping? It's not illegal, immoral, or unethical."

"You aren't wearing a ring," Angie said, accusation clear in her voice. She made it sound as if Dori didn't have on any clothes.

Dori held out her left hand and looked at her empty third finger. She had had a ring. Trev had married her with her mother's ring, slipping it on her finger with vows of undying love and fidelity. They had talked about which ring to use, his mom's or hers. They'd decided on hers because that left Trev's mom's for Phil to use some day.

Dori had taken the ring off and placed it on the TV just before she left six years ago. Many times she'd regretted that move. Now she no longer had her mother's ring, one of the few things she'd had to remember her by.

"No time to get the ring," she said brightly. That was true too. It dawned on her that Trev would have to give it back to her, and she would have to wear it for the next six months whether she wanted to or not. Somehow that seemed the most fraudulent of actions. Her parents had loved each other deeply. She remembered laughter and affection freely shared. To compromise what that ring represented seemed horribly wrong, criminal even.

"Is he here with you?" Judy asked, looking around as if she expected Trev to jump out from between the Oreos and the Chips Ahoy.

Dori shook her head. An easy question. "No, he's visiting Barry in jail and Mary who has kidney stones."

"Some honeymoon," Angie said, clearly pleased that Trev wasn't with Dori.

Dori shrugged. "That's what impulsive gets you. We'll have to go away later."

Angie and Judy just looked at her, and Dori realized with a start that they didn't believe she and Trev were married. She frowned at them. Did they think that Trev, their pastor, would fake a marriage to cover an affair? And that she would cooperate? Sure, pastors fell into sexual sin all too frequently, but she doubted that even the most brazen brought their girlfriends home to masquerade as their wives.

Resentment washed through her. Dori knew she needed to move on and quickly before she said something she'd regret or that Trev would regret.

She smiled, imagining pointed shark teeth ready to take a bite out of Angie or Judy. "If you'll excuse me, I need to get on with my shopping so I'm there when Trev gets home. We hate being apart for even a single minute." She pushed gently on her cart, still blocked by Angie's, as she heard the lie she'd just told. Somehow it would come back on her; she just knew it. Getting caught was the story of her life.

"Paul," Angie said as she pulled her cart back to her side of the aisle. "His name is Paul."

Dori tried to feel sorry for Angie, but there was something nasty about the girl's manner that wiped out her usual compassion. "To those of us who love him, it's always been Trev." With a breezy wave, Dori moved on down the aisle.

In frozen foods she grabbed a pair of pizzas, the vegetables she wanted, and a bag of frozen chopped onions. You could never have too many onions. As she picked up a package of precut boiled ham and another of American cheese, she replayed the conversation with the Warringtons. She grabbed an African violet and two planters of flowing ivy from the flower department and wondered how she should have handled things. As she checked out and drove home, she began to realize just how difficult a position Pop had put Trev in.

She pulled up to the curb in her red Taurus and climbed out. She opened the trunk and was reaching for the grocery bags when Trev appeared beside her.

"I didn't think you were home yet," she said, giving him an automatic smile. "I didn't see your car."

"It's in the garage off the alley." He waved that away as of no importance as he glared at her. "Where have you been? I thought—" He stopped himself and cleared his throat.

She felt a chill as she realized what he had thought. "You thought I'd left again."

He colored but made himself look her in the eyes. "Yes."

"I wish I could," she said and watched him turn pale. He grabbed two grocery bags and stalked up the walk, but not before she saw the hurt in his eyes.

"Trev." She grabbed a pair of bags, slammed the trunk shut, and hurried after him, her bags bumping against her. "That didn't come out the way I meant it."

He kept walking. She followed him up the stairs and into the house. "I just meant that I wish Pop hadn't done this to us, locking us in this untenable situation. It's so unfair to you."

He dumped the bags on the kitchen counter. "I know what you meant." His voice was chill.

She set her bags down, grabbed his arm, and turned him to her. "No, you don't. I met Angie and Judy Warrington at the store, and they began asking questions. As I skated about, trying to be truthful but careful—" except for that one little misstatement about never wanting to be apart—"I realized how much is at stake for you, and how complicated things are. When I said I wished I could leave, it had no bearing on you personally, just the hard situation. I don't like having to try to explain every little move."

He looked at her without expression for a moment, and she held her breath. A couple of hours ago she had wanted to boil him in oil, and now she couldn't stand the fact that she'd inadvertently hurt him. These fluctuating emotions were going to make her crazy.

When he nodded understanding, she sagged with relief. He looked toward the front door. "Where'd the car come from?"

"I rented it."

"Really?" He looked impressed. "You sure move fast."

"Self-preservation. I opened the refrigerator." She began unloading the bags while Trev watched with interest. "By the way, you're allowed to help."

Trev rolled his eyes as he reached in a bag and began dragging items out.

"So how was Barry?" Dori asked.

Trev sighed. "He's in deep trouble this time. They're going to make it as hard as possible for him to get out. There's a bail hearing Tuesday, but I don't think the judge will allow bail."

"Maybe that's good."

"Maybe. Obviously he can't control his compulsions, and he can't be allowed to continue to scare women so badly. It's especially hard on the younger victims. They expect to be attacked. So far there seems to have been some inner control that's never let him go farther than flashing or streaking, but who knows if and when that might change." Trev slid the pizzas in the freezer. "Such a waste of a life."

"And Mary with the kidney stones?"

"She's uncomfortable to put it mildly. They'll probably shoot the stones with ultrasound on Monday. Knowing Mary, I wouldn't be surprised if she tried to tell the doctors how they should do it."

They laughed softly together, and she became aware of him staring at her.

"What?"

"I've always loved to watch you laugh," he said. "You have such a wonderful smile."

She looked at him, totally surprised, not knowing how to respond.

"But what I really need to say to you is that I'm sorry." He crumpled a plastic grocery bag in his hand. "I should never have spoken in such anger earlier. I said some things I'm ashamed of. Please say you forgive me."

Dori nodded as she put the milk and juice in the refrigerator. "I know. Me too." She put the twelve-pack of Coke on the bottom shelf. "Do you realize we've never spoken to each other in anger before in our whole lives?"

He opened the freezer and slid in the chicken and the roast. "Now that you mention it, I think you're right."

"I know I'm right." She picked a cupboard at random for the cookies.

He folded the bag. "Anyway, as an apology, I'd like to take you out to dinner tonight."

Dori stilled. "Yeah?" She pulled a dead leaf off the ivy plant, then set it in the middle of the kitchen table. She turned to him with a smile. "Sounds very nice. I'd love to go."

"Good." He opened the refrigerator door and dumped the potatoes and carrots in the crisper drawer. He grinned at her over his shoulder. "Good."

She cleared her throat. "That's the first time you've ever asked me for something that could even loosely be termed a date."

He was quiet for a minute, but she could feel his eyes on her as she put the African violet on the windowsill. Then he came to her and turned her to him. His arms encircled her and hers automatically slid around his waist. He studied her with eyes full of regret and something else she couldn't quite define.

"I'll see if I can do better this time around," he said softly. He bent and kissed her forehead. "Now go put on the best thing you've got with you."

With an unsettling mix of regret and relief, she stepped out of his embrace and hurried upstairs. As she thought over the clothes she had with her, she realized that she hadn't packed anything particularly dressy. She'd expected to be at the hospital or at Pop and Honey's. Neither place called for anything but slacks and tops.

Her navy slacks and white T would look nice with her chenille jacket, but it was a long way from elegant. She hoped Trev wouldn't be disappointed because he wanted to take her somewhere fancy. After Tuesday when Randy brought her things, she could go anywhere Trev wanted to take her. Tonight he'd just have to make do with her as she was.

She stood at the side of the bed and smiled. Trev had asked her out. On a real date. How long had she dreamed he'd do so? Feeling somewhat giddy, she lifted her big suitcase onto the bed. It didn't matter to her what she wore or where they ate. Anywhere with him would do.

She threw open the lid of her larger suitcase and stared in disbelief.

"Trev!" she shouted. "I've got the wrong suitcase!"

Fourteen

JOANNE PULLED THE BLACK SUITCASE behind her as she went through the automatic doors back into the Philadelphia airport. She shuddered. Even being close to the huge planes filled her with dread.

As if Vinnie's attitude wasn't enough to fry her circuits. She could practically see the anger rising off him in waves, like heat from the sand in high summer. He had never been so abusive before. Even thinking of the names he'd called her and the way he'd wrenched her arm made tears come to her eyes. Sure, he got angry sometimes, but never like today. Not like when he realized the paintings weren't there because she had taken the wrong bag.

Well, the whole mess would be over soon. She'd get the right suitcase, and Vinnie would forgive her. Even more important, Mr. J would never know.

Oh, please, God, please, God, please, God, let it be so.

The only trouble with her prayer was that she wasn't certain God listened to people like her. Didn't you have to go to church and stuff to be on His good side? Still, He was her best bet, and sad to say, her only bet.

It was all the fault of that lady.

"This is my bag," she'd said and pulled it right out of Joanne's hands. Talk about rude!

Joanne stopped inside the airport doors and looked around, not certain what to do. Since Vinnie's car heater wasn't working well, she could barely feel her feet in their stiletto-heeled boots. As she wiggled her toes, trying to get some sensation back, she hoped she looked cool and smart. She was afraid she just looked lost and dumb.

For want of a better plan, she went back to where she'd gotten the suitcase. The room with the three baggage carousels was empty except for a man working in a glass booth on the street side of the big room. Several suitcases stood beside his little office, and three stood inside it. She squinted and tried to see if any of them had a red tie on the handle. It didn't look like it. But maybe the tie had come off and the suitcase was here, just waiting for her. She brightened for a moment.

But if the tie had come off, how would she be able to tell it was hers? The little black cloud that had begun raining on her the moment she got the wrong case dropped another bucketful of water.

"How do you know that's yours?" the man in the booth would ask her. "There's no name and no red tie."

"It's got stolen paintings in it."

Right.

She hesitantly went into the office. "Hello."

The harried-looking man glanced up from his work. "Yes?"

"I got the wrong suitcase."

The man didn't move. He just let his eyes slide shut. Joanne could just imagine what he was thinking: another dumb blonde.

"Bad day?" she asked, hoping to make him not be angry at her.

He opened his eyes and gave her a slight smile. "You wouldn't believe."

Joanne thought that she would because she knew all about bad days. Lots of her days were bad days. And just look at what today had been like. The baddest of the bad. "I took the wrong suitcase," she told him again.

"Name?"

"Joanne Pilotti."

The man consulted some papers, then shook his head. "No

one by that name has called about a missing suitcase."

"Oh, no." Joanne leaned on his high counter. "I'm Joanne Pilotti."

"Ah." He went back to his papers. "No suitcase belonging to a Joanne Pilotti has been turned in. Where did you come from?"

Joanne blinked. "Seaside." Why did that matter?

The man looked at her without saying anything for a minute. "No, I mean where did you fly in from."

"Oh." Joanne felt herself turn scarlet. Definitely a dumb blonde. "Chicago."

The man consulted his magic list once more. Then he pointed. "I have two unclaimed suitcases from O'Hare."

Joanne felt hope like when the sunshine slips out from behind a rain cloud.

The man pointed. "That olive green one and that fake leather one."

Feeling her hope collapse as surely as big hair in the damp sea air, she shook her head. Vinnie was going to kill her.

"You got a name and an address on that case?" the man asked, indicating the one she pulled.

Joanne nodded. "Dori MacAllister. But she lives in San Diego."

"Maybe if you call, someone at that address can tell you where she's staying while she's here. Maybe she can meet you, and you can trade."

Joanne stared at the man. What a good idea! Why hadn't she or Vinnie thought of that? "Thanks!" Rushing away to find Vinnie and tell him about this good idea, she ignored the man as he called, "Hey, give me your address and phone number in case that other woman calls."

Pulling the wretched suitcase behind her, she hurried to the curb where Vinnie waited in the car. She opened the passenger door and sat, the suitcase still on the sidewalk.

"You make the exchange?" he asked. She could tell by his manner that he was still furious with a little bit of scared thrown in. It was the scared part that worried her. If he was scared—and he hadn't even made the big mistake of losing the suitcase, though asking for her help might be seen as his big mistake—how should she be feeling?

"The other one's not here." She flinched, waiting for his reaction. She half expected him to hit her.

When nothing happened, she opened her eyes. He had both hands wrapped around the steering wheel, probably wishing it was her neck, and he was very, very pale.

She hurried to tell him about the great suggestion from the luggage man. "So we call this lady's house," she finished. "We get them to tell us where she's staying, and we go there and make the exchange."

Slowly Vinnie turned to look at her. "I don't believe it. You actually have a good idea here."

Joanne preened under his praise, her cheeks flushing. "Thanks."

They drove away from the airport, following the signs for I-95. Just before the ramp to I-95 north, Vinnie pulled over on the shoulder of the road. He pulled out his cell phone and punched up information. "I need the phone number of Dori MacAllister," and he read her address off the suitcase label.

Joanne pulled out a pen and a receipt from her last trip to Wal-Mart. "Repeat it and I'll write it down."

"858-555-2394," he said and punched out. Immediately he punched in the new number. Joanne watched him, thinking how handsome he was with the three studs in his one ear and the snake tattoo that wound around his wrist, across the back of his hand and up his middle finger.

"858-555-5627?" he said, pointing at her. "You got that?"

She wrote furiously. She was pretty sure she had it right. If she had known he was going to throw another number at her like that, she wouldn't have been daydreaming. "What's this number?"

"Something called Small Treasures. If you don't get an answer at the first number, you're supposed to call Small Treasures."

"Are they the guys who sent the picture for Mr. J?" Joanne asked.

"You and the picture came from Chicago." He gave her that you-are-so-stupid look.

"Yeah, but this Dori person was on my plane, and she came from California. Maybe the picture did too."

Vinnie looked at her with something very like surprise mixed with admiration. "Maybe you're right." He hit his hand against the side of his head. "Twice in less than ten minutes. I can't stand it." And he grinned at her for the first time since she'd opened the suitcase.

She sighed. Things were going to work out. She just knew it. And she had another idea. "And the pictures are like small treasures, aren't they?" she asked again. "Maybe they came from the Small Treasures place."

Vinnie lifted his hand, and Joanne willed herself not to flinch. She'd thought she had such a good idea. Instead of the slap she expected, Vinnie patted her gently on the shoulder. "Not bad, Joanne. Not bad at all."

She glowed.

Fifteen

REV COULD HEAR Dori yelling, but he couldn't make out her words. He took the steps two at a time, Jack thundering beside him. "Dori! What's wrong?"

He stopped in the doorway of the master bedroom. She stood at the bedside, hands on hips, staring at the open suitcase in front of her. Jack stopped beside her, sniffing the contents of the case, curious about what had upset her so.

"What in the—?" Trev walked over to the bed and stared.

The contents of the case looked like a collection of very worn clothes just dropped off at Goodwill without the prerequisite washing. Shabby T-shirts, torn pajamas, kids' jeans with holes in the knees. All were neatly folded and carefully packed.

"I took the wrong bag." Dori said unnecessarily. Her voice was laced with frustration and thick with unshed tears. It was obvious to him that the last two days had brought her close to the breaking point.

He slid an arm around her shoulders to offer comfort just as he had countless other times as they grew up. Interesting how he still saw himself as her protector, her guardian and defender. This time, however, she didn't lean into him and accept his support.

Sighing inwardly, he let his arm drop. Marriage had

a way of interfering with friendship; at least their marriage did.

"So whose is it?" he asked.

"Oh." She slammed the lid shut and began searching for a name tag. "There's no name." She threw her hands up in aggravation.

He leaned quickly to the side, just missing an inadvertent swat in the head. "Well, let's call the airport and see if your suitcase is there. If it is, we'll go get it."

She sank down on the bed. "I don't have any clothes." Jack laid his head on her knee, his dark eyes watching her in commiseration.

"Don't worry. We'll get your stuff back."

"I don't have any shoes. Just these." She held out a sneaker-shod foot.

She looked so forlorn that his heart turned over. Poor Dori. "I'm going to go call. You just sit tight."

She nodded and immediately got up and followed him downstairs. Jack, who seemed as much under her spell as Trev himself, sat at her side when she collapsed into a kitchen chair. She fondled his ears and rested her cheek on his silky head.

Trev called information, then the airport. He punched his way through several prerecorded options until he finally had someone on the line. He dropped into a chair across from Dori and rested his elbow on the table.

"That's right. A black bag with the name Dori MacAllister on it. It has a piece of red yarn tied to the handle. Yes, from O'Hare." He repeated the flight number. As he talked, he stared at the container of ivy growing lush and green on the table. He blinked. Ivy? He reached out and touched one of the leaves. It was real, all right. Where had it come from?

"Nothing? You're sure?" He paused and listened. "Seaside? You're sure? Yeah, thanks."

He hung up. "Someone named Joanne Pilotti from Seaside came in looking for this suitcase. She has yours."

"And she's from Seaside?" Dori rose. "Phone book?"

"Top drawer beside the dishwasher."

She opened to the p's in a flash. "Do you think it's Pilate like the exercise program or Pilotti like Italian?"

"Look up both and see what's there."

There was neither a Pilate nor a Pilotti.

"I bet she only has a cell phone," Dori said. "So I still don't have any clothes." She straightened. "And my books! She's got my books."

Trev eyed her cautiously. "What books?"

"My books to read. You know I never go anywhere without something to read."

He hadn't known that though now that he thought about it, she frequently had her nose in a book growing up.

"I finished the one I had in my carry-on last night when I couldn't sleep and you were snoring happily away. How will I ever get to sleep tonight without a book to shut off my mind?"

"By closing your eyes?"

"Funny. But closing your eyes doesn't turn off your thinking. Reading does that."

"Oh." Trev didn't want to disagree, but closing his eyes had done it for him for years and years. "You know, Ryan and I both have books. You can borrow one of ours."

"Bioethics and the evangelical community? Though I guess that would put me to sleep, wouldn't it?"

He watched her smile and purposed to do everything he could to help her smile a lot. Absently he fiddled with the ivy leaves.

"You like it?" Dori asked.

"What? Sleeping? Yeah, I like it a lot. Or reading? I like it too."

"No, you idiot." The light tone took away any sting. "The ivy."

He stilled his hand and studied the plant. "Yeah. It's okay."

"Okay? That's the best you can do?"

She sounded mildly offended, but then he suspected it wouldn't take much for her to be offended, given her circumstances. Years ago she would have been goading him for the fun of it. Now he wasn't sure. He looked at her carefully, not certain what she wanted from him. After all, he'd lived in this house for two years without ivy. In fact, he hadn't even realized he was missing ivy. And it was only ivy, not the cure for cancer. "It's fine."

She glared at him, and he knew he'd failed again. Suddenly this marriage thing seemed harder than he'd realized. Then in the far reaches of his mind, he had a flash of Pop and Honey looking at a flower of some kind that Honey had put on the living room coffee table.

"Isn't it lovely?" Honey'd said.

"Absolutely," Pop had answered. "But not as lovely as you."

And Honey had melted into his arms. When she left the room, Pop put the plant on the floor. "It blocks the TV when I lie down," he'd said to Trev and Phil. "And it's just going to die. I don't get women and flowers."

Well, a pot of ivy wasn't lovely, but he could try. "It's nice and green and bushy." She still looked unhappy. "Thank you."

Home run. She smiled sweetly. "Can we still go out to eat even if I can't put on clean clothes and real shoes?"

"Hey, this is a resort town. You can go out to eat in almost anything except bare feet."

"Which aren't a problem this time of year." Dori looked out the window at the black night held back by the warmth and light of the house. "Should I buy some snow boots?"

"If you want, though it doesn't snow much here because of the ocean."

"What?"

"The Gulf Stream and its warmth usually mean rain, not snow." He stood. "How about after dinner we run to the mall, and you can buy some clothes to tide you over until we recover your suitcase."

They settled for the family side of Dante's at the Dock, a restaurant that also had a fancy side.

"Sometime when you have your stuff back, we'll eat in the pricey side. They have great stuff over there."

She looked around the Formica-topped tables with their paper place mats and napkins and bottles of ketchup. "This section is fine, but—" She glanced at the wall that separated them from the linen tablecloths and napkins and fine glassware. "I'd love to eat over there." She turned back to him. "I'll hold you to that offer."

Trev grinned. They said that the way to a man's heart was through his stomach. Well, he bet that applied to a woman too, but in the sense of food at a fine restaurant. It had to be one of the

138 ~ Gayle Roper

most successful courting ploys known to man.

Courting.

His breath caught as a very real and terrible truth struck home. Never once had he courted Dori. First there were all those years he'd kept his heart in check lest Pop have a snit and follow through on his threat to send one of them away. Then when he had declared himself, they ran off immediately and married because they couldn't stand the idea of just sleeping together.

"I'm a Christian," Dori had told him. "I can't just live with someone, even you. Besides, Pop would kill us."

While her first argument meant little to him, her second point was one he accepted readily, and he knew that with Phil around, Pop was bound to find out sooner rather than later. Of course they knew he wouldn't be pleased with the marriage either, but at least it was honorable.

Then she'd disappeared for six years.

He *had* to court her this time. He could see it so plainly. Certainly they had issues to discuss and discard, forgiveness to offer and receive, but there had to be more if they were to establish a solid home and family. He had to woo her, to show her clearly that she was special, that quite simply she was his heart.

"Remember the night you confronted me about my drinking?" he asked after the waiter took away their salad dishes and left their entrees.

She nodded, busy putting butter on a fragment of roll.

Of course she remembered. Minutes later she'd been in his arms. He cleared his throat.

You broke all those promises. You broke your vows. He could see those words in the note she'd left on the TV with her mother's ring.

Oh, Lord, help me do this right.

"You were right, you know. I was drinking too much. Way too much."

She looked at him, her roll stalled partway to her mouth. "It worried me terribly."

"I know I said I'd stop, and I really meant to."

She just watched him, waiting. His heart pounded out his anxiety, and he had to force the words around the constriction in his throat. So much rode on her understanding how repentant he was, on her accepting his changed life.

"I really didn't mean to drink again because I knew it meant so much to you that I stop. It was just that once."

Dori didn't say anything, just continued waiting, her big eyes fixed on his face. He took a deep breath and forced himself to go on.

"On that Monday after Las Vegas when I went to class, I was so tired I could hardly stay awake. As I'm sure you remember, the weekend hadn't been filled with much sleep." He smiled at her, inviting her to acknowledge that fact.

She remained solemn, unmoved, and he swallowed. She was obviously not going to make this confession any easier, and he supposed he couldn't blame her. He'd hurt her dreadfully, though he still didn't think it was bad enough for six year's worth of *dreadfully*. That prick of self-expiation eased his tension a bit. It no longer felt as if his heart would crack his ribs with its pounding.

"The guys started teasing me," he continued. "They thought I'd had a wild weekend, and that's why I kept falling asleep." He heard his words and grinned before he could stop himself. "Well, in a way I did, but not in the way they thought."

Dori suddenly became very interested in putting everything on her baked potato. She piled sour cream on top of a huge gob of butter and shook salt and pepper over it all as if she were sprinkling chocolate jimmies on ice cream.

Trev cleared his throat. "They insisted that I come with them because they had the perfect cure for what they thought was a hangover. I couldn't tell them what I had really done over the weekend because we still hadn't decided whether to tell people or keep it a secret."

"We kept trying to second-guess Pop's reactions and what would get us into the least trouble with him," Dori said, staring at her plate.

Trev sighed in relief at her comment. She was listening. "Anyway, right or wrong, I went with them. The next thing I knew, I woke up on the living room floor of the apartment, lying face-down in my own vomit."

Her eyes were on him again, and she flinched slightly at the last bit. Well, so did he. It was hard to believe that he had once thought being drunk was cool.

"I haven't had anything to drink since that day."

She nodded. "That's good, Trev." She smiled. "I'm glad."

He smiled back, relief flooding him. "So I'm forgiven?"

"Of course. I'm sure your congregation appreciates not having to peel you off the floor so you can preach."

His smile dimmed a bit. "While I care what my congregation thinks, I'm more concerned about you. I know I broke my promise to you, but I swear, that was the only time."

She looked at him, obviously pleased with his confession. She reached out and gently squeezed his hand resting on the table beside his iced tea. He turned his over and gripped hers. He studied her. Something was wrong here. Why wasn't she reacting more strongly?

Like a bolt of lightning knocking out a power station, the realization that his drunken performance wasn't what had driven her away short-circuited his brain. He stared at her, unable to think, unable to talk. For six years he'd thought he understood what was bothering her, and for six years he'd been wrong. For six years he'd been able to wrap a cloak of self-protection about himself because he thought she'd overreacted. Regardless of what he'd done, she'd done worse.

He was okay; she was not.

Now he was totally lost. He just stared at her, her hand still clutched in his. She stared back, puzzled.

"Ahem."

Trev actually jumped. He was so intent on Dori that he hadn't noticed anyone or anything else. Now he looked up and saw the Shaw family staring from him to Dori. In a brief moment of panic he wondered what they'd heard. What great material to hang him with—our pastor, the drunk.

But they were all smiles, all eight of them, Frank and Janie and their six little stair steps.

"We heard the news, Pastor Paul." Frank beamed at him. "We just wanted to say congratulations and wish you well."

Trev stood, struggling to pull himself together. "Thanks, Frank. This is my wife, Dori."

"You are such a lucky woman!" Janie rushed to Dori and

embraced her. "Pastor Paul is such a prize."

Dori didn't roll her eyes or throw up at Janie's comment, but Trev had no doubt she wanted to. In fact, she smiled warmly at Janie and returned the hug.

Janie bulldozed on. "I don't know how many times we've said that Pastor Paul needed a godly woman by his side."

"And he's gotten a mighty pretty one, too," Frank said gallantly.

Trev's thanks and Dori's thank you stepped on each other, and everyone laughed. Did he and Dori sound as strained to the Shaws as they did to him?

"Now you two go right back to your dinners," Janie said. "We don't want to butt in on a private time." Then she added sotto voce, "Though, Pastor Paul, I'd think you'd want to take your bride to the fancy side."

Trev felt himself flush. How to explain?

"I lost my suitcase," Dori said. "No other clothes than the ones I'm wearing."

"Oh, my!" Janie patted Trev on the arm. "See what happens when I jump to conclusions?"

Trev smiled at Janie to show he understood her apology. "We're going to the mall after dinner so Dori can get what she needs until the confusion is resolved."

Frank took Janie by the hand. "Come on, honey. We've got to let these nice people eat." He turned to the six sets of bright little eyes, all fixed on Dori. "Stop staring and say good-bye, kids."

The Shaws walked away in a flurry of good-byes. Frank's words drifted back. "Staring is very impolite, guys."

"Yeah, I know," piped one little carrying voice. "I think she's prettier than Angie."

Several little heads bobbed in agreement.

"At least they seem more welcoming than the Warringtons," Dori said, watching them crowd into a booth across the restaurant.

"Frank's an elder, and he's one of the best. He's still relatively young, but he's got a good head on his shoulders, and he loves the Lord."

Trev felt relieved to be away from the painful conversation they had been having, and Dori seemed more than happy to steer clear too. Why she was glad to be done with it he didn't know, but for himself, he needed to think. Every preconceived notion had just been knocked awry, and he had to have time to regroup, to analyze things anew.

For the rest of their meal, he talked about church and his vision for it. Dori listened as if she actually cared, even asking questions at appropriate places.

Catastrophe momentarily averted.

Trev was at the cash register paying their bill when a man and woman came through the door.

"Hello, Bob, Penni." He nodded at them, knowing he couldn't have planned a more upsetting meeting if he'd worked at it. Even Barry running around undressed would have been better than this.

"Oh. Pastor." Penni looked at him with the deer-in-the-headlights big eyes that were her forte. Personally he thought she looked like an exaggerated cartoon character when she pulled that move, but apparently Bob liked it well enough.

Bob gave him an abrupt nod. "Heard you just got married."

Trev put his arm around Dori's waist. "This is my wife, Dori, and, honey, this is Penni Aaronson and Bob Warrington."

Dori smiled at Penni. To Bob she said, "I think I met your family?"

There was a moment of horrified hesitation that Trev was pleased to see went right past Dori. With an innocent smile, Trev said, "We saw your parents and Angie up in Pennsylvania this morning."

"Oh." Penni's eyes returned to near normal.

"Ah." Bob sounded like a tire going flat. "They said they were going away overnight. Things have been rough at work."

Trev agreed things had been tough, but he doubted that the father-son car dealership was the problem.

"I saw your mom and Angie again in the supermarket this afternoon," Dori added.

Penni went wide-eyed again and looked up at Bob. "Oh, honey, I just realized. Poor Angie." She shook her head.

Bob narrowed his eyes at Trev. "Come on, Penni." He grabbed her hand. "Our table's waiting."

Zipped against the blustery cold that seemed a few degrees warmer than Bob's manner toward them, Trev and Dori hurried to the car. Once inside, she turned to him. "That Bob's as charming as his father and mother."

"That Bob was dying a thousand deaths, as was Penni. And terrible man that I am, I couldn't help but enjoy it a bit too much." *Oh, Lord, forgive me.*

"Trev, what are you talking about?"

"You remember that you said you'd met Bob's family?"

"Yes. So?"

"Well, he has a closer family than his parents. He's got a wife and two little kids."

Dori raised an eyebrow. "I take it Penni's not the wife?"

"No. Her name's Shannon. He left her for Penni about two weeks ago."

"Ouch. And how did the Warringtons take that?"

"Believe it or not, they keep defending Bob, at least publicly." Trev wondered if Jonathan wasn't a bit more critical in private. The problem was that the congregation needed to see public distress for Bob's actions from an elder of Jonathan's standing, son or no son. Wrong was wrong.

"But how can they justify what he's done? Nothing can excuse a man for being unfaithful."

"I agree. They can't, of course. So they've gone after Shannon."

Dori made a disgusted sound. "Did she do something terrible that would cause Bob to leave?"

"Like have a boyfriend or gamble away their house in Atlantic City?"

She nodded.

"Nope. Shannon's a very nice girl. She's not the greatest house-keeper, but she's got a three-year-old and a three-month-old baby." Trev pictured the svelte Penni. "I think it bothers Bob that Shannon's had a tough time losing her pregnancy weight. In short, she looks and acts like a thousand other tired, overweight young moms."

"I bet she can't make big eyes like Penni." Dori widened her eyes and blinked rapidly.

Trev laughed. He couldn't help it. Still, he also couldn't help wondering how he could confront Bob about his and Shannon's troubled marriage when his own was little more than a farce.

Sixteen

Dori MacAllister.
Dori MacAllister Trevelyan.
Dori Trevelyan.

Dori looked out at Trev's congregation and remembered how as a child and teen she had yearned to be a Trevelyan. Then she would feel she belonged, and the world would know she belonged. She would no longer be the one in the family with the different name.

Not that Pop and Honey had ever done anything to make her feel unwanted. In fact, they had done all the right things to make her feel included. Not only had they told her they loved her; they had shown her. They had come to her school plays, listened to her school concerts, and cheered at her field hockey games with the same faithfulness and enthusiasm they had given to Trev and Phil. They had listened to her opinions with respect even when they disagreed with her reasoning, and they wrapped their arms around her and hugged her with embarrassing frequency, regardless of where they were.

Then the miracle of miracles had happened, and Trev married her with promises of undying love. Surely now she would belong for she was finally and undeniably a Trevelyan.

Ha!

She had dropped the name even before she boarded her plane for San Diego all those years ago, at first because all her proofs of identity read MacAllister, then permanently because the name hadn't made her belong.

In fact, the assumption of the name had led to the cataclysmic shattering that tore the fabric of her world and created a chasm of separation that she didn't think could ever be crossed, no matter how much her heart yearned. And it had yearned, even as her stubbornness held her fast in California.

Now as she stood on the platform of Trev's church, clutching his hand nervously and smiling at his people, she was named Trevelyan again for all the world to hear.

"I've been living in California for the past six years," she told the congregation. "It's good to be back East again. I'm looking forward to being here in Seaside with you—" she nodded at the people—"and with Trev." She turned and smiled at him.

What a liar she had become.

Then Trev smiled at her, and any dream she'd ever had of happily ever after rose to taunt her.

It's just fatigue, she told herself as she felt her answering blush. *Utter fatigue.*

As Dori gave the congregation a final smile and turned to go back to her seat in the first row, Janie Shaw rushed up the aisle.

"Wait, Dori," Janie ordered as she mounted the steps to the platform. She was slightly breathless when she stopped beside Dori and Trev. "Excuse me, Pastor, but I have an announcement to make."

Dori feared she knew what was coming. As if he understood her discomfort, Trev stepped to her and slid his arm around her waist. She allowed herself to lean against him, but it was only because of the fatigue that she gave herself that latitude.

Janie grinned at the congregation. "It's not every day that our pastor gets married." She turned her grin on Dori and Trev. "You might have thought you could escape all the hoopla by keeping everything quiet." She turned back to the people. "But they can't! Because Wednesday night we're having a party in their honor. Right here at 7 PM."

Dori forced herself to smile and look pleased when all she

wanted to do was groan and take the world's longest nap. Trev stepped back to the pulpit, dragging Dori with him.

"What a kind gesture," he said with a sincerity that made Dori think he might just mean it. But then Trev always did like a party. "We are honored that you'd go to all this trouble for us."

Dori nodded. "Thank you so much. We look forward to it."

As the last words left her mouth, Dori's eyes collided with Angie's. Dori felt the resentment and anger blazing in the young woman like a slap in the face. Vaguely she heard Frank Shaw join Janie on the platform, heard him say that he was there to congratulate her and Trev on behalf of the church and welcome her to the Seaside Chapel family.

Dori pulled her attention from Angie to the kindness being extended her. She smiled as she shook Frank's hand and returned the hug Janie gave her. As she resumed her seat to the clapping of the congregation, she swallowed against nausea. Nerves and fatigue. And Angie. She wasn't used to people disliking her, especially so obviously. She swallowed again, deeply regretting the piece of raisin toast she had forced herself to eat for breakfast. And wasn't there supposed to be some magic ingredient in Coke that settled your stomach? Little good her breakfast portion was doing her.

God, please don't let me get sick!

Maureen pulled into the parking lot at Seaside Chapel hoping no one noticed her. She planned to slip into the back pew, observe, then leave during the closing prayer.

After Friday's fiasco at the hospital, she had staked out the Trevelyan house, spending more boring hours freezing. But it had been worth every moment of discomfort when she saw Paul carry the black suitcase into the house late Saturday morning.

Immediately she called Greg Barnes at the police station on Central Avenue.

"It's here."

"Let me send someone to relieve you," Greg said. "I want you to come in. We need to talk."

Uncertain what "need to talk" meant, she reported for the

meeting. She found not only Greg in the small conference room, but Fleishman too, still unhappy about being bumped from his car.

"Where's my magazine?" he asked, looking extra grumpy.

Maureen thought of the disgusting periodical she'd found on the floor of his car. "In the trash where it belongs."

"What? Why'd you do that? You had no right—" Fleishman began, but Greg held up his hand.

"Not now, boys and girls. We've got work to do. Let me get the chief in here."

Chief Glenn Gordon arrived, and the four of them reviewed all their information, including studying the pictures Maureen had taken at the airport.

"I have a hard time seeing the Trevelyans, any of them, involved in the Matisse case," Maureen told the men. "They just don't seem the type."

Cary Fleishman looked at her with an expression so blatantly dismissive that Maureen wanted to gnash her teeth. "There are bad guys who are nice looking and well educated," he said in the tone one uses with a not-too-bright child. "The better to trick the naïve."

She took a deep breath and swallowed her anger. "Granted. But a pastor and a pharmacist? And both Trevelyans have been here for over two years."

"Smart planning on someone's part," Fleishman said. "And everyone knows that 'men of the cloth' are all phonies."

Maureen glowered at him. She was almost certain that he was just baiting her for the fun of it. Surely no one was really as dumb as he appeared to be. "Do you ever go to church, Fleishman?"

He started. "What's that got to do with anything?"

"I go regularly."

"Now why am I not surprised."

She ignored him. "Believe me when I say that two and a half years is a long time to fool people who listen to you and work with you every week. Besides, certainly they checked his resume before they called him."

"Called him what?" Fleishman asked with a nasty grin. "Jimmy Swaggart?"

Maureen looked at her white running shoes sticking out

below her jeans and wished she had on her heavy uniform brogues instead. Not that she'd ever actually have the nerve to kick Fleishman in the shins—unfortunately Mom had done too good a job instilling manners—but it was an interesting thought. "Called him period, as in asked him to be their minister."

Fleishman grunted understanding.

"They've only asked him to be their interim," Greg said. "They've never called him full-time. Now why is that?"

"Interim for over two years?" Maureen asked, surprised. "That's a long time. Usually an interim is there to cover the time after one pastor leaves and before the next one comes. Six months, a year tops."

"And then there's the strange marriage situation," Fleishman said.

Maureen thought of Phillip telling her about his brother's wife living in California for six years. There was definitely a story there, but she doubted it had anything to do with the missing paintings, so she kept her own counsel.

"What I want to know," Chief Gordon said, "is where the brothers got their money."

"What money?" Maureen asked.

"For one, the money to come to town right out of seminary and immediately buy a brand new house. You know what real estate costs in this town. And the other brother, the pharmacist. Where does he get the money to buy a pharmacy? He's only thirty years old."

"The offering plate?" Fleishman suggested.

The chief shook his head. "A church the size of Seaside Chapel couldn't generate that much money in that short a period of time, and even if they could, I think someone would notice if an amount that large went missing. There's another source, and we need to find out what it is."

Maureen felt her heart pinch. Could she be wrong? Were the Trevelyans so good at creating the desired image that she'd mistaken mere façade for substance?

"I know we have questions," she said, "but I still think it was just an inadvertent mix-up of suitcases."

Fleishman gave her a dirty look. "Come on, cutie. Even you

have to see that the timing is suspicious. The little wifey just happens to come back now, the very time the paintings come here? And she just happens to bring them with her in her suitcase?"

Maureen stared at him, her gaze as steely as she could make it. "My name is Officer Galloway."

"I like *cutie* better," he said blandly. "And it's a compliment."

"I don't, and it's not." She spoke through gritted teeth.

"Enough!" Chief Gordon's voice was a whiplash.

Maureen was afraid to breathe as the chief looked at her. Had her pique at Fleishman made her appear petty or unprofessional? She was the only woman on the Seaside force and the youngest besides. She had to be so careful. *Don't take me off the case. Please don't take me off the case.*

"Officer Galloway," he said slowly and distinctly, then flicked his gaze to Fleishman to see if he had heard.

Fleishman flushed and began studying the scuffed linoleum underfoot.

Chief Gordon turned back to Maureen. "Officer Galloway," he repeated, "I want you to make the Trevelyan family your best buddies."

She tried to keep her smile under control, but she was as pleased as a kid with five bucks to spend at the ice cream truck. She was still on the case.

"I want you to study them," the chief continued. "Get to know them, learn everything there is to learn about them. It is your responsibility to prove they are as innocent as you obviously believe."

"Yes, sir." She knew her smile stretched from ear to ear, and she was careful not to look at Fleishman. "My pleasure, sir."

So here she was in the parking lot of Seaside Chapel. She found a space and climbed out of her car. She studied the building as she walked toward the front door. Dark brown cedar siding, freshly stained. A sharply slanted roof shingled in brown. A small steeple, its white spire pointing, appropriately, to heaven. Three arched stained glass windows above the small portico. All in all, it was a very attractive, well-maintained building.

She climbed the steps, crossed the narthex, and took a seat in the next-to-the-last pew. Immediately her eyes were drawn to the circular stained glass window above and behind the pulpit, a picture of Jesus kneeling in prayer. Sun streamed through the colored glass, bathing the platform in dazzling light.

Paul Trevelyan stood behind the pulpit, obviously at ease there. Maureen always marveled at people who made their living by speaking to other groups of people. In all the lists of things people feared most, speaking was always at or near the top, way ahead of dying even, and Maureen understood completely. The idea of standing before a congregation, a club, a class, anyone who breathed, was too terrifying to contemplate.

Paul smiled at his people. "I know many of you have heard the rumors swirling." His smile broadened to a grin. "Well, for once they happen to be true." He looked down at the front pew on the left. "Dori, come on up."

The woman who took the suitcase from Joanne Pilotti climbed the four steps to the platform. Today she wore a winter-appropriate outfit of light gray slacks, a red turtleneck, and a black blazer. A large silver pin accented one lapel, and silver flashed at her ears. Her dark brown hair fell sleek and shining to her chin.

Maureen's hand went automatically to her mass of uncontrollable black curls and the dangling, wildly colored butterflies hanging from her ears. She sighed. Sophistication was never to be hers.

The pastor held out his hand to Dori, and she placed hers in it. He drew her close, smiled at her, then turned to the congregation. "My friends, I'd like you to meet my wife, Dori MacAllister Trevelyan."

Dori smiled at the people. The light streaming through the circular window backlit her, making it look as if she had a halo suspended over her head. Maureen wanted to laugh. All in all, a good effect for a pastor's wife.

"Well, well, look who's here."

Maureen knew that whispering voice. She turned to Phil, standing in the aisle, and put a finger to her lips.

He slid into the pew beside her. "My sweet Irish rose."

She looked at him, startled. Where did that come from?

"I was hoping you'd drop by." He leaned so close that her hair stirred when he exhaled. "You are irresistibly drawn to my person."

He said it so seriously that for a minute Maureen didn't know how to react. She drew back. Then she saw the twinkle in his eye, and she knew he delighted in teasing. She sighed. If she was honest, she liked being teased, at least by him.

Watch it, Galloway.. Conflict of interest! He's a suspect.

"Came to check me out, did you?" Phil asked, his breath warm on her ear. He nodded to the platform. "Or them?"

Flustered, worried that he knew who she was, she did her best to stare him down. It didn't work, but as he grinned, he moved a church-decent space from her. Her pulse steadied, and she worked at ignoring him for the rest of the service. She concentrated on Paul Trevelyan's words, noticing in her peripheral vision that Phil also paid attention, taking careful notes on the sermon.

Her instincts told her that both Phil and Paul were just who they seemed to be, pharmacist and pastor, but instincts weren't proof, especially to Fleishman. She needed hard information, undeniable substantiation of their innocence. Therefore when Phil asked her if she wanted to get something to eat after church, she readily agreed. What better way to begin to prove their innocence?

Finally the service was over, though Dori couldn't have told anyone what Trev said. She stood and made herself smile at the people who came up to her, kind people, Trev's people, grinning their pleasure, accepting her at face value. She shook hands and returned hugs. She agreed again and again that Trev was indeed wonderful and that she was most fortunate. Her cheeks hurt from smiling, and a headache blossomed above her right eye.

At least she had a ring on today. Trev had given it to her last night just before they'd retired to their separate rooms. He'd taken her hand in his and slid her mother's ring back onto her third finger, just as he had six years ago. As he moved the ring over knuckle and flesh, he looked her straight in the eye and said, "With this ring, I thee wed."

Her heart sputtered, and she put her hand over his mouth. "Trev, don't."

"Ah, Dori, whether it's for six months or sixty years, you are my wife."

She tried not to let her mix of apprehension and exaltation show, but she knew her serene face wasn't successful with him.

"Don't worry," he said. "While I don't plan to let you go a second time, I won't ask anything of you that you don't want to give. Marriage is giving, not demanding." He leaned over and kissed her on the forehead. "Sleep tight."

Dori sat in bed long after Trev went to his office, trying to read the paperback she'd picked up when she'd bought her new clothes, trying to shut her mind off. At least a wall separated them rather than the too-intimate acres of that huge bed at the motel, but somehow that fact hadn't allowed her to relax. Sleep only came in the early hours of morning.

Now as she tried to smile at Trev's people, her eyes felt gritty and red.

A pastor's wife. Never in her wildest dreams would she have imagined that marrying Trev would bring her to this pass.

"Dori," said a woman with short brown hair liberally sprinkled with gray. "I'm the other woman in Pastor Paul's life."

The woman's smile was so engaging Dori knew right away that she would like her. "How's that?"

"I'm Nancy Powell, and I'm Pastor's office administrator." She gave Dori a hug. "I can't tell you how delighted I am that he's found a wonderful, godly woman. I used to worry about him, such an inviting prize for some lucky woman. I knew several who had their eyes on him, and I didn't approve a one."

Not even Angie? But Dori didn't ask.

When almost everyone was gone, Trev walked to her with three older women following him. They looked at Dori with avid interest.

"Dori, I have here three very special women who say that you are an answer to their prayers," Trev said.

"Oh, my dear," the oldest of the trio said, her wrinkled cheeks creased in a smile. "We have been so concerned for Pastor Paul."

"Oh, yes," said the one with bright spots of rouge like a large pair of polka dots in front of her ears. "It is not good for man to be alone."

"It's not good for us to be alone either," said the third, a somber woman dressed in navy slacks, a navy sweater, and a formidable expression. "Not that we have any choice."

"Now, Gracie, don't change the subject," admonished the polka-dot rouge lady. "We're talking about Pastor Paul, not us."

"These are Seaside Chapel's three Graces, Dori." Trev grinned at each woman in turn. "We have Grace Fellows, Gracie Wilder, and Grayce Warrington."

"That's Grayce with a Y," said the one with the polka dot rouge.

"What a lovely way to spell the name," Dori said. "Grayce Warrington? Are you related to Angie?"

"Her grandmother."

"But don't hold it against her," said the somber Gracie. "It's not Grayce's fault that Angie's grumpy, Bob's a scoundrel, and Jonathan thinks he's God."

Dori blinked. There was forthright and then there was forthright. She looked at Grayce to see if her friend's comments had upset her.

"Thank you, Gracie," Rouged Grayce said. "You're a good friend. Maybe if Merit had lived longer, things would be different."

"Merit was your husband?" Dori asked.

"Wonderful man," Rouged Grayce said. "He died of cancer when Jonathan was twelve, and he made the mistake of telling the boy that when he went, Jonathan would be in charge as the man of the house."

"Jonathan interpreted his daddy's comments rather broadly," said Wrinkled Grace. "He thought Merit meant that he was in charge of the world, especially the chapel."

"But we've been taking care of Pastor Paul," Rouged Grayce said. "We like him and don't want the same thing to happen to him that happened to all the others."

Dori looked a question at Trev, but he was busy listening to the old ladies.

"*You* could make it happen," said Somber Gracie, pointing her index finger at Dori. "So we'll take care of you too."

Trev made a peculiar choking sound and began to cough.

Somber Gracie pounded on his back with enough strength to make him stagger.

"By the way, Pastor," she continued after he seemed to be breathing normally again. "You once again put the object of the preposition in the nominative case. How many times must I tell you it should be the objective case? You said, 'They sent money to he and Paul.'"

"I did not. I couldn't have."

"Yes, I'm afraid you did." Somber Gracie shook her head at the tragedy of it all.

"It's *him*," Dori said with a smile.

"Ah," said Somber Gracie. "Listen to your wife, sir."

"And listen to me, too," said Wrinkled Grace. "We sang three of those praise songs this morning. Right in a row! Isn't that a bit many?"

"But, Grace," Trev said, "we also sang 'The Old Rugged Cross.' All verses."

"Well, yes, that was very nice, but the Collins boy was up there playing his guitar to it." Wrinkled Grace was incensed.

Dori thought of the guitarist, who had to be forty if he was a day, and bit her lip to keep from smiling.

Wrinkled Grace continued, "I think an organ is the only proper instrument to be played in church except for maybe the piano."

"We don't have an organ," Trev said, his smile now somewhat strained.

"We should." Obviously a little fact like reality wasn't about to stop Wrinkled Grace. "Every church should."

"Do you play the piano and organ?" Grayce Warrington asked, squinting at Dori over her glasses.

"Me?" Dori asked, taken by surprise. "No, I'm not very musical."

Grayce shook her head. "That's a shame. The best pastor's wives play the piano. They also cook very well. All those church dinners, you know. Do you cook very well?"

Knowing she was about to confess another weakness, Dori tried to look extra confident. "Well, I've lived alone for the past several years, and I haven't had much chance to improve my cooking skills."

Rouged Grayce raised an eyebrow, weighing the answer. Then she nodded, deciding to give the bride the benefit of the doubt. "Practice on Pastor Paul, dear. That's the secret, you know. Practice."

Trev reached for Dori's hand. "If you'll excuse us, ladies, we need to get home."

"Oh, I just bet you do." Wrinkled Grace winked at them. "Practice."

Dori felt herself flush and refused to look at Trev. If the Graces only knew!

"Grace! Mind your manners," Somber Gracie said with a glare.

Trev pulled Dori toward the door, the Graces following.

"He's wearing a sweater and shirt again," Wrinkled Grace whispered to her friends in a voice that would carry throughout an auditorium much larger than the Seaside Chapel sanctuary. "He should be wearing a suit. A black suit."

"Next thing you know, Grace," Rouged Grayce said, "you'll be wanting to put him in one of those white backwards collars."

"Well, why not? Then everyone knows he's the minister."

"When I grew up," Somber Gracie said, "my minister wore vestments and a robe. And there was no guitar!"

Dori managed not to laugh until they were a safe distance away. "Oh, Trev, what a hoot!"

Trev's smile was somewhat pained. "Easy for you to say. You don't hear from them every week, week in and week out. 'Now I'm only saying this for your good, Pastor.'"

Dori was thoroughly taken with the idea of Trev being assaulted by these women every week. "They like you and want to help you."

"I know. I remind myself of that every Sunday when they corner me. I have nightmares about what would happen if they ever decided they didn't like me."

A brisk wind blew off the ocean, and when they turned the corner for the two-block walk home, it slapped Dori in the face. She shivered.

"Cold?" Trev pulled her close.

"I'm fine," she said, very conscious of him, of his arm around her shoulders. "It's just that San Diego is never like this." She yawned, slapping her hand over her mouth. "What I am is tired."

"Did you have trouble sleeping last night? Isn't the bed comfortable?"

She wanted to deny her sleeplessness, but she knew she couldn't. She also didn't want him to know he was the reason she couldn't sleep. He might misinterpret. "Jet lag." At least that was true as far as it went. "And the bed's fine."

They turned up the walk to the house and found Ryan sitting on the top step, his duffel bag at his feet, his green and white Eagles jacket swamping his slight frame.

He stood as they approached. "I forgot my key."

Trev nodded as he pulled his out of his pocket and opened the front door. He put out a hand to catch Jack before the animal could lick all of them to death. "Try and find it before we eat, okay?" he said as he wrestled Jack back into the house. "Back door. Backyard," he told the dog, pointing. Jack gave him a look of deep disappointment and headed for the rear of the house.

"Wouldn't it be easier if you just took me to the hardware store, and they made us about five more keys?" Ryan asked.

"Easier for who?" Trev asked.

"For whom," Dori said. "Watch it. Gracie will get you."

Ryan grinned broadly, but Trev merely rolled his eyes. "Ry, there's already at least ten keys to my house spread around Seaside, and you've only been here for three weeks!"

"Yeah," Ryan agreed as he let his coat slide off his thin shoulders. He grabbed it just before it hit the floor. "I'm not good with keys. But none of them has an address on them, so no one can break in."

"And that's supposed to make me feel good?"

Ryan shrugged. "It makes me feel good. No bad guys in the night is something to be happy about, you know?"

Dori grinned as she hung her coat in the hall closet. She suspected that Ryan gave Trev more than a run for his money. "What kind of sandwich would you like, Ryan?"

"What do you have?"

"Well, I can do egg salad, grilled cheese, or a BLT, though the tomatoes look a little woody."

Ryan looked at her with stars in his eyes. "Really? No PB&J?"

"Sure, if that's what you want."

"No, I don't want!"

Trev looked at the boy with mock hurt. "You mean you haven't liked my cooking the whole time you've been here?"

Ryan blew a raspberry. "No offense, Pastor Paul, but variety is the spice of life. Grilled cheese, Dori."

In a few minutes they were sitting at the table eating their grilled cheeses with chips, pickles, and apple slices on the side.

"Hey!" Ryan pointed to the center of the table. "We got a plant!"

Dori nodded. "Ivy."

Ryan stared at it a minute. "Grandmom always had an African violet on the table." He sniffed. "She must have fifteen different ones all over the house, and she puts whatever's blooming on the table. She even has a couple at the bookstore."

Dori's heart kicked. "You miss her."

Ryan nodded and swallowed hard. Jack, back inside after his quick trip to water the garden, seemed to sense the boy's distress and came to lay his head on Ryan's knee.

"Just remember that she's doing very well," Trev said as he put a couple of apple slices on his plate. "It won't be long until you can be home with her." He reached over and dropped two pieces on Ry's plate.

Ryan nodded. "I know." Absently he picked up a slice and crunched on it while he ran his other hand over Jack's silky head. "Then I'll miss Jack." He stopped midcrunch and narrowed his eyes.

Dori watched the boy with interest. What had his astute mind come up with now? With a look of innocent longing, Ryan turned to Trev. "You wouldn't want to give Jack to me, would you, Pastor Paul? You could make a lonely boy very happy."

Trev laughed. "Nice try, kiddo, but I'm afraid Jack's here for the duration, aren't you, boy?"

The big animal lifted his head, stared briefly at Trev, then walked to the front door and barked.

Dori rose and began collecting the dirty plates. "Someone obviously wants out again."

"He wants to go to the beach." Trev popped the last apple slice into his mouth, then rose and carried his dishes to the sink.

At the word *beach* Jack began charging back and forth between the door and Trev, threatening anything or anyone in his path with dire injury.

"I'll take him," Ryan offered.

"Thanks, tiger," Trev said, "but I was hoping my wife would help me walk Jack."

He looked at Dori.

"Okay," Ryan said. "We can all go."

Dori opened her mouth to tell the guys that she didn't really want to catch pneumonia on the beach in January. They should go while she took her much anticipated nap.

But Trev spoke first. "Not this time, Ry. This will be just Dori and me. Sort of like a date, you know?"

Ryan's eyes got big. "But you're married."

Trev nodded. "So?"

"Married guys don't date."

"Sure they do." He slipped his arm around Dori's shoulders. "And kids get to do the dishes."

"What?" Ryan looked highly offended. "I can't walk Jack, but I can wash dishes? You do know that I'm a boy child, right? Boy kids walk dogs. Girl kids wash dishes."

Dori started to laugh. "Oh, Ryan, do you have a lot to learn about life."

"Besides," Trev said as he held out Dori's coat to her, "we don't have a girl kid available at the moment."

"Then have one!" Ryan ordered, carrying the remaining dishes and his grump to the sink.

Dori pulled on her red beret and gloves. She tried to make believe she didn't like it when Trev pulled a plaid scarf off the top closet shelf and wound it around her neck.

"Got to keep the California girl cozy," he said softly.

Jack set a brisk pace, and soon Dori was warm in spite of the cold. They walked the two blocks to the beach, then crossed the sand to the packed strand left by the tide. Jack raced in and out of the water, snapping at the little waves like he could catch them, sputtering periodically as he got an unexpectedly big mouthful of salt water.

"He's crazy," Dori said. "That water's got to be freezing."

Jack came racing to them, his mouth open, his tongue lolling.

"Don't you dare!" Trev ordered, turning his back.

Jack gave a doggie laugh and shook as hard as he could. The flying pellets of frigid salt water slapped Dori in the face.

"Jack!" she screamed, rubbing her coat sleeve over her face. "You rat." She turned to Trev. "And you're not much better. You turn your back but neglect to tell me to turn mine."

"You've got a dog. I thought you'd know." His eyes danced.

"Like Trudy would ever be so gauche." Dori leaned over until she was nose to nose with Jack. "She's going to eat you alive, big guy. You just wait. I'll get my revenge."

Jack wiggled with delight and kissed her.

She laughed and glanced at Trev to find him studying her.

"Phil told me you were prettier now than when you were young," he said. "I couldn't imagine how since I thought you were beautiful then. But he was right."

"Trev." She sounded breathless. "Don't. This is hard enough without you playing the moonstruck swain."

His eyes bored into hers. "Who says I'm playing?"

Suddenly it was too much—the emotion, the fatigue, the situation, even Ryan and the Graces. She felt her eyes fill and her chin quiver, and she folded her arms protectively about herself even as she told herself she would not, she absolutely would not cry.

"Poor Dori."

Trev's voice was so soft and kind that first one tear, then another and another slid down her cheeks. He reached for her, and she fell into his arms. She gripped him as tightly as she could.

"Oh, Trev, I'm so scared," she whispered as the tears kept falling.

His arms tightened. "I know, sweetheart. I know. Me, too, if you want the truth. Oh, Father, we need You right now, both of us. Please teach us Your will. Please make something of this marriage."

Dori froze. He was praying right here on the beach? Did he ever think she might feel awkward praying in public? And he wanted to make something of the marriage? What if she didn't?

"Easy, Dori," Trev whispered into her ear. "Relax. There's no timetable, no hurry, no foregone conclusion. Just relax and we'll see what happens."

She nodded and forced the tension from her shoulders.

"We used to laugh a lot together," he said. "Remember? Maybe we can learn to do it again."

She sniffed. "Maybe."

"That's all I ask for now." He rested his cheek on the crown of her head, and she relaxed into him. They stood that way for several minutes as Jack sat beside them, first merely curious, then whining with feelings of abandonment.

"Well, nothing I like better than seeing a happy couple wrapped in each other's arms," boomed a voice so near that Dori jumped. She pulled back to see a disreputable-looking man with a long gray ponytail sticking through the back of his baseball cap, a diamond ear stud blinking in the weak, lemony sun, and a metal detector in his hand.

Trev stuck out his hand. "Clooney."

"Pastor Trevelyan."

They shook hands somberly, Jack sticking his nose into the middle of the transaction.

"No need to feel jealous, Jocko." Clooney rubbed the dog's head until Jack's eyes closed in ecstasy. Then Clooney turned his attention to Dori who was busy trying to hide the evidence of her tears, scraping her gloves back and forth over her cheeks.

"So this is the much-talked-of bride, wiping away her tears of joy," Clooney said.

As if he didn't know they weren't of joy, she thought.

"This is Dori," Trev said. "And, Dori, this is Clooney, Seaside's premier beach bum."

Dori blinked. "Trev, what a thing to say."

"Oh, no, not at all, ma'am, for that is exactly what I am," Clooney said with a tip of his cap brim. He continued to study her, but he spoke to Trev. "I'll say this for you, Pastor. You sure know how to pick 'em. This is one beautiful woman."

Dori blushed, first at the compliment, then at Trev's warm look of agreement. "Thank you," she managed.

Clooney turned to Trev. "How'd you keep her such a secret?"

"If I tell you," Trev said easily, "then it's no secret anymore."

Clooney nodded, content with the nonanswer.

"We missed you in chapel this morning," Trev told Clooney.

Dori was surprised. She never would have expected Clooney to be a churchgoer of any sort.

"Just like you miss me every week, Pastor," Clooney said without the slightest appearance of remorse. "And will continue to miss me. You know God and I don't do well together."

"Don't you think it's time to stop blaming Him for men's sin and put the past away?" Trev asked.

Clooney gave him a sardonic look. "I can't. My memories of 'Nam and of other injustices are always present."

"Vietnam was thirty years ago, Clooney."

"To you maybe. But I thank you for trying to change my rebellious heart. It's kind of you."

Clooney turned his attention back to Dori. "You got a good man here, Mrs. Trevelyan. He's God's man through and through, but he's not obnoxious about it like some I could name."

Dori glanced at Trev, uncertain what to say. Trev as a believer was an idea she had yet to come to terms with. He smiled back, that wonderful wry smile, and it struck her that Trev *was* a good man and always had been. One fall from grace didn't nullify his overall character.

She took a deep, somewhat shaky breath. *All this time I've been dwelling on the one negative and ignoring the many, many fine qualities. I'm just like Clooney. He can't get over Vietnam, and I can't get over my hurt.*

Seventeen

$\mathcal{M}$AUREEN LOOKED UP at the sign that read Seaside Pharmacy in big black letters on a white background. Each letter was outlined in crimson. Below the sign the brick wall was broken by a picture window that gave a clear view of the interior of the store. Since the store was on the corner, the entrance was angled for access from either street. A bell jangled when they entered.

"Look around for a few minutes." Phil waved his arm. "I need to check with my pharmicist in the back."

She was watching him walk down the aisle, thinking again about her certainty of his innocence, when he turned suddenly and caught her looking. He grinned and winked, and she flushed like she was back in junior high and got caught staring at the cutest guy in the class. She knew he thought she was interested in him *that* way when all she was doing was her job. He was whistling jauntily when he disappeared into the back.

Maureen wandered up and down the aisles, letting her flushed face cool. As she studied the shelves full of products, she suddenly found she needed lots of things. She had a collection of cosmetics, toiletries, and over-the-counter medications in her hands, everything from polish remover to sinus tablets, when Phil returned.

He glanced at her full arms. "On the house."

"Oh, no," Maureen began. Could this be construed—or mis-construed—as a bribe?

"Oh, yes." He began placing her purchases on the checkout counter. "Hand me a bag, Midge," he asked the Reba McIntire look-alike manning the register.

Maureen felt something close to low-grade panic. She couldn't take these items as a gift. Even if she wasn't a cop on the job, she couldn't, but as a cop surveilling a suspect, she *really* couldn't.

"Phil, I'm serious. I want to pay."

"Nonsense," he said, his arm extended to Midge for the bag.

"Phil."

Something in her voice caught his attention, and he looked at her. "I like to give things. That's all."

She nodded. "I appreciate that, and I like to receive. But not today. I'm paying."

He stepped back, clearly unhappy but acquiescing politely. As Maureen handed Midge her money, a woman who looked to be eighty if she was a day walked to the register, a bottle of over-the-counter pain medication in her hand.

"Hi, Mrs. Prescott," Phil said, pitching his voice several decibels louder. "How are you today?"

"You don't want to know, young man," she said, her head shaking slightly on her thin neck.

"What are you getting today?" Phil asked.

She held up her bottle.

"And what's your prescription?"

Reluctantly she held out the bag.

Phil shook his head. "Mrs. Prescott, what am I going to do with you?"

"You could mind your own business," she answered tartly.

Phil grinned. "And miss sparring with you? Never." He became serious. "You know that this over-the-counter medicine isn't to be used with your prescription. They react badly to each other."

"When I use them together, I never feel anything bad. In fact," Mrs. Prescott stared him straight in the eye, "I always feel better."

"For the moment, maybe," Phil said. "But terrible things are happening to your liver, and you won't know it until the damage is done."

"Prove it," the old lady challenged.

Maureen watched, fascinated, as Phil thought for a minute.

"Aha!" He grinned at Mrs. Prescott. "Now don't you go any-where, my lovely. I'll be right back. And, Midge, whatever you do, don't let her buy that pain med."

Mrs. Prescott folded her arms over her bony chest and watched Phil stride back up the aisle to the pharmacist's working area. She gave a cackle of a laugh. "Ain't he grand?" she asked Maureen. "Enough to get your blood pumping and your heart singing, no matter your age."

Maureen started to laugh.

"But don't tell him," Mrs. Prescott ordered. "It's too much fun fighting him."

Phil returned holding a small computer in his hand. "This contains information about every drug out there, and it'll tell us if you've got a bad combination there."

"How do I know it's not outdated information?" Mrs. Prescott demanded.

"Because it's updated weekly." He pushed some buttons, screens flickered, and he said triumphantly, "There! See?"

Mrs. Prescott squinted at the little machine. "Well, I'll be. You're right."

Phil took the over-the-counter medicine from her. "Let me get you the kind that won't have any bad reactions."

As soon as he walked away, Mrs. Prescott looked at Maureen again. "Couldn't see that blasted little print on that silly little machine if you paid me a million dollars. But don't tell him. It makes him feel good thinking he's got the upper hand."

Finally Mrs. Prescott was checked out, proper medicines in her bag. Just before she walked out the door, she leaned to Maureen. "He always makes my Sundays. He's more fun than any of them preachers on TV." And she was gone, hobbling down the street toward her home.

Midge looked at Phil from her station behind the cash register. "You were late today. She was getting tired of waiting."

Phil nodded. "Service went longer than usual. My brother had to introduce his wife to the congregation."

Maureen noticed Phil didn't say *new* wife.

"So the rumors are true? Paul got married?" Midge leaned forward with interest.

Phil nodded. "That he did."

"Poor Angie."

Phil rolled his eyes. "Any romance with my brother was all in Angie's mind, believe me."

"Oh, I know that. Most people do." Midge straightened the counter as she spoke.

"Did Mrs. Prescott chew your ear off before we got here?" Phil asked.

"No worse than usual. But I'll need a raise if you're late next week."

Maureen shook her head. "She thinks she's pulling one over on you, but you've been onto her all along, haven't you?" She buttoned her royal blue coat, the one that made her eyes more vivid than they were naturally.

Phil shrugged as he led her outside. "That's the fun of a small town pharmacy. You get to know your clients, even the nutty ones. Do you like seafood?"

"Um, love it."

The air was damp and chill with just enough wind to rearrange her curls. She very much feared her nose was turning as red as Rudolph's, not that it mattered, of course. She was merely conducting police business.

"Let's go get some, either a late lunch or an early dinner, however you want to look at it."

He took her Seaside Pharmacy bag from her and stopped to put it in his car. Then he took her hand and led her across Ninth Street. Maureen slowed and peered into the window of the store directly opposite Phil's, a Christian bookstore named Harbor Lights. An old-fashioned children's sleigh sat in the window, and colorful children's books filled the sleigh, tumbling out onto the artificial snow to mingle with little mittens, boots, and hats. Maureen turned her head this way and that to read the titles and authors.

"You like to read?" Phil asked.

"Love it, especially fiction." She turned to him and grinned. "It's one of my biggest weaknesses. I can't imagine a worse fate than having nothing to read." She went back to the books, making a mental note of titles she wanted to remember for later purchase for her little nieces and nephews. "I stopped here several times last week because I wanted to get a new novel, but the store was always closed. I ended up at the library."

"It's cheaper," Phil said.

"But you have to give the book back."

He laughed and squeezed her hand, but she was barely aware. She finally heard what she'd said. She just indicated she lived here in Seaside or at least shopped here. *Ack. Ack.* She froze, waiting for Phil's reaction.

He didn't seem to notice her slip. He continued to peer in the window, shaking his head.

"What?" she forced herself to say. "You don't like books?" How could she ever like a man who didn't like books?

He shrugged. "I like them as well as the next man. I was thinking of Mae Harper, the lady who owns the store. She fell a couple of weeks ago right there behind that second shelf." He pointed through the window, and Maureen squinted to see where he meant. "She was up on a ladder changing some lighting and boom! She did a real job on her hip and leg. I don't know when she'll be able to work again."

Maureen made a sympathetic noise.

"She was alone at the time," Phil continued. "No one, including Mae, is quite certain how long she lay there before old Mrs. Prescott walked in and found her."

"Your Mrs. Prescott?" Maureen was fascinated.

"She's a very good screamer." Phil started walking again. "She scared Midge and me half to death."

"Poor Mrs. Prescott." Maureen imagined that even as hearty an octogenarian as she would find such an experience upsetting.

"Oh, she was fine, tough old bird that she is. It's more poor Mae. The store is the only source of income for her and her grandson, Ryan, who lives with her. It'll be weeks before she's out of rehab and back at work."

"No workmen's comp?"

"None, and minimal health coverage. Trev's been working at getting the chapel to fill in a lot of the needs."

Not a sign of a clever criminal at work, Maureen thought, ever more convinced that Paul Trevelyan was just as he seemed, the pastor of a small Seaside church.

"Here we are." Phil stopped in front of a hole-in-the-wall restaurant named Moe's.

Maureen looked at Moe's, then at him. "You're sure we can trust the food in here?"

"The best seafood in town, I promise. This is where all the locals eat."

"And how long have you been a local?"

"Two years."

"Do you like it here?"

He reached around her for the door. "I do. But what I really like is having my own store. I worked for a couple of years for one of the chains, and I didn't care for it. I enjoy being my own boss. I also like being part of the community, corny as that sounds."

"That's not corny. That's nice." Maureen was impressed in spite of herself.

They entered Moe's, and the hostess lit up at the sight of Phil. "Hey, handsome. Your usual table?"

"Sure, Monica." Phil didn't seem to notice Monica's obvious interest in him, a fascinating fact since she was a spectacular red-head. "Meet my good friend Maureen, as sweet an Irish rose as ever there was."

Monica's smile dimmed significantly as she nodded to Maureen who smiled warmly back. *Good* friend, huh? As sweet an Irish rose as ever there was? Even if Phil wasn't as oblivious as he seemed and that was his way of defusing Monica, Maureen knew she'd warm herself by those words for many a cold winter's night.

As they made their way to their seats, several waitresses called to Phil by name. He waved genially to all. Maureen shook her head. The man was a babe magnet.

"They all like you," she said as they sat down.

"Who?" He seemed genuinely confused.

"The waitresses."

"Oh." He nodded. "I guess. What do you want to eat? Everything's good."

"You're not interested in any of them?" *I hope not.* "You've already got a girl?"

He looked vaguely around. "I'm not interested." He turned to her. "I don't have a girl, but I am looking."

Maureen felt the heat rise. "Have you ever heard the word *subtlety?*"

"Believe me, Irish, compared to what I was in my BC days, I am the height of subtlety."

"BC days?"

"Before Christ. You know, like in dates, calendar ones, not girl ones."

She laughed. "It must have been interesting knowing you then."

With a completely serious face, he said, "You wouldn't have liked me." He turned to their waitress and gave his order. Maureen did the same.

"Why wouldn't I have liked you?"

"I was a wild man. Women and drink." He studied his hands. "I look back and wonder what in the world I was thinking."

It was obvious that the topic was painful to him, so she changed it. She needed current information anyway. "I've been wondering about Mae What'shername, the bookstore lady."

"Harper."

"Right. Where's her grandson while she's in the hospital and rehab?"

"He's been living with my brother."

"Really? With Paul?" Phonies didn't take in stray grandsons, did they? Too much trouble. Another plus for Trevelyan.

Take that, Fleishman.

Phil started to laugh as he reached for his coffee.

"What?" Maureen asked, enjoying the way he enjoyed life.

"I was just imagining what having a thirteen-year-old in the house is doing for Trev and Dori's reunion!"

Eighteen

JOANNE AND VINNIE STOOD in front of the big brick house with the name Trevelyan on the mailbox. Even with the lawn frost-killed and the flower beds empty of everything but shriveled azaleas and rhododendrons with their leaves puckered shut, it was still a beautiful place.

"I always wanted to live in a house like this," Joanne whispered. "It's like a house someone on TV lives in. Not a dumpy little three-room apartment on the third floor of some shabby old boarding house but a real house with lots and lots of rooms."

"I don't care if the Sopranos themselves live here. You just get that suitcase, idiot girl."

"Not the Sopranos." Joanne shook her head. "The good guys. The Nick at Nite guys. They all live in real nice houses just like this one."

The yearning for the better life that came with the big house filled Joanne. She knew that people in these big houses loved each other and helped each other. Just look at the Brady Bunch, though she had to admit she didn't have as much need for a celebrity to sing at her prom as Marcia Brady did, especially since she quit school and never went to a prom. Still, their lives always worked out. Hers never did, no matter how hard she tried.

Except maybe for Vinnie.

"Like you think TV's real?" Vinnie straightened his leather coat, twisting his neck like his tie was too tight, except he wasn't wearing a tie. He was wearing a snug blue sweater that showed off his hard abs. Eye candy. "You think they actually live in those houses you see shots of? They're just front walls, not real houses."

"They are not!" She stamped her stiletto-booted foot. "They're real!"

"Sometimes you're so dumb it scares me."

"Dumb! I am not. What about when you see them in their living room, huh? Or their kitchen? That's real, Vinnie. They have such pretty kitchens." Joanne sighed, then continued in her feathery whisper. "And I'd have my own pretty bedroom and a bed with a canopy thing over it."

Vinnie threw her another of his scornful looks. "Why do you want a stupid canopy? It just collects dust. And who do you think you are? Some prissy little princess?"

"Just because I want the better things in life doesn't mean you can mock me," she hissed. Sometimes he made her so mad! "So just shut up, Vinnie."

He scowled at her for a minute, his eyes real narrow and mean, and she knew she'd better watch it. He didn't like it when she spoke like that to him.

"Sorry," she mumbled.

"Yeah, yeah. That's what they all say." He wasn't convinced.

"I am. Really. Really, really." She put as much sincerity as she could behind her whisper.

"What's with all the whispering anyway?" Vinnie asked.

"Shh! Mind your manners. I don't want they should get a bad impression of us."

He just stared. "Like they're watching us out their window." His voice dripped scorn.

Joanne jabbed him in the ribs.

He grunted and glared at her. "You got sharp elbows, idiot girl."

"Like you actually felt that through your coat." Joanne glared back. "You think they got a pool out back?"

"What?" Vinnie scowled. "Who?"

"The however-you-pronounce-its." She gestured to the brick house. "These guys."

His lip curled. "When we go to the front door, idiot girl, why don't you ask them?"

"Are you scared?" Joanne whispered, studying his face.

"Scared? Me?" He wouldn't look at her. "I'm never scared."

"Whenever you're scared, you get snippy and mean. Like you're acting now."

He held out a clenched fist. "You get up to that door, Jo, or I'll show you what mean really is."

Joanne rang the doorbell with a shaking finger. Talking face-to-face with people was so much harder than asking questions over the phone, and that was hard enough. Yesterday afternoon after Vinnie had called Dori McAllister's house and gotten the number for Small Treasures, he'd made her make that call. Her palms had been so sweaty she could hardly hold the phone.

A lady answered with the words, "Small Treasures. May I help you?"

"Is Dori there?" Jo asked in a small voice. Her throat seemed to have closed off, and forcing words out was very difficult.

"I'm sorry. She's not here now. May I take a message?"

"Yeah. See, I got her suitcase by mistake at the airport and she got mine."

"In Philadelphia?"

Jo nodded, then remembered the Small Treasures lady couldn't see her. "Yeah."

"Oh, dear. As if her grandfather's illness wasn't bad enough."

"Yeah. So do you know how I can find her?"

"I do. She's visiting her family because her grandfather is very ill."

"Oh. Um, that's too bad." That was probably why she was so rude-like at the airport. "Well, I won't bother her. I just need my things, and she must want her stuff."

"I'm sure she does. Just a minute while I look up the address and phone number of the Trevelyans."

"Thank you so much," Jo said and wrote very carefully. She even read the numbers back to the nice lady.

"Tell Dori that Meg sends her love," the lady said and hung up.

When Joanne handed the address and phone number to

Vinnie, he smiled at her, his deep brown eyes crinkling at the edges. He wrapped his arms around her and kissed her. Jo's heart sang. He really did love her.

Amhearst, Pennsylvania. Vinnie had to go out and buy a Pennsylvania map before they knew exactly where Amhearst was.

"We'll drive up there tomorrow," Vinnie said. "It's only about two hours. Then we'll call when we're almost there to be sure someone's home, and bingo-bango, we get the paintings. Mr. J will never know there was a problem."

"Don't you want me to call to be sure the suitcase is there?" Jo asked.

"Like where else could it be? We know it's not at the airport."

"But what if we get there and no one's home?"

"She's visiting her sick grandfather. They're not going to the mall."

"I was thinking the hospital."

"Then we wait until someone comes home."

In spite of Joanne's misgivings, they followed Vinnie's plan, leaving at ten in the morning and calling the Trevelyans as they neared the house. They got a busy signal.

"Good," Vinnie said. "Someone's home. That's all we need to know."

It wasn't all they needed to know, Joanne thought. They needed to know where the house was. "Stop and ask directions. Please."

Vinnie waved away her suggestions. "I can find it myself."

By the time they finally located the house, it was midafternoon. All Joanne wanted was something to eat, but she didn't dare suggest it. Vinnie was way too surly and mean from driving all the twisty country roads.

Now they stood on the front porch of the big brick house waiting for someone to answer the doorbell. Dori MacAllister's suitcase rested at their feet.

Nineteen

As THEY WAITED FOR THEIR MEALS, Maureen looked around Moe's with its menus on the place mats, its sodas served in red plastic tumblers with red and white straws sticking out at a jaunty angle, its flatware wrapped in large white napkins, its scuffed dark red linoleum floor, and its flaking white paint on several of the mismatched chairs at the motley collection of tables.

"Very posh." She grinned at Phil. "I'm impressed."

"Never say I don't take a girl to the very best places." He leaned toward her. "Just wait til you see where I take you next time."

Her grin broadened. "My heart goes pitter-pat with anticipation." He didn't need to know that there was truth in her comment. She waved her arm to indicate the chaos that was Moe's. "But to better this place—I don't know. It'll take some doing. I don't think there's another place like it within miles, at least not that I've been to."

Maureen froze. What had she just said? Surely he'd realize she'd once again shown knowledge of Seaside and its surrounds. Greg would kill her if she blew this assignment, especially since she'd lost the pastor and wife on Friday. Sure, she'd found them again, but that didn't stop Fleishman from commenting and Greg from speculating.

And she had to keep reminding herself that it was an assignment, not a date.

Phil nodded, accepting her words at face value. "This is my favorite restaurant in town, but I usually don't look forward to the meal as much as today. I mean, who wants to eat alone in a lovely place like this?" His hand indicated the stained ceiling tiles and the tattered posters on the wall. "This is where a guy brings a favorite girl."

Favorite girl, huh? This guy could really lay it on. Usually flirts made her very uncomfortable, but there was something about Phil that made his outrageous statements charming instead of repulsive. Maybe it was because for a very long time no one except her father had indicated in any way, shape, or form that she might be a favorite girl, and her father didn't count. He was supposed to feel that way. Whatever the reason, she soaked up Phil's comments like a neglected piece of furniture soaked up wax.

Did that make her pathetic or what?

As she straightened her place mat over the cracked Formica of their table rather than look at Phil and risk seeing that his comment meant something—or worse yet, nothing—she realized that she had held the world, especially the male half, at arm's length since Adam's death. No involvement, no pain. No relationships, no danger. But she liked this man with his over-the-top humor and kind streak. And he took notes on his brother's sermon!

She took a deep breath to steady herself and said lightly, "You expect me to believe that you eat alone all the time?" With women like Monica eyeing him as a fox eyes a plump chicken, it was impossible to believe he didn't have a harem following him around.

"Eat alone. Live alone." He tried to look woebegone. "My life is a sad, sad thing."

She laughed. "I am not convinced."

For a few seconds he looked at her, suddenly serious. "Will you answer a question truthfully?"

She blinked. "Sure."

"What does a good girl like you think of a guy like me?"

"What do you mean, 'a good girl like me'?" He made her

sound five years old, and just when she was really starting to like him.

"Easy, Irish. It's a compliment. All I mean is that if I read you right, you're not into wild living."

She nodded, mollified. By that definition she was a good girl. "What do you mean, 'a guy like me'?"

"You know. A wild guy."

"You're a wild guy?"

When he nodded, Maureen struggled not to laugh. "A wild guy who takes notes on sermons?" But what if she had read him wrong, and he really was a wild guy, one cleverly playing a role, one involved somehow with stolen art. *Please, God, no.*

Phil gave her a halfhearted smile. "I'm going to tell you something I have told very few, but for some reason I refuse to analyze at the moment, I want you to know."

Pressure built in Maureen's chest until it actually hurt. She found herself rubbing her sternum and forced her hand to her lap. She was stunned by how much she feared what he was about to say.

He began to draw lines on his place mat with the tines of his fork, studying the results as if they were great works of art. His hand paused, and he put the fork down. He looked at her.

"I've only been a Christian for a little over two years, and it's still new and feels awkward to talk about. It happened after Trev came to Seaside Chapel, and I bought the pharmacy. I started going to the chapel as much to razz Trev as anything. I kept thinking that I'd find the holes in his new life. Not that I thought he was a phony or anything. Even before he got religion, Trev was always one of the good guys. I just thought I'd find all the flaws in his reasoning, his logic."

Phil stopped as their waitress set their meals before them. Maureen took one look at her crab cakes, and her mouth started to water. She took a bite and closed her eyes in pleasure.

"Told you," Phil said as he forked a bite of his flounder smothered in crab imperial.

They ate in silence for a few minutes, giving the delicious food the attention it deserved. Then Phil began to talk again.

"When I realized that I needed Christ desperately, I came to

Him as someone who had lived his life very selfishly. Not that I was a terrible person or anything, but I usually managed to arrange things the way I wanted them."

Maureen listened carefully, relieved that he wasn't announcing his complicity in the Matisse case, knowing there was something more going on here than just the recital of a personal journey.

Phil looked at her with an intensity that would have been unnerving from anyone else. "I bet you've been a Christian all your life, haven't you, Irish?"

Surprised a bit by his change of direction, Maureen nodded. "I grew up in a home where Christ was much honored. I knew I was a sinner at five years of age."

Phil grinned. "Some sinner. A little curly-haired sweetheart with a dark past."

Though he made light of her sinful little self, she sensed a sadness beneath his words. "No big sins," she agreed. "I got mad at my brothers. I lied to my parents. I disobeyed their rules. But even in my young heart I knew that I had a lousy attitude. And I knew it didn't please God." She shrugged. "Big sin, little sin. God hates it all."

"I know," Phil said. "But how can a sweet, godly woman like you ever accept a wild man like me who's been around the block many too many times?"

Well, now she knew the reason for that gentle, unspoken sorrow. He thought she was too good for him, or worse still, he thought she'd think herself too good for him. Maureen frowned.

"Sweet, godly woman," he'd said. Like she was beyond sin and struggles.

She remembered the battles she and Adam had had keeping themselves pure, especially when he was about to leave the country for dangers unimaginable. She and he had grown up knowing each other forever, going to the same church and youth group. They'd even committed their lives to the Lord at the same youth retreat. Adam was as much a constant in her life as her parents and her brothers. That he might actually die in his military service was something she knew intellectually. But after his death, she learned that in her deepest heart she had believed that since they had been obedient King's kids in spite of their yearnings, then God was obligated to protect him.

When word came of Adam's death, Maureen was rocked to her core. It was like God had reneged on His part of their bargain. After a life of espousing chastity, she found herself deeply regretting their purity. Now she'd never know the magic of physical love, and it broke her heart. She resented her obedience and God for asking it of her.

"Oh, I know all about struggling and doubting," she said, an edge to her voice.

Phil looked like he was waiting for more, but she wasn't going to pour out her deepest heart. Not yet anyway. Still, there were safe things she could say.

"I was engaged several year ago." She stared over Phil's shoulder as she spoke. "Adam was killed in Bosnia. Land mine. When he died, I was so angry. I felt that God had cheated me, cheated us both. We had always followed Him. He owed us."

She suddenly felt the need to pay attention to her last two bites of crab. "So you see, I'm not that godly after all."

She could feel his concern as he asked, "Do you still feel cheated? Are you still mad at God?"

She shook her head, remembering God's patient nudging, returning her unerringly to His standards. As she looked back, it hadn't taken her that long, though it had felt like forever at the time. A life of thinking in a certain pattern and hewing to a certain standard was hard to change, especially when the Holy Spirit impressed the wisdom of that standard on her heart.

"'Do you still want to argue with the Almighty?' That's what He thundered at Job. I slowly realized that while by His grace God gives me much, He owes me nothing." She shrugged. "I finally stopped fighting and accepted that truth."

"Wow. That sounds like godly to me." He gave her a sad half smile. "All I have is belated propriety. Secondhand purity. Late-blooming morality."

Maureen's heart melted. "In other words, you're a new man in Christ practicing godly living and godly standards."

He perked up a bit. "It sounds so much nicer phrased that way."

She reached across the table and took his hand. "I think that is one of the most wonderful things I've ever heard." She smiled. "It's what you've become since you met Christ that matters, not what you were before. Never forget that."

He turned his hand over and gripped hers so hard that it hurt. He swallowed before he spoke, and his words trembled a bit. "Thank you, Irish. You'll never know what your words mean to me. I've been terrified that no nice girl would ever be interested in me."

"If Christ can forgive all your offenses, neither I nor anyone else has the right to hold them against you."

"I don't care all that much about the others, but I find I care inordinately about your opinion."

Maureen swallowed and looked self-consciously away, right into the cynical gaze of Fleishman sitting two tables away with a pleasantly plump woman she assumed was his wife.

Much as she didn't want to, she flushed. What must it look like, her sitting here deep in conversation with Phillip Trevelyan, holding hands with him no less. She pulled her hand free and tucked it into her lap.

"What a lovely meal," she said, all chirpy, but her stomach suddenly knew that the crab cakes still had claws.

Phil frowned slightly at her almost flippant manner, but the waitress appeared with the bill and distracted him. He pulled out his bank card and slapped it on the table. The waitress disappeared to do the electronic magic of fund transfers.

Phil leaned back in his seat and gave her a look that immediately made her crab claws even more active. He definitely had something on his mind, and this time it wasn't pleading his case.

"So you're like a PI?" He seemed intrigued by the idea.

Maureen's heart tripped. "What?"

"You're a PI. A private investigator."

"No, I'm not."

"Yeah, but that's what you've got to say, or you'll compromise your investigation, right?"

Maureen stared at him. She could feel her mouth hanging open and snapped it shut.

"Who hired you?" Phil asked. "Pop? He wants to make sure Trev and Dori stay together, and he hired you to keep him informed."

Out of the corner of her eye she saw Fleishman and his wife getting out of their seats. She felt her shoulders relax as he headed for the door. At the door he stopped and turned. He stared at her, a contemptuous glare that told her quite clearly what he thought of her. Then he turned on his heel and left.

Maureen forced herself to forget Fleishman and concentrate on the job she had to do. "Phil, I don't know where you got that absurd idea, but I've never met Pop, and I've certainly never been hired by him."

Phil seemed to gauge her words, to weigh them in some mental balance like a merchant weighing produce in a bazaar. She couldn't tell his conclusions from his expression.

He reached across the table and fingered one of the enameled butterflies hooked in her ear. His fingers tickled, but all she could think was how glad she was that Fleishman was gone. If he'd seen this move—she couldn't even bring herself to think of his reaction.

"Cute," Phil said, tugging ever so lightly. "Like you. Pop's our grandfather. He and Honey raised the three of us after our parents were killed."

Maureen forced herself to ignore his hand against her neck. "Pop's who Dori came east to visit in the hospital?"

"As if you didn't know." Now his fingers played with one of her curls, twisting it gently.

She raised a hand like she was making a pledge. "I didn't."

Phil narrowed his eyes and sat back in his chair. He folded his arms across his chest and studied her for several moments. It was all she could do not to fidget. She couldn't keep one hand from pushing the curl he had played with behind her ear.

"Then why are you following them, Maureen?" The bantering tone was gone. In place of the charming tease was a man who stared implacably across the table, his whole demeanor demanding an answer to his question, a reminder that new men in Christ weren't pushovers or idiots.

She tried to dissemble. "What makes you think I'm following them?"

He didn't even bother to answer.

She looked down at her empty coffee cup, studying the dram of liquid still sitting in it.

Oh, Lord, I'm about to go with my instincts here. If I'm wrong, please show me in the next five seconds or so.

She took a deep breath and looked at Phil. His brown eyes remained fixed on her as he waited.

"I'm not a private investigator," Maureen began.

Phil raised a doubtful brow.

"I'm a cop."

At this announcement, Phil blinked. "A cop?"

She nodded and sighed inwardly at his disbelieving look. She would miss his friendship, his humor, his outrageous behavior.

"What's a cop doing watching Trev and Dori?"

"I'm not watching them. I'm watching her suitcase."

"You're watching Dori's suitcase." He repeated her statement as if it made no sense, which, of course, it didn't out of context.

"We have a very reliable tip that that particular suitcase contains stolen goods."

The temperature at the table cooled dramatically. "You're saying that Dori is a thief?"

Maureen shook her head. "I don't know who the original thief was. I don't think anyone does. All we know is that the stolen goods were being transported to Seaside. My job was to watch for the courier and follow her back to Seaside."

"So where does Dori come into this?"

"She picked up the suitcase."

"The one with these stolen goods inside." He made it a statement.

Maureen nodded.

"How do you know she took that specific one? So many suitcases look alike."

"It had a piece of red yarn tied on the handle and a streak of white chalk down the side."

He was silent a minute, and she suspected that he was seeing that damaging red yarn attached to the case Dori wheeled to his car.

He shook his head decisively. "But Dori would never transport stolen goods. I know she wouldn't. She's not that kind of person, and besides, Pop'd have her hide."

"My feeling is that she took the wrong suitcase." Maureen saw again Joanne Pilotti and Dori reaching for the same bag. "Everyone else I work with isn't quite as certain of your innocence as I am, so—"

"My innocence?" He looked highly offended that it was ever in doubt.

"Not you as in Phil specifically."

He grunted approval.

"You as in all you Trevelyans."

His expression told her what he thought of that absurdity.

She sighed. "I'm supposed to be ingratiating myself into your family to ascertain your degree of involvement in this whole mess."

Hurt flashed in his eyes, quickly banished. "So that's why you came to lunch with me." And he had poured out his heart to her.

"Yes."

He compressed his lips, disgusted with her.

"But no." She was desperate for him to understand.

"What is it? Yes or no?"

She slumped in her seat. He'd surely hate her now. "Both. I had to come, but I wanted to, too." She wet dried lips. "I-I really wanted to."

"And I'm supposed to believe that, fall under your spell, and confess my evil machinations—oh, pardon me, *our* evil machinations."

"Wow." She managed a half smile. "I never heard anyone use that word in real life, and you used it twice in one sentence. And I don't think any of you had anything to do with the stolen goods."

She watched a slow smile grow on Phil's lips and felt hopeful.

"You think we're innocent?" he asked.

"I thought I already said that. I'm either very naïve or very perceptive, but I do."

He suddenly stood. "Well, let's go prove you're right." He came to her chair and pulled it back for her. "Let's go ask Dori to let us see in that suitcase."

Twenty

AN OLD LADY with white hair cut short and combed back from her face answered the door. Joanne thought that she was very pretty for being that old, and that she looked like she went with the house. She was the grandmother who made cookies and stuff, sort of like Aunt Bee did for little Opie back in Mayberry, only she was way prettier that Aunt Bee.

Joanne opened her mouth to explain about the suitcases, but Vinnie beat her to it.

"We're looking for Dori MacAllister. My girlfriend here," he pointed to Joanne and she smiled, "and Dori mixed up their suitcases at the airport. We drove all the way up here to make the exchange." He smiled at the lady who looked at the suitcase on her doorstep in dismay.

Suddenly she pushed the storm door wide open. "Come in, please. It's too cold to stand out on the doorstep."

Joanne and Vinnie stepped into a warm hall with lots of photographs clustered on one wall. Three kids at various ages smiled in the pictures, and Joanne fell in love with the idea of pictures of her own kids hanging up like that. All she had to do was get Vinnie to marry her so she could have them. She would never have a kid without getting married first.

She grew up with three brothers, and all four of them had a different last name. Her mother had never married any of the fathers. In fact, Mom always said she didn't even know who Joanne's father was. She gave Joanne her last name by putting the names of boyfriends she could remember in a hat and drawing one.

"I'm so sorry," the white-haired lady said, pulling Joanne back to business. "But Dori isn't here."

Joanne's heart skipped a beat. Had she gotten something mixed up? Vinnie'd kill her if she had. Maybe she'd written down a wrong number? Maybe they weren't even at the right house. She thought back over her talk with the Small Treasures lady named Meg. No, Jo was sure she had everything right. Besides, the white-haired lady seemed to know who Dori was.

Joanne's heart skipped another beat as she thought of something so scary she feared she'd be sick on the spot. Dori had found the paintings! She'd found them and done something with them, like maybe gone to the police. The guys on Nick at Nite always went to the police when something wrong happened. Law and order was important to them. They didn't transport stolen goods. She was the idiot who did that.

The white-haired lady smiled. "She's sort of on her honeymoon."

Honeymoon? "I thought she was visiting her sick grandfather," Joanne blurted.

The lady nodded. "She was, but Pop wasn't as sick as we first thought. In fact, I brought him home today." She smiled, obviously pleased.

Joanne found herself smiling back. Was Pop like Mr. Huxtable, the grandfather on *The Cosby Show*? Did he have a gentle voice and play in a band?

"When it became obvious that Pop wasn't as sick as we had thought, Dori and Trev left."

"Who's Trev?" Vinnie asked.

"Our grandson, Paul Trevelyan."

Joanne thought for a moment. "Isn't Dori your granddaughter?"

The woman nodded.

"Your granddaughter married your grandson?"

The woman nodded again. "Sounds funny, doesn't it?"

"Can you do that?" Joanne asked, fascinated. Maybe weird stuff did happen in the Nick at Nite houses after all. Maybe not knowing your dad's name wasn't really so terribly bad.

"Dori's our adopted granddaughter, so it's all right."

"Oh, that's good." Joanne felt a surge of relief as the world righted beneath her. She looked at Vinnie and caught the hint of panic in his eyes.

Forget grandsons and -daughters, Joanne. Think paintings. Think Mr. J. Think poor Vinnie.

"So where are they?" Vinnie asked. "Did they go to one of those places in the Poconos? The ones with the heart-shaped tubs and all?"

The lady laughed. "No. That's not their style."

Joanne couldn't imagine why anyone wouldn't want to go to one of those resorts. She wanted to go there when Vinnie finally got around to marrying her. The very idea of the heart-shaped tubs was so exciting! Or maybe the tubs that were like champagne glasses, the ones you had to go to the second floor to climb in.

The lady thought for a minute. "They've probably gone home by now."

"Back to California?" Joanne squeaked.

The lady reached out and patted Joanne's arm. "No, no. Back to Seaside."

"Seaside?" Joanne and Vinnie said together. "New Jersey?"

The lady nodded.

"We live there," Joanne told her. How great was that! "We can get the suitcase real easy."

"Let me give you Trev's address," the lady said and did.

They were halfway back to Seaside before Vinnie spoke. "I can't believe you led me astray like that." He turned and glared at Joanne.

Jo's mouth dropped open in surprise. "How did I lead you astray?"

"Making me go all the way to Pennsylvania when the suitcase was in Seaside all along."

"I told you to call first, but no—" she started when Vinnie's cell phone interrupted with "The Daring Young Man on the Flying Trapeze."

Joanne grabbed the phone from his belt.

"Don't answer!" he yelled at the same time she said, "Hello. This is Vinnie's phone."

"And this is Neal Jankowski," a deep, brisk voice said. "Give me Vinnie."

Eyes wide with awe, Jo passed Vinnie the phone. He held it like it was going to bite him. He took a deep breath and swallowed. She saw his Adam's apple bob up and down.

"Hello, Mr. Jankowski, sir," Vinnie said. "How may I help you?"

All Joanne could hear was the low rumble of Mr. J's voice.

"I'll take them over to your assistant first thing in the morning, sir. You don't have to worry about a thing."

More rumbling, and Joanne watched Vinnie's Adam's apple bob up and down again several times.

"Well, yes, I should have taken them Friday evening. I know that. It's just that there have been—" He cleared his throat. "—complications."

"*Complications?*"

Joanne heard Mr. Jankowski roar the word as clearly as if she'd had the phone to her ear. Then he went back to a rumble.

"B-barney Noble, sir?" Vinnie made a gagging sound. "Really, sir, I don't think I need his help."

Joanne slapped her hand over her mouth. Barney Noble! Vinnie'd told her all about him. He was Mr. J's cleanup guy. He did everything from collecting on overdue loans to doing away with troublesome people.

And when Mr. J heard about her mix-up, he'd think she was about as troublesome as you could get.

Joanne shuddered as her blood froze as solid as the water in the puddle right outside her apartment's front door.

Twenty-One

$\mathcal{D}$ORI WALKED HOME with Trev and Jack, her mind full of Clooney's comments about Trev. About her *husband*. She tried to make sense of her confused emotions, but she was so tired she could barely think, let alone sift through chaotic feelings that shifted from moment to moment with all the subtlety of tidal shifts in the Bay of Fundy.

Trev squeezed her hand. "Thanks for coming with me and Jack. I know it was selfish of me to ask and gracious of you to agree, but I wanted some time alone with you. As soon as we get home, you climb into bed and sleep as long as you can. I promise not to wake you."

How wonderful that sounded. "Thank you, thank you!" Sweet sleep to knit up her raveled sleeve of care. Or something like that.

They had just rounded the last corner, Jack walking contentedly beside Trev now that he'd had his outing, when Trev said, "Uh-oh."

Climbing out of a car in front of their house were Phil and a dark-haired woman.

Dori wanted to cry at the sight. There went her nap.

"We'll get rid of them as fast as we can," Trev said. "I promise." He released Jack's lead and the dog, now straining toward Phil, dashed headlong toward his objective. Phil, wise man that he was, shoved his companion behind him as Jack bore down. The dog reared up, planted his paws on Phil's shoulders, and washed his face with doggie kisses.

"Down, you big oaf," Phil ordered as he rubbed Jack's ears and neck. "You'll make Maureen think you have no manners."

At that, the dark-haired woman stepped around Phil and began running her hands up and down Jack's back. In a flash Jack abandoned Phil and focused his affections on the newcomer.

Dori watched the young woman with interest and Phil with even more. He was watching the woman with a goofy smile unlike any Dori had ever seen from him before.

"Who's she?" she whispered to Trev as they drew near. Curiosity had pushed the need for her nap aside for the moment.

"I have no idea."

"He likes her. A lot."

Trev frowned. "How can you tell? All I see is a girl scratching Jack."

"Don't look at her. Look at Phil."

"Ah. I see what you mean. He looks sort of like I probably do when I look at you."

Dori's pulse kicked. What was she to do with these wonderful comments he threw out when she was least expecting them? She was saved from having to respond at the moment by Jack remembering who fed him and racing over to Trev to share a wiggle or two. Then it was back to the young woman.

"Hey!" Phil greeted. "This is Maureen, and have we got a story for you!"

Maureen looked up from Jack and offered an infectious grin. "I love your dog. We had one like him when I was growing up. Ours was a police dog injured in the line of duty and retired from active service." She looked back at Jack, rubbing his ears. "He could have been your papa, handsome, you look so much alike."

Jack, who knew a compliment when he heard one, kissed her with a great sweep of his tongue.

"Not fair, buddy," Phil muttered as he pulled Jack away. "You got to kiss her before I did."

Dori, biting her lip to keep from laughing at Phil's put-upon expression, shot a glance at Maureen. She stood, face red, making believe she hadn't heard a thing.

"Come on in," Dori said, patting Maureen's arm sympathetically. These Trevelyan men! "We're dying to hear your story."

Led by the delighted Jack, the four of them went inside. As they took off coats and gloves and hung them up, Ryan came downstairs to join the action.

"I did the dishes," he informed Trev in a martyr's voice.

"Good," Dori said without an ounce of compassion for his extreme suffering. "We'll make a man out of you yet."

Ryan frowned at her. "You're worse than my grandmother."

She grinned back. "Thanks. Knowing how much you miss her, I take that as a compliment."

Ryan rolled his eyes.

Dori scanned the living room, suddenly aware that seating would be a problem. A sofa and a chair. Four seats, five people. "How about we sit around the kitchen table. We've got enough chairs out there, I think."

As she led the way into the other room, she thought of her green and peach love seat and the two white wicker chairs in her living room in San Diego. Certainly they wouldn't fit in the car being driven east by Randy Reynolds. She'd have to find another way of getting them here. How expensive would it be? The question of how they would mesh with Trev's oversized furniture was secondary to the fact that they would then be able seat more than two guests at a time, a situation that seemed desirable for a pastor's home. Too bad Randy wasn't driving a U-Haul truck.

When they were all settled at the table, sodas before them, Phil looked at Maureen. "Do you want to tell them how we met and why you're here, or shall I?"

Maureen grinned at him. "Can I trust your version?"

"As much as you can trust me," was Phil's wiseacre reply.

Maureen studied him for a minute, then nodded. "Go ahead. You tell."

There was a moment of startled silence as Phil's gaze locked with hers.

Dori bit back another grin. Though she had no idea of the hidden connotations in the byplay between the two, the trust

Maureen was showing meant something special to Phil. Her brother-in-law looked like someone had just hit him over the head with a substantial stick. The man was a goner, no two ways about it.

Ryan looked like he wanted to stick his finger down his throat and make gagging noises, clearly affronted by the romantic vibrations in the air, but he politely restrained himself. Dori was impressed and patted his hand. He looked at her, startled, then returned her smile.

Trev cleared his throat. Phil jumped and actually flushed. Maureen just smiled softly to herself and waited. Dori knew she was going to like this woman. Anyone who could discomfit Phil was a woman worth knowing.

"I met Maureen Friday," Phil began.

"Before or after I got in?" Dori asked. She didn't want to miss a detail of this juicy story.

Phil scowled at her. "After. Now don't interrupt. It's a long story."

Dori held her tongue as she, Trev, and Ryan listened, fascinated. Phil told the tale with all the drama it deserved. "And so I convinced her that you were not a courier for organized crime, and that you would be more than willing to let her see your suitcase."

Ryan stared at Maureen, eyes wide. "You're really a cop?"

She nodded.

"But you're a girl."

Dori shook her head. "Ryan, we really have to work on your gender issues."

"There are lots of women police officers these days," Maureen said.

"But what if the bad guys are big?"

"I've been trained to overcome situations like that."

Ry nodded. "And you've got your gun, right?"

"I do, but it's a last resort. My father's been a cop his whole life, and he's never fired his gun in the line of duty. I hope for the same record."

Ryan looked disappointed, trained as he was by TV blood and guts. "But you fire it *out* of the line of duty?"

Maureen nodded. "But only on the practice range. We have to keep our skills sharp should the need to use the weapon ever arise."

"Are you good?"

"I am very good." She made the statement quietly but with a certainty that left no doubt about her claim.

Ryan nodded, somewhat mollified. "Where's your gun now?"

"In my locked glove compartment."

"What good does it do you there?"

"Well, I didn't think I should wear it to church. Then I went to the pharmacy, then out to dinner, and from dinner directly here." Maureen looked around the room, frowning intently. "Is one of these guys a lot more dangerous than he looks? Should I go get it?"

Ryan giggled. "These guys are all wimps. I bet you could take them out with your little finger." The giggle became a full-fledged laugh.

Dori smiled. There was truly nothing like junior high humor.

"I think we're getting just a bit off track here," Phil reminded everyone. "We need to see Dori's suitcase."

Dori rose. "Come on. But it's not my suitcase, just as you guessed, Phil. However there's no name or anything identifying on it. And if there's stolen masterpieces in it, I haven't found them."

Ryan led the charge upstairs, the others following. In the master bedroom, Dori dragged the suitcase out of the corner where she'd put it. Trev lifted it and deposited it on the bed. He made to open it.

"May I?" Maureen asked, laying a hand on his arm to stop him.

Trev stepped back as Dori said, "I'm afraid that if there was any evidence that would help you, I contaminated it when I went through the contents looking for some identifying information of some kind."

Maureen shrugged. "It can't be helped." Carefully, she studied the case, the latches. She searched the outer pouch, then opened the bag. Then item by item, she lifted out the collection of used clothes, examining each one thoroughly.

"There aren't any labels on anything," she commented. "Did you notice?"

Dori hadn't.

"Cut out so you can't trace stuff, huh?" Ryan's eyes sparkled with excitement.

Maureen nodded. When the suitcase was empty, she ran her hands carefully over the lining, taking special care at the seams. Dori watched with interest, seeing nothing suspicious.

"Ah." Maureen smiled and began to pick at one corner where the lining covered the bottom. With just a little work, the lining peeled back and there lay two small unframed canvases.

"Henri Matisse," Maureen said as she laid the paintings on the beige duvet.

Dori couldn't tear her eyes from the glowing canvases. To think they had been in her possession, and she hadn't even known it. Shouldn't things this beautiful give off vibrations or emanations or something that let you know they were near?

"They're small." Ryan looked disappointed. "I thought master-pieces were big, like in museums, you know?"

"Small or not, they are very valuable." Maureen studied them with a faint smile. "They belong to a private collector on the West Coast, someone I'd never heard of before we got involved," Maureen said.

"So now you give them back to him." Ryan smoothed the duvet around the paintings, his small hands quick and careful. "And the mystery is solved." He looked up with a delighted grin. "Wait until I tell the kids!"

"Well, uh."

Dori turned to Maureen as did the others. For the first time she looked somewhat uncomfortable.

"Well, uh, what?" Phil asked. "We're not allowed to tell?"

Maureen waved her hand in a motion of dismissal. "I'm not worried about you telling, though of course you can't."

"Rats," Ryan said with feeling. "That's what I was afraid of. Finally something worth talking about at school, and I can't talk about it."

Maureen looked sympathetic. "Sorry, guy. See, the thing is that we don't want just to recover the art. We want to catch the receiver of the stolen goods. That's why I was at the airport. My partner and I were to follow the suitcase and catch the guy red-handed."

"And you expected it to come to Seaside?" Dori asked.

Maureen nodded. "Though you were a surprise."

"I'll bet. But why here? I mean, Seaside is hardly a hotbed of crime."

Maureen thought for a moment. "We don't know who the original thief was, and that's not our major concern. We'll leave that part of the puzzle to others. We're involved because the paintings were to be delivered to Seaside to a crime boss named Neal Jankowski."

"How do you know this?" Trev asked.

"A CI who wants Jankowski to fall."

"A CI?"

"A confidential informant."

"And this crime boss lives in Seaside?" The disbelief was clear in Phil's voice.

"He works out of Atlantic City, but he likes living in our quiet little town. A better environment for his kids."

Phil blinked. "Am I the only one to hear the irony in that statement?"

Maureen shrugged. "He's got four kids he's crazy about."

"Jankowski," Ryan said. "I've got a Jankowski in my class. Eric." The boy's face darkened. "He's a bully."

Maureen picked up one, then the other of the oils and put them back in the suitcase. She gently covered them with the lining.

Dori hated to see them go, they were so beautiful, so full of color. "Can you imagine actually having treasures like that in your house?"

Trev cocked an eye at her. "Pastor's salaries don't go that far."

Ryan had been studying Maureen rather than the pictures. "You're saying Eric's dad is Mafia?" Ryan gave a nod of understanding. "Well, that explains a lot."

Maureen grinned at the boy's comment. "Not to burst your balloon, but he's not Mafia. He's his own man, small-time in the eyes of many, but he's managed to successfully work out deals with other local crime figures, each getting his cut of the illegal businesses out there, of which, unfortunately, there are many. Our main concern on the Seaside PD is that he has bought a home here in Seaside, a big, window-filled mansion in the Gardens, right on the beach where he can see the lights of Atlantic City across the inlet. He wants that nice family atmosphere for his family I told you about."

"Eric." Ryan made a face. "Some family."

"He's got two younger daughters and another son, two years old. Anna is ten and Lucy is eight. His wife is a beautiful lush. I figure she drinks so heavily to escape from her marriage the only way she can."

Maureen began neatly placing the used clothes back in the suitcase. "We would be more than happy to have the means to get Jankowski out of our hair for a very long time. Seaside neither deserves nor wants him and his ilk. But he's clever. Though he's been arrested several times through the years on various charges, there has never been enough solid evidence to convict him. His clever lawyers have seen to that. Catching him with paintings this valuable would be a fine first step in bringing him down. It would also provide federal agencies with the chink in his armor they need to compile a more complete case against him because you can bet he didn't pay taxes on them."

"So how do you manage to catch him now that the wrong people—that's us—have the paintings?" Dori asked.

Once again Maureen looked uncomfortable. "We—ah, that is, the Seaside PD—would, ah, appreciate it if you—"

"Bait!" Ryan shouted. "She wants us to be bait!" He punched the air. "Yes!"

Bait. The word hung in space.

"Well, I don't know if I'd actually say *bait*," Maureen began.

"What else would you call it?" Phil asked, the edge to his voice sharp enough to cut steel. "I didn't bring you here to endanger my family."

As she watched Maureen meet Phil's angry look without blinking, Dori wondered if she was seeing the death of a relationship before it began. If so, it was very sad because Maureen was just the woman Phil needed. She knew it.

She also knew Ryan had it right. Bait. She examined the idea carefully. "You want someone to steal the suitcase from us so you can follow it to Jankowski himself."

Without breaking her staring contest with Phil, Maureen nodded, her black curls bouncing. "That's it."

"We don't have to try to prevent the theft or catch the thief?"

Maureen broke from Phil and looked at Dori, clearly appalled at the very idea. "Absolutely not! We don't want you to be endangered in any way."

Dori nodded. "Okay."

"Okay?" Maureen grinned at all of them. "Thanks!"

"Now wait a minute, Dori." Trev moved to Dori's side and placed a hand on her shoulder. "Let's think this through more carefully." He turned to Maureen. "What if we run into this thief while he's in the process of taking the case? He's not in on our we-won't-interfere plan. You could be asking Dori or Ryan or even me to put ourselves in danger."

Dori knew Trev wasn't worried about himself. She was his concern, though she didn't think she would be in any danger. Still, it felt surprisingly good that he was protective of her. And Ryan, of course.

Ryan. Trev—and by extension she—was responsible for him and his safety. How would they ever be able to explain to his grandmother if something happened as a result of their willful choice? She looked at the boy, his eyes bright, his cheeks flushed. He'd be just as likely to throw himself at the thief in order to be a hero as not.

On the other hand, how could they look Ryan in the eye if they refused to help? He might end up spending the rest of his school career bullied by Eric Jankowski, and it would be all their fault, to say nothing of the don't-get-involved message the boy would read loud and clear.

Maureen correctly read the hesitation in Dori's face. "You wouldn't have to worry," she said. "I could stay here for the duration to provide protection. I'd just be Phil's friend, visiting." She shot him a look as if daring him to challenge her. "And when I'm not here, someone would be keeping the house under surveillance to follow whoever happened to drop in uninvited."

Suddenly Phil beamed at her. "Okay."

Maureen's eyes went wide with surprise. Then she gave him a beautiful smile that brought that bemused swain look back with a vengeance.

"You just like the idea that Maureen will be here for you to visit." Trev sounded as testy as Dori had ever heard him.

Phil shrugged. "Yeah. So?"

Ryan looked at Trev, deeply distressed. "Pastor Paul, you're not thinking of saying no, are you? How can you say no? You're the pastor!"

Dori watched Trev squirm as all the things Ryan meant in his "You're the pastor" comment sank in. She laid a hand on his arm. "It'll be okay. Isn't this where you're supposed to say, 'The Lord will protect us'?"

"Tell that to all the victims of crime," he muttered.

"Good." Maureen shut and latched the suitcase. "You guys are the best. Now let's put this back where it was and settle back to see what happens."

"No," Trev said, his face set. "Not in here. Out in the hall closet."

"Fine," Maureen said. "No problem."

Ryan was practically jumping out of his skin. "Can I tell the kids after it's all over? After you catch the bad guys? Can I? Please?"

Maureen nodded. "But you have to wait until I tell you that you can talk about it. There may be legal ramifications that will put you under a gag order for a while."

"A gag order." He shook his head in delighted wonder. "Will I have to testify? Please?"

Maureen grinned at him. "That's up to the lawyers, Ry. I just catch the bad guys."

"Gotcha." He was practically vibrating with delight. "This is almost worth Grandmom falling." He saw everyone's shocked looks. "Almost, I said."

Suddenly the stuffings went out of Dori, and she sagged against the wall. It was all she could do to hold herself upright. She tried to smother a huge yawn but failed.

Trev saw. "Okay, everybody. Out. I promised Dori a nap, and I can't let her down." He smiled at her.

Phil and Maureen left immediately, Ryan trailing behind, throwing one last excited look at the suitcase. Trev reached over the pillows of his bed and pulled the covers down. Then he turned to Dori, still propping herself against the wall.

Trev walked to her. "Come on, sweetheart. Not that you need any beauty rest since you're beautiful already, but I know exhaustion when I see it."

Before she realized what he had in mind, he scooped her into his arms and carried her to the bed. Automatically her arms went around his neck to steady herself as he moved. She burrowed close. When he lowered her onto the mattress, her arms still around his neck, his face was inches from her. Silently they looked at each other. He blinked first, smiling that wonderful wry smile.

"Well, I guess this will have to do for the moment." He bent and quickly kissed her cheek. "But only for the moment."

Her cheek burned where his lips touched it. "Trev, I can't—" She didn't even know how to finish her sentence.

"I know. Just relax and sleep."

He stood and after slipping her shoes off, pulled the covers over her. She watched him walk to the door, the suitcase in his hand. He turned back. Again their eyes met and held. This time she broke the moment as the mother of all yawns exploded.

Trev laughed. "I'm going to take Ryan for a quick visit with his grandmother while you sleep. I'll make certain Phil and Maureen stay here until I get back." He blew her a kiss and shut the door.

She wanted to think about him, about her tangled emotions, but no sooner had she heard the click of the door latching than oblivion overtook her.

Twenty-Two

"THEY KNOW ABOUT the paintings." Barney Noble made the pronouncement with absolute certainty.

Joanne looked at the big man beside her. She was squeezed in the front seat of his car between him and Vinnie early Sunday evening. Barney had met her and Vinnie at her apartment after their return from Amhearst. She wasn't certain yet what she thought of Barney, but he wasn't anything like she'd imagined. The way Vinnie talked about him, she expected something like the Hulk in a very, very bad mood. Although Barney could certainly give the Hulk a run for his money sizewise, he was handsome and very pleasant, at least to her. He was also very smart.

"How do you know they know?" she whispered. She'd been watching the gray house just like he had, but all she'd seen was a man and a woman with dark, curly hair come out and take a big black dog for a walk around the block. They had just gone back inside.

Barney looked down at her and smiled. "You don't have to whisper, sugar. They can't hear you."

Joanne blushed. "Sort of stupid, huh?"

"Sort of cute," Barney corrected.

Joanne stared straight ahead even though she could feel Barney looking down at her. Had he just complimented her? She didn't have the nerve to look back at him and find out.

"But to answer your question, sugar, you saw that couple walking the dog?"

She nodded, aware of Vinnie sulking silently against the passenger door.

"He's Phil Trevelyan, the brother of Paul Trevelyan who's married to the suitcase lady."

"He lives here in Seaside too?"

Barney nodded his bald head. Joanne had never realized how much she liked bald heads before, at least on young men who made them bald on purpose. "He has the drug store at Ninth and Asbury."

"Yeah?" Joanne was impressed. "I shop there sometimes. They got great sunglasses, you know the ones with the funky frames that look so cool?" She frowned. "I never saw him there though." She gestured at the house.

"That's 'cause you're never sick, idiot," growled Vinnie. "You never have to get medicine. He gives out the drugs and stuff."

"Oh," she said in a small voice. Vinnie could make her feel so bad so quick.

Barney leaned forward and glared at Vinnie. "You will never speak to the lady like that again."

Vinnie looked startled, then angry. "Not that it's any of your business, but I'll speak to the 'lady' any way I want."

Barney reached a huge arm across the seat behind Joanne's head and gripped the back of Vinnie's neck. "I beg your pardon?" he said pleasantly, but he must have squeezed hard because Vinnie flinched and went white.

"S-sorry," he stuttered.

"Don't apologize to me. Apologize to her." Barney still spoke pleasantly, but Joanne could see why he had such a fearsome reputation. She certainly wouldn't want him squeezing her neck like that.

"S-sorry, Jo," Vinnie managed.

"That's more like it," Barney said. "Maybe there's hope for you after all." He released Vinnie's neck, but he didn't pull his arm back. Instead, he let it lie across the back of the seat, his fingers skimming the back of Joanne's neck.

Squeezing would be bad, Joanne thought again, but skimming, tickling—wow!

"Now Phil Trevelyan doesn't concern me," Barney said, all business once again except for the tickling fingers. "But the woman with him—she's another matter. She's Maureen Galloway, the latest addition to the Seaside PD. She's been in town about two weeks. Before that she worked in Camden in the juvenile unit. She got burned out dealing with the poor kids and the perverts who hurt them. I guess she figured a little town like Seaside would be a safe, quiet place to work. They're probably using her on this job because they think no one will recognize her."

"That cute lady with the black curls is a cop?" Joanne couldn't believe it.

Barney shrugged. "Sad, isn't it?"

"How do you know that?" She was fascinated that he knew such a fact.

"It's my job to know things like that," he said simply. "And see that car parked down the street in front of the white house with the green shutters?"

Joanne squinted through the darkness. "You mean the black one?"

"Good girl, sugar." Barney gave her neck a light squeeze, and goose bumps spread up and down Joanne's arms. So squeezes could be good too, in the right circumstances. "There's a cop inside."

"There is?" Joanne squinted, but she still couldn't make out a figure.

"An idiot named Fleishman."

"It's a stakeout!" Joanne couldn't believe it. It was just like TV.

Barney nodded. "They want us to take the suitcase so they can catch us with stolen goods. But there's a potentially bigger problem than the cops."

"What could be bigger than the cops?" Vinnie asked with a trace of his old swagger.

"That dog," Barney said. "I don't like to kill dogs or kids."

Joanne's heart swelled. What a great guy Barney was. "I don't like it either. It's mean, and it's not like they did anything wrong."

He nodded. "People get very upset if you hurt their pets and kids. It makes the media crazy, too. We don't want the attention. We'll have to drug him." He tapped the steering wheel in a syncopated rhythm as he talked. "Mr. Jankowski gets home from his vacation in Aruba next Sunday. We have until then to get the case."

"The paintings are worth a lot, aren't they?" Joanne found herself leaning closer and closer to Barney.

Barney's fingers stilled on her neck. "How do you know about the paintings, sugar?" Though the words were spoken in a soft voice, his whole body was on alert. She could feel it.

"Vinnie told me?" The question wasn't because she wasn't sure of her answer. It was because she wasn't sure of Barney's reaction. She knew all too well what Vinnie did when he was displeased with her. She held her breath and only relaxed when his fingers began skimming again.

Barney skewered Vinnie with a look. "You do talk too much, don't you?"

Vinnie seemed to shrink before Joanne's eyes. She knew Barney was scaring him big-time.

"Don't be mad at him." She laid a hand on Barney's thigh. "He thought that since I was courier—"

Vinnie grabbed her arm and squeezed. "Shut up, Joanne," he hissed.

Barney went very still. "You were the courier, sugar? I thought you just pulled the wrong suitcase off the belt."

Joanne closed her eyes and hunched her shoulders. Here it came, all the trouble that Vinnie had said Barney was good at making. She waited for those caressing fingers, now stilled, to grab her by the neck and shake the life out of her. She had messed up big-time, and now that Barney knew—and from her own stupid mouth!—she would have to pay. She waited for the pain. When it didn't come, she cracked her eyes open a slit.

Slowly Barney leaned past her and put his face right in Vinnie's. "*She* was the courier?" he said in a very quiet, very scary voice.

Joanne looked from man to man. Something was going on here that she didn't understand.

Vinnie nodded, his eyes wide. Joanne could feel him shaking where his leg touched hers.

"That was *your* assignment." Barney loomed over Vinnie. He loomed over Joanne too, but she wasn't scared because he was looking at Vinnie, not her. Vinnie who apparently was the one in big trouble, not her.

"I was there when Mr. Jankowski laid out your responsibilities." Barney's voice was still soft but scarier than ever. "'Go to Chicago and bring back the suitcase.' How difficult is that?"

Vinnie looked ready to be sick, and Joanne hoped he'd turn away if his stomach did heave. She didn't want him to spatter her with anything so vile. She wouldn't be getting her thousand dollars if she read the situation right, and without the money, she wasn't getting new clothes. He'd better not ruin the few she had.

"I—" Vinnie swallowed and tried again. "I can't fly."

Barney looked blank.

"I can't fly," Vinnie repeated. "I got like this phobia."

Suddenly Joanne understood. "You can't fly because you're scared? And you made me fly?" She was outraged.

"So why didn't you just drive, idiot?" Barney asked.

With a disgusted snort, Barney put the car in gear and drove back toward the center of Seaside, one hand draped casually, possessively across Joanne's lap. When he dropped Vinnie off, he snarled, "I need to make plans, and you need to be ready to do whatever I tell you, moron."

"Sure, Barney, sure," Vinnie bleated as he backed away from the car.

"And one more thing." Barney glanced down at Joanne who still sat plastered to his side, though there was now room to move away, not that she wanted to. "She's mine."

Vinnie looked startled, and that made Joanne frown. What did he think? She was chopped liver? Nobody but him could be dumb enough to like her?

"Got that?" Barney smiled at Vinnie like the shark in *Finding Nemo,* all teeth ready to bite if Vinnie made the wrong move. "Mine."

"Sure, Barney, sure." Vinnie nodded like a bobblehead doll. "All yours."

Joanne wondered if she should be insulted that Vinnie gave her up so easily, but when Barney looked at her like he was looking now, it was hard to even remember that Vinnie existed, let alone be upset by his quick giving her up.

"Mine, right, sugar?" Barney whispered just before he kissed her.

Twenty-Three

"WHAT IF GRANDMOM loses the store because she can't pay rent because she's not making any money?" A woebegone Ryan sat at the dinner table Sunday evening after his visit with his grandmother. "She's had such a hard life, and the store is her special project, the good thing she does. She can't lose it!"

His head was propped on one hand while he played with his spaghetti with the other. "And what if we lose the apartment because we can't pay rent? Where will we live? There's no family but us." He didn't even mention his mother as a possible source of help, which saddened Dori immensely.

"Don't worry so, Ry," Trev said as he twirled a forkful of spaghetti. "The church will never let you be homeless, and we'll do all we can to make sure Mae doesn't lose the store. The elders and I have already talked about it, and Mr. Warrington has pledged to make up any difference the congregation can't meet."

Ryan wasn't impressed with the assurances. "Like that will happen. Mr. Warrington is real mad at you right now because of Angie."

"Maybe," Trev said, "but he won't take his anger at me out on you. He likes to help people."

"When it helps him or makes him look good,"

Ryan said cynically. "But if helping us was your idea to begin with, we're in deep trouble."

Dori looked at Trev who didn't bother to refute Ryan's comment. "I take it Jonathan is fairly well off?"

"*Rich* is the word, I believe."

Ryan nodded. "He owns half the businesses on the boardwalk as well as his car dealership."

"An exaggeration, but only slightly." Trev dumped more salt on his pasta. "Got to keep my blood pressure up," he said when he saw Dori's raised eyebrow.

Ryan stirred his spaghetti around and around his plate. "If I was older, I'd quit school and take care of things myself." He sighed. "I hate thirteen!"

"You know you couldn't quit school even if you were older," Trev said. "Mae'd never allow it."

Ryan made a face and stuffed much too much spaghetti into his mouth. Utterly dejected, he chewed for a moment. Suddenly he sat up and looked at Dori.

"You ran a gift shop, didn't you?" he asked around his mouthful of food. It sounded more like, "Uo ra a gi sha, din ou?"

Dori put her hands up, palms out to ward off the suggestion, and shook her head. Her life was already too complicated.

"Why not?" He looked at her slyly. "You could be the heroine and save my grandmother from all kinds of financial calamity."

"Please don't ask me, Ry." Though what else she was going to do with her time she didn't know.

"I think it's a great idea," Trev said. "It'll give you something to do that you enjoy and know. And by the way, these are great meatballs."

She glared at him. "A gift shop and a bookstore are vastly different. Thanks. Four eggs for every pound of hamburger."

"Four eggs?" Trev shrugged. "And retail is retail, right?"

And ignorance is ignorance, she thought but managed not to say.

"Please think about it," Ryan said. "Please, please." A basset hound couldn't have looked any sadder or needier.

That night Dori stared at the ceiling of Trev's room, talking to herself about why she shouldn't take on the bookstore. The main reason for not getting involved was that it would become another link in the chain binding her to Seaside, a chain whose weight was already pulling her under.

But what if Ryan was right, and Mae would lose her store? What would happen to her and Ryan then? But why was saving them *her* responsibility? Trev said the church was going to help. Wasn't that one of the reasons for churches—to help people?

She finally fell into a restless sleep and woke on Monday feeling groggy and disoriented. The day passed slowly for her with Ryan in school and Trev at work. She wandered the house, making little adjustments here and there, noting things that needed to be bought like decent sheets and colorful towels to replace the mud brown ones.

She read for a while, did the crossword in *The Philadelphia Inquirer,* and eyed the weights a few seconds before sanity returned. She even put on her new black down coat and red beret and took Jack for a walk. She did not think about working at the bookstore, at least not much.

"Bet you haven't had a bath in all the years he's had you," she said to the dog as they entered the house after their walk. She hung up her coat, then led him to the bathtub. She lifted his front legs into the tub, then scooted his hindquarters in. He stood there cooperatively, but he obviously had no idea what she was doing. When she leaned in to turn the spigot, he kissed her lavishly. She sputtered and laughed and gave him a hug.

"You are a wonderful dog. Just don't tell Trev or Trudy I said so."

He grinned compliance.

She turned on the water and Jack promptly began drinking. As he drank, she played with the temperature until she felt it was right. Then she dropped the stopper.

As the water rose up his legs, Jack looked nonplussed. Still, he stayed put. He was, after all, a water dog. When she began pouring water over him, he gave her a woeful look, but when she began shampooing him, he seemed to take it as a great scratching. He turned glassy eyed with pleasure. She rinsed him, crooning to him about what a good boy he was. He gave her a slurp from chin to hairline.

She released the water, and he jumped out. Before she had a

chance to duck, he shook, sending thousands of tiny water drops flying around the bathroom. Dori was convinced that an abnormal percentage somehow found her. Still it was worth it. He smelled like Pert and felt soft to the touch.

Just then the phone rang. She ran, dripping, into the bedroom to answer. It might be Meg, or it might be something about her suitcase. "Hello?"

"I need to make a visit," Trev said without preamble.

If she didn't know better, Dori would have thought he sounded nervous, but Trev was never nervous. "Okay." Why he was telling her she wasn't sure. Did he think he needed to report in any time he left the office? Or get her permission?

He cleared his throat, that special little click. He was nervous! "Would you go with me?"

"Me?" Her voice squeaked. Now *she* was nervous, and being bored suddenly looked a lot better than it had a half hour ago. "Why?" Did he want her to go visit a dying person? Or a shut-in? Certainly he wouldn't take her to visit Barry the Flasher, though that would be a visit worth the time. She was very curious about him.

"I have to go visit Shannon Warrington, and I don't want to go alone for several reasons. I know it's an awful lot to ask of you since you've never even met the woman, but please come along?"

Bob Warrington's abandoned wife. Jonathan and Judy's daughter-in-law. Angie's sister-in-law. If anyone needed an extra friend after life with that bunch, it would be Shannon.

"Sure, I'll go."

"Thanks, Dori."

The relief in his voice made her glad she'd said yes, though she wasn't sure what kind of help she could be. One thing was for certain. She understood everything that Shannon was feeling. Watching your marriage disintegrate was agony in the extreme.

"I'll be home for you in about ten minutes."

Good. Time enough to towel Jack a bit and still change out of her wet clothes.

She was ready when Trev walked into the house and looked at his still moist dog. "Did Dori take you for a walk on the beach, big guy? Have you been in the ocean?"

Jack wiggled with joy at having him home, even if only for a few minutes. Trev reached to pet him and froze. "He smells like a perfume factory."

"He smells wonderful," Dori corrected. "And he's so pretty and clean, aren't you, boy?" She crooned the last at him and he wiggled his way to her. "You smell beautiful, and don't let the mean man tell you differently."

"Yeah, Jack. You're beautiful."

She laughed at Trev's sarcasm and pulled her coat from the closet.

"Say," he said. "I have a turtleneck just that same color."

She looked down at the crimson shirt with the cuffs rolled up three times. "Not anymore."

Trev sighed as he followed her to the car. "First you wash my dog, then you steal my clothes. What next?"

She grinned at him. "Be afraid. Be very afraid."

Shannon Warrington lived bayside in a large new house with lots of glass, an immense screened back porch looking over the marshes and bay, and a dock at the edge of the lawn. Dori could only imagine the size of the Warrington boat hibernating for the winter in some nearby marina.

"Bob and Shannon must be doing pretty well for themselves." Dori eyed the rest of the neighborhood full of oversized but beautiful homes, all with backyard docks. "Or else they're in hock to their ears."

"He sells cars," Trev said as he rang the doorbell. "Lots of cars. Shannon hasn't worked since the kids came along."

The front door opened a crack, and Dori saw a little girl with two lopsided ponytails sticking out on either side of her head and a one-eyed blue teddy bear tucked under her arm. Even though it was almost two in the afternoon, she wore a frilly cotton nightie with Cinderella, Jacques, and Gus-Gus on the front. She was a skinny mite who didn't look tall enough or strong enough to handle a huge front door.

"Hi. I'm Serena. I'm three. Who are you?"

"Hi, Serena. I'm Pastor Paul and this is Dori. Remember me?"

Serena squinted at him. "Nope."

Dori smothered a smile.

Trev tried again. "Is your mom home?"

"Sure. Her's sleeping on the sofa. Come on in." She turned and ran. "Mommy! There's a man and a lady here."

Hoping the child didn't invite all unknown adults in, Dori pushed the door open, then entered, Trev right behind her. She heard a baby crying off in another room. When Serena came dancing back, Dori asked, "Is that your brother crying? Is he all right?"

Serena nodded, completely unconcerned. "That's Jonny. He always cries. He's got colic bad. He's named after Grandpop Jonathan."

A chubby woman with pasty skin and red eyes padded into the foyer. She wore old, faded navy sweat pants and a spotted red sweatshirt that read SEASIDE, NJ in navy stitchery. Seashells and a breaking wave backed the words. Its sleeves, which ended inches above her wrist bone, were badly frayed. On her feet were white socks fast losing their white.

Dori saw a woman who had probably once been cute but who had lost her vitality. She looked—hollow. Her hair needed a good shampooing, and the circles under her eyes evidenced sleepless nights. Dori wanted to hug her, to tell her it would be all right, but she knew there was a good chance it wouldn't.

"Pastor," Shannon whispered, her hand going to her uncombed hair and pushing it back from her face. "I'm sorry I wasn't at church yesterday. I was afraid I'd see—" Her chin trembled, and she brought her hand up to still it. A lone tear slid down her cheek.

"Mommy's crying," Serena announced. Her little face scrunched up.

Quickly Dori knelt in front of the girl. "Don't you cry too, honey. We have to be brave for Mommy, okay?"

Serena looked at her for a minute, and it was touch and go on the tears. Then the little girl gave a brisk nod. "Brave."

Dori smiled at her. "Good girl."

"Let's sit down, Shannon," Trev suggested.

Shannon nodded wearily. "Serena, honey, why don't you go watch a video?"

"The mermaid," Serena said.

Shannon nodded and turned toward the back of the house. "I have to set it up for her. I'll be right back."

Serena danced after her mother, then danced back. "I'm going to be Ariel when I grow up. That's 'cause mermaids get to swim all over the world." She grinned, then turned and ran from the room.

"How could anyone leave a charmer like that?" Dori asked as they walked into the living room. It was full of elegant beige and white furniture, totally unsuitable for a young family as evidenced by the grape juice stain on one of the beige chairs and a smudge on the pale carpet. A cream chenille throw lay crumpled on the floor beside the cream and beige striped sofa.

They sat in silence as they waited for Shannon. When she walked in, her shoulders were slumped and her steps dragged. She collapsed onto the sofa and pulled the chenille throw onto her lap like a security blanket.

"I went to the grocery store this morning," she said. "They wouldn't accept my debit card. They said there was no money in the account." She gave a great, heaving sob. "Bob said he'd put some money back. He promised."

Trev pulled out an envelope and handed it to Shannon. "Here's a gift card to the grocery store for a hundred dollars. It'll get you through the next few days."

Shannon took it in a shaking hand. "Thanks," she whispered, obviously embarrassed to take charity. She wrapped her arms about herself and began to rock. "I can't believe this is happening to me. I just can't believe it. I thought we were so happy."

Dori felt her own heart being ripped open with empathetic pain.

"Have you spoken with Brewster Robbins yet?" Trev asked.

"I don't want to go to a lawyer." Shannon's voice was suddenly stronger. "I don't want a divorce. I want Bob to come back!"

Why she'd want a rat of a man who had left her and their kids, taken all their money with him, and moved in with his girlfriend was more than Dori could understand. She sure wouldn't want him.

"I hope you can reconcile too, Shannon," Trev said. "Brewster will just protect you and the kids. He'll see that things like an empty account get fixed and real quick. He knows what buttons to push to get Bob to assume his legal responsibilities. He's a

Christian too, Shannon, and he hates divorce as much as you and I do. He won't push you in that direction, I promise. Please call him."

"I can't afford him." She sniffed, then ran the back of her wrist under her nose.

Trev shook his head. "Money's not an issue. Brewster has made helping women in circumstances like yours his special ministry."

Serena danced into the room, a bag of potato chips in her hand. "Can I have some, Mommy? I'm hungry."

"Sure, baby. Why not?"

Serena grinned, revealing a mouthful of chip crumbs. Her request was obviously a case of better late than never. Dragging the bag behind her, she danced away.

"I usually give her fruit and cheese and good things to eat," Shannon said helplessly as she watched her daughter disappear. "Chips and junk food of all kinds were Bob's favorites. But—" She waved her hand vaguely.

Dori knew. No money, no more good stuff.

Trev captured Shannon's waving hand. He held it in both of his. "Lord, Shannon needs You to wrap Your loving arms around her and hold her tight. Be real to her, Father, and comfort her. Be her husband and a father for Serena and Jonny. And, Lord, break into Bob's heart and bring him home."

Dori knew he no more expected that miracle than she did.

On Tuesday boredom hung heavily once again, and Ryan's *please, please* kept ringing in Dori's ears as she rearranged the kitchen to suit her preferences. When she called Mae early in the afternoon, it was most assuredly not to talk about the store but to introduce herself since she was now living with Ryan and Trev. However when Mae talked about the store, Dori listened carefully.

"At least I was smart enough to fall after Christmas," Mae said. "Otherwise I'd be really, really worried. Now I have the luxury of being just plain worried."

Dori decided she liked the woman's attitude even as she

thought of Small Treasures. While it was a sound little store, it wouldn't take much of a forced closing to put them in financial difficulty. Bills like rent, electricity, and insurance continued whether income did or not.

Mae sighed. "It's not that winter is such a great season in a resort town like Seaside, but I do have my regulars. And it's my planning time for what's to come. I also get orders through our web page, and no one's filling them."

"You have a web page?" Dori wouldn't have expected a fifty-something proprietor of a small bookstore to have one, which she was certain said something about an age prejudice she hadn't realized she had. After all, Meg had a Small Treasures web page.

Mae gave a burst of laughter. "I've got Ryan. How could it be otherwise?"

Dori grinned. "Point taken."

When Randy and his friend Sam showed up late Tuesday afternoon with Dori's car full of her clothes, treasures, plants, and most important, Trudy, Dori was still not willing to admit her growing compulsion to work at Harbor Lights. She was only too happy to dwell on her dog and her things, familiar and comfortable in a way her new life wasn't.

"You'll stay for dinner, won't you?" she asked Randy and Sam who, all bleary-eyed and bristly jawed, looked like they had driven straight through from California.

"Can't," Randy said. "We want to get to New York today so we can get a decent night's sleep before the new job tomorrow." He gave her a kiss on the cheek. "Thanks though. I'm just sorry I don't have time to wait and meet the husband. Mom's dying to know what he's like."

Dori stood in the living room with Trudy dancing around her feet. "I'm sorry you won't get to meet him too. You'd like him and Ryan."

"Who's Ryan?"

"A kid from Trev's church who's living with him—with us—while his grandmother's in rehab for a bad fall."

Randy grinned. "You've got a kid living with you? How old?"

"Thirteen."

Randy started to laugh. "Only you, Dor," he said setting the last box of her things down. "A husband you haven't seen for six years and a thirteen-year-old in residence to watch the reunion."

"It's not that funny," Dori said as his hoots filled the room, but she had to laugh too. How had her life become such a soap opera?

She followed Randy out to the car, snuggling Trudy under her black coat, the dog's fluffy head peeking out under Dori's chin. As she nuzzled Trudy's ear, a school bus stopped at the end of the street, and a slight figure in an oversized Eagles coat climbed off.

"Ryan?" Randy asked.

"Ryan," Dori confirmed. She waved. Ryan didn't wave back.

When he got closer, she could see his glasses weren't sitting on his nose right. When he reached her, she saw one bow was missing. From his stormy face, the story of what happened wasn't good.

"What's that?" Ryan asked abruptly as he eyed Trudy, all fluffy light topknot and panting pink tongue.

"This is Trudy." At her name, Trudy turned and kissed Dori under the chin.

"What is she?"

"She's a Dandie Dinmont terrier."

Ryan frowned. "What does Jack think of her?"

"Jack hasn't met her yet. I put him in your bedroom for the time being."

"He'll eat her for lunch." His tone said it was nothing less than the little puffball deserved.

Trudy leaned toward Ryan, her little feet scrambling for traction inside Dori's coat. She managed to climb out, teetering for a moment on the V of Dori's coat. Then she launched herself at Ryan. She hit the front of his slick coat, surprising him completely, and began a quick slide to the ground. Dori made a little yelp and reached for the dog, but Ryan was faster. He grabbed Trudy just as she slid off the bottom of the coat and, pulling her to him, cradled her in his arms.

Trudy reacted with a happy little bark and a dainty slurp of a kiss. Just like that Ryan was smitten. He slipped her inside his coat and held her close while they said good-bye to Randy and Sam.

Just before he climbed into the driver's seat of Dori's rental, which he was going to return in New York, Randy took Dori by the arms and looked at her with concern. "Are you okay, Dor? Are you going to be happy?"

"Of course she's happy," Ryan answered for her, and she was glad. She didn't know what her true answer was. "She lives with two great guys, and she's running my grandmother's bookstore."

Randy brightened. "You got a job?" For some reason Dori couldn't fathom, that seemed to satisfy him about her welfare. It must be that jobs were some kind of guy sign of happiness. At any rate, he pulled her into his arms for an exuberant hug, gave her a kiss on her cheek which she returned, climbed in the car, and drove off, leaving her waving on the curb.

She turned to see Ryan and Trudy frowning at her. "What?"

"He kissed you," Ry accused. "And you kissed him back."

"He's an old friend." She held out her arms to Trudy who came only after bathing Ryan's face and sending his glasses flying. "Friends sometimes kiss good-bye."

Ryan bent and picked up his glasses. "Well, I won't tell Pastor Paul if you work at the bookstore."

"That, sir, is called blackmail." She buried her face in Trudy's soft fur. "Come on. Let's get you something to eat and drink."

"Who are you talking to?" Ryan demanded. "Me or the dog?"

"Are you hungry or thirsty?" she asked.

He nodded.

"Then I'm talking to you."

She led the way inside and to the kitchen, which smelled strongly of pot roast overlaid with brownies. Ryan let his coat slip to the floor and dropped into a chair at the table. Dori cut a large piece of the brownies and put it and a glass of cold milk on the table.

"Enjoy." She sat at the table across from him. He shot her an angry look, then proceeded to inhale the food and drink. When he finished he swiped the back of his hand across his mouth and slouched in the chair. Dori swallowed the urge to say, "Ever heard of napkins?"

"You must have had a very bad day," she said instead, taking her clue from the fact that he hadn't bolted from the room. He wanted to talk.

He glowered at her, then pulled off his glasses and held them out. "Eric Jankowski."

The crime boss's son. "He broke your glasses?"

"Grabbed them right off my nose, dropped them on the floor, and stepped on them."

"Oh, Ryan." Humiliation was hard to take at any age, but especially at thirteen. She cast around for something, anything she could think of that would help him feel good again. "Why?"

"Bullies don't need reasons." He looked at her with a faint smile. "But he did have one this time."

This time. Dori's heart contracted, and she turned away so he wouldn't see the pity in her eyes. How could she help him feel better about himself? The kid was such a wonderful, funny, smart guy, but he didn't realize it. She remembered all the encouragement Pop and Honey had given her and how it had helped her through the dark days of junior high. Certainly there was something she could do for Ryan. Her glance rested on the weight bench in the dining room. *Ca-ching!*

"In gym I made a last minute basket that made his team lose." There was pride in his voice.

Dori laughed and high-fived him. "Way to go, Ryan. I didn't know basketball was your game."

"It isn't. Nothing's my game. I hate team sports, even though Pastor Paul and I shoot baskets over at the park on Thirty-fourth Street sometimes." He snorted. "Today was luck, pure and simple. I was only playing for the last five minutes of the game because Mr. Kline makes everyone play. Eric was guarding me, which is sort of like Goliath guarding David. He was bumping me, elbowing me, and I knew he was just waiting for Mr. Kline to look away before administering real pain."

He made a face. "I don't like pain. I threw the ball in a panic before he could get me. When it went through the hoop, I knew I was dead."

Dori held out her hand for the glasses. "Let me see. Maybe I can fix it with a toothpick to hold things together. You do have the broken bow, don't you?"

Ryan reached in his pocket and pulled it out. "A toothpick

won't do it. It didn't just come apart at the hinge. He actually broke the hinge. The only good thing is that I think he wanted to break the lenses. He was getting ready to stomp again when Mr. Kline walked over."

Dori looked at the unrepairable glasses. "Is your optometrist nearby?"

"Just off island."

"We'll make arrangements to run over tomorrow."

He sighed. "You know, between Grandmom and Eric, this is turning out to be the worst year of my life."

Been there, kiddo. I know all about worst years. "I talked to your grandmother today. She's a nice lady. Funny."

Ryan didn't even react.

"She told me all about the store."

He turned toward her, his face still downcast, but she thought she saw a spark of interest in his eyes.

Forcing a smile, Dori spoke the inevitable. "I'm going in tomorrow morning to see what I can do to help her out."

Ryan turned away quickly, but not before she saw the tears he wanted to hide. "Thanks," he said, his voice thick. "I have to go change." He grabbed his backpack and started for the stairs.

"Before you go, I've got a question for you."

He didn't look at her, but he also didn't run from the room.

"Do you know how to use the weights in the dining room?"

"Dining room? That's the weight room. Just ask Pastor Paul." He turned. "Sure I do. He's been coaching me."

"Is it hard?"

He looked at her, and she knew she'd asked a girl question. He raised his hands over his head, his fists closed around an imaginary bar. "You just lift what you can."

"Do you enjoy it?"

"Yeah, sort of. It's not a team sport, so there are no Erics to make my life miserable. I only compete against myself."

Dori followed him to the doorway where they both stood looking at the bench, the bar, and all the weighted disks.

"Show me, then help me?" Dori asked.

"You want to lift weights?" Ryan looked disbelieving.

"Don't you dare do that girls-keep-house and boys-lift-weights thing, kiddo."

"Nah, I know girls lift weights. I just didn't know you wanted to look like the babes in the weight magazines with muscles all over."

"You don't go for that look?" she asked as he took off one of the large disks and managed to keep it from slamming to the floor. He rolled it aside and replaced it with a much smaller one. He did the same on the other side. Then he lay on his back and slid under the bar, which rested on supports several inches above him. He wrapped his hands tightly around the bar and lifted. He raised and lowered the weights several times. Dori noticed that his arms were beginning to shake.

"Now let me try," she ordered.

The bar clanged into its resting spot, and Ryan slid out from under. Dori lay on the bench and positioned herself under the bar. She clutched it.

"Wait!" Ryan positioned both her and her hands. "If you're not positioned right or if your hands are too close together, you'll hurt yourself and lose lifting power."

"Gotcha," Dori said. "So I'm good to go now?"

He nodded.

"You're a good coach."

He looked at her with one raised eyebrow. Whoops. Mustn't lay it on too thick. The kid was too smart to fall for overblown flattery. Grinning at him, she pushed the weights up, surprised at how heavy they felt for how little they looked. No wonder she couldn't move the big ones when she tried the other day. She began to perspire, and her bangs stuck to her forehead.

"You know, girls don't have the upper body strength of boys."

"So I've heard." And after this little exercise, she believed it. "Thanks for the encouragement." She forced herself to concentrate and lifted the bar again.

"Come on, Dori." Ryan clapped his hands. "You can do it. Just straighten those elbows!" He clapped again. "In case you don't realize it, I'm encouraging you."

"These things are heavy!"

"That's the whole idea," he said, making a strange gurgling sound. "That's why they're called weights."

"Are you laughing at me?" she asked as she let the bar clang home. She looked at him and was delighted to see a huge grin at her expense. Grunting, she forced the weights up again. Her arms were beginning to shake.

"I'd never laugh at you," he said and began to laugh.

She let the bar crash home again and glared at him.

"I'm not laughing at you," Ryan choked out. "It's him. You should see his expression!"

Dori twisted and saw Trev standing in the other doorway, amazement writ large across his face. At that moment Trudy, who had been pacing in agitation at this new and unnerving activity in this new and unnerving place, rushed to her, jumped onto the bench, and climbed onto her chest, stepping on all Dori's tender places in the process. She began to lick Dori's wet face.

"That's Trudy," Ryan informed Trev. "She likes me."

"She's a beige powder puff with no legs," Trev said as he came into the room.

"Hey, buster." Dori pushed herself to a sitting position, no easy task with the bar and the animal impeding movements. "Speak no unkind words about my baby." She cuddled Trudy in her lap.

Trev dropped down on the bench beside Dori and began tousling Trudy's topknot. Trudy immediately abandoned Dori for this new person.

"She's a little licking machine," Ryan warned as Trudy went up on her hind legs, braced her front legs on Trev's chest, and greeted him wetly.

"Nothing like being welcomed home with a kiss," Trev said and leaned to Dori. She didn't even hesitate. She turned her face to his and met his kiss.

"Come on, Trudy," Ryan yelled. "Time to leave them alone!" He grabbed his backpack and fled upstairs, Trudy at his heels.

Dori leaped to her feet. "Jack!" She rushed after Ryan, Trev right behind her.

"What's wrong with Jack?" he called.

"You'll see."

They hit the top of the stairs just as Ryan opened his bedroom door, and Jack dashed out. Trudy saw what she thought was an attacking giant and went into confrontation mode. Jack saw a snarling beige fur ball who raced under his belly, yipping and nipping. It was hard to tell who was the most dismayed, the big black dog who rightly understood that his home was no longer his domain or the little fluffy dog who had never had to share her position as Princess Trudy with another. All night they eyed each other with distrust, Trudy from her throne on Dori's lap, Jack from his seat at Trev's feet.

Because Trudy loved Ryan from the moment she saw him and didn't hesitate to show it by rubbing against his legs or pawing him for attention, the boy was torn. Every time he patted Trudy, he rushed to pat Jack.

"Don't worry, boy. I still love you best," he'd say as he threw his arms around the dog's neck.

Jack looked at him with sad eyes and gave him a slobbery kiss.

Then Trudy struck again, pawing Ryan as she pranced on her back legs.

It wasn't even nine o'clock when Ryan said, "I can't handle this anymore. I'm going to bed."

Dori and Trev looked at each other and smiled, sharing the humor in Ryan's dog dilemma like two people who knew each other well. Once again Dori marveled at how her husband was exactly the same and yet completely different from the young man she'd deserted.

"By the way," Trev said as Ryan's door slammed shut, "I'll be away overnight Friday."

"Overnight?" Visions of the black suitcase being spirited away by a dark figure who wreaked havoc upon her and Ryan rose in Dori's mind.

"I'm sorry," Trev said. "Lousy timing, I know, but I've been committed to this conference for several months now."

"We'll be all right," Dori said, trying to convince herself as much as Trev.

He studied her for a minute, and she tried to exude confidence. She didn't like the idea of being here with only Ryan for company, but at least she wouldn't have to struggle with the distressing confusion that came each night as she watched Trev go to his office to sleep while she went to his bed to stare into the night.

"I'll just cancel," Trev said as enthusiastically as a boy turning down a new video game. "I don't have to go."

"Sure you do," she said. "I bet you've been looking forward to it. Ryan and I will be fine. After all, we've got Jack and Trudy, and maybe Maureen can come and spend the night. Besides, the suitcase will probably be gone by then anyway. In fact, I'm surprised it's still here."

"Me, too. I thought they'd grab it the first night."

"Well, the house will be empty all day tomorrow, so that would be a good time for them to strike. In fact, I should write a note, a large one, and stick it on the front door. HOUSE EMPTY. COME AND GET IT."

Trev laughed. "Where are you going tomorrow?"

Feeling very self-conscious, Dori said, "Harbor Lights."

Trev straightened in his chair, reached across the distance to the sofa and captured her hand. "Dori Trevelyan, you are a very nice woman."

Feeling selfish to the bone because she didn't really want to go but felt she had no choice, Dori flushed.

"Lord, thanks for Dori's willingness to help Mae. Bless her for her kindness."

Guilt made her sharp. "For Pete's sake, Trev, do you pray about everything?"

"I try to," he said without embarrassment.

His expression as he looked at her was warm and loving. It scared her because of the deep yearning it aroused in her. "I think I'll go to bed so I'm in good shape for tomorrow," she blurted.

Trev stood and pulled her to her feet, dislodging an unhappy Trudy. He continued to pull until she was in his arms. They both ignored the complaining Trudy yapping at their ankles.

"Did you know that I came to California to get you not long after you left?" he asked suddenly.

She blinked. "What? When? How come I never knew?"

"I got tired of you never answering my e-mail or talking to me on the phone. I flew out with Pop's words ringing in my ears. He told me in no uncertain terms that if you were happy, I wasn't to bother you."

"And you thought I was happy?"

"You were moving into an apartment that day. You had who I know now were Meg and her family helping you. Then all I saw were three handsome guys fetching and carrying for you, and you were laughing and having such a good time. Meg and her husband appeared, and you all went off to a picnic in some park after the moving was finished. You played Frisbee, and the biggest of the guys kept hugging you."

Dori remembered that day clearly. She had been filled with overwhelming grief because the move made the break with Trev seem that much more final. As a result she had forced manic laughter so she wouldn't dissolve into tears. Young Ron Reynolds had understood and hugged her to comfort her, each time bringing her closer to tears with his kindness.

And Trev had been there, watching.

"I was so jealous," Trev said, voice thick. "There you were, so happy without me, with them. How could I compete with all that joy after I had broken your heart?"

"Oh, Trev." Her own voice was thick as she laid her cheek on his shoulder. "That was one of the saddest days of my life."

"Yeah?"

She gave a teary nod. "It was too much my new life." *Without you.*

He put a hand under her chin and lifted her face to his. "I love you, Dori. I've never stopped loving you." And he kissed her.

Dori's heart pounded and her senses swam. This was Trev, her Trev, and he loved her. She returned the kiss. Surely she could forgive him for all that had happened. After all, it was only that one time.

Wasn't it? What if it wasn't? Well, he had certainly changed now, hadn't he? He was a Christian, a pastor. He prayed at the drop of a hat, for Pete's sake. Couldn't she find it in herself to forgive him, to let go of the hurt and bitterness? She felt angry with herself. Why was forgiveness, the letting go of old hurts, so hard for her?

He must have felt the difference in her as the doubts once

more sliced through her. He pulled back. With his wry smile he looked at her.

"Go to bed, Dori. Tomorrow will come soon." He turned to Jack. "Come on, fellow. Let's walk around the block."

And he left her.

Twenty-Four

*D*ORI SLID THE KEY into the front door of Harbor Lights at seven-thirty Wednesday morning. She pushed the door open, happy to step inside and out of the damp, penetrating cold of the late January morning. The store, musty and shut up, dank and chill as it was, didn't feel all that much better.

She kept her coat on as she searched for and found a thermostat. It was set at fifty-five. No wonder it felt nasty in here. She pushed it to seventy-two, wishing for the sunny warmth of San Diego in spite of the warm red fleece top Trev had bought her as a surprise and which she wore under her parka.

She wandered around the store as she waited for it to heat. She remembered how Small Treasures had caught her from the moment she looked in the window. She waited for Harbor Lights to grab her the same way. It didn't. In fact, the store made her shake her head in dismay.

Mae Harper might have the finest inventory in the Christian book business, but you'd never know it. In spite of her wonderful attitude and her genius of a grandson, she had no sense of how to display items to their advantage, no sense of making the store anything but utilitarian.

Beautifully framed pictures sat in bins while the

walls sported advertising posters for books and records, many old, many curling at the edges. Books were crammed on shelves, all spine out, arranged by some system that Dori couldn't immediately grasp. If she couldn't figure it out, she guessed that most customers couldn't either. Music tapes and CDs were crammed into a small area just outside the store bathroom. There was no way to preview the music before you bought, and the artists were arranged alphabetically, regardless of type of music.

The cash register and computer sat on a counter by the front door surrounded by so many little novelties—stickers, pencils reading Jesus Loves Me in gold, VeggieTales erasers, flyers for long-past events, a jar of Testamints, and wallet-sized laminated cards with a calendar on one side and the prayer of Jabez on the other—there was virtually no space left to lay a purchase down. A long dead grape ivy hung above the counter while its fallen, crisp leaves spread over everything below it in a brown, crackling carpet.

She sighed as she hung her coat in the small back room. How she yearned for Small Treasures, for Meg's friendly and efficient presence. Straightening her shoulders, she gathered the stack of mail that lay on Mae's desk. Several boxes bearing publishers labels or gift company return addresses were stacked against one office wall. Clearly someone had come in once in a while and gathered the mail and the shipments, probably the girl who worked part-time for Mae. Dori knew she had a key.

Last night while Trev walked Jack, Dori had called Mae from the bedside phone, hoping she wasn't calling too late. Mae answered, wide awake and delighted to talk some more about Harbor Lights. When Dori volunteered to open the store and try to keep things running, Mae was ecstatic.

"I've been praying about this, Dori, dear."

Great, Dori thought as she listened with half an ear for Trev's return. *Another pray-er. Just what I need.*

"I can't tell you what a relief it is to have you take over. The girl who works for me volunteered, but she's going to college. She just wouldn't have time to do everything, and I don't think she has the experience. But with your retail background, you are just what the Lord ordered."

Yeah, right. "Do you think she'd be willing to come in and help me?" Dori asked as she absently petted Trudy, snuggled down on the duvet beside her.

"I don't know why not," Mae said. "I'll call her and ask if she can drop in tomorrow. What time?"

Dori heard the front door close and knew she was no longer the only adult in the house. It wasn't until she felt the tension draining away that she realized how anxious she had been. Friday night was going to be very long and very stressful.

Jack's toenails clicked on the stairs as he came up to spend the night with Ryan. At the sound, Trudy's ears perked up, and she looked at Dori who shook her head. Trudy sighed and lay back down.

"Tell her to come in anytime," Dori said, listening for Trev to come upstairs. "I plan to be there all day."

"Will do," Mae assured her. "Oh, one big thing that needs addressing right away is contacting all the local churches about their Sunday school material for the next quarter. Put that at the top of your list," Mae insisted. "All the records of previous sales of that type are in the computer as are the contact people at the various places. At Seaside Chapel it's Judy Warrington."

Angie's mom. Wouldn't you just know.

"And I'm afraid Christmas things are still out. They need to go away, and spring or Easter books, music and gift items need to be brought out."

So here Dori was, still shivering slightly as she spent an hour opening mail and sorting it into three piles: urgent, pressing, junk. She'd have to call Mae to be certain she had it all right, then run to Mae's rehab to get checks written and signed to cover all the bills. She couldn't go tonight because of the party at church for her and Trev. She gave a slight shudder at the thought of it. Maybe tomorrow over lunch.

Next she went to the file cabinet to check when the last pink sheet had been run. January 3. Mae had fallen January 4. No pink sheet for that date. The record of transactions was still locked in the computer. Dori glanced at the bottom lines on the January 3 pink sheet. The figures of product sold and money received were off by thirteen cents. Not bad for a day's totals, and hopefully not an omen. *At least*, she thought, *it isn't 666.*

Don't be an idiot, she chided herself. *This is a Christian book-store. No omens here. Besides, Trev prayed for me this morning.*

Her heart warmed a little at the memory. She had been stand-ing by the closet explaining to Jack why he wasn't allowed to eat Trudy while they were all gone. Jack hadn't looked convinced, but Dori wasn't worried. Trudy was safe in her crate in Dori's room. Trev walked to her, took her hand, and pulled her to him. When he bowed his head, she automatically did the same.

"Lord, be with Dori today as she goes to Harbor Lights. Help her as she tries to sort things out. Use her experience at Small Treasures, and bless her for helping Mae."

She felt his arm go around her waist and pull her closer.

"And Lord, please repair our marriage for Your glory." His voice was soft and urgent.

At that moment, just in time to keep her from leaning against Trev, Ryan came tearing down the stairs. Trev didn't miss a beat but merely raised his voice.

"And, Lord, be with Ry today. Keep him safe from predators like Eric, and work a miracle on his behalf. Help him to actually enjoy school."

They'd all left the house smiling, though Ryan's smile was more sarcastic than happy.

Now she went to the computer and turned it on. Harbor Lights used different software than Small Treasures, but hopefully with a bit of study, she'd get the hang of it.

At nine-thirty she unlocked the front door and put the OPEN sign in the window. Then she went to work on the easiest and most obvious need, cleaning and reorganizing the inventory so it invited anyone who stepped inside to browse and hopefully buy more than originally intended.

She began with the checkout counter, tossing the old flyers and collecting all the little items to place elsewhere, though at the moment she wasn't certain where *elsewhere* was going to be. She looked at the plain white plastic bags behind the counter and made the first of many notes: *Is there a Harbor Lights logo? Design one? Print it on bags.*

In the music department she pulled all the Christmas music. In the gift area she put away the Advent wreaths and the ceramic

Christmas trees. In the fiction area she pulled multiples of the same title to make room for turning as many books face out as she could. Since she was no more familiar with Christian fiction than she was with Christian music, she made her face-out selections based on the covers that appealed to her.

She was staring at the Christian living, psychology, and theology sections with panic when the bell over the door jangled. With a feeling of great relief, she went to meet her first customer.

After just a few steps she jolted to a halt. "Angie!"

Angie froze in the middle of taking her coat off. "What are *you* doing here?"

"I'm helping Mae out by keeping the store open. Uh, can I help you?"

"You're who's going to save the store?" Angie was incredulous.

"Well, I don't know about save the store, but—"

"She turns down my help and accepts yours. Isn't that just another perfect slap?"

Dori felt her stomach flip. "Are you the girl who works for Mae part-time?"

"I'm the girl who works for *Mae* part-time," she spit as she shrugged back into her coat. *"Mae."*

A loud and completely unconvincing cough sounded from the front of the store. Dori hurried forward, aware that sniping employees were very bad for business anywhere, but it must seem especially bad in a Christian bookstore.

Standing uncertainly inside the door was a delivery woman from Seaside Flowers, two carefully wrapped bouquets in her hands. "Dori Trevelyan?"

"That's me." She looked at the bouquets with delight. "Put them here." She tapped the checkout counter.

"There's one more in the truck," the woman said. In minutes she was back with a third carefully wrapped arrangement.

"Can't be too careful of flowers in this weather," she said as she accepted Dori's generous tip and left.

Smiling, Dori tore at the green wrappings around the first of the flowers. *With a heart full of gratitude, Mae* read the card with a bouquet of lavender mums, pink carnations, statice, and baby's breath in a green glass vase. Dori was sniffing the carnations when she became aware that Angie was standing just behind her.

"Impressive," the girl said, her voice dripping with sarcasm. Or was it jealousy? Hurt?

"It's from Mae," Dori said. "Wasn't that nice?" She pulled the wrappings from the second gift, a huge and very healthy philodendron.

Make Harbor Lights a small treasure Seaside can be proud of, love, Phil and Maureen.

Dori laughed as she held the card toward Angie. "Phil. He must have peered in and seen the plight of the deceased ivy."

"Who's Maureen?" Angie asked abruptly, curious in spite of herself.

"She appears to be Phil's special friend. She was at church with him last Sunday."

"Well, last Sunday was certainly a big day, wasn't it?" Angie looked as if she'd just swallowed vinegar. "Phil shows up with a girl and Pastor Paul with a wife."

Dori pulled a chair up to the counter so she could reach the hook in the ceiling and climbed up to hang the living plant in the place of the dead one. As she was climbing down, Angie reached out and ripped the green paper from the last gift, revealing a gigantic cyclamen in rich fuchsia. Angie read the card in a voice that thickened as she went.

"Dori, I'm so proud of you. All my love now and forever, Trev."

There was an electric silence when she finished. Dori knew the words hurt the young woman and felt bad about it, but she didn't know what to do to relieve her pain.

Angie made a noise that was half sob, half furious scream. She tore the card across again and again until only confetti remained. She hurled it at Dori, the little pieces of pasteboard raining over the counter. She reached for the plant with the obvious intent to backhand it to the floor, but Dori moved faster. She grabbed the cyclamen and hugged it to her.

Before she could suggest that Angie ought to leave, Angie turned and fled, but not before Dori saw the tears starting to fall.

For a few minutes Dori just stood, the plant in her arms. She was appalled at Angie's behavior, but she sort of understood. When she'd thought Trev was gone forever, she'd been devastated.

She'd just never thrown anything in the guilty party's face.

She put the plant on the table and began to collect all the little pieces of Trev's note. Maybe she could piece them together. She frowned as she laid the confettied card on the counter and began arranging it. Maybe she'd never thrown anything, but she'd been pretty nasty to Trev. The realization made her shiver.

"Doing a miniature jigsaw puzzle?" asked a voice behind her.

She swung to find Maureen peering over her shoulder.

"Maureen!" She gave her new friend a quick hug. "A friendly face!"

Maureen hugged her back. "So that was Angie I saw storming out of here a few minutes ago."

"You know about her?"

"Phil told me."

Dori rolled her eyes. "I can just imagine his version."

"He defended Trev," Maureen said, quick, Dori noted, to defend Phil.

Dori nodded. "Good for him. I should have known." She told Maureen about Angie's visit. "And now I'm trying to put Trev's note back together, but I'm missing a few pieces." She sighed.

"You're wearing them." Maureen reached out and plucked several scraps of paper from her hair.

With the help of a large roll of tape that Dori found in a drawer behind the counter, they managed to reassemble Trev's note.

Maureen looked at it. "Why all this effort over an ordinary gift note?"

"It's the first time Trev's ever given me flowers," Dori said softly as she slid the reconstructed message into her slacks pocket.

Maureen grinned at her. "I like him, Dori."

"You like Phil," Dori retorted.

"I'm keeping him under surveillance," Maureen said primly.

This time it was Dori who grinned. "Right. Now how can I help you?" She waved toward the books.

"I'm looking for a good novel." Maureen moved toward the fiction rack.

Dori followed. "I don't think I've read a Christian book in years," she said. "I'm not the best person to have in a bookstore like this one, not that I'm telling the customers."

"After Adam died—"

"Who's Adam?"

"My fiancé. He died six years ago. It broke my heart, and I read all kinds of books on death and mourning." Maureen pointed to the Christian living section. "They helped, but I was over-whelmed by all my emotions. I needed to read something lighter. I tried some novels and found I could lose myself in the story. For a while my sorrow diminished as I lived the struggles of the characters."

Dori listened with fascination as Maureen lifted first one novel, then another, glancing at back copy, reading first pages. She thought of all her romantic suspense novels. Certainly she'd used them as a means of escape, but she'd never thought of them as a means of healing.

"And I loved the fact that Christian novels offered me hope," Maureen continued. "Not that they candy-coated life. They acknowledged pain and sorrow and sin, but they didn't stay mired there like so many secular books do. My life was awfully bleak back then, and the stories taught me that living isn't static but evolutionary. New plateaus of forward development would always be open to me if I stuck with the Lord. Hope was always there if I chose to grab it."

She held one book out to Dori. "Sermon's done. I'll take this one."

Long after Maureen left, Dori thought about their conversation. Adam must have died somewhere around the time she herself moved to San Diego. Maureen knew pain, but she had turned to the Lord to get through it.

Just like Trev had turned to the Lord. And Dori had turned *from* Him.

What that all meant she wasn't yet sure, but it raised one very hard question: How could she be a pastor's wife if she wasn't following God? She shivered as she considered the corollary: How could Trev be a pastor with an unbelieving, no, a badly lapsed wife? She hadn't become an atheist, saying there was no God. To her that was foolish. There were too many proofs that God was there, from creation to the complexity of the human body, to say nothing of male and female. She'd always wondered how evolutionists explained two sexes.

But she had become hostile and anti-God. She paused. No, she wasn't anti-God. If He helped someone, good, fine. Let them believe. She'd just decided to ignore Him because she felt He'd failed her.

Ah, Pop, I know you didn't realize some of the ramifications, or you wouldn't have done this to Trev and me. It's not just the awkwardness we're experiencing or even the issues of love and trust we need to work through. Because of who Trev is, it's the issue of faith. Me and faith.

Burdened, she slipped her hands into her slacks pockets as she thought about it all. Her fingers brushed the taped-together card.

A warm feeling washed over her. Certainly there were difficulties, but Trev loved her. He'd told her so last night; he'd written it in the note today. He'd shown it by buying the red fleece top and by remembering to send the plant.

She sighed. It was time she faced the fact that she was starting to love the now Trev as much as she'd loved the old Trev. At the thought, she waited for the familiar fear to wash through her, dislodging the sweetness of this growing realization. Nothing happened. She felt slightly stunned as she returned to work.

When she finished clearing all the Christmas bric-a-brac from the gift shelves, she placed Trev's cyclamen next to a pair of cream candlesticks and a ceramic statue of a little girl sitting in a rocker reading the Bible. She placed Mae's bouquet on top of the fiction shelf and stacked some of the duplicate novels artistically around the vase.

She went to the door and turned, looking in, trying to see the store as a customer might. She grinned. Better already.

After a quick lunch, Dori called Mae who walked her through the intricacies of her software. Dori made copious notes so she would be able to remember how things worked tomorrow and all the days after.

She worked steadily through the afternoon without another customer. While she regretted the lack of business, she was happy to be able to spend time familiarizing herself with the store, the inventory, the catalogues, and the new supplies. She called all the local churches about their Sunday school materials. She actually got to speak to four directors of Christian education who placed orders immediately. The majority of the churches, smaller in size, had volunteer Sunday school directors or superintendents who would return her calls soon.

As the day wore on, she decided that things at Harbor Lights were very different from Small Treasures, yet they were the same. She realized she was going to enjoy the challenge of getting the store back in business, maybe even returning it to Mae's keeping with improvements in sales. She smiled to herself as she washed her dirty hands preparatory to leaving at five. She was drying them on the last paper towel on the roll when she heard the bell over the door ring again.

"Coming," she called. She hurried out to find Trev waiting.

"Hi," she said, suddenly shy. He looked so wonderful, tall and strong, full of character and depth, a man worth knowing. A man worth being married to. She swept her hand toward the cyclamen. "Thanks. It's beautiful."

He grinned, pleased. "How did today go?"

"Fine, thanks." She'd tell him about Angie later. "The strangest thing is not knowing the inventory."

"Well, I've come to take you away from it all." He shoved a gift bag at her.

"For me?" She felt bemused. Two chivalrous moves in one day! She looked at the brightly patterned bag with tissue paper stuffed in the top. She pulled the paper out and put it on the counter by the register. She reached back in and pulled out a flat rectangular package. "A pair of navy tights?"

He grinned. "Keep going."

She reached in again. Another flat rectangular package. "A navy leotard."

"Keep going."

She reached in a third time, and her hand touched a cold silky fabric. She pulled out a pair of nylon navy running shorts.

"We're going to the fitness center." He spoke with all the delight of someone who had just presented his true love with tickets for a Caribbean cruise.

She laughed. "Oh, you mad romantic!" She hugged him.

He looked very pleased with himself. Then a thought hit her.

"Did you pick these out yourself or did you send your secretary?" Dori tried to imagine him slinking though the women's department searching for these items.

He looked surprised. "I got them myself."

She smiled. Either way, the items had been his thought, but knowing he went out of his way to buy them himself made the gesture extra special.

"But what about Ryan?" she asked as she put everything back in the bag.

"Phil and Maureen will see to him."

"And the suitcase, I've no doubt." Dori looked down at herself. "I guess it doesn't matter that I don't look all that great as a result of pushing dust bunnies and spiders around all day."

"This is a resort town, remember? Casual's in. You look fine."

He was the one who looked fine, she thought, in his khaki Dockers, a navy turtleneck, and a cobalt blue sweater that made his blue eyes absolutely riveting.

"Can we get me home in time to change before that party at church tonight? You look so great that I have to dress up to your standard before your congregation, or they'll think me unworthy."

He grinned at her compliment. "Sweetheart, you look wonderful no matter what you're wearing, but not to worry. We'll get home in plenty of time."

He waited while she turned back the heat, shut off the lights, and locked the door. They climbed in Trev's car for the short drive to the fitness center.

As they drove, Dori told Trev about Angie's visit.

"I didn't know she was Mae's part-time help, and she didn't know I was opening the store for Mae." She pulled out her reassembled gift card and held it for him to see. Passing lights reflected brightly on the many strips of tape.

He made a distressed noise deep in his throat. "I knew she had her sights set on me, but I didn't realize how bad it was." He ran a hand through his dark hair. "Please believe me when I tell you that I gave her no encouragement."

Dori grinned at him as she slid the precious card back in her pocket. "It's all your own fault, you know. You're just irresistible to

the ladies and always have been. Remember Gladdy Morris?" She
started to laugh.

"The very name makes me shudder."

"Sixth grade. She thought you were wonderful!"

"If she'd been an adult, she'd have been called a stalker," Trev
said, disgruntled. He pulled into the fitness center parking lot and
handed her a nylon zipped bag that he pulled from the backseat.
"Towel, soap, sneakers, and stuff."

The man had thought of everything. Or had he? Blow dryer?
Curling iron? She could get pneumonia leaving the center with
wet hair on a night like this.

They parted for the changing rooms. Dori found an empty
locker to stash her belongings in and changed into the leotard and
tights. She pulled the shorts on, thankful he'd gotten them. They
did a lot to relieve the am-I-really-wearing-something feeling of
the leotard.

When she left the changing room, Trev was waiting for her in
the hall. He looked at her very carefully, top to toes. He grinned.
"You look even better than I imagined."

She flushed with pleasure.

An attractive woman in a red leotard walked by, looking like
she'd never broken a sweat in her life. "Hi, Paul," she said, her
voice definitely flirty.

Trev glanced up. "Oh, hi, Melody." No flirtiness.

Dori shook her head as he reached around her for the door.
"Ladies' man."

He snorted.

"Amy Skolnik," she said over her shoulder as she walked into
the room noisy with clangs and grunts and redolent with sweat.

"At least she was cute," Trev muttered.

Was she ever! In eighth grade Dori had been so jealous of her
naturally curly red-gold hair and her braceless teeth. "And Jeannie
Markowitz and Jordan Darlington and—"

"Enough, woman!" He led her to the first machine where they
waited for the large man with the black back brace to finish his
reps. "What do you want me to do—start mentioning the guys
you dated? Rob Baldwin? Hal Commons? Denny Lipinski?"

She just smiled sweetly at him. "A list of guys I dated wouldn't come near the list of girls you dated. Add to that the ones who chased you unsuccessfully, and you have the Chester County phone book."

"I'm a changed man," he said, hand over his heart, as he stepped back for the large man to get up.

"Hey, Trevelyan," the man said as he mopped sweat from his face with a ratty, once-blue towel that had lost most of its loops. "I hear you got married."

Trev nodded. "This is my wife, Dori."

The man nodded. "Hey, Dori. Nice to meet ya. And congratulations on your marriage. You've broken the hearts of all the women here, you know." He turned and wiped the moisture from the leather bench he'd been lying on. He turned back, looking concerned. "Not that he ever gave them any encouragement, you understand. They just all liked him. Personally, I never understood what they saw in him, him being a minister and all." He grinned. "When they could have had me."

Dori laughed as the man walked away. Trev bent to adjust the weights on the machine to a level he thought Dori could handle.

"And just what did they see in you, you being a minister and all," she teased, wagging a finger at Trev.

He grabbed the offending finger and opened his mouth to retort.

"Well, aren't we having a good time," said a snide voice.

Twenty-Five

*B*OTH DORI AND TREV swung toward the man standing just inside the weight room. Bob Warrington stared at them with Penni Aaronson, her lush curves accented by her black leotard and tights, huddled at his side.

"What can I do for you, Bob?" Trev asked. Dori noticed that all traces of his laughter disappeared when he saw Bob. Her own stomach gave a little jump. These constant meetings couldn't be good for anyone's digestion.

"I got a letter in the mail today. So did Penni."

Penni nodded energetically. "That was mean, Pastor Paul." Her lower lip trembled.

Dori looked from Bob to Penni to Trev. Mean? Trev? No way.

Trev looked quickly around the weight room. "Here is hardly the place for this conversation, Bob. Why don't you call me at the office for an appointment? I'll be glad to talk whenever it's convenient for you."

"You know you can't get away with this," Bob said, his voice shaking with anger. Apparently now was the convenient time and talking in the weight room didn't bother him at all. Neither did the people at the machines who looked on with interest. "If I don't play on the church basketball team, we'll lose the championship. Believe me, no one will appreciate that. We've won for the past three years."

Undoubtedly all because of Bob.

Trev ignored him as he held out his hand to Dori. She took it, letting him pull her out into the hall.

Bob and Penni followed them. Dori's shoulders twitched. It felt like Snoopy's evil twin was doing Snoopy's vulture act, staring at them with malevolent eyes.

Bob hissed, "Wait until my father hears. He'll have a few words to say. Don't think he won't."

Once they were in the hall, Trev glanced around. "Let's find an empty room to talk. I'd just as soon not all of Seaside knew the chapel's family problems."

Dori had no doubt that Bob would be happy to air them to the world, but Trev was right. Some discussions should be private. "You think you run this church," Bob said, his voice spiteful. "Well, you don't. No one crosses my father and lives to tell about it."

A chill slid over Dori. Even assuming that Bob was exaggerating, his threat was ugly. Was this the kind of thing pastors faced often, this animosity? This defiant challenge? Her only Christian experience was Young Life back in high school. She knew so very little about what a pastor's life was like. Or a pastor's wife's life, for that matter.

Never once did she think Trev was in the wrong, whatever had set Bob off. The little she knew about Bob and Penni left no doubt in her mind that they were facing some consequence of their brazen actions, and like most sinners caught in their own web, not liking it.

Trev tried a couple of doors, found one that was unlocked, and flipped on the lights. It was a small office with little more than a desk and two visitors' chairs.

"We'll borrow this for a few minutes."

Bob and Penni followed him in. Dori pulled the door shut behind them and came to stand beside Trev. To say the room was crowded was understatement, and it would be impossible to overstate the animosity pouring off Bob. Dori shivered. Trev leaned back against the desk. "Lord, give us wisdom and strength and the ability to act in a manner that honors You."

For once his prayer didn't aggravate Dori. She wasn't certain whether that was because she was becoming used to his praying anytime, anywhere, or whether it was so obvious that this conversation needed Divine guidance that the prayer seemed more than appropriate. Either way, she supposed it signaled an advance in her own spiritual reawakening.

Trev began. "Penni, you said you thought I was being mean. I'm sorry you see it that way. That's not my intent at all. I'm just following church policy." He turned to Bob. "Policy that your father helped write, Bob. When someone is involved in continual sin, has been confronted about it, and won't change his mind or actions, that person can't participate in church-sponsored activities."

"So because I love Bob, I can't sing in the choir anymore?" Penni's chin started to wobble again, and her big eyes filled with tears.

Trev shook his head. "You know that's not what it is, Penni. The discipline is because you are having an ongoing affair with a married man. If we let you continue to sit up there in the front row of the choir loft and sing, it'll be like we approve of what you're doing."

"But I love him!" Penni's voice had become loud and whiney. "And I'm scheduled for a solo this Sunday. I can't leave Rosetta in the lurch."

Dori watched Penni with interest. She didn't want to leave Rosetta—the choir director?—in a lurch, but she was willing to leave Shannon without a husband and the kids without a father. *Can you say 'warped thinking'?*

"Rosetta knows not expect you," Trev said. "The choir will manage."

"You told her about us?" Penni all but shrieked.

Dori couldn't help but compare poor, heartbroken Shannon with Penni, all wide eyes and hard edges. No question, Bob was not only wrong; he was nuts.

"Told?" Trev looked flabbergasted. "Come on, Penni. You're living very openly with Bob. We saw you together at Dante's and now here at the center. I didn't have to tell anyone anything. Rosetta already knew. She came to me about it."

Penni turned a tragic face to Bob who rose to the occasion.

"It seems to me, Paul," he spat, "that we're entitled to live our lives as we want."

Did Trev notice that Bob had dropped the *pastor* from his name? Whether he did or not, he gave no indication.

"You can say you're entitled to live as you want, but what about those you're hurting by your choices? You've got a wife who is brokenhearted and two kids who don't understand why their father suddenly disappeared."

Bob waved his hand in the air like his family was of no account. Dori thought of the adorable Serena and poor, colicky Jonny, named after Bob's own father, and couldn't understand Bob's easy dismissal of them. Had he never loved them, his very own children?

Bob decided to try another tack. "Doesn't the Bible say love is of God and God is love? So what we feel for each other, Penni and me, comes from Him. And if He didn't want us to be together, He never would have let us feel the way we do for each other."

Nothing like blaming God for your sin, Dori thought, astounded at the man's gall.

Trev just shook his head in appalled amazement. "God does not condone adultery, Bob. He never has, and He never will. The Bible is very firm on that point. You can manipulate Scripture all you want, but you know what it says. You know very well."

For a moment there was silence in the little office.

Then suddenly Penni pronounced, her voice sharp and dismissive, "Shannon is a mess."

Dori frowned at her and her cruelty. Penni glared back, though her cheeks did flush.

"Well, she is," Penni said defensively. "She calls all the time. She begs Bob to come back. She cries. She asks for money. She claims that she can't pay the mortgage or the grocery bill."

Dori couldn't keep quiet any longer. She glared at Bob. "So you let the church pay for your family's food and housing." Her tone was scathing. "Talk about deadbeat dads. Men go to jail for that, you know."

Bob ignored her and looked at Trev. "We've gotten off topic here." He sounded stiff and self-righteous.

"Have we?" Trev asked. "I thought we were talking about the consequences of abandoning your marriage, of breaking the vows you made to your wife. Remember 'what God has joined together, let no man put asunder'?"

Dori wanted to ask the sixty-four thousand-dollar question but wasn't sure she should. This pastor's wife stuff was going to be tricky. She glanced at Trev. "Can I ask a question?"

"Go ahead. Ask whatever you want."

She hesitated a minute, then blurted out, "Is this the first time you've been unfaithful to your wife?"

Bob and Penni stared at her, their mouths agape. Trev lowered his gaze, but not before she saw the amused approval in his eyes.

"Well?" she prompted.

"It's not a matter of being unfaithful," Bob said, carefully dodging the question. He pulled Penni close to his side. "It's a matter of loving Penni."

"Don't try to put a nice face on it, Bob." Trev sounded disgusted. "No matter how you try to explain it, it's adultery. Don't kid yourself with nice words. If you choose to continue in this pattern, I can't prevent you. But before God, know that you are wrong. Marriage vows are forever, not until a Penni comes along."

"Look who's talking," Bob spat, clearly tired of being on the defensive. "You and your sudden marriage. I'm not even sure I believe that she is your wife."

Trev glanced at Dori and grinned. "Oh, she's my wife all right."

Dori looked at Bob and Penni and smiled as sweetly as she could.

Bob shook his head. "There's something weird going on here," he persisted. "It's just too sudden. My dad has been checking, and we'll find out the truth. I hope you can deal with that!"

"There is something unusual about our marriage," Trev admitted.

Dori closed her eyes and prayed as earnestly as she ever had. *Lord, let him keep his mouth shut. Please! Strike him dumb. Bob is making enough trouble as it is. Please don't let Trev play right into his hand.*

"I didn't marry Dori this past weekend."

"I knew it!" Bob punched the air.

"Well, I never." Penni sniffed and looked down her nose at them. "And you're a pastor!"

"I married her six years ago," Trev said calmly.

Bob and Penni stared. "What?"

So much for answered prayer.

"We've been married for six years," Trev repeated. "We've had some difficulties in the past, but we're working to resolve them."

"Six years?" squeaked Penni, eyes as big as Dori had ever seen them.

Bob grinned, a very nasty, smug grin. "Well, well, so that's the story. A pastor who couldn't even keep his marriage together."

"You have a lot of nerve lecturing us!" Penni sneered. "And if I can't sing and Bob can't play, you can't preach. It's only fair."

Trev nodded. "Maybe it will come to that, though I hope not. After all, neither of us is running around town with someone else. In the meantime, you know the church's position on your actions. If you want to fight the decision, you'll have to go to the board of elders. You did notice that the letter was also signed by Ed Masterson, chairman of the board?" He nodded toward the door. "I think we've all said everything that needs to be said for the moment, and Dori and I have a party to attend."

With ill grace, Bob and Penni stalked out, slamming the door behind them.

Dori turned to Trev. "Should you have told them about us? I'm worried that he will do something to hurt you because of me."

He pulled her into a hug. "It's going to come out anyway, Dor. Better I say it than someone like Jonathan."

She wrapped her arms around his middle. "I didn't mean to be such a problem to you," she said in a small, unhappy voice.

He kissed the top of her head. "Sometimes life is a problem no matter what you do. There's no easy way to deal with things and no easy or painless solutions."

Too true, she thought. *If I stay away, I'm trouble. If I stay here, I'm trouble.*

"But understand that you are one problem that I delight in."

Dori looked up. "Really?"

In answer he kissed her.

Twenty-Six

JOANNE WATCHED BARNEY as he dressed and thought again how handsome and strong he was. He liked to wear pin-striped suits and dress shirts to make himself stand out in a town where everyone wore casual clothes most of the time. He flipped the broad end of his tie over the narrow end and made a perfect knot.

"Well, babe, it looks like Friday will be the night. And just in time too. Mr. Jankowski is due home Sunday."

Joanne had noticed right off that Barney never called Mr. Jankowski the shortened Mr. J that Vinnie did.

"You have to give your boss respect," he explained when she mentioned it.

"Why Friday?" She stretched, reaching over her head and touching the padded headboard of the great king-size bed in Barney's suite overlooking the ocean. She loved the glitz and flash of Atlantic City. She played the slots for hours each evening on Barney's unlimited credit while he attended to various business responsibilities. Once she even won five hundred dollars. That evening she couldn't wait for Barney to come take her for their now-customary late dinner so she could show him her prize. By the time he actually arrived, most of it had gone back into the machines, but he'd been real happy for her anyway.

"Trevelyan's going to be away."

"He is? How do you know?"

"People who keep their calendars on their computers share their plans with the world."

Joanne was impressed. "You're a hacker?" She'd learned the term from TV where she saw the Sandra Bullock movie about breaking into computers.

"No, but I've got friends who are."

Jo shrugged. It was still amazing, all the stuff he knew.

"With him away," Barney said, "that means only the girl, the kid, and the dogs."

Joanne sat up abruptly. "You aren't gonna hurt the dogs, are you? You said you never did." The idea of making one of them cry just about broke her heart. Her eyes actually got teary thinking about it. "I-I wouldn't want you to do anything that mean, baby."

She said the last softly because she was still feeling her way with Barney. She hadn't been away from him since they met Sunday except for the short stints when he had to work. He hadn't taken her home to get any clothes or anything. He'd simply bought her new, and they were gorgeous! She knew she could never go back to Wal-Mart, and even Sears and Penney's were ruined for her after the exclusive boutiques he'd taken her to.

Every day she liked him more, and she loved his style of living.

Barney looked at her strangely. "You don't think I'm mean?"

She shook her head. "I think you're wonderful." She smiled sweetly at him, thinking of all the gentleness he had shown her these past few days.

He studied her for a minute longer, looked out the window at the ocean, then turned back to her. "You do know what I do for a living, right?"

"Oh, yeah. You do Mr. Jankowski's necessary work. But dogs—I don't know. Dogs is different."

He smiled, and she melted. How had she gotten so lucky?

"So, okay," he said. "We won't hurt the dogs."

"Promise?"

"Promise."

She stood on the bed and threw her arms around his neck. Standing on the bed she actually got to look down on him a couple of inches. "Thank you! Thank you!" She rained kisses all over his face, and he grinned like a happy man.

"How about you and me taking a vacation after Mr. Jankowski gets home?"

"A vacation?" Joanne clapped her hands. "A real vacation?"

He nodded, smiling at her excitement.

"I never been on a vacation before."

"Never?"

She shook her head. "My father said they were a waste of money." Like being a drunk wasn't. She felt her spirits start to sag. It always happened when she thought of him and his heavy fists. She took a deep breath.

No more sad thoughts about him, Joanne. He can't hurt you any more. You've got Barney. With Barney she had only happy.

"So where do you want to go?" Barney asked. "You pick the spot. Hawaii? The Bahamas? Paris?"

"Paris?" she squealed. "That's in Europe! We could really go there?" Of course she'd have to fly, which made her shudder, but with Barney holding her hand, maybe it wouldn't be that bad.

"Paris it is," he said. "I'll make the arrangements."

She shook her head. "I was just thinking how far that was, that's all. I really want to go somewhere warm since it's so cold here."

"The Caribbean somewhere." He reached into his inside jacket pocket and pulled out his wallet, a long, sleek leather one, not the bent and beat-up thing Vinnie stuffed in his back pants pocket. "Don't you worry your pretty little head. I'll take care of everything. Here's a few hundred. Get a new bikini for the trip, and a couple of those floaty dresses for our nights on the town. Anything you want. I'll be back for you in time for our midnight dinner."

She took the money with wide eyes. Would she ever get used to having so much? "I'm going to get a massage." She gulped down a giggle. "They make you take off your clothes."

Barney took her chin in his hand. "Just remember, sweetheart.

You belong to me." He gave her one last hard kiss, then strode out the door.

Joanne hugged herself. Life like those TV shows could be hers after all, she thought, and the reason was Barney.

She was falling in love.

Twenty-Seven

DORI TURNED TO TREV as they walked up the aisle of the deserted church after the welcome party. It had gone better than she'd expected. People had been so kind and friendly to her that the conversation had flowed without her having to contribute much. She'd just smiled and nodded and agreed that Trev was indeed wonderful.

"How do you do it?" she asked.

"Do what?" He took her coat from her and held it out. She slid into it.

"Talk all evening like that."

He looked blank.

"It's like you always know just what to say."

He shook his head as he started to zip her coat for her. It was obvious he didn't understand what she meant. "There's no great secret here. You just talk about whatever comes to your mind."

She pushed at his hands. "I can zip my own coat."

He continued to pull the zipper up. "I know. I taught you how."

"You did not. I knew how to do that long before I came to live with you."

"Well, I would have taught you if I'd been around."

She rolled her eyes. "But *what* do you talk about?"

He shrugged and zipped his Lands' End jacket over his cobalt blue sweater. "Stuff."

She gave him the evil eye. "That's a big help."

He laughed. It was strange that she'd forgotten how adept he was socially. She walked into a room and saw people as threatening challenges. Somehow she had to figure out what to talk to them about, and that was hard enough when you knew the people. It was murder when you didn't. Trev walked into a room, any room, and everyone was his instant friend. Conversation never lagged.

"I bet you love cocktail parties." It was an accusation.

He nodded. "Except pastors don't end up at too many cocktail parties."

"Then church socials like tonight."

"I love church socials. It's a great time to get to know my people."

His people. Interesting. Another sign of the way he looked at life these days. She remembered when making himself happy was his chief goal, and partying was an end in itself. Of course, it was most people's goal at nineteen and twenty, left over from being teenagers when the world revolved around you and your search for happiness. She remembered angst from those years. He probably remembered fun.

Like the time Alyson Bailey had a big party, and Dori wasn't invited. Now a certified social outcast, she had died a thousand deaths over her exclusion. Trev, also not invited because he had dated Alyson once and never again in spite of her dogged pursuit, threw his own party for all the non-inviteds. He had a wonderful time, and in retrospect she realized his party was a great success. She, however, had been too conscious of the fact that everyone present was also a party pariah to enjoy herself.

She could definitely be a glass-is-half-empty girl.

She suspected that this tendency toward melancholia was what made forgiving Trev so difficult. Her standard for herself was perfection with everything done to the best of her ability. Since perfection was impossible, she spent a lot of her time berating herself and trying harder and harder to meet her own standards. In spite of the fact that she failed regularly and knew it, imperfection in others was as hard to accept as was her own, especially from someone she loved so fiercely.

248 ~ Gayle Roper

Somewhere there had to be someone who could satisfy her need for doing right, being right, and acting right. When Trev had failed so spectacularly, she hadn't been able to accept that this man she loved, this man who was supposed to make up for all her flaws, had feet of clay. That he hurt her so badly when she planned to spend her life doing everything she could to make him happy was what made her reaction to his breach of promise so strong. It also made letting go of the horrendous hurt so impossible for her.

Not that she liked this overly touchy part of her personality. Many times growing up she wished she were more like Trev. Not Phil. He took living the fun life a bit too far for her. But Trev always seemed to know what to say and when to back off. What a gift, especially for a pastor.

"Well, I'm not good at gatherings like this evening's," she said, pulling her red gloves on.

"You did great, Dori. You had them eating out of your hand."

She shrugged. "I like it when there's a specific purpose to a get-together."

"Mingling and getting to know each other isn't specific enough?"

She shook her head. "I like to know what we're going to be talking about. I like to know exactly what is expected of me. Then I can perform as I should. Like at the store. People come in, and we talk product and purpose. 'You're looking for a gift? What's the occasion? Your mother's birthday? Her fiftieth? How about a nice—' And we're on our way."

"Then where's your spontaneity?"

"My what?" she asked with a self-deprecating smile.

He laughed and gave her a gentle hug. "Believe it or not, I always admired your sensitivity and tender heart."

"What?"

"I've watched you with Ryan. You are so kind and understanding with him."

"You're not so bad yourself."

He waved her comment away. "I gave him Jack."

"You gave him a lot more than Jack."

"And remember Gail Mercer?"

Dori did, though she hadn't thought of her in years. Gail was a sad girl, a pariah in junior high school. She didn't dress right, bathe regularly, or even brush her teeth half the time. Her father was in jail, and her mother was rumored to be the town prostitute.

"You were always so nice to her. I couldn't even stand to be near her—she smelled half the time—and—"

"She thought you were so cute."

"—you would purposely sit by her."

"I always felt sorry for her."

"See? That's what I mean. And there was Fat Alma."

"Trev!"

He shrugged. "That's what the guys all called her."

"I know. So did she."

"See? That's what I mean. As I've grown in the Lord, I've tried to model myself after that part of you."

She stared, openmouthed. She couldn't have been more astonished. Surely this was Trev, teasing as usual. But one look at his face in the dim emergency lights told her he was serious.

He opened the door for her. The wind whipped in and suddenly the two-block walk home seemed more like two miles. She pulled her red beret low on her head, forsaking chic for warmth.

Trev carefully checked to be certain the door was locked behind them. As they began walking, he took her hand.

"You always impressed me because you cared for people," he said. "Because you could talk issues, substance. I just tell stories and make people laugh. Remember how Pop used to despair that Phil or I'd ever have a deep thought in our heads? You, on the other hand, have always thought deeply and made everyone else think. You delve down, and I skim the top. That's probably why you became a Christian in high school, and I didn't until I had no choice."

Skim the top? She thought of the stack of books by his chair. "Six years has changed you a lot, Trev. I doubt that you skim anything anymore."

He grinned. "Dull and pedantic, that's me."

"Yeah, right." Trev couldn't be dull if he tried. He was the one who had always brought joy to her life as they were growing up.

She'd fall into one of her despairing moods, and he'd make it his goal to make her laugh. As far as she could remember, he'd always succeeded. "Don't worry. You still tell stories better than anyone I know, and you can still charm the birds from the trees when you set your mind to it."

"How about a shopkeeper from California?" he asked softly.

A short electric silence vibrated between them while she searched wildly for an answer. No thought emerged as he bent and kissed her, a soft kiss full of yearning and love.

When he pulled back, she stared up at him, mouth dry, heart pounding. More and more every day, every hour, every minute, she wanted to be with him forever. She watched him with Ryan, doing everything he could to make the boy feel safe and secure. She watched him pray at any moment and listened to him pray for her specifically. She saw his interaction with his congregation. She'd heard him be compassionate with Shannon and firm with Bob and Penni. She agreed more and more with the assessment of Clooney, the beach bum.

"You got a good man here, Mrs. Trevelyan. He's God's man through and through."

There were only two problems standing in the way. She was no longer God's woman, and there was the pink elephant standing firmly between them. She blinked and looked away from him, uncertain how to fix either.

"We've got to talk about it, Dori," he said with that uncanny ability to read her.

"I know. It just scares me so. I like how things are going between us. I-I like being with you." She *loved* being with him. "I even like Seaside. I'm afraid talking will upset everything. I'm afraid we'll lose what we've found. I'm afraid—of myself." The last was a whisper.

"I guess I've got more faith in you that you do," he said. "You're not nineteen anymore. You're older, wiser. I'm older, different. Whatever it is, we can work through it. I know we can."

Wasn't she the one who said she liked specifics to talk about? Well, here was as specific a topic as ever there was. The words to explain, to ask for his explanation, crowded her throat, clawing for release, but she couldn't, just couldn't make herself risk saying them.

They walked a full block in silence as she swallowed and swallowed and swallowed, choking the dangerous words down. She closed her eyes in distress and disgust. Sometimes she disappointed herself so much!

"Dori?" he finally said, his voice encouraging and hopeful.

With false brightness she said, "I noticed that Jonathan and Judy didn't come to the party tonight. He's out to get you, you know."

Trev smiled wryly at her change of topic but didn't push. She wasn't sure whether she was grateful or dismayed.

He nodded. "I've known since I came here that someday we'd have trouble, he and I."

"Beware the man at the airport?"

He nodded again. "He's chased the last three pastors away."

"Why am I not surprised? How does he do it?"

"He learns stuff."

"Stuff?"

"Dirt, or what he twists into dirt, about the pastors."

"Like?"

"My immediate predecessor had trouble with porno on the Internet when he was younger. He had a nanny program on their computer that only his wife had the password for."

"But that's wise," Dori said.

"I think so, too, but Jonathan made the man sound like a pervert."

Dori stopped abruptly and turned to face her husband. "What will he do to you?"

Trev grinned. "Me? I have no secrets."

Dori winced. "What happens if Jonathan pushes for you to leave? Does he have enough power to get the congregation to vote you out? And wouldn't that mean an ugly fight?"

He looked up and studied the sky like the answers to her questions were written there. "I don't know. All I know is that I don't want to leave Seaside anytime soon. I'd like to become the permanent pastor now that my personal life is back on track. Or at least going in that direction."

"Are you sure that's not just your stubbornness talking?"

"What? You think I'm stubborn?" He affected shock. Then he

turned serious. "I'm not being stubborn, Dori-girl. I've known for a long time that if I stayed here, there would come a day when my personal issues would surface. That day is probably here. Maybe I'll survive. Maybe I won't. All I know is that I love Seaside Chapel and its people. Until God shows me differently, I'm here."

"Sort of like Martin Luther at his heresy trial? 'Here I stand, so help me God'?"

"Sort of. This morning I read a psalm that said it all: 'I wait quietly before God, for my salvation comes from him.' And listen to this part. 'To them I'm just a broken-down wall or a tottering fence. They plan to topple me from my high position. They delight in telling lies about me. They are friendly to my face, but they curse me in their hearts.'"

"That sounds all too applicable, at least where Jonathan is concerned," Dori said.

"'My salvation and my honor come from God alone. He is my refuge, a rock where no enemy can reach me.'" Trev shrugged as they walked up the front walk to their house. "We just have to trust the Lord to take care of us."

She stopped, looking out into the cold, blustery night. "Your commitment to God is like the winter winds, isn't it, blowing everything else before it?"

He thought for a moment. "Winter winds are capricious," he finally said. "They blow where they want, when they want, and as hard as they want. In that sense I hope my commitment to the Lord is more constant. But you're right in that it blows so strong and hard that it's impossible to miss. Loving the Lord with all your heart, mind, soul, and strength is a consuming thing. But it's in loving Him with all that's in us that we become people unafraid to risk loving and serving others, even men like Jonathan."

"So what about when you take that risk, and it backfires? Where's God then?" She heard the edge in her voice and didn't care. God and Trev already knew how she felt.

"Right where He always was, beside you, waiting to pick up the pieces and fill in the holes left by the people who failed you." Trev looked at her with compassion. "You do realize that people will inevitably fail you, don't you? It may not be on purpose, but no one can be everything to someone. No one can be perfect."

She knew he was no longer talking about Jonathan, but himself. "But you should be able to trust the people you love." Unexpected tears sprang to her eyes.

"You should." He cupped her cheek gently, his leather glove cold against her skin. "But they're only human, and sometimes—" He paused and looked away. "Sometimes they let you down bigtime." She knew that now he was talking about her.

"So what do we do?" she asked quietly. "How do we fix it?"

He looked back at her with great intensity. "Offer each other what God has offered us in Christ."

"And that is?" she asked, though she knew what he was going to say.

"Forgiveness."

Exactly the answer she'd expected. "So just like that, you're supposed to overlook years of hurt and loneliness and pain? You make believe nothing ever happened?"

"Not just like that. It's a willful choice to let go of something you know happened. There's no denial in forgiveness. God knows full well that I've done many wrong things, but He has chosen to put them away. In the same way, we have to choose to let go of the wrong done us, the hurt dealt us by another."

Dori felt truth pressing in on her. *God, I can't! I just can't!*

Won't? said a quiet voice inside.

Can't! And once again she chose safety.

"So when Jonathan goes after you, you're just going to forgive him? Does that mean you're going to stand by and watch him ruin your reputation?"

He frowned, and she knew he was disappointed in her. She swallowed against the pain that realization brought, but she didn't back down. "You're just going to wait for Jonathan to strike?" She laid her hand on his sleeve. "I don't want him hurting you because of me." She had never meant anything more.

He looked at her, and the love and understanding she saw in his eyes nearly brought her to her knees.

Ryan threw the door open and saved her from saying or doing something she wasn't yet ready for.

"Hey, Pastor Paul." He had a bowl of cookies 'n' cream ice cream in his hand, his eyes fixed on a great spoonful as he brought it to his mouth. Jack stood beside him, watching the spoon as avidly as Ryan.

"Didn't you get enough to eat at the party?" Trev slipped his arm around Dori and led her inside. "We'll finish this conversation another time," he whispered softly in her ear.

"He didn't get enough, and neither did I," called Phil from the living room. He held out his own dish of ice cream as Dori and Trev began shedding their coats.

"I did," Maureen called, holding up empty hands.

"Such a good girl," Phil said, but his affectionate tone muted any sarcastic bite.

Ryan shoved the ice cream in his mouth, and Jack's shoulders slumped. Ry smiled beatifically as he savored his treat. He swallowed. "Did you know Bob Warrington is living with Penni? Are they having an affair or something? And I hear you won't let him play on the church basketball team. We're going to lose the championship now, you know. And is it true that Penni can't sing in the choir? Now it's just the old ladies who warble." He demonstrated, letting out a long *ahh* as he pounded himself on the chest multiple times.

"You could always join the choir and keep the old ladies in line," Trev said.

"Yeah, right." He spooned up some more ice cream. "How long do you think it'll be before Mr. Warrington goes for your throat?"

As a welcome home greeting, Dori thought, it was a lulu.

When no one answered him, Ryan shrugged. "Not something to talk about in front of the kid, huh?"

Trev grinned and ruffled Ry's hair. "Good try though."

Ryan offered his spoonful of ice cream first to Jack who took several licks, then to Trudy who demanded equal time. "Dori, there's a package here for you." Without a thought to dog saliva or germs, he plunged the spoon back into the cookies 'n' cream. "I found it on the porch when I got home from school. I brought it in and forgot about it." He pointed.

Trev picked up the box and offered it to Dori. The return address was Pop and Honey's in Amhearst. Dori sat on the sofa and opened it. She pushed aside the tissue paper covering the contents and stared at a red Lands' End Squall with navy lining. She could see DORI written in block letters on the iron-on tape Honey had affixed all those years ago so people could tell which jacket belonged to which person.

She raised tear-filled eyes to Trev who was hanging up his red Squall. "They saved it," she whispered. "They actually saved it."

Twenty-Eight

FRIDAY MORNING BEFORE going to the store, Dori stopped at Mae's rehab center and gave her all the catalogues that had accumulated since her injury.

"Go through them and tell me what to order," Dori said.

Mae nodded. "I'll call later."

Dori looked at the collection of get-well cards taped to the wall beside Mae's bed. "How much longer will you be here?"

Mae made a face and shook her head. "I have no idea, but I'll tell you I'm bored to tears! How many crossword puzzles can one woman do? At least I know Ryan's being taken care of."

"He's having a ball with Jack and Trudy. Trev and I are there to feed him and take him where he needs to go, but it's the dogs that make missing you manageable." She told Mae the story of Trudy falling in love with Ryan, making it sound as comic as she could.

Mae smiled. "I keep telling myself I should feel bad that he's with you and pastor as you start out your marriage, but I'm truly delighted. He needs to be around a godly man to see how one lives, and they don't come much better than Pastor Paul."

She sounded just like Clooney, the beach guy.

Mae sighed. "Sometimes I feel so badly for Ryan it actually hurts to breathe." Tears filled her eyes, and only by blinking furiously did she keep them from spilling down her face. She sniffed. "What would we ever do without the Lord?"

The question haunted Dori as she drove to Harbor Lights. Any way you looked at it, Mae's life had been as full of disappointments and hurt as Ryan's, yet she still had a strong, vibrant faith. Instead of centering on the abandonment issues and rejections in her life, she centered on the Lord, just the opposite of what Dori had done.

What would we ever do without the Lord?

Dori knew the answer to that question, at least as it pertained to herself. She had become bitter, resentful, and unforgiving. The new question was, what was she going to do now?

The new question stayed in the back of her mind as she continued familiarizing herself with the store and its products. Aside from the spiritual confusion—conviction?—the new question aroused, the day passed uneventfully until well after lunch. Then Gracie Wilder and Grayce Warrington came to call. When they walked into Harbor Lights, their eyes lit up immediately.

"My, my," Gracie said in her somber way. "You have made the place look lovely."

"Indeed you have," Grayce agreed, her rouge circles particularly bright under the fluorescent store lights. "And just who sent you the flowers?" Her tone was sly.

Dori was most pleased with their approval of the store, and she laughed at their delight in the cyclamen.

"You've got to love a man who sends flowers," Somber Gracie said. "Harold bought me a bouquet every single week for almost forty-five years."

"What a thoughtful thing for a husband to do," Dori said

"Oh, I never married him," Gracie said. "I was afraid he'd stop with the flowers."

Not knowing whether to laugh or cry at that observation, Dori smiled and said, "Are you two out without your buddy today?"

"Oh, no," Rouged Grayce said, peering at the figurine of the little girl in the rocker reading the Bible. "Grace is parking the car. It always takes her a long time to parallel park anymore."

Dori shuddered at the thought of Wrinkled Grace, who

looked like she could give Methuselah a run for his money, out parallel parking. She was thankful she was parked in the slot behind the store.

The two Graces looked around, handling this gift and that book until the third Grace arrived. The three gathered briefly behind the fiction shelf, and if her eyes weren't deceiving her, Dori thought they were praying. At least their heads were bowed, and she didn't think they were all looking at a novel on the bottom shelf.

The three turned and came toward Dori as she stood behind the counter dodging the tendrils of Phil and Maureen's philodendron.

"Dori, dear," Grayce said, her face paler than ever beneath the rouge circles.

One look at her face, and Dori knew something unpleasant was coming. What was it about the Warringtons? She braced herself and waited.

"Go on, Grayce, dear," Wrinkled Grace encouraged. "It's your job to tell."

Dori sucked in her stomach and straightened her shoulders. Rouged Grayce straightened her shoulders too. "It's Jonathan."

Dori waited for more, but Grayce seemed stuck. After a minute Dori asked, "What about Jonathan?"

"He's called a meeting." Grayce looked stricken, and the other Graces patted her back consolingly.

"A meeting?"

"At church tonight, dear." Somber Gracie couldn't keep quiet any longer.

"Seven-thirty," added Wrinkled Grace.

"Because he knows Pastor Paul is out of town," Rouged Grayce finished, her neck turning scarlet with embarrassment. "I'm so sorry."

"Let me get this straight," Dori said, not certain why a meeting was bad. "Jonathan has called a meeting tonight even though Trev is out if town."

The Graces nodded. Dori looked at them blankly.

"She doesn't understand," Somber Gracie said.

"She's too nice to see the skullduggery," Wrinkled Grace said.

Dori blinked. Skullduggery?

Rouged Grayce sighed. "Jonathan wants Pastor Paul out."

Dori frowned. Then it clicked. "Out of the chapel? He wants Trev to leave Seaside?" Dori took a deep breath. So this was Jonathan's strategy. Wait until Trev left town, then go for his jugular. Why was she surprised? Trev had said this would happen.

The Graces nodded, expressions sad.

"I'm so sorry," Grayce Warrington said. "He's my son, but he's wrong."

Dori patted Grayce's hand. Another parent disappointed in a child, just like Mae Harper. "It's not your fault, Mrs. Warrington. Jonathan's an adult who makes his own choices."

Rouged Grayce sniffed. "That's very kind of you, dear."

The other Graces sniffed. "Very kind, very kind," they agreed. "Pastor is so lucky to have you."

"He's my son." Rouged Grayce said again, her head bowed. "Sometimes he shames me so."

"No, no, Grayce," Somber Gracie said. "Like Dori said, it's not your fault."

"It's not," agreed Wrinkled Grace. "We know. We were there the whole time you were raising that mischief maker. You did everything right. He just didn't listen."

Grayce gave a wan smile, her clown cheeks brilliant against the pallor of her face.

"How do people know about this meeting?" Dori asked.

"Judy's been working the phones all day," Somber Gracie said. "As soon as Angie gets home from classes, she'll help. That's how they always do it."

"But they didn't call us," Somber Gracie said. "They never call us anymore."

"They know we won't cooperate," Wrinkled Grace said.

"Mae called me," Rouged Grayce said. "She knew I'd want to know."

"But how can Jonathan call a meeting just because he wants one?" Dori's fingers beat a tattoo on the counter. "What authority does he have to do something like this?"

"He's on the elder board," Somber Gracie said. "He thinks that gives him the right."

"Does it?" Dori asked.

"Oh, no. He's not the only elder, you know."

"They're supposed to agree on things." Wrinkled Grace reached in her bag and pulled out a pill bottle. She dumped out a pill and slid it under her tongue.

Dori's eyes widened in concern, but the other Graces seemed not in the least concerned that their driver was having heart problems severe enough to require digitalis.

"I doubt he even contacted Ed Masterson, who is the chairman, and the others on the board with him, like Frank Shaw, such a fine young man." Wrinkled Grace looked quite militant as she patted her aching friend Grayce on the back. "He knows that they'd say things need to be done decently and in order."

"I called Ed," Rouged Grayce said. "I can't let Jonathan bully the congregation again."

"He's done this before, hasn't he?" Dori thought of the earlier pastors that Jonathan had managed to get to resign.

Sadly Grayce nodded. "It's his modus operandi."

Dori came out from behind the counter. "Thank you so much for coming to me with this news." She leaned in and kissed each of them on their withered cheeks. She gave Grayce Warrington an extra hug.

"What are you going to do?" Wrinkled Grace asked. Three pairs of expectant eyes settled on Dori.

She shook her head. "I don't know, but I'll think of something."

"We will be praying," Somber Gracie said, patting Dori's arm.

"And we'll be at the meeting," Wrinkled Grace said, squeezing Dori's hand.

"We'll do our best for your Trev," Rouged Grayce said, putting her hand on Dori's cheek. "After all, he's our Trev too."

The Graces left, subdued but relieved.

As soon as the door closed behind them, Dori raced to the back room and grabbed the phone. She dialed the number Trev had given her when he left that morning. A recorded message kicked in telling her to dial the extension she wanted or hold for a receptionist. She held, but no receptionist answered.

"Come on, come on!" She hung up and dialed again. Same

thing. She dialed Trev's cell phone and got his voice mail.

"Trev, Jonathan is having a meeting about you tonight. What do you want me to do?"

She hung up, knowing that Trev probably had his phone turned off for the meetings. He might not even check it for messages until much too late to do any good.

She raced across the street to Phil's pharmacy. He took one look at her face, pulled her into his office, and closed the door.

"What's wrong?"

"He's going to get them to fire Trev!"

"Who? How?"

"Jonathan Warrington at some meeting tonight. And I can't get hold of Trev!"

"Good old Jonathan." Phil shook his head. "Trev always said he'd be trouble some day. How did you find out?"

"The Graces."

"Ah." Phil ran his hand through his hair. "I wish I could help you, but when Maureen said she was spending the night with you, I gave my pharmacist the night off. I have to work until nine."

Dori waved her hand. "Don't worry. I didn't expect you to fix things. I just needed someone to share the bad news with. And someone to pray."

Phil nodded. "Will do."

"Don't you find it, oh, I don't know, *upsetting* that a Christian would do this to another Christian?"

"Personally, I think *upsetting* is much too nice a word." Phil stuck his hands in his trouser pockets and leaned back on his desk. "I don't have much experience in churches yet, but even I know that going after a man when he's not around to defend himself is punching way below the belt."

"Trev's done a great job here, hasn't he, Phil? You've seen him in action longer than I have."

Phil nodded. "Again I don't have any means of comparison, but it seems to me that he's given above and beyond no matter how you look at it."

Dori nodded. "That's what I thought. So I'm the issue here." She felt tears burn behind her eyes. "If Pop had only thought!"

"He would have done the same thing." Phil reached for Dori

and gave her a hug. "You're more important to Pop than any church. To me, too, and to Trev. If he loses this pulpit but gets you back, he'll consider it a great bargain."

Dori could no longer contain her tears.

"But the issue isn't really you," Phil continued, ignoring the stream coursing down her cheeks. "It's that Trev never told anyone about you."

Dori sniffed. "It makes him look like a deceiver." She reached for a tissue from the box on Phil's desk. "But even if he was wrong in keeping quiet about us, it's still wrong to stab a man in the back when he's not there to defend himself."

"What I want to know," Phil said, "is how one man can just call a meeting of the church. I think there's a rule somewhere in the church policies or constitution or something that tells the way meetings get called. I looked through all that stuff when I joined the chapel, but it was a while ago. I wasn't thinking I'd need to know that little fact later."

The phone beside Dori rang, and she jumped at the sound.

Phil grinned at her as he reached for the receiver. "A bit nervous, are we? Hello, this is Phil Trevelyan."

Suddenly he was all business, and Dori slipped out of the office thinking how proud she was of him for the success he'd made of his life. Now the question was what should she do on behalf of his brother to avert catastrophe tonight? She was so lost in thought that she almost bumped into Maureen before she saw her.

Maureen's smile dimmed as soon as she got a good look at Dori's face. "What's wrong?"

The tears came again, and Dori batted at them. "There's a meeting at church tonight to talk about Trev and me and our strange marriage, and he's not even in town."

Maureen took Dori's arm and drew her into the corner by a carousel of reading glasses. "Start at the beginning."

Dori did and concluded, "So I don't know what to do!"

"I'd suggest you get hold of someone you trust who is in church leadership and ask him what's the story on calling meetings."

Dori nodded. "Yes, that's what I'll do."

"You do know someone you can call, don't you?" Maureen asked.

"Frank Shaw. He's an elder, and he likes Trev."

Maureen took Dori's hand. "You do understand that liking Trev won't be the issue, don't you?"

Dori nodded miserably. "It's me."

"Well, yes and no. What you need to remember is that a pastor's private life isn't really private. His congregation wants to know that his marriage is strong." Maureen wrinkled her nose. "Even more, they want to know if he's married. The fact that he never said anything about you or your marriage and your separation will be the issue. If anyone has an ax to grind, they can make Trev look very bad."

"It's funny, but if this were a regular job, nobody'd care whether we were married, separated, happy, or sad."

"But it's church," Maureen said, "and things are different. People expect more of a church leader, and the Bible even says more is required of one."

"I don't know anything about how churches work," Dori said. "My only exposure to Christians was in Young Life as a teenager. Nobody in our family went to church, and even though I went with some of the Young Life kids my senior year in high school, as soon as I got to college, I stopped."

"Well, I've gone to church my whole life. My mom took me for the first time when I was two weeks old."

"Really?" Dori was fascinated.

Maureen nodded. "Over the years I've seen Christians do lots of very unkind things to each other, especially to their pastors. I remember one lady who stood up in a business meeting when they were seeking approval for a raise for the pastor that would bring his income a tad above minimum wage. She said, 'Why should we give him a raise? All he ever does is fish!' And once there was a group who disliked the pastor so much that they left church by the back door every week rather than go out the front and have to shake hands with him."

"All the first guy did was fish," Dori said.

"I always thought he did it to feed his family," Maureen said. "They sure weren't paying him enough. Of course they got mad when he stopped fishing and his wife got a job. She should be home with the kids, you know."

"What did the guy they wouldn't shake hands with do that made them so mad?"

"He didn't agree with their ideas on music and suitable activities for the youth program."

"He liked fast and they liked slow?"

Maureen nodded. "And he liked rowdy and fun where they liked serious and quiet."

"Poor Trev." Dori wrapped her arms around herself. "All he's ever done is love me."

Dori went back to Harbor Lights and closed for the day. In the gloom of the early winter's evening she drove home. Ryan, Trudy, and Jack met her at the door.

"So Mr. Warrington is making his move tonight, huh?"

Good grief, Dori thought. *Even the kids know!*

"Sort of makes you proud to be a Christian, doesn't it?" Ryan looked like he'd swallowed something foul.

Dori dumped the cheesesteaks she'd picked up on the kitchen table. Jack immediately put his chin on the table and began salivating. Trudy jumped onto a chair and then the table, drawn by the smells as strongly as Jack. Dori reached out and brushed Trudy to the floor and pushed Jack back.

Ryan pulled potato chips and coleslaw from the paper bag Dori had dropped on the counter. He twisted the top on a bottle of Coke and listened with closed eyes to the fwish of the vacuum being broken.

"Gotta love a meal like this!" he said, unrolling the paper wrapped around his cheese steak. "Pure cholesterol."

Dori dropped into the chair across from him. "Lord, thanks for this food, and help me know what to do tonight."

"Yeah, God. They want to get Pastor Paul. Don't let them."

They ate for a moment in silence, savoring the blend of chipped steak, melted cheese, spicy onions, and tangy ketchup. Ryan was guzzling his bottle of Coke when Dori spoke.

"You know, Ryan, all Christians aren't like Mr. Warrington."

Ryan shrugged and kept eating.

"How long have you lived with Trev?"

"Almost four weeks."

"Is he like Mr. Warrington?"

Ryan looked affronted at the idea. "Of course not."

"Then don't lump all Christians together. It's like lumping all seventh graders together and saying Eric Jankowski represents them all."

Ryan looked at her for a moment in silence, not wanting to acknowledge her logic. Then he dropped his eyes and stared at the ketchup-stained paper in front of him. "But what if he can get people to turn against Pastor Paul?" When he looked at her again, his eyes were bleak. "I remember when he did it to Pastor Jackman."

He pulled a piece of meat from his sandwich and dropped it to Jack. Trudy immediately put her little white paws on his knee and demanded some too. "I liked Pastor Jackman. So did my grandmother. He was a very nice man."

"And you like Trev too."

Ryan nodded. "But what's he going to say about you, Dori? Mr. Warrington, I mean, not Pastor Paul." He gave a devilish little smile. "I already know what Pastor Paul says about you."

Dori couldn't help but grin as she remembered this morning. They'd all been leaving the house at the same time. After Trev had prayed for each of them, he'd turned to Ryan.

"Take good care of her for me, Ry. We don't want to lose her again." He'd pulled Dori close in a hug while Ryan made believe he was gagging. "She's too good a cook." And he'd kissed her while Ryan laughed and ran for the bus.

That's when he'd said, "I'll miss you, sweetheart. After the pleasure of being with you this week, even one night away is much too much."

Her heart had expanded, knowing she felt the same way. "Hurry back," she'd whispered.

Now she wished him home with all she had in her.

Twenty-Nine

DORI STOOD IN the church lobby but off to the side where Jonathan Warrington couldn't see her. She huddled in her red Lands' End Squall, stomach in knots, and listened to him attack her husband. She shuddered with a chill that didn't come from the winter's winds but from the icy vitriol pouring from the man up front. She slid her hands into the jacket's pockets and rolled them into fists to stop their shaking.

"Integrity is a characteristic we need, we deserve, in our pastor," Jonathan said, sounding so sincere, so full of spiritual common sense. "We must be able to trust our pastor, have absolute confidence that he is the man of God he claims to be. Where is integrity in keeping a marriage secret?"

When Dori had decided to come, leaving Ryan at home with Maureen and the dogs, she'd known it would be difficult to listen to the things that Jonathan said. She just hadn't realized how difficult.

Jonathan paused a moment, then said with more than a touch of cynicism, "A marriage, I might add, that is in serious trouble."

But it's not now, she wanted to yell. *We're working it out. He loves me, and I love him.*

She froze as she heard her own thoughts. She loved him? Yes, she loved him. Whatever had happened six years ago no longer mattered. He was a different man now in so many ways. He would never hurt her like that again. She knew that as surely as she knew the sun would rise tomorrow morning. These years had honed him, tempered him, taken all the things she had always loved about him and strengthened them, making him a much better man than she deserved.

"He lied to us," Jonathan told the partially filled auditorium. "Oh, he never said he wasn't married. That's true enough. But he never said he was married either."

As Dori looked honestly at herself and Trev, she could see that she was the one who was lagging far behind in character development. She was the one who had set God aside rather than embracing Him and asking His help. She was the one who held a grudge of such major proportions that she had kept the two of them apart for years.

Oh, Lord, forgive me! Dori closed her eyes in pain. *And, Lord, please protect Trev. You know he never meant to deceive these folks. He just didn't know what to tell them. Help us build a strong marriage. Make me a wife Trev can be proud of.*

"You all know that my son is going through a hard patch in his marriage." Jonathan sounded troubled and sad. "You know he has been told he can no longer play on the church's athletic teams because of it, and by a man who has a troubled marriage himself! Where is integrity in that?"

Dori felt her shoulders tighten in frustration and panic. Where was integrity in denying the little fact that Bob was living with Penni, being unfaithful to Shannon, and ignoring his children? Trev never behaved in a manner that would bring such dishonor on the Lord and the chapel.

Where was the man or woman who would stand up and defend him?

"You also know how Paul Trevelyan led my daughter on." Jonathan sounded about ready to weep. "Just imagine her distress and hurt when she found out he had been married the whole time he courted her!"

When he paused, Dori heard only silence. Did all these people for whom Trev had worked and prayed and cared think for themselves so little that they believed the shrewd web of half-truths

Jonathan spun? Was this how he had gotten rid of the last few pastors? An illegal meeting? A clandestine vote? An opposition of such pressure and numbers that the men hadn't been able to take the strain?

A huge anger rose up in Dori. If no one else would speak for Trev, she would. She'd tell these people exactly what she thought of Jonathan Warrington and his lies, of them and their malicious silence.

As she gathered her courage, she was vaguely aware of the door behind her opening. Cold air raced around her feet, but she ignored it. She stepped toward the door into the sanctuary.

"No, Dori." Strong arms slid around her and held her in place. "Don't march in there with that avenging angel look. It'll create more dissension, exactly what we don't want."

She spun. "Trev! What are you doing here?" She threw her arms around his neck and kissed him.

"Wow," he said softly. "I think I'll go away more often if this is the welcome home I get." He gave her a quick, hard kiss.

She smiled at him and thought how much she loved him. She had been a fool to stay away. Maybe she could blame her youth for her original running, but she could blame nothing but her stubbornness and unforgiving heart for the length of her desertion.

Here I stand, so help me God, she thought. *Right here at Trev's side. I'll never run again.*

"I tried to call you and tell you about this." She tipped her head toward the auditorium. "Several times."

"I got the messages on my cell phone. I tried to get hold of you then, but somehow we never connected. I did get through to Ed Masterson though."

"Ed's in there? Why hasn't he said anything?"

Trev shook his head. "Jonathan would never carry on like this if he thought Ed was around. He's in the room off to the right, out of sight just like you. Two other elders, Frank Shaw—remember him?—and Jerome Player, are with him. They've been waiting for my call that I'm here."

He pulled his cell from his belt and punched in a number. "I'm in the narthex." He nodded, hit off, and returned the phone to his belt. He held out his hand to Dori. "Now come and stand with me in the doorway."

"All right!" She nodded, thinking how good it would feel when Jonathan finally got his comeuppance.

"You look ready to cut out Jonathan's innards," Trev said, a restraining hand on her arm. He smiled that wry smile she so loved. "My fierce Dori. I thank you for caring so deeply. It's a very wifely attitude."

"That's because I'm your wife."

He studied her face for a long moment and must have seen things there she wasn't aware were showing, not that she cared.

"I love you, too" he said, "but you have to promise me not to say a word."

"What? You didn't hear all the things he said! And everyone else is too cowardly to even challenge his version of things. Somebody's got to defend you."

He gave her a quick hug, chuckling softly. "Dori, the idea here is to keep peace, not declare war."

"Jonathan already declared it," she said, feeling a holy militancy.

He put his hands on her shoulders. "Let Ed take care of it, sweetheart. Promise."

Her eyes fell to the bottom of the vee in the yellow sweater he wore over a navy and yellow plaid shirt and beneath the red Lands' End Squall that hung open. She took a deep breath.

She lifted her eyes to his. "You've been talking to the Lord a lot more than I have in recent years, and you undoubtedly have a better feel for what He'd want. I'll keep quiet."

He gave her a little shake of approval. "That's my girl." He released her, took her hand, and led her to the doorway into the sanctuary.

In the few minutes Dori had been talking to Trev, she'd missed part of Jonathan's rant. She'd also missed his mother rising to her feet. She stood, rouged cheeks vivid against her pallor. Her voice shook as she spoke.

"Please don't do this, Jonny."

Jonathan looked appalled. "Mother, take your seat."

"I haven't said anything when you spoke against the others,

but I know I was wrong then. I don't want to be wrong now."

"Sit down, Mother. You don't know what you're talking about."

"I know about lots of things, Jonny." Tears started to run down her cheeks right through her rouge circles. "I know you're only telling half-truths, and it shames me that you would do that in the house of the Lord. It shames me."

With a sigh, Grayce collapsed into her seat, and the other Graces, one on each side, began comforting her.

Jonathan was so intent on his mother and the giant monkey wrench she'd just thrown into his pseudospiritual, self-righteous plans that he didn't notice Ed Masterson until Ed was standing on the platform beside him.

"Excuse me a minute, Jonathan." Ed was obviously nervous, but he stepped toward the microphone anyway.

Jonathan, taken off guard, sputtered but could do nothing but move to the side. Anything else would look petty, and he was going for the high road of principle, at least in his words.

"Good evening, folks," Ed said. "I want you to know that Jerome, Frank and I appreciate your caring enough about Seaside Chapel to come to this meeting tonight." Ed indicated the two men who had come to stand beside him. "I also want you to know that we're going to adjourn in just a couple of minutes."

"Now wait a minute," Jonathan roared. "We have things to discuss!"

Ed nodded. "I agree with you. We do. However, we want to do it according to the chapel's bylaws." He opened the folder he had in his hand and began to read from the paper in it. "'Any business meeting of this assembly may be called by the majority of the board of elders, the congregation being given two weeks notice of said meeting.'"

Ed looked at the people in the pews. "In keeping with this specifically spelled-out policy, the majority of the four-member board of elders—Jerome, Frank, and I—call a meeting for two weeks from tonight." He turned to Jonathan. "We know that you will agree with us that following already-legislated church policy is by far the best way to do things."

Jonathan looked ready to explode, but he again had no choice but to agree.

Ed turned back to the people. "At that time we shall address any and all issues affecting Pastor Paul Trevelyan, in particular the circumstances of his marriage. In the meantime, we request that you all be in prayer about this meeting. Our main objectives are to air all issues honestly and to do so in a spirit of Christian love and concern."

Dori stood by Trev, amazed at the way Jonathan had been defanged, and all without the spilling of any blood. Suddenly Trev pulled her hand, and she found herself walking down the center aisle beside him.

"And to close tonight, I've asked Pastor Paul, who was out of town at an important conference but who rushed back to be with us in this potentially divisive time, to close with prayer."

Trev walked onto the platform, pulling Dori with him. A united front. She couldn't wait to hear his prayer. In fact, she hoped he said a few pointed words first.

"Lord," Trev began as he stopped at the mike. "We are your people. Seaside Chapel is but one small part of the Body of Christ, but it is our part, and we love it. We want above all that Christ be glorified here. Come lead us. Show us what, given our present circumstances, is the best way that we can bring glory, not dishonor, to the name of Christ through whom we pray, amen."

Ed stepped to the mike again. "Good night, everyone."

In mere minutes the church was empty.

Thirty

MAUREEN, SOMETHING'S WRONG with Trudy." Ryan held the little dog in his arms. Instead of her usual lavish licking of his face, she lay inert, her little paws drooping listlessly.

Maureen looked at the too-still dog and felt instant alarm. She laid her hand on the animal's chest.

"Is she dead?" Ryan's eyes were huge.

For a moment Maureen thought the answer was yes, and she paled at the thought. Ryan didn't need another loss; he'd faced more than his share in his short life. And how would she tell Dori that her dog had died on her watch?

"I feel a heartbeat," she cried, her knees going weak with relief. She ran her hand over the little dog's head. "What happened?"

"I don't know." Ryan hugged the animal close. "She went out back with Jack a few minutes ago. She doesn't like the cold weather at all, so I didn't wait too long before calling for her to come in. She came, walked funny to her water, took a few slurps, and sort of fell over."

Maureen frowned. She had known from the beginning that the main flaw in the plan to have the suitcase taken was always the dogs. But if the dogs were removed from the scene... "Where's Jack?"

"He's still out."

Maureen flew to the back door and threw it open. "Jack!" she called. "Jack!"

No big black dog bounded to her.

Ryan pushed in front of her, Trudy still in his arms. "Jack! Come here, boy. Come on, Jack. Come on."

No dog appeared.

"Maybe he's being stubborn," Ryan suggested, his eyes worried behind his replacement glasses.

Maureen doubted it but had to acknowledge the possibility. "He could be out there, and we'd never see him in the dark. The porch light doesn't reach that far."

"There's a light on the garage," Ryan said. "It shines on the backyard so you can see when you come in from the alley."

Maureen hit all the switches by the door. The kitchen and porch went dark, but the spotlight on the garage poured brightness onto the fenced yard.

"The gate's open!" Ryan yelled and began running. "We never leave it open!" Maureen was right behind him. They stopped at the gate, and Maureen looked carefully at the sturdy latch that had to be opened by sliding it up the heavy support pole. There was no way that latch had been opened by a dog, even one as big and smart as Jack.

"Was it open when you let the dogs out?" Maureen asked as she studied the yard, especially the shadows behind the edge of the garage.

"I don't think so," Ryan said. "But I'm not sure. I never thought to check because we always keep it shut." He peered into the darkness and called, "Here, Jack. Come on, boy!"

Maureen laid a hand on his sleeve. "Don't bother. If he's escaped, he's not hanging around. He's out running."

"The beach." Ryan's voice was firm and certain. "He'd head there. He loves it."

Maureen nodded. It was as good a guess as any, probably better than most. "One gate mysteriously open, one dog missing, and the other unaccountably unconscious."

"The suitcase!" Ryan's eyes were big.

"Probably. Let's go in. I'll call Greg and Fleishman. Then I'll get you out of here."

"What? No way!"

"Way," Maureen said. "Nonnegotiable. And we've got to get Trudy to the vet's."

Ryan stopped with his hand on the back doorknob. "They drugged her, didn't they?"

Maureen shrugged as she pushed him inside. "Probably." She reached for her cell.

"How about Jack?"

She punched the quick dial number. "I wouldn't be surprised." The phone was answered, and she turned her attention to it. "Hello, Greg. Tonight's the night. The dogs have been drugged."

"We can't just let him be sick out there," Ryan wailed. "We've got to find him! We've got to!"

"Ryan and I are the only ones here. Everyone else is at church, work, or out of town." She put her hand over the mouthpiece and spoke to Ryan. "Get a blanket and wrap Trudy in it. Find a couple of flashlights."

"So we can look for Jack?"

Maureen nodded. "Get going and wrap yourself up well, too."

The boy charged from the room.

"Get yourself and the kid out of the house," Greg said in Maureen's ear. "We want that suitcase as accessible as possible. Fleishman is lurking down the street behind a hedge. Great shadows to hide in. His car's around the corner. I'll alert him. And I just took up position in the back alley."

"All my time on this case, and I'm going to miss all the fun!" She knew she had no choice with Ryan and the dogs, but it was a distinct letdown to know she was going to miss the collar.

"Go, Galloway. That's an order." And he hung up.

She was pushing her arms into her bright blue coat when Ryan rushed into the room with Trudy lolling in his arms, a green fleece blanket wrapped around her so that only her head with her glassy, unfocused eyes, black button nose, and floppy little ears showed.

They rushed out of the house to Maureen's car parked along the curb out front. Maureen blinked to keep the tears of frustration and aggravation from doing anything more than sting the backs of her eyes. She was a professional. She could take disappointment. Besides, the kid and the dogs needed her.

She drove to the end of the block and turned toward the beach. She parked illegally at the break in the dunes where a path led to the beach. She and Ryan jumped out, leaving Trudy snug in her blanket on the backseat.

The cold bit through her coat, making her shiver as they rushed onto the sand. The night was very dark, the moon a mere sliver covered by clouds much of the time. Since the homes lining the beach were mostly summer residences, there was no artificial light to help them find a black dog on a black night.

In the distant north, Atlantic City was just visible, more a brightness reflected against the clouds than actual lights, and several blocks to the north, light poured from the windows of two homes onto the beach. Neither was close enough to be of help. A small bobbing light appeared closer, but again it provided them with no aid.

To the south it was all black. Directly ahead the ocean's ebony was relieved by the muted curling of the foam-flocked waves as the sea relentlessly tried to reclaim the beaches that the taxpayers had paid for and the Army Corps of Engineers had dredged up and piped in.

"If he ate something drugged like Trudy did, he can't be too far, can he?" Ryan asked as he peered into the darkness.

"I wouldn't think so." Maureen gave him a quick hug. "Don't worry. We'll find him."

"Yeah." But Ry didn't sound convinced. "Which way?"

"You go left. I'll go right," Maureen said. "Call if you see anything."

She turned south, and a feeling of helplessness overcame her. How would they ever find him? And how long could they afford to hunt for Jack before Trudy was truly endangered by the delay in seeking treatment for her?

Lord, let us see Jack and fast. Help us find him! Day and night are alike to You. Lead us to him.

"Maureen! Maureen! I found him."

She turned and ran toward Ryan's voice. The beam of her flashlight found him crouched beside a black bulk that lay inert on the sand. Ry was stroking Jack's head, crooning to him in that soft, caressing voice used instinctively on invalids and babies.

She dropped to her knees beside Ryan and slid her hand down the dog's chest. She went limp with relief when she felt a heartbeat.

"We've got to get him to the car." She stood and looked back at the break in the dunes. She turned and stared at the unmoving Jack. She walked behind him, bent, wrapped her arms around him under his forelegs, and pulled.

Nothing. Absolutely not one inch.

Vaguely aware that the bobbing light was getting nearer but paying it no attention, she straightened. "Maybe we can roll him on the blanket and pull him to the car that way."

"What about Trudy? She'll freeze if we take her blanket."

"It'll only be for a little while. Unless you have a better idea, guy, I don't see what else we can do." She turned and ran back to the car, her flashlight beam jumping with each step, the sand dragging against her feet. She skidded to a stop beside her car and opened the back door. She grabbed the green fleece and the little dog wrapped in it. She reached into the blanket with trepidation and felt Trudy's chest. Her heartbeat was still faint but steady.

Holding Trudy firmly against her chest inside her jacket, she hurried back to Ryan, finding him still on his knees beside Jack. Suddenly a flashlight beam struck them.

Blinking against the sudden light in her eyes, Maureen called, "Who's there?"

"Clooney," came the answer.

Clooney? The name meant nothing to her.

Ryan jumped to his feet. "Clooney? It's Ryan Harper. Pastor Paul's dog is sick."

"Well, hello, young Ryan." A man with a long gray ponytail halted in the light of Maureen's flashlight beam. He wore a ratty green down ski jacket and jeans with a hole in one knee. A Phillies cap sat on his head, his ponytail pulled through the hole in the back, and he had on a pair of well-worn dark leather gloves. A huge sparkler, surely a cubic zirconium, pierced one ear.

"You know him, Ryan?" Maureen asked.

"Everyone knows Clooney," Ryan said as the man dropped to his knees beside the boy. Ry jerked his thumb toward Maureen. "She's Maureen Galloway, the new cop in Seaside."

"Ah," Clooney said. "I'd heard we had a lady on the force." He looked over his shoulder at Maureen who hovered behind him. "Pleased to meet you, Officer Galloway. That a blanket you've got there?"

"We were going to get Jack on it and pull him to the car," Ryan explained.

"Exactly the plan I would suggest." He stood and reached for the blanket. Trudy's little head lolling out of Maureen's jacket caused him a slight jerk of surprise. "This one sick too?"

"Someone seems to have drugged them." Maureen ran a hand over Trudy's head.

He pinched his lips and shook his head. "Some people are cruel."

Clooney shook the blanket open, let it fall to the ground beside Jack's back, and pushed the edge as far beneath the animal as he could.

"Help me roll him, young Ryan."

The two circled the blanket, took hold of Jack's legs, and swung them over his body until he was lying on his other side and on the edge of the blanket. Then Clooney knelt and slid first Jack's head and shoulders, then his hindquarters, until the animal was resting in the middle of the blanket. The only sign the dog gave of being aware of the people manipulating him was a deep sigh.

Clooney and Ryan stood. Clooney looked from Ryan to Maureen and back.

"Young Ryan, I don't want you to take this wrong, but I think you should hold the little dog and Officer Galloway should help me pull."

"I'm strong for my size," Ryan protested. "I can pull."

"Let's put it this way, boy." Clooney bent as he spoke and picked up a corner. "You can take over for her when she tires. After all, she's only a girl."

Understanding that Clooney was trying to save Ryan's sense of self, Maureen puffed herself up and said, "*Only a girl?* What do you mean by that, mister?"

Ryan giggled and reached for Trudy.

"You have her tucked inside your coat?" Maureen asked as she bent for her corner of the blanket.

"Already done," Ryan said.

They began their slow progress across the beach. It was astonishing how heavy Jack was, lying there unable to help at all. Maureen dragged first with one hand, then the other, then both, walking forward, then walking backward. Clooney pulled like Jack weighed as much as Trudy.

"What are you doing up here at this hour of the night?" Ryan asked as he walked beside them. "Isn't this a bit late for beachcombing?"

"A bit cold, too," Clooney added. "And I forgot my spade and detector."

Maureen watched Clooney from the corner of her eye. He was well-spoken and intelligent, and her instincts told her he was safe. Ryan certainly trusted him. But had she heard right? A beachcomber?

When Clooney said nothing more, Ryan said, "So? Why are you here?"

Clooney cleared his throat. "Something just told me I had to come." He sounded apologetic, as if they wouldn't be able to believe him.

Not something, Maureen thought. *Someone.*

"What do you mean?" Ryan asked.

"I don't rightly know," Clooney said, his voice still uncertain. "I was in my house watching some TV when all of a sudden I got the feeling that I needed to go to the beach. I tried to shrug it off. After all, it's well after dark on a midwinter night. It's not the best time or weather for detecting."

"But the feeling wouldn't go away?" Ryan's voice was excited.

Maureen didn't say anything, but she felt pretty excited too. It had to be God supplying an answer to her prayers for Jack before she even prayed them.

"The feelings wouldn't go away," Clooney agreed. "I even knew I was to come to this area of the beach." He shrugged. "So I did."

"Wow!" Ryan was clearly impressed. "It's like ESP!"

Maureen stopped and turned to Ryan. "It's like God, kiddo. It's like God."

Thirty-One

BARNEY, JOANNE, AND VINNIE sat in Barney's black car parked in the drive of a summer house across the street and three doors down from Trev's. Joanne was toasty sitting in the curve of Barney's arm, except for her feet. The boots with the stiletto heels might make her legs look great, but they were no good at keeping her feet warm.

The three of them had been sitting here for a couple of hours now, except for when Vinnie delivered the doped meat. She grinned. Barney had warmed her up very nicely while Vinnie was gone. Now he was back, and the cold was beginning to seep up her legs even though she wore jeans over tights.

"Can you turn on the heat for a few minutes, Barney?" she asked. "I'm getting cold."

He shook his head. "We can't because the cops would see the exhaust."

"What cops?" She leaned forward and scanned the street. It looked completely empty to her.

"See that hedge?" He pointed in the direction of the house they were watching, the one where Dori MacAllister now lived.

She didn't, but she nodded. She didn't want Barney to know her eyes were so bad. Like her mom always said, guys don't go for girls with glasses.

"There's a cop behind it," Barney said. "He's been there ever since it got dark."

Joanne was surprised, but she didn't question Barney's statement. Barney knew everything. "He must be freezing!"

Barney looked at her, and she could hear the amusement in his voice when he said, "You worried about him?"

"Not really worried." Joanne tried to wiggle her toes again. "But being cold's no fun."

"He's wrapped up in a sleeping bag," Vinnie said, looking straight ahead out the windshield. Joanne knew he was doing his best to pretend she wasn't there. "He's probably warmer than we are."

"A sleeping bag?" Joanne blinked. "Wow, what a good idea. I wish I had one."

"There's also a cop in the alley," Vinnie said. "He showed up just as I was leaving the meat." He held up a hand and said quickly, "But he didn't see me."

Joanne looked at him. "You didn't hurt the dogs, did you? I told Barney I didn't want them hurt." She turned to Barney. "I don't want you to hurt that girl either. Or the kid. Or the minister."

Barney gave her a squeeze. "It's sort of hard to do my job if I can't hurt anyone."

"Well, you can't. You're way too nice to keep doing mean things like you used to."

Both Barney and Vinnie made choking sounds.

"Well, you are," she said with passion. "I know."

Barney leaned over and kissed her temple. "And you, baby, are a wonder."

"Yeah?" She felt herself puff with pleasure. "That's really good, isn't it? Being a wonder, I mean?"

"If you don't mind, how about we get back to business," Vinnie interrupted. He sounded like he'd just tasted something very bad. "After I put out most of the dog food, I left the gate open behind me. I put the rest outside the gate to lure the big dog out."

Barney nodded, looking impressed. "Not bad, Vin."

Joanne smiled at her ex-boyfriend. She was glad he had done well, but she was also glad she was now with Barney. She snuggled closer to the big man, wishing there was some way he could hug her feet.

"Yeah," Vinnie continued, still not looking at Joanne. "He ate most of the stuff in the yard. The little dog—its name is Trudy; can you believe it?—got some too. Then Jack—that's the big dog— came through the gate, ate the rest, and took off just as the back door opened. Trudy went in when they called, but Jack kept running. He was heading for the beach."

Joanne tried to wiggle her toes but couldn't feel them. She sighed and wanted a sleeping bag real bad. Barney's arm tightened around her as if he understood her problem and sympathized.

Suddenly the front door of the house they were watching flew open. The kid and a lady who was not the suitcase lady but the cop lady raced out. The kid—skinny little thing—held something crushed to his chest. Joanne squinted, trying for better focus. She hated not seeing things far away.

Last night at the casino, she wouldn't have known it was Barney who came into the restaurant if it wasn't for his size. She was able to smile her welcome way before she could really see him. Sometime she was maybe going to have to get glasses in spite of what Mom said, but not until she had to, like when she couldn't read a stop sign anymore.

"I guess they got that Trudy dog wrapped in that blanket," Vinnie said, staring like he had x-ray vision or something. "She should be out cold. Taking her to the vet's, you think?"

"I think." Barney looked over Joanne's head and smiled at Vinnie. "That means an empty house."

Vinnie nodded. "Give me twenty minutes. It probably won't take that long, but I'd rather have too much time than not enough. I'll stay hidden until the time's up."

"Be careful." Joanne couldn't help it. The words sort of slipped out. Some habits were hard to break.

Vinnie looked at her for the first time all night. "You too," he said stiffly and reached for the door handle. He glanced up at Barney. "Dome light still off?"

"Still off. Your car just around the corner?"

Vinnie nodded and opened the door. "See you at Mr. J's house."

"You mean Mr. Jankowski's house?" Barney's voice was ice.

Vinnie glanced back. "Yeah. Mr. Jankowski. Whatever." Dressed entirely in black with black stuff smeared on his face, he disappeared into the night almost immediately.

Barney stared after him. "I don't know about that guy. He's not too smart, and he's disrespectful. Bad combination." Barney glanced at his watch. "Twenty minutes." He looked at Joanne. "Come here, baby."

Joanne went willingly. She was starting to shudder with cold and knew he'd fix her in no time flat. Maybe he'd even rub her feet to get them warm.

Barney pulled her into his lap, and she twisted to face him. She wrapped her arms around his neck even as she curled her legs up so she could tuck her toes, boots and all, behind him. When he pulled back and said, "Time's up," she was toasty all over, even her feet.

She blinked. "That's twenty minutes?"

"Ten. And it's time for you to do your bit."

She uncurled herself and picked up the black watch cap that had fallen on the floor. She hated the hat and what it did to her hair. She spent so much time getting every little strand just right, and now she had to crush it, but she understood that she had to hide the blonde curls. They were too visible even on a dark night like tonight. She crammed her hair up inside the cap, trying not to flinch at the thought of how ugly she'd look when she took it off. When she was finished, Barney reached over and adjusted it for her. Then he gave her a quick kiss.

"You look just like a longshoreman." He grinned. "A cute longshoreman."

She grinned back, uncertain what a longshoreman was but knowing he was teasing her. He teased so nicely, not with the edge that Vinnie had always had.

"You know where the suitcase is hidden?" he asked.

"Behind the shrubs on the left side of the porch."

"I want you to go down to the end of the block before you cross the street." He pointed to the left, away from the hedge where the cop was hiding. "I don't want him seeing you prematurely."

She nodded and climbed out. "But it's okay if he sees me when I get close?"

"I hope he doesn't, but if he does, it'll be okay."

"See you in a few minutes." She got out of the car, crouched low, and ran as fast as her boots would let her, keeping to the shadows of the trees and shrubs and houses. Five houses down she took a deep breath and raced across the street. Her heart was beating so fast she felt almost as light-headed as she had on the plane. But Barney was counting on her, and she would keel over dead before she'd disappoint him.

She hid in the shadows again as she slipped ever closer to the Trevelyan house. When she dashed across the last bit of lawn to hug the side of their house, she rested a minute. She couldn't remember the last time she'd run on purpose. As she felt nervous sweat trickle down her spine, she remembered why. "Never let 'em see you sweat," Mom always said. "Nobody likes a sweaty woman."

Oh, Barney, please don't mind. I'm doing this for you.

She felt behind the shrubs, found the suitcase, and pulled it out. With a mighty heave, she pushed it over the porch rail. It was a good thing no one was home because the thud when it landed would have brought everyone running. She climbed over the rail after it. She pulled up the handle and wheeled the case to the front door, lost in the shadows of the porch roof, grateful that the lady and the kid were in such a hurry that they had forgotten to turn on the porch light. She pulled off her watch cap, stuffed it in her pocket, and with her free hand fluffed her matted-down curls back to life.

Taking a deep breath, she pulled the suitcase to the edge of the porch and looked down the road toward Barney. She waved her hand in signal. With a roar he pulled into the street and screeched to a stop in front of the house. She raced down the front walk, pulling the suitcase behind her. She ripped open the car's back door and stuffed the suitcase in while Barney leaned across the seat and threw open the passenger door. She jumped in, and they took off.

She couldn't stop laughing.

Thirty-Two

REV AND DORI DROVE their separate cars home from church. When first one, then another car sped past Trev going much too fast for the residential streets, he frowned. He slowed to turn into the alley behind his house just as a third car roared around the corner, forcing him to hit the brakes and wait for it to pass. He watched in his rearview mirror as it turned south at the light, tires screeching.

Shaking his head and praying no one was killed by any of those thoughtless drivers, Trev parked his van in the garage. Dori would be parking her car at the curb. Hopefully there were no more wild drivers out there endangering her. He couldn't stand to lose her again.

As he climbed from his van, Trev looked at the clutter filling the other half of the garage. He was definitely going to have to clean things up as soon as possible, freeing the other side of the garage for its intended purpose. Dori needed to be able to park her car out of the weather.

In fact, he thought as he walked to the back door, *I should give her my slot immediately. I'll park out at the curb.*

As far as he was concerned, nothing was too good for Dori, especially this evening. She had been so angry at Jonathan, and all because he attacked Trev. She had stood with him on the platform, a unit presented to the congregation. But most important, she had looked at him with love, not the uncertainty and fear he'd seen in her eyes far too often since she'd come home.

Of course she hadn't said she loved him aloud yet, but he knew it was coming. He gave the air a discreet punch, though he really felt like turning cartwheels of joy. Just how soon could he get rid of Maureen and get Ryan into bed? He wanted his wife to himself and in their bedroom. No more of this office stuff. Never again would he sleep apart from her. Never again would he let anything come between them.

He was grinning like a loon when he went inside. The first thing that struck him was the silence.

"Jack?"

No black retriever barreled his way to greet Trev. Come to think of it, no little fluffy mutt yapped at his feet either.

"Hey, Dori, where is everybody?" he called as he walked through to the living room.

"I don't know. I was wondering the same thing." She turned from hanging her coat in the closet. Her cheeks were red from the cold and her eyes sparkled. With love? For him?

He hung up his coat and pulled her into his arms. "Thank you for being there for me tonight."

A thud sounded upstairs, and they both turned toward the steps.

"Anyone there?" Trev called. "Ryan? Jack?"

"Trudy?" Dori called. "Maureen?"

Silence was their only answer.

"It's Jonathan," Trev whispered dramatically, "come to get his revenge."

"Oh, Trev, he made me so mad!" Her face clouded at the memory. "He said such terrible things about you! And it was all my fault." Her lower lip began to wobble.

He brought up a finger and waved it gently in front of her nose. "Don't go taking on yourself all Jonathan's bad behavior. Remember I told you he's done this before. The Lord will hold him accountable for his half-truths and shaded facts, not you."

"Well, yes," she agreed. "But it's our strange marriage that's made all the trouble."

"But it's not strange anymore, is it? We're committed to each other now, aren't we? Or did I misunderstand?" Trev held his breath.

"'No, you didn't misunderstand." She melted against him. "I love you. I always have, and I always will. I was just so hurt and so young that I didn't handle things well. Forgive me?"

"Done." He set her back so he could see her face. He knew he should probably quit while he was ahead. After all, she was happy, and their bed was waiting. Still, there were some questions he had to have answered, or they'd fester in his heart and poison their reconciliation as the corruption spread. "What made you decide I was trustworthy after all?"

She smiled and reached a hand to rest it on his cheek. "I watched you. I saw the kind of man you have become, the best of all the old traits melded with the new man in Christ you now are."

"That's it? It wasn't the flowers or the dinners out or the gifts? By the way, the garage is yours from now on. I'll take the street."

"Thanks. That's very nice of you, but I'll keep the street, at least until you get an electric garage door opener. The alley's too spooky."

It was? He'd never thought it so, but that was beside the point. "We'll shop for an opener tomorrow."

"See what I mean? The old Trev would have told me to save my pennies. Maybe he would have volunteered to take me to the store—if he wasn't too busy."

"The old Trev was busy protecting his heart against this wonderful girl he wasn't allowed to love. Part of that protection was not doing all he wanted for her."

"And the new Trev? The now Trev?"

"He'll do everything he can to be what you want in a husband and to bring you joy."

"See? That's what I mean. You have become a truly wonderful man. I won't ever have to worry about a Rosalee Germaine ever again. I know it as surely as I know my name's Dori Trevelyan."

He looked at her, confused. "Who's Rosalee Germaine?"

The joy in her face vanished. Just that quickly, uncertainty took its place along with what looked like disappointment. She stepped well away from him.

"Please, Trev, don't play games." Her voice shook.

What games? All he'd done was ask who Rosalee Germaine was. He shut his eyes and stared into his memory. She had to be someone from their common history. That meant someone from Amhearst or college. He sifted through all his mental files and folders. Nothing. He went through them again because it was obvious his present and future happiness depended on his remembering. Still nothing. He looked at Dori, hands spread in question. "Who is she?"

The disgust he read in her face made his stomach turn. "You don't even remember her name?" Condemnation rang its shrill chime. "And you cared so little for me that you could be unfaithful with someone you didn't even know?"

One word hit him between the eyes. "Unfaithful?"

"I'm sure you thought you could get away with it, but my last class was cancelled, and I got home much sooner than expected. I raced up the steps, hoping you were home too. After all, I hadn't seen you for six hours." Her tears fell, dripping off her chin onto her ruby sweater. "Well, you were home all right, all tucked up in bed with Rosalee."

He felt like she'd slugged him. "Never, Dori. I'll swear on a stack of Bibles if you want me to. I don't even know who Rosalee Whoever is, and I certainly never slept with her."

"And I thought you'd changed." Her scorn bit deeply. "I saw you, Trev. I saw you!"

He shook his head and kept shaking it. No, she hadn't seen him. He had never been unfaithful. From the moment he said, "I do," he had never touched another woman.

"Remember how you could see the whole apartment from the front hall?" she asked. He remembered that little fact just fine. The place wasn't the best or the most beautiful, but he and Phil had found it more than satisfactory, and Pop liked the monthly fee.

"I came in, and there you were, lying on your stomach, sound asleep, and Rosalee was cuddled beside you on her side, her arm thrown across your back. Your bare back."

For a moment all Trev could do was stare at her, still shaking his head. Then slowly the shock of her accusation began to wear off, and a fierce and terrible anger took its place. He glared at her.

"So that's why you left me," he ground out. "You thought you saw me in bed with someone else, and you ran."

"You killed something in me that day." Her voice wobbled. She sniffed and looked around for a tissue. He did not offer her his handkerchief. Let her nose drip all over her. She deserved it!

He leaned in close to her and said slowly and coldly, "I did not go to bed with anyone ever after we married. Never. Not once. I don't know what you thought you saw, but it wasn't me—as you would have found out had you bothered to stick around long enough to check things out."

His nose was almost touching hers when he finished, and she drew back. He saw with pleasure that she looked uncertain.

He continued in the same low, cold tone, "I was off getting drunk with the guys, remember? And to think that I thought for years that you left over that drunkenness. But no, you left because you *thought* I was unfaithful."

"But I saw you," she whispered.

"Not me, Dori. If you think just a little bit, something you obviously haven't done for six years, maybe you'll see an alternative."

With that he reached over her head and grabbed his red Squall from the closet. He stalked out the front door, slamming it behind him. As he zipped up, he thought what an idiot he had been to buy another jacket just like the ones Pop had given them all that long-ago Christmas. Like he could keep the family intact even as it splintered.

Stupid, stupid, stupid!

Six years he'd pined after her. Six years! Six years he'd tried to imagine what he had done that would upset her so, and he hadn't done anything. Not one thing.

His conscience kicked him. Yeah, well, he'd gotten drunk after he promised not to drink anymore, but that was a far cry from what she fancied he'd done. Did she think so little of him that she thought he'd ignore the vows he'd made to her? They might have been made under unusual circumstances in an unexpected place, but that didn't make the saying of them any less binding.

Even back in those days he'd had a great respect for marriage. He remembered his parents loving each other, laughing together, making a warm and happy home for him and Phil. Then he'd watched Pop and Honey and seen another marriage that was rock solid. A good thing, too, since it had to survive the invasion of three youngsters. Pop had honored Honey, treated her as if she were the most special woman in the world—which she was to him.

He had planned to treat Dori the same way.

And, by George, he expected the same courtesy and trust to be reciprocated. It was only right. And it was his due.

She had ruined it all by running. She had ruined it by refusing to talk. He had tried to be gracious, gentle, and kind, and she'd been distant, snippy, and accusatory.

The farther he walked and the more he thought, the higher his temperature rose.

God, I've tried to do it right, and this is the thanks I get? I do not deserve her accusation, and she does not deserve me.

If Phil had only kept his hands to himself! But, no, not Phil. He was too busy enjoying the freedom of being big man on campus as he did his graduate work for his DPharm. And girls were his biggest joy.

When he saw Phil again, he was going to strangle him. Maureen could then arrest him, and Jonathan could with great honesty tell the congregation just what a rotter Paul Michael Trevelyan was as he spent the rest of his life behind bars.

Two things struck him at almost the same time. It had begun to snow. Flakes like little needles slapped him in the face and brought him out of his red haze. He looked around in surprise. He had walked miles, and across the street was Phil's pharmacy, closed and dark for the night, the clock above the front door reading nine-fifty. Close at hand was Harbor Lights where Dori had been working so hard to help Mae and Ryan.

Dori. And the second realization ripped through him. He was furious at her, not for the false accusation, though he certainly didn't like it. He was livid because she left him, because she caused him such pain, and because she hadn't returned of her own free will.

He stepped into the recessed doorway of Harbor Lights to get out of the weather. He leaned against the door and with genuine

290 :~ Gayle Roper

dismay knew himself as guilty as Dori. She had run, but he had
raged and been too blind to even realize it. She hadn't had the
courage to discuss things with him, but he had put on a garment
of godliness, not seeing the giant moth holes of pride, false
humility, and wrath.

He heard Dr. Quentin saying, "Just be careful of that anger. It
could sink your love boat before you're even out of port."

For years he'd thought Dr. Quentin was speaking of Dori's
anger, and he'd long planned to be mature and sensitive to her to
defuse that anger. Now he realized his mentor had been speaking
of Trev's own anger, anger he had seen simmering, but which Trev
hadn't even realized was there.

*Oh, God, forgive me! Here I have been saying the Pharisee's
prayer—Thank God I'm not like her—when in my own way, I've been
worse. I've been a self-righteous prig, proud of my godly attitude, when
underneath I was furious at her for deserting me, embarrassing me, and
hurting me.*

I have to talk to her. He stood up straight. *I have to ask her forgiveness.* He started to run. *God, help me! I've made such a mess of
things. Help me!*

Thirty-Three

$\mathcal{J}$OANNE FOLLOWED BARNEY into the Sea Whisper Restaurant located ten minutes south of Seaside. She had worked on her hair in the car, but as she glimpsed herself in a mirror on the wall, she knew it looked terrible, like someone caught in the rain and wind.

She was never wearing one of those cap things again, not even for Barney.

"Don't worry, baby. You look fine."

She looked at him skeptically.

He grinned. "In fact, better than fine. I like your hair like that."

"You can't be serious."

He nodded. "It doesn't look so stuck-up, you know? It looks like I could run my fingers through it, sort of like this." He slid his hand into the blonde mass until his palm cradled the back of her head. "Now I can hold you still while I kiss you." And he did.

The throat clearing of the hostess made Joanne gulp and break the kiss. Barney grinned at her, not the least embarrassed.

"Table for two," he said as he winked at Joanne.

The hostess led them into the dining room where she sat them near the fireplace with its cozy gas flames. As she took the seat Barney held for her, Joanne knew she was going to keep her hair like it was, loose and flowing, sort of untamed, like he made her feel. It'd sure be easier than all that teasing and curling and spraying and moussing.

They had just given their orders to their server when a man wearing a police uniform and a name tag that read Lt. Greg Barnes walked up to their table.

"Excuse me," he said. "Miss Pilotti?"

Joanne gave a little bleat. Cops always scared her. "Yes?"

Barney had coached her and told her not to say anything more than she was asked.

"Never offer a thing," he said. "You like to help people. Don't help the police."

"I'm Greg Barnes of the Seaside Police Department."

Joanne nodded. "This is Barney Noble." As if he didn't know.

"Are we still in Seaside?" Barney asked. "I'm just asking because I'm wondering why you're here out of your jurisdiction."

The policeman nodded vaguely at Barney, ignored his comment, and concentrated on Joanne. She felt like twitching under his unblinking stare.

"May we talk to you in private, Miss Pilotti?" Lt. Barnes asked.

"What about?" She didn't have to try to look scared like Barney had told her. She felt scared for real. "Did something happen to my family?"

She loved that question. Barney had said it would make her look completely innocent because that would be the big reason the cops would come see someone who was really innocent.

"Excuse me, but can't you see you're scaring her?" Barney rose and came over to Joanne. "I'll go with you, Jo. It'll be all right, I'm sure." He pulled her chair back for her and helped her rise.

Lt. Barnes didn't look happy to have Barney along, but there wasn't much he could do about it short of making a scene in the restaurant. They walked to the parking lot.

"Is that your car?" Lt. Barnes asked, pointing to Barney's black car gleaming softly in the parking lot lights. A man in rumpled clothes leaned against its side.

"It's mine," Barney acknowledged. "Why? And get off my car, please. Go lean on someone else's."

"But yours is the nicest one here," the man said, but he straightened.

"And I'd like to keep it that way," Barney said.

"This is Sergeant Cary Fleishman," Lt. Barnes said with a hard look at Sergeant Fleishman.

"Also of Seaside PD?" Barney asked.

Lt. Barnes looked at Joanne for a minute, then at Barney. "Would you mind opening the car for us and showing us the suitcase you have in the backseat?"

Joanne made her eyes very big. "How do you know we have a suitcase in the back seat?"

Lt. Barnes ignored the question. He motioned to the car.

"It's okay, baby," Barney said, pulling out his keys.

In a moment the black suitcase with the red yarn tied around the handle sat in the middle of the parking lot, the four of them staring down at it.

"Where did you get the suitcase, Miss Pilotti?" Lt. Barnes asked.

"At the airport," she answered. "I picked up the wrong one by accident." She stepped to the suitcase and held out the name tag. "See? Dori MacAllister." She shook her head. "Boy, did I feel dumb."

Lt. Barnes frowned as he studied the name tag. He walked around the suitcase and muttered something impolite under his breath.

"Please open the case," Sergeant Fleishman ordered.

Joanne looked at Barney who nodded. "Go ahead, baby."

Joanne set the case on its side and unzipped it. Dori MacAllister's clothes and gifts, all except the necktie with the books on it that Barney really liked, lay there for all to see.

Lt. Barnes's cell phone rang. "Excuse me a minute." He walked several steps away so he could talk privately.

Fleishman pointed to the case. "Empty it."

"In the dirt?" Joanne was horrified.

"In the dirt. And why were you at the home of Reverend Paul Trevelyan at eight-thirty this evening?"

"That's where she lives." Joanne grabbed the luggage tag. "I wanted to give it back to her."

Barney had told her, "Don't mention that you wanted to exchange it for the other one. That's offering information that they can make trouble with."

She remembered and kept her mouth shut about any exchange. It was Sergeant Fleishman who brought the subject up, just like Barney said a cop would.

"You were going to exchange this case for yours?" Fleishman watched the pile of clothing on the parking lot grow and the pile in the case diminish.

"I don't know if she's got mine or not." Joanne kept her eyes down as she spoke. That was the one lie that she had worried about telling convincingly. Not having to look at the cop made it easier.

Lt. Barnes hurried up. "Forget it," he said to Joanne. "Come on, Fleishman." He took off for his car at a run. Frowning, Fleishman followed.

Barney stood with his arm around Joanne as they watched the two policemen careen out of the lot and speed down the road toward Seaside. He turned her in his arms.

"You did great, baby! I'm so proud of you." He hugged her.

Joanne glowed at the praise. "Really?"

"Really. You couldn't have been better." And he hugged her again.

"I'm starting to feel like a real professional." She felt all hyper inside, full of fizz. She giggled, then laughed aloud. The world couldn't be better. "First I'm a courier. Now I'm a decoy. What next, do you think?"

"We're going to the Caymans."

"Now?" she asked in surprise. "We're going now? This very minute?"

He took her arm and led her toward the passenger door. "Come on. We need to hurry."

"But I don't have any clothes. And I don't have my passport yet."

Barney reached into the inside pocket of his black leather coat and pulled out two small books bound in navy blue. They both read PASSPORT and United States of America. An American eagle sat in the middle of the covers. He held them out to her.

She flipped one open. There was her picture under a fat USA. Beside it was a name, Jo-Ellen Barnhouse and some address in Pittsburgh. When the light caught the page right, an eagle showed over the picture and name. She frowned and flipped open the other passport. There was Barney's picture, but the name read Tom Barnhouse, and his address was the same one in Pittsburgh.

"Do I look like a Tom?"

She got it all of a sudden. Just like *Alias* on TV! "Do I look like a Jo-Ellen?"

"I wanted the names to be somewhat similar so that if we slipped up, no one would think anything of it. If you forgot and called me Barney, people would just think it was a nickname for Barnhouse."

She stared at him for a minute, awed. "You are so smart! But why do we have to leave? I mean, right this minute? I thought we did everything the way you and Mr. Jankowski planned."

"We did our part in getting the paintings to Mr. Jankowski just right, but I'm willing to bet anything that the call Barnes received had to do with Vinnie. If I'm right, Seaside is not a safe place for any of Mr. Jankowski's people at the moment, especially me. So we're going where it's safe—and where I've got money stashed. We can make up a whole new life, Jo-Ellen. Anything we want."

"You won't have to do mean stuff anymore? You won't have to hurt people ever again?"

"I can be Tom Barnhouse, nice guy."

She grinned. "Are we ever coming back?"

Barney thought for a moment. "Is there any reason why we should?"

"Uh-uh. None I can think of."

"Then we won't come back. We'll sit in the sun forever." He opened the car door. Joanne saw the clock on the dash reading 9:58.

"Oh! Just a minute." Joanne ran back to Dori's suitcase lying open and empty behind the car. She fell to her knees beside the pile of clothes and fumbled through them. "Got it," she yelled and ran back to Barney. She held up the glass ball with the beautiful swirls of color in it.

Thirty-Four

DORI STARED AT the closed door, the sound of Trev's angry slam reverberating in her ears. For a moment she couldn't think, didn't feel. Then the disbelief and pain kicked in.

What had just happened? How had she gone from such hope and joy to such despair? One moment she was in Trev's arms, vowing to be his forever. The next he was storming out of the house, more furious than she had ever seen him in all the years she'd known him.

Years of patterned thinking asserted themselves, and she found herself feeling resentful and used. How dare he walk out on her like that! That's what happened when you tried to dislodge the pink elephant. Better to leave it alone and just step cautiously around it, leaving it behind as you pressed into the future.

Except there was no future now.

The thought hit with all the subtlety of a sledgehammer pulverizing stone. The ache was so intense she doubled over, her arms wrapped around her stomach. The pain was too deep for tears. She'd known from the beginning that if he rejected her again, she'd die somehow. Oh, not physically. That would be too easy.

Oh, Lord, I can't stand this agony! Help me!

No immediate surcease came, no lifting of the black cloud that enveloped her, no reconstructing of the heart the sledgehammer of his rejection and anger had crushed.

With a sigh she pulled herself to her feet. She climbed the stairs slowly, each step its own little Everest. Halfway up she heard a little slither of sound over her head, but when she stopped to listen, the sound disappeared.

When she reached the top of the stairs, she noticed the door to the hall closet was partially open. She pushed it shut and continued on to her room. She pulled her little suitcase from under the bed and threw in as much as it would hold. She zipped it shut and pulled it to the floor where it landed with a thud. She jerked up the pull handle and wheeled it to the top of the stairs. There she grabbed the short handle on the case's side and lugged it down to the living room.

She opened the closet to get her coat, and the red Lands' End Squall seemed to jump out and grab her. A sob rose as she deliberately reached around it and got her black down-filled coat. She pulled on her red beret and her red gloves, grabbed her purse and suitcase, and left the house.

She thought suddenly of Trudy, off somewhere with Maureen and Ryan. Poor Trudy, moved at the whim of people whether she wanted to move or not. A picture rose in her mind of Ryan seated on the floor laughing as Trudy gave his face a bath. Another surfaced of Trudy lying head to head with Jack, barking and teasing him to come chase her. And the sweetest picture of all—a grinning Ryan lying on the floor with Trudy's head lying on one shoulder and Jack's on the other, both dogs blissful as he fondled their ears.

She'd leave Trudy here as a gift to Ryan. Someone might as well get something positive out of this catastrophe. Certainly Trudy was small enough that Mae wouldn't mind having her in the house.

Oh, Lord, I don't want to leave!

But she knew she had no choice. Trev didn't want her. It was that simple.

As she drove through town, it began to snow, slowly at first, then with increasing force. She felt a momentary flutter of fear—it had been so long since she'd driven in snow—but the emotional chaos consuming her pushed the snow problem to the side. She made certain she didn't pass Harbor Lights or Phil's pharmacy. It would be too painful. She sniffed.

I'm sorry, Mae. Forgive me for letting you down. And, Phil, be careful you don't let Maureen get away. She's just right for you.

Tears sheened her eyes as she thought of the two of them getting married. She wouldn't even be able to come to their wedding because Trev would be there. With Angie?

For a minute she thought she might throw up.

As she drove over the Ninth Street Causeway, she glanced at the clock on her dash. Ten o'clock. She'd been in Seaside for six days and eight hours, give or take an hour. That wasn't very long, but she felt utterly bereft.

Trev.

She allowed herself to go back to that fateful afternoon six years ago. She saw herself open the door, so excited about seeing her new husband again, so hungry for his arms about her. She saw the open bedroom door and the dark-haired man and the blonde woman sleeping in what was to have been her bed, hers and Trev's. She felt the slam of horror all over again, saw her hand come to her mouth to smother the agonized scream, saw herself turn and run back to her dorm room where she'd stuffed whatever came to hand into her backpack and headed for the airport.

Suddenly a conversation long forgotten surfaced. She was at the apartment one Friday not too long after her first semester had begun. Phil was already in graduate school, sharing the apartment with Trev, a junior.

"How come you've got the big bedroom?" Phil asked as he walked out of his tiny room. "I can barely turn around in there."

Trev shrugged. "I got here first on moving day?"

"But oldest gets first dibs. Haven't you ever heard of primogeniture?"

"Right. I want to know where that rule is written down," Trev groused. "I think some oldest kid somewhere just decided it should be that way and told all the other oldest kids he knew who told all the oldest kids they knew and on and on."

"What's wrong with your room?" Dori asked, peering in the door of the room under discussion. "Aside from the socks and underwear on the floor and the dust bunnies under the bed, I mean."

"Well, the bed, for one thing. It's too small."

Dori frowned at Phil. "It's a standard twin bed. What's the problem?"

"Two don't fit well."

"But there's only one of you," she answered reasonably.

"Most of the time," he said with a significant look at Trev.

Dori felt her face heat as it dawned on her what her brother was talking about. "I don't want to hear this. I do not want to hear this."

Trev laughed at her discomfort. "Look, Phil, feel free to use my bed anytime you need to, provided I'm not sleeping in it, of course."

"Better yet," Phil said, "we'll trade. One semester yours, one semester mine."

As the memory unrolled, Dori began to shake, her whole body trembling under the enormity of her discovery.

He was right, and she was wrong!

All these years she had been so certain of her position. He was wrong; she was right. Sure, she was an emotional coward. Sure, she had run. Sure, she had refused to talk about the situation out of a combination of fear and self-protection.

But he had been wrong, and she had been right.

Oh, Lord, what have I done? I've killed my marriage to the only man I've ever loved or will love, and I did it not once but twice. How can he ever forgive me? How can You ever forgive me?

Great wracking sobs began to shake her. The road wavered through the flood of moisture that filled her eyes. She slowed so she wouldn't have an accident. Snowflakes slapped the wind-shield, one after another. She groaned and turned the wipers to high speed. Even the weather was against her.

She peered into the night. Shouldn't she have come to the entrance to the Garden State Parkway by now? It hadn't seemed this far when Trev drove it. She frowned. It hadn't looked this rural either. She had no idea where she was. She thought she was driving north, and Philadelphia was north, wasn't it? Philadelphia and the airport. She'd just keep driving, and she'd get there eventually.

This time, Lord, I won't turn away from You. I at least learned that much in my short time here.

Trev had taught her. She'd seen in him what a Christian should be. She'd even seen mesmerizing glimpses of the loving husband he would have been if she hadn't messed it all up.

And I believe in marriage so strongly, Lord. That's the irony of it all.

She dashed a hand across her cheek. At the rate she was weeping, she'd have chapped skin before she got halfway to the airport.

Six years without a move to divorce was proof of her commitment to marriage, wasn't it?

She thought for a minute, and honesty forced her to rephrase. It didn't show commitment to marriage but rather to the concept of marriage. If she'd been committed to marriage itself, wouldn't she have been here, fighting for it instead of abandoning it?

Her parents had been committed to marriage, not the idea of marriage. They had lived together every day, been happy together, sad together, bored together, angry at each other, dazzled by each other. The same with Pop and Honey.

Pop wasn't always an easy man to live with, and Honey had been independent for over forty years before they married. Both were highly opinionated. Their fights were dillies, and at first the young Dori, already uncertain in her new surroundings, still raw from the loss of her parents, had been frightened by them. When Honey had realized how the little girl was being affected, she sat down with Dori.

"Dori, love, you mustn't worry. Pop and I are fine. Since no one can be everything that his or her partner wants, there will always be struggles and disagreements in a marriage, even between people who love each other deeply like Pop and me. It can't be avoided. A marriage without struggles isn't a marriage. It's only two people living in the same house, not caring enough to work out the issues between them."

"But you yell," Dori said in a small voice.

Honey smiled. "That we do. Some people cry. Some people get real quiet. Some people turn away. We yell. But this is the fact you need to always remember, honey. We love each other, Pop and I. When we stood before the minister and said our vows, we both knew that we were promising to be together for life. I'm not going anywhere. Pop's not going anywhere."

"You're sure?"

"Absolutely positively. And you're not going anywhere either." Honey hugged her close. "We're family, and family stays together even in the hard times. Especially in the hard times."

"No!" the adult Dori shouted into the black night and cranked the steering wheel to the left. "I am not running again. Families stick together, especially in the hard times. I'm fighting this time. Oh, God, give me courage!"

The car turned, crossing the white center line, all but invisible under the carpet of snow. The nose swung toward Seaside, and Dori was filled with determination and hope. She would get down on her knees and ask Trev's forgiveness, then get up and help him build their marriage, one that would reflect their love and commitment to each other and to the Lord.

When the right front wheel slid off the shoulder into a slight ditch, she felt the jolt of the undercarriage coming to rest on the ground from her tailbone to the base of her skull.

Thirty-Five

MAUREEN LEANED AGAINST the headrest on the passenger side of her car and let her eyes slide shut. She was more than content to let Phil drive her and Ryan back to Trev and Dori's.

What a night! The dogs were both expected to recover completely, but it had been close. They were staying at the vet's until tomorrow afternoon, just to be safe. Even now the thought of having to tell Trev and Dori that their dogs had died made her shudder. At least it made telling them that the animals were only ill seem like a piece of cake.

"You okay?" Phil asked, his hand reaching over and grasping hers.

She turned her head and looked a question.

"You shivered."

"Ah. Just thinking about how close a call it was."

When she and Ryan had left the vet's, she hadn't been able to resist stopping at the pharmacy. It was mere moments from closing time.

"Want a candy bar?" she asked Ryan as she parked beside the store.

"Sounds good."

So Ry got his candy, and she got Phil. Comfort food for both of them. Phil had insisted that he drive them out to Dori and Trev's.

"You don't have to." She felt she had to protest, but she really hoped he wouldn't listen. "The suitcase was undoubtedly snagged while we were gone. Greg Barnes and Cary Fleishman have the culprits in custody by now."

"I don't care whether that blamed suitcase is there or not. I'm taking you home, and I'm spending the night on the couch to be certain you're safe."

"So who's arguing?" she asked.

Now she shut her eyes again and fell into that hazy half sleep that occurs when there's too much on your mind to actually allow slumber.

Ryan lay on the backseat, half-asleep.

"Maureen! Look!"

Phil's anxious, excited hiss brought her awake. They had just turned onto Heron Lane. Scooting down the sidewalk was a slight man all in black pulling a black suitcase behind him.

Instantly alert, Maureen ordered, "Drive around the corner and park. Don't look at him as you go past. Just drive."

"It's the suitcase!" Ryan was completely awake now, too, bouncing up and down in his excitement.

"Get down, Ryan," Maureen ordered. "We don't want him to see you. And don't get up until I tell you."

Ryan frowned in disgust but did as he was told. So did Phil. She noted out of her side vision that the man checked his speed when they drove past, like he expected something to happen. When they kept moving, he resumed his near run. They rounded the corner onto Beachcomber and Phil pulled to the curb.

"Kill the engine." Maureen reached into the glove compartment and grabbed her gun. She noted Phil's start of surprise as she stuck it in the waistband at the small of her back. She also fished in her purse and pulled out her small camera. Quickly she reached across Phil and flipped the knob that turned off the dome light. She opened her door and slid out.

"Stay put, both of you. I mean it. If he comes around the corner, duck."

She slid into the shadows back toward Heron. Where were Barnes and Fleishman? They should be shadowing this guy, but neither they nor their cars were anywhere to be seen. She huddled behind a large hydrangea, wishing her coat weren't royal blue, and watched the man in black come steadily in her direction. As he got close, she could see in the light of the streetlamp that his face had been blackened. She held up the little camera and sighted. How wise her dad had been giving it to her. *Click. Click.*

Then she hunkered down and waited to see what he would do. He rounded the corner onto Beachcomber. She scarcely breathed as he stopped at a beat-up light blue car mere feet from her and threw the case into the trunk. He climbed behind the wheel, and as his motor turned over, Maureen took a picture of the car, license plate on the rear visible. The suitcase thief did a 180, and drove up Beachcomber to the stop sign at Central. He turned right toward town.

Maureen raced to her car and jumped in. Phil already had the motor running and took off toward Central without her saying a word.

"He's going one of two places," Maureen said.

"Atlantic City and Jankowski's offices there," Phil offered as he turned onto Central.

"Or Eric's house." This from Ryan.

"So don't lose him." Maureen kept her eyes fixed firmly on the battered baby blue car ahead. "But don't get too close. There's not much traffic around here this time of year."

"All we need to know is whether he crosses the Ninth Street Causeway. If he doesn't, we can get to Jankowski's house by another route."

Maureen looked at him in surprise. "You know where he lives?"

"That I do. Aside from the fact that he lives down the street from friends at church, his wife also uses our pharmacy. When this mess all started, I looked up the house number just in case." He grinned proudly.

Maureen rolled her eyes. "Look, Phil, please don't get to thinking you're a cop here. You are not."

"Of course I'm not. I know that. I'm just the cop's chauffeur."

"And don't you forget it!" She pulled her cell from her purse. "If anything ever happened to you—" Her throat closed. She looked out the side window as she struggled to regain control.

How could she feel this intensely this quickly?

"Hey, Irish." Phil pulled gently on one of her curls.

"What?" she asked in a thick voice.

"Look at me."

"Look at the road."

"Look at me, Maureen." His voice was firm.

Reluctantly she did. She saw a man with strength behind his gentleness and humor, a man who had learned to love the Lord and showed it in the changes in his life. She saw a man she was falling head over heels in love with.

She also saw a highly interested thirteen-year-old face watching from the backseat.

Phil ran a hand over her cheek. "Don't worry, Irish. You're in charge. And this is Seaside, not Bosnia."

She laid her hand over his and held it to her face. "Like Jankowski's goons are going to care about the locale."

"Hey," Phil said. "Now you're making me worry about you."

"Well, he didn't turn at Ninth Street," Ryan announced. "In case you two were too busy to notice."

Maureen dropped Phil's hand and hit speed dial for Greg Barnes. She glanced at the clock on the dash. It was just after ten o'clock. "Where are you?" she asked without preamble.

"About ten miles south of Seaside at the Sea Whisper with Joanne Pilotti and Barney Noble."

"And Fleishman?"

"He's with me."

"Well, get yourselves back here. The suitcase is en route to Jankowski's. We're tailing it as we speak."

She could hear Greg gnashing his teeth. "We're on our way."

Next she hit the chief's number and got him at home, courtesy of call forwarding. She reported what was happening.

"Keep everyone under surveillance," he ordered. "Backup's on the way."

As the blue car drove in a straight line toward Jankowski's oceanfront home, Phil cut off and went by another route, speeding in an attempt to arrive first. Even though there was no traffic and speed was of the essence, Maureen still flinched as they ran three stop signs.

"You're having way too much fun," she said sourly.

Phil just grinned and rounded the corner onto Ocean Drive with his lights off.

"It's the one with the white stones instead of grass," Phil said.

As a car began to turn off Central, he pulled into the drive of the darkened house two down from Jankowski's and killed the motor. In silence they watched the blue car roll to a stop in the driveway of Neal Jankowski's magnificent house. The man got out, went to the trunk, and got the suitcase. Maureen took a picture.

"Eric's house looks dark," Ryan said. "Maybe the guy wasn't supposed to come here."

No sooner had he finished speaking than the light beside the front door came on for a brief minute, flicked off, and the door began to open. There was probably a peephole in the door, Maureen thought. The person inside flicked on the light to check the identity of the man on the porch before opening the door. Then he doused the light for secrecy's sake.

Quickly, before the door was fully open and the man could look up and down the street, Maureen slipped out of the car, paused a moment to send a don't-you-dare-leave-this-car look at Phil and Ryan, and ducked behind the low but tightly woven fence of the property next door to Jankowski's. She put her eye to a slight crevice between two boards in the fence and managed to see the front door. Maureen put the camera to the crevice and clicked.

"You're late." Neal Jankowski stood in the doorway, looking his guest up and down with distaste.

Jankowski himself! What was he doing here? He wasn't due back in town until Sunday. He must have come home early to check on the problem of the paintings.

"I got trapped," Vinnie whined. "That place is a madhouse."

"Like I care." Jankowski scanned the street. "Get in here."

When she heard the front door close, Maureen stood and stared at the house. She felt like she should do something, but she wasn't sure what. Certainly she was not going to do anything to attract the attention of anyone inside. The last thing she wanted was shots being fired. What if his kids were in there? They certainly weren't in Aruba. She knew that because of Ryan's run-in with Eric. So where were they? No kid should see his father in a shoot-out with the police.

She scanned the house carefully. The curtains in most rooms were open with no lights showing. Too dark for a family of six. She was willing to bet no one was home but the big guy himself. Suddenly a splash of light fell onto the dunes behind the house. Someone had turned on a light in one of the back rooms.

She crept from behind her fence and hurried down the short drive past the baby blue car, around the side of the two-car garage, and into the backyard, such as it was. Seaside was not a big island, and even million-dollar homes like this one didn't have much property. The spill of light illuminated an empty patio, large terra-cotta urns empty of flowers, and a pool with a top stretched snugly over it. A black cat sat in the middle of the pool cover.

Maureen slid cautiously along the back of the house past darkened floor-to-ceiling windows. She wanted to get close enough to the lighted room to see what was going on. The only problem was how to see them without them seeing her.

"Hey!"

She jerked to a stop, her hand going to her gun. She looked behind her.

"Hey! Over here!"

The words were hard to hear over the constant sound of breaking surf just yards away. Maureen scanned the perimeter of the yard, then farther back into the dunes, their sea grasses undulating in the wind. There she saw a hand waving, then a grinning face emerging. The hand beckoned even as the face disappeared behind the grasses.

She was going to kill him. When she got her hands on Phil, she was going to string him up by his thumbs. She was going to arrest him for interfering with police business. She was going to send him to jail for years and years.

First, however, she was going to join him for what had to be a great view of what was happening in that room. Then she would string him up.

She scooted back the way she'd come, got behind the neighbor's fence once more and followed it until it ended at the dunes. She found both Phil and Ryan lying on their stomachs, watching the lighted room. She fell down beside them.

"I thought I told you guys to stay in the car."

"You did. And please put that away." Phil pointed to the gun she held in the hand nearest him.

She snorted and stuffed it back in her waistband. Then she turned her attention to the house. The view was unbelievable. There was the opened suitcase on the coffee table. There was the slight man who had brought it, tossing the ratty clothes onto the floor. There was Neal Jankowski watching like a hawk, then reaching to slit the lining and get his treasure.

Maureen pulled out her camera and recorded the whole process. Her coup was the shot of Neal Jankowski pulling one of the paintings, a beguiling swirl of primary colors, from the suitcase and gazing at it lovingly.

Suddenly Chief Gordon rounded the side of the house, moving silently through the shadows. Maureen pushed to her knees, ready to join them.

"Stay put," she hissed to Ryan. She glared at Phil. "You too."

He grinned unrepentantly, leaned up to give her a quick kiss and said, his voice completely serious, "Be careful, Irish. You mean the world to me."

She hurried through the dunes and joined Chief Gordon in the backyard.

"I got it all," she said in a low voice, holding out her camera.

His smile was blinding. "Good girl."

"You alone?" She sincerely hoped not.

He shook his head. "Uniforms out front. Barnes and Fleishman on their way. ETA ten minutes. How many people in the house?"

"As far as I can tell, just the two in that room. At least I haven't seen anyone else."

The chief nodded. "Probably keeping knowledge of this picture deal limited to as few as possible." And he stepped out into the light streaming from the window, gun in hand. "Police," he yelled. "You're under arrest for dealing in stolen goods."

The two men looked up in surprise, then anger, at least on the part of Jankowski. He reached for the drawer of an end table. Without hesitation, Chief Gordon shot through the window.

Though he hadn't aimed at either man, they both froze.

"Open the door, Vinnie," he yelled to the slight man.

Vinnie looked at Jankowski, then at the chief. With a resigned expression, he moved toward the glass door.

"Who's he?" Maureen asked. She too stood in the light now, her eyes fixed on Jankowski and her gun leveled at his midsection.

"Vinnie Testa, a small-time would-be wise guy. He works for Jankowski. Just an errand boy."

Vinnie slid the glass door open and stepped aside. Chief Gordon stepped through, pulling his cuffs from his belt as he moved. Maureen followed him inside.

"Keep him covered," the chief ordered as he holstered his gun and moved behind Jankowski. The cuffs clicked over Jankowski's wrists.

"Go open the front door," the chief told her as he stepped back and pulled his gun again. "Sit," he barked at Jankowski who lowered himself onto the sofa. He looked with loathing at the chief, then with longing at the paintings.

Maureen hurried down the hall to the words of the Miranda warning being read in Chief Gordon's voice: "You have the right to remain silent . . ." She unlocked the door and raced back, two uniforms rushing after her. All seemed as she'd left it, the chief putting his printed card with the full warning written on it back in his pocket.

Except Vinnie was gone.

"He just went out the door," Chief Gordon said, pointing with his gun.

Maureen raced for the door and burst onto the patio, gun at the ready. She saw Vinnie picking himself up, one of the large terra-cotta planters lying on its side in several pieces.

"Stop right there!" she yelled, legs spread, gun held before her. *Oh, Lord, please don't make me have to shoot him!*

Vinnie glanced back at her and ran, limping from his collision with the planter. She raced after him. She would catch him and tackle him and not have to shoot.

"Watch out!" she yelled, but it was too late. He was so busy looking back at her that he didn't see the pool with its dark cover. He took two steps onto the cover, and the material gave way under his weight, plunging his leg through to his hip. His forward momentum caused him to topple forward onto his face, his other leg sprawled out behind him. Slowly, slowly the material of the cover began to tear further.

One of the uniforms joined her at the pool's edge as they watched Vinnie struggle to free himself without other extremities going through.

"Stay on your stomach," Maureen called. "Keep the weight distributed."

Even as she spoke, the top gave way some more, and Vinnie slid into the water to his waist. His hands scrabbled desperately at the taut cover, seeking purchase so his whole body didn't fall into the frigid water.

"Help me! I'm going to fall in!" He looked beseechingly at Maureen and the uniform who stood steady, their guns aimed at him. "The water's freezing. I'm gonna get hypothermia! And I can't swim!"

Maureen looked at the uniform who shrugged. "You might as well tell him," the uniform said.

"Vinnie," Maureen said, trying not to smile, "you're in the shallow end."

Vinnie looked momentarily disconcerted. Then he lowered his legs, found the bottom just as Maureen had said, and stood. He was shuddering with cold.

"Well, don't just stand there," she ordered. "Turn around and climb out." She shook her head. He was worse than a kid.

When he stood dripping on the patio, Maureen cuffed him and read him his rights. She turned her back while the uniform helped him out of his wet pants and wrapped him in a towel.

"Whee-oo! That was great!" Ryan clambered over the dune, all smiles. "Better than TV any day!"

Phil followed, a huge grin on his face.

Maureen made believe she'd never seen either of them in her life.

Thirty-Six

*D*ORI STEPPED ON THE GAS. The engine roared, but the car didn't move. Not that she was surprised. She knew something strange had happened, and she was afraid she knew what. Ditch. Could life get worse?

Sure. Serials killers stalking snowy back roads came to mind.

Even as she told herself that possibility was highly unlikely—surely serial killers didn't like getting cold and wet any more than regular people—she looked cautiously around, scanning what little she could see of the countryside through the falling snow.

It was all the suspense novels she read. They gave her too many ideas about the many things that could befall a woman alone and stuck in the middle of nowhere. A woman running.

She frowned as a thought crossed her mind. All those novels with the covers of fleeing women. Had she bought them because subconsciously she was that woman, a fugitive from her personal horror? Interesting possibility, but now certainly wasn't the time to ponder it. Besides, she wasn't a woman running anymore.

She'd forgotten how rural parts of New Jersey were. No help in sight, but no serial killers either. If one should happen to show up and do her in, would the police think to tell Trev that the car was turned toward Seaside? So he'd know she was coming back? That she planned to fight for their marriage? That she loved him with her whole heart?

She climbed out of the car and slipped and slid around to the far side. She had on the dress flats and good slacks she'd put on to go to the church and face down Jonathan Warrington. They were no protection against the weather. Snow seeped over the edges of the shoes whose soles skated on the snow like a figure skater's blades on ice, forcing her to hang on to the car for stability.

She groaned when in the glow of the headlights she saw the right front wheel dangling in the air. It was just as she'd thought. It made no difference that the bottom of the ditch was only a matter of inches from the tire, and the road was only a matter of fewer inches. It might as well have been miles. She assumed the front axle or whatever it was called these days was resting on the road. She tried to peer under the car to see if she was right, but it was too dark.

Flashlight! She hurried back to the car and began rooting in the glove compartment. She found an expired insurance card, a booklet about the car that she'd never read, a map of southern California, another of San Diego, a packet of never-opened Kleenex tissues, another insurance card that expired in a month, and no flashlight.

She was sure she had one somewhere. Maybe the trunk. But the trunk was as unhelpful as the glove compartment.

While she was checking the trunk, she checked the exhaust pipe. She was getting very cold, but the last thing she wanted to do was turn on the heater and asphyxiate herself if the pipe was damaged somehow or blocked by snow. People died from blocked exhaust pipes all the time as fumes backed up into the car. Good. There was no danger. The rear of the car was elevated as usual, though the right rear tire was very close to the ditch. If everything stayed stable, she could probably keep the heat on at least in spurts, until help came.

A soft plop made her jump and scan the copse of trees clustered just past where she was stopped. Shivering with cold and fear, she told herself it was just snow falling from the branches, hitting the ground with a thud. Still, she climbed back into the car as fast as she could, pressed all the locks, and told herself she was safe.

Lord, I didn't realize I was such a fraidy cat. Please keep me safe, and get me home to Trev. Please.

She turned on the motor to get some heat. Why, oh why hadn't she joined AAA? Then she could call for help. Some poor serviceman would come rushing out into the storm and free her, and she could rush back to Trev and fall at his feet in supplication.

Trev. She could call him. She hesitated. What if he wasn't home yet? What if he never wanted to speak to her again? What if he didn't care if she froze to death in a snowstorm?

What if she had lost her mind? Even if he didn't want to be married to her anymore, he would certainly be willing to help her. At the very least, he'd send Phil.

Phil. Her brother. He felt so much safer, so much more a known quantity than Trev at the moment. She picked up her cell phone and called 411 for his number. She ignored the niggling thought that she was being a coward again. She felt her shoulders slump as she got his machine.

"Phil, call me! It's an emergency."

She tried Maureen's number. Again a machine. "Maureen, call me! It's an emergency."

In spite of the thin stream of heat flowing over her legs, she was getting colder by the moment. It was amazing how much less heat the car produced when you were stationary. And outside her windows the snow was getting deeper by the moment.

She sighed and knew that she had no choice unless she wanted to hike back the way she had come. She looked out at the black night. She looked down at her already-wet shoes and slacks. Trev it was. She took a deep breath, preparing herself for his anger, and dialed his home. Her home.

The phone was picked up on the second ring.

"Dori? Sweetheart? Is that you?"

Dori blinked. Trev sounded desperate, worried, not angry. "Yeah, it's me."

"Oh, thank God! I've been so worried! Are you all right?"

"I'm fine." She started to cry. "But my car's not. I'm stuck. I want to come home!"

There was a moment of silence.

"Trev, are you still there?"

"Home where, Dori? San Diego?"

She could hear the uncertainty in his voice, the pain, and her heart broke. "I'm sorry," she blubbered. "I'm sorry! You were right. I was wrong." By the end of her confession, she was crying so hard the words were barely understandable.

"Take a deep breath, Dor. Deep breath. Where are you?"

"I don't know!" She sniffed and hit the button on the glove compartment. She tossed everything out until she found the tissues. She blew her nose. "I was going to go back to San Diego. I thought you hated me."

"Never, love. Never in a million years."

"But I got lost. I missed the Garden State Parkway entrance. I guess I'm on that road farther along. I turned around to come back home, back to Heron Lane, and I ran off the road. I'm stuck!"

"You were coming back to Heron Lane?" She heard the hope in his voice.

"If you want me back," she managed to whisper. She was terrified of his answer.

"Oh, I want you back all right. And when you get here, I'm never letting you go!"

"Then come get me. I'm freezing, and I want to come home!"

"I'm on my way."

Dori settled back to wait, warmed by the knowledge that Trev was on his way, that he was coming to get her and take her home. If only it wasn't so dark and silent, so spooky out there, the wait wouldn't seem so long. She hit the lock lever again, just to be certain. The snow fell harder, and she suddenly had a new fear. What if someone came up behind her and because of the weather didn't see her rear end sticking out in the road? What if they hit her? She had her lights on, but they might not be visible in the weather.

Taking a deep breath and telling herself that all the ghosties and ghoulies were at home around their fireplaces instead of out in the snow, she unlocked her door and stepped out. She breathed a sigh of relief. She was off the road. She was safe.

A halo of light bathed her. A car from the direction of Seaside. She hadn't seen it coming through the snow, and the suddenness of the lights made her jerk which in turn made her slip which caused her to fall. The inch of snow did nothing to cushion the shock of hitting the macadam with first her rear, then the back of her head. She lay, stunned.

She was dimly aware of the car skidding to a stop. Could it be Trev? Could he get here that fast? She didn't think so. Well, if it was a serial killer, she was out of luck. The world was still spinning too wildly for her to make an escape attempt.

One door opened and closed, then another. Suddenly a giant with a bald head and a gold hoop earring loomed out of the snow. He was scowling fiercely as he stared down at her.

She knew it was the end.

Oh, Lord, I'm sorry I didn't get a chance to live for You like I wanted. Forgive me for my sins. And thanks for that last conversation with Trev. At least he knows I meant to come home.

A blonde woman peered around the giant. "Oh, Barney, is she okay?" The woman looked nice, sort of angelic with the snow starting to coat her hair like a fluffy halo. She looked much too nice to hang out with serial killers who looked remarkably like Mr. Clean.

The giant knelt beside Dori. "Are you okay? Where did you hit?"

Dori just stared, waiting for the coup de grace.

"I think you're scaring her, Barney." The blonde gave the giant a little shove. "I know you're a pushover, but she doesn't. She just sees a big, bald guy scowling at her."

"I am not scowling."

"Yes, you are. Let me talk to her."

The giant moved over a bit. The blonde knelt and took Dori's hand. "Can you sit up? I don't think you should be lying here in the snow."

"Okay," Dori said, finally realizing they were here to help. Messengers from the Lord? The giant slid an arm under her and helped her sit up, then assisted her to her feet, the blonde chattering the whole time.

"Can you believe this snow? I haven't seen anything like this here at the shore for a long time. What are you doing out here? Are you going to Seaside? We just left there. Me and Barney are going to—"

"Jo-Ellen, honey, why don't you go open her car door so I can help this nice lady inside?"

The blonde stared at him a minute, then with a wide grin sashayed to Dori's car on stiletto-heeled boots that Dori knew would have given her cramps in her calves, to say nothing of bunions for life.

"That's my wife, Jo-Ellen Barnhouse. I'm Tom," said the giant.

Dori heard a gurgle of laughter from Jo-Ellen who stepped aside so Tom could lower her to her seat. Whatever was so humorous to Jo-Ellen was going right over her head. It was proba-bly the thunk it had taken.

"Thanks for your help," Dori said, holding out her hand. One thing the blonde was right about. The giant—Tom—was a nice man. "My husband's on the way to get me."

"Do you want us to wait with you?" Tom asked.

"Say," Jo-Ellen said. "Do I know you?" She was squinting at Dori as she sat in the glow of the dome light.

Dori studied the woman. "I don't think so. I'm—"

Headlights cut through the snow, distracting her. A car slowed and stopped behind the Barnhouses'. The driver's door flew open, and Trev jumped out.

"I'm Dori Trevelyan," she said, getting to her feet. "That's my husband, Pastor Paul Trevelyan."

Jo-Ellen and Tom looked at each other in amazement and laughed some more as they made their way back to their car, but Dori barely noticed. Her eyes were fixed on the man running to her.

"Dori, Dori!"

She moved toward him, all aches forgotten. She opened her arms. "Here, Trev. Here forever, my love."

Epilogue

*D*ORI ADJUSTED THE WHITE VEIL that hung down her back. She hadn't planned to wear a lovely bridal gown, all *peau de soie* and seed pearls, but Trev had insisted.

"It's a waste of money," she'd protested. "I'll just get a pretty dress I can wear afterward."

"You were cheated of the fun and splendor of a wedding the first time around. This time we're doing it up right. Get a gown. Let Pop walk you down the aisle to me. I want to see a vision of grace and beauty."

She didn't know about the grace and beauty, but she did feel like a princess. She fiddled with her veil again.

Maureen batted at her hands. "Uh-uh. I'm maid of honor. Fixing the veil is my job. You leave it alone. It looks great. You look great. A beautiful bride."

Dori grinned. She stood in the narthex of Seaside Chapel, ready to walk down the aisle to her husband. Pop had wrung the promise from them that they would live together just six months ago, so today's date was an anniversary of sorts. Pop stood beside her, ready to escort her to her husband, happily convinced that he was solely responsible for today's event.

"I've looked forward to this day for years," he said, handsome and healthy in his tux.

Dori reached up and adjusted a tie that didn't need adjusting. She kissed his cheek. "Have I said thank you? For everything?"

"About a million times, but you can say it again."

They grinned at each other.

Dori turned to Honey, ready to be escorted to her seat on Phil's arm. "And to you, too, Honey. What would we have done without your none-too-gentle push?" The women embraced, both blinking back tears. The last thing either of them wanted were raccoon eyes from runny mascara.

"I love you, Dori. And I can't tell you how wonderful it is to be the mother of both the bride and groom." She kissed Dori, then Maureen, smiled a come-hither grin at Pop, and walked into the church on Phil's arm. He seated her in the second row, right in front of the three Graces, who kept peering over their shoulders for their first glimpse of the bride.

The music changed. Randy and Sam had driven down from New York City to play for the day, much to her delight. She couldn't imagine where they had found an arrangement of "Jesu, Joy of Man's Desiring" for keyboard and guitar, but it sounded amazingly good. And seated in the audience were Meg and Randy, Sr., who had flown in from San Diego a week ago. What a joy to spend time with them and let them come to love Trev too.

Maureen recognized her cue. Dressed in a royal blue that made her eyes brilliant and carrying a bouquet that was a floral rainbow of summer blooms, she started down the aisle. Dori watched her friend go, knowing that in a month she would be trading places with her. She would be matron of honor as Maureen and Phil married.

There were a satisfyingly large number of people in the pews, come to witness the renewal of vows of their pastor and his wife. Mae Harper was one of them, still walking with a cane, but back at Harbor Lights and delighted at the cosmetic changes Dori had made to the place.

They had reached an agreement that had Dori working part-time and responsible for the look of the place as well as the development of the fiction and music areas. Their business over early summer was strong, and Mae was a happy woman.

Dori surveyed their guests. She hoped that Trev understood

that their presence was but one more proof that Seaside Chapel was delighted to have him as their pastor. The meeting in which all the secrets of their strange marriage were aired had been hard on Dori. She had felt so foolish and so responsible.

"Trev's only mistakes were to love me and to love you," she told the people that night. "He didn't want to deny either. Don't punish him for that. Our marriage is now stable and getting stronger each day. Our commitment to each other is total, as it has always been. Dr. Roger Quentin, Trev's mentor from seminary, talks with us weekly for marriage coaching. I am growing daily in my walk with the Lord, and my primary model for the Christian life is my husband. He is a man who loves God with his whole heart. With your agreement, we would like the opportunity to remain here in Seaside and serve you."

"It was never my intent to deceive you," Trev said, facing his congregation. "I came originally to be interim for the summer. I thought my marital state wouldn't make a difference for that short a time. But I didn't leave. I should have told you from the beginning about Dori and me, and I ask your forgiveness for not doing so. Please know I never meant harm to the chapel or the cause of the Lord. We would love to stay and continue to serve the Lord with you here in Seaside, but even more than that, we want God's best for this church. May the Lord give you wisdom as you decide."

"He's all a charade," Jonathan Warrington had railed when it was his turn to speak. "He and his 'wife' have come here to steal the testimony of Seaside Chapel. They make a mockery of marriage and of commitment to the Lord. They are wolves in sheeps' clothing, an embarrassment to all of us. He must go. If he doesn't, I fear that we Warringtons cannot stay, and I'm sure there are others of you who feel the same."

Dori always thought it was that ultimatum that was the deciding factor. Whatever the reason, the vote was strongly in Trev's favor.

The Warringtons had left as threatened, and Jonathan, Judy, and Angie were attending another church where, if rumor was correct, Jonathan was already making waves. Bob Warrington was in the process of divorcing Shannon so he could marry Penni. As far as Dori knew, the two of them weren't attending anywhere.

Shannon herself still had plenty of bad days, but they came less frequently. She and Grayce Warrington had become family for each other since Jonathan no longer spoke to his mother or his ex-daughter-in-law. After all, they had supported Trev. Dori and Shannon met together weekly with the Graces who prayed over them both. Dori didn't know about Shannon, but she herself was growing in the Lord by leaps and bounds under the godly tutelage of these amazing older women.

The music changed again, and Dori knew it was her turn. She and Pop moved to the doorway. He patted her hand.

"Ready?"

Foolish question. She looked down the aisle to Trev, so handsome as he waited for her. Phil and Ryan stood beside him, Ryan so proud he could hardly stand it. Of course the boy had made the required complaints when told he had to wear a tux, but when he saw himself in the mirror at the fitting, he'd blinked in surprise.

"Whoa! Cool."

Though he had gone home with Mae two months ago, he frequently came over to visit. Dori suspected Jack and Trudy were the real draws, but Ry was polite enough to refrain from saying so. He and Trev took the dogs for long walks on the beach, each holding a leash. Sometimes they let her come along, but she was careful to see that Ryan often had Trev's undivided attention. What better way for the fatherless boy to see what a real man was like?

Her hand resting in the crook of Pop's arm, Dori kept her eyes fixed on her husband who watched her approach with a smile that melted her heart. She thought of the wonderful secret she and her husband shared.

The bride was three months pregnant.

They planned to tell people the happy news after they returned from their two-night stay in Cape May. Their real honeymoon had to wait until fall because of the demands of the summer season. Then they would relax on a two-week trip through the Southwest, making a loop of the national parks: Grand Canyon, Arches, Canyonlands, Bryce Canyon, and Zion. Dori had booked them into either the park accommodations or the most interesting bed-and-breakfasts she could find. She'd be quite chubby by then, and long hikes wouldn't be part of the program, but just being together alone would be enough.

The ceremony began. At the proper time Pop placed her hand in Trev's and went to take his seat beside Honey. Trev wrapped his large hand around hers and held tightly. He lifted their joined hands and kissed the back of hers.

"I love you, Dori-girl," he whispered. "Now and forever."

Dr. Quentin continued with the service while Dori's heart swelled to bursting. God had been so good to her, even when she didn't deserve it. He had preserved Trev for her until she was wise enough to value him and her marriage and was strong enough to fight for them both.

The winter winds that had blown through their lives had often been painful. The coming year would bring the baby, and with him more changes, more adjustments, but this time the winds would be gusts of love, zephyrs of joy.

And as always at the center of it all there would be Trev, only Trev.

The publisher and author would love to hear your
comments about this book. *Please contact us at:*
www.letstalkfiction.com

Dear Readers,

Have you ever watched a couple married for many years and thought, *They are as comfortable together as someone is with a favorite pair of old shoes?* What we tend to forget is that making those shoes comfortable was for that person a matter of time and effort.

We have great expectations when we buy the perfect pair of shoes, knowing they will complete our outfit and make us a fashionable whole. It's disappointing to realize that our feet are still as big, our ankles still as thick, our thighs still as heavy. On top of that, the shoes are stiff on our feet. They even chafe a bit until we add that slight lift in the heel. Just when they finally seem right, they get scuffed or dirty and need a good polishing. Then the heels run down and have to be torn off, and new ones have to be nailed in place.

Developing a comfortable marriage is a long-time process, too. We have great expectations that our new mate will complete us and make us whole. How disappointing to learn that he cannot fulfill our expectations no matter how hard he tries. Then the need to impress—our "stiffness"—slowly falls away, and the real person appears. Perhaps differing ideas on issues like money cause chafing, and the answer isn't anything as simple as a lift in the heel. Compromise that lets both parties function satisfactorily may be hard to find and harder still to live out. Often one or the other gets scuffed or dirty as anger, jealousy, a snippy tongue, or any of a hundred problems appear. A good "polishing" by the Holy Spirit is definitely needed. Sometimes the problems are quite serious, and the old habits and bad thinking patterns must be ripped off and replaced with things that are good and pure and right, a painful process.

But marriage merits the time and effort and even the pain. As the traditional vows say, it is a worthy estate. Nowhere else do we get to offer as much of ourselves, to be Christ's servants, to the same extent. Nowhere else do we learn as completely to lay down our lives for another. While no union will ever be perfect, my prayer is that yours will be strong, resilient, and filled with wonderful moments of great joy.

Drop me a line. Ask me a question. Tell me your story, good

or bad. I love to hear from readers at either gayle@gayleroper.com or www.gayleroper.com.

Gayle Roper

Sadly I have to qualify my above comments by saying I do not encourage anyone to stay in an abusive marriage. Sin must never be allowed to flourish in the name of submission.

Discussion Questions

1. Dori's big issue is forgiveness. Have you found that some people have a harder time than others with this issue? Why do you think this is so? Personality? Severity of the offense? Read Ephesians 4:31–32. What escape hatch are we given on the issue of forgiveness?

2. In chapter 27, Trev says that forgiveness is "a willful choice to let go of something you know happened. There's no denial in forgiveness. God knows full well that I've done many wrong things, but He has chosen to put them away. In the same way, we have to choose to let go of the wrong done us, the hurt dealt us by another." Read Isaiah 44:22. To what does Isaiah compare God's forgiveness of us? Is lack of forgiveness clouding your life?

3. Many times we hear, "Forgive and forget." When God forgives us, does He forget? Can He forget? Read Isaiah 43:25. What is the alternative to forgiving and forgetting?

4. Bob and Shannon justified their affair by their feelings for each other. Is their argument valid? Read 1 Corinthians 6:18–20. What are God's standards for us as believers?

5. In what ways do Pop and Honey's actions mirror those of the Lord? Read Psalm 68:5 and Hebrews 12:7.

6. Dori, Joanne, and Maureen all suffered severe hurts in their lives, but they reacted differently.
    Dori reacted as follows: "Keeping pace with the depth of her anger at Trev was her bitterness at God for letting her be so hurt. He'd snatched happiness from her twice, first with the

death of her parents and then with Trev's treachery. How could she ever trust Him again?"

Joanne thinks that "the only trouble with her prayer was that she wasn't certain God listened to people like her. Didn't you have to go to church and stuff to be on His good side?"

Maureen tells Dori, "My life was awfully bleak back then [when Adam died], and the stories taught me that living isn't static but evolutionary. New plateaus of forward development would always be open to me if I stuck with the Lord. Hope was always there if I chose to grab it."

How does God work in each of these women's lives? What lessons can we learn for our lives?

7. Have you ever gone to church with someone like Jonathan Warrington? What personality traits and actions make someone like him a poor spiritual leader? Read Philippians 3:17. What example is Paul talking about? Read Philippians 3:12–16 to find out.

8. What is God's standard for the church? Read Romans 15:5–7. Does your church exemplify this standard? Is this standard lived out in your own life?

9. It's a major turning point for Dori when she realizes that not filing for divorce "didn't show commitment to marriage but rather to the concept of marriage. If she'd been committed to marriage itself, wouldn't she have been here, fighting for it instead of abandoning it?" Why is the concept of marriage so much more comfortable than marriage itself?

10. What do you find to be the hardest thing about being married? Why? What is God's standard for relationships? Read Philippians 2:3–8.

TEARS ARE FALLING LIKE SPRING RAIN...

"Gayle Roper is in top form with *Spring Rain*. Her storytelling skills make this one a page-turning experience readers will love."

—JAMES SCOTT BELL,
author of *Blind Justice* and *Final Witness*

Spring Rain **by Gayle Roper**
Seaside Seasons, Book One:

Leigh Spenser, a young teacher and single mother of ten-year-old Billy, is thrown into conflict. Clay Wharton, the boy's estranged father, comes home to Seaside, New Jersey, to await the passing of his twin brother, Ted—now dying of AIDS. Threats against Billy's life ratchet the tension tighter, as Leigh wrestles with both tough and tender feelings for her old flame. Clay's own conflict, as he seeks to come to grips with his brother's lifestyle choices and the needs of the boy he fathered, underline the issue of God's forgiveness in the hearts—and lives—of this modern-day family. An emotionally gripping read!

ISBN 1-57673-638-5

YEARNING FOR SUNSHINE, ABBY FINDS DANGER, LOVE, AND LAUGHTER IN THE SUMMER SHADOWS

"A highly entertaining tale with just the right touch of mystery. I'm already looking forward to my next visit to Seaside."

—DEBORAH RANEY, author of *Beneath a Southern Sky*

Summer Shadows by Gayle Roper
Seaside Seasons, Book Two

The accident that killed Abby Patterson's husband and daughter has left her with a limp and chronic pain. Abby strikes out, determined to build a new life for herself. She finds the perfect home: a cottage on the beach. At least, it would be perfect except for one tiny irritant: Marsh Winslow, her landlord. But when Abby witnesses a hit-and-run accident and the trauma leaves her with amnesia, she finds an unexpected source of help: Marsh! When mysterious events make it clear that Abby is now a target, she and Marsh join forces to uncover a dangerous secret. Together they discover that God is in the business of putting broken lives back together so that they are more beautiful—and more perfect—than ever.

ISBN 1-57673-969-4

SOMEWHERE BETWEEN WISHES AND REALITY...
LIE DREAMS

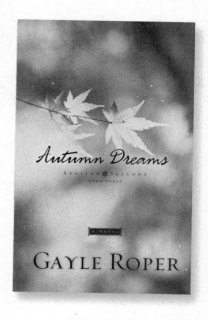

Autumn Dreams by Gayle Roper
Seaside Seasons, Book Three

The proud proprietor of her own bed-and-breakfast in sleepy Seaside, New Jersey, Cass Merton is intrigued by Dan Harmon who arrives at SeaSong for an extended stay. Management and finance specialist Dan Harmon is there to contemplate his life's significance as a result of witnessing the tragedy of 9/11. Meanwhile, Cass struggles to care for her feisty teenage niece and easy-going nephew for a whole year while their parents work in the Middle East. Add Cass's aging, deteriorating parents, and her emotions swirl like the quickly rising hurricane that's fast approaching Seaside.

But everyday cares aren't Cass's only problems. A troubled young employee unknowingly endangers her as well. When an alarm sounds in the middle of the night, bullets fly, and Cass is taken hostage by a gunman. Dan looks urgently to the Lord for help and recognizes a new emotion within himself: love.

ISBN 1-59052-127-7

Visit
www.letstalkfiction.com
today!

Fiction Readers Unite!

You've just found a new way to feed your fiction addiction. Letstalkfiction.com is a place where fiction readers can come together to learn about new fiction releases from Multnomah. You can read about the latest book releases, catch a behind-the-scenes look at your favorite authors, sign up to receive the most current book information, and much more. Everything you need to make the most out of your fictional world can be found at www.letstalkfiction.com. Come and join the network!